The Men of Lancaster County Series
By Mindy Starns Clark and Susan Meissner
The Amish Groom

The Women of Lancaster County Series
By Mindy Starns Clark and Leslie Gould
The Amish Midwife
http://bit.ly/AmishMidwife
The Amish Nanny
http://bit.ly/AmishNanny
The Amish Bride
http://bit.ly/AmishBride
The Amish Seamstress
http://bit.ly/AmishSeamstress

Other Fiction by Mindy Starns Clark

THE MILLION DOLLAR MYSTERIES
A Penny for Your Thoughts
Don't Take Any Wooden Nickels
A Dime a Dozen
A Quarter for a Kiss
The Buck Stops Here

A SMART CHICK MYSTERY
The Trouble with Tulip
Blind Dates Can Be Murder
Elementary, My Dear Watkins

STANDALONE MYSTERIES
Whispers of the Bayou
Shadows of Lancaster County
Under the Cajun Moon
Secrets of Harmony Grove
Echoes of Titanic

The Amish Groom

MINDY STARNS CLARK
SUSAN MEISSNER

HARVEST HOUSE PUBLISHERS
EUGENE, OREGON

THE AMISH GROOM

Copyright © 2014 by Mindy Starns Clark and Susan Meissner
Published by Harvest House Publishers
Eugene, Oregon 97402

ISBN 978-1-61129-203-9

For the Akamines
Brian, Tracey, Hannah, and Emiko
with love and thanks
for your faith and your friendship

ACKNOWLEDGMENTS

Our sincere and heartfelt thanks are extended to

Kim Moore, editor extraordinaire, and the entire Harvest House team, for being so gifted and dedicated in all you do.

Chip MacGregor, our literary agent, for pairing two good friends on such a wonderful collaborative journey.

John Clark, for assistance with plotting, brainstorming, research, and so much more.

Ben Riihl and the Daniel and Liz Fisher family, all of Lancaster County, for opening your Amish homes to us, sharing your insights and friendship, and showing us such warm hospitality.

Emily Clark, Lauren Clark, Tara Kenny, and Christy Koustourlis, for help with brainstorming and problem-solving.

Erik Wesner and Sherry Gore, for assistance in our research.

God, who walks alongside all of us on the search for our true place of belonging.

ONE

The surface of the pond was glassy smooth, a deep liquid oval beckoning through the trees. I headed down the path, my dog at my side. When we reached the clearing, Timber darted forward, chasing a duck into tall reeds. I came to a stop right at the edge of the water, work boots and pant cuffs damp from the morning dew, and paused to take it all in.

This secluded little farm pond was always so striking, so peaceful, but never more so than at this time of day, when the sun was just coming up—not to mention at this time of year, when the trees lining its banks offered riotous bursts of reds and yellows and oranges among the green. Whatever the season, I could never get enough of it. The fish that darted in and out of sight below. The dense and rocky overgrowth on all sides. The weeping willow at the far end, its branches dangling down to the water, tickling the surface.

I set down the tools and other items I was carrying and then turned my face upward just as the sun broke across the stillness. I watched as the horizon lost its sleepy purple cast, turning auburn. There wasn't a cloud in sight, and I knew a perfect day lay in store for my cousin Anna's wedding. As if on cue, Timber barked from somewhere off to my right, reminding me that there was much to do between now and then. Time to get to work.

Not far away, the old wooden rowboat rested upside down on the grass where I'd left it the last time I'd used it, the oar tucked securely underneath. I flipped it over and brushed out a few spiders who'd been living inside. Then I put the oar and the stuff I'd brought into the small craft and slid to the water. When it was all loaded, I glanced around for Timber and was glad to see that although the duck had flown off, the yellow lab was now fully occupied with sniffing his way around the pond's perimeter.

I placed one foot in the boat's hull and gently pushed off with the other, the small vessel cutting through the water with ease. When it slowed about ten feet short of my goal, I lowered the oar into the water and paddled toward the buoy that floated near the center of the pond. As I did, I breathed in the new morning air, filling my lungs with its earthy, October fragrance.

According to my grandmother, this pond had been my mother's favorite place to go when she was young and wanted to be alone with her thoughts. She had come here often, and I had a feeling I knew why. When the morning sun slashed across the top of the trees on mid-autumn dawns like this one, I could see my reflection in the water as clear as in the mirror in my bedroom back at the farmhouse, as if there were another me beyond the surface, looking back. I was always drawn to that other place, to the what-ifs of it all. No doubt my mother, who was so full of wanderlust, had felt the same.

Easing the boat alongside the buoy, I brought it to a stop once the floating brown orb was within easy reach. I rested the dripping plank beside my feet, gave the straw hat on my head a pat to make sure it was secure, and then slid my hands into the cold water, feeling under the buoy for the rope. Grasping it, I began to pull slowly upward, working my hands along the taut line, wishing I'd thought to wear gloves for a better grip. The more I pulled up, the slimier it grew, coating my palms in a nasty brown goo that smelled of mud and dankness and rot.

I'd known last spring that something needed to be done when the ice began to melt away and I'd spotted more than a few silver, bloated bodies floating sideways in the black water. Too many fish had not survived the winter, which confirmed what I'd suspected for a while, that there was a problem with the aerator.

Not that this pond mattered all that much in the grand scheme of things. No one ever even bothered with it except me anyway—and, in her youth, my mother. Hidden among the trees on a far back corner of my grandparents' farm, it was no longer necessary once wells were dug on the farm, but that didn't mean it was unimportant—at least not to me—or that it could be ignored. Busy with my work in the buggy shop, I'd managed to put off dealing with the issue for months. But now that fall was here, and another winter just around the corner, I knew it was time to get this thing repaired.

As I pulled on the rope, an old airstone emerged from the surface, with long strands of what looked like seaweed dangling down from its round head. I put it into my lap—wetness, slime, and all—pressed my elbow against the boat's rim to hold the tubing in place, and then grabbed the wrench to disconnect the rusting adapter. After considerable effort, I finally broke the valve free. The rest of the installation was easy by comparison, and soon I had the new diffuser attached and ready to go, while the old one lay in a puddle at my feet.

I released my elbow hold on the tubing, gripped the rope, and began lowering the new diffuser into the water a little bit at a time.

I wasn't sure how long it would take for the bubbles to start appearing at the surface, but I didn't mind sitting in the boat, waiting. My time was usually spent in quiet reflection, standing on the bank, but being here in the middle of the pond was giving me a unique vantage point, so I took in the scenery, gulping it down like liquid to a thirsty man.

For years I'd been coming to the pond once every few weeks or so, but lately I'd found my way down here almost daily. As blessed as I was to have this place where I could escape and contemplate life in private, I knew the increase in frequency didn't bode well. My mind had become such a jumbled mess, and it seemed all I wanted to do was be alone to think and pray and try to make sense of the conflict raging inside of me.

Much as my mother had done, long before I was born.

Not far from the path, a cluster of rocks and boulders formed a natural sort of sitting area, and I often imagined her as a young woman, perched there and doing the very same thing, begging God for clarity and direction as she tried to soothe her troubled soul. She had been just eighteen years old when she turned her back on the farm for good, leaving behind her parents and siblings and the Amish life she no longer wanted. She'd thrown in her lot for a life among the *Englisch*, eventually marrying my dad, moving to Europe, and giving birth to me.

Then she died, suddenly and unexpectedly, when I was just six years old.

After that, I had been her family's consolation prize, so to speak. The little boy with the football jerseys and blue jeans who had known a smattering of Pennsylvania Dutch but otherwise hadn't a clue what it meant to be Amish. At my newly widowed father's request, my grandparents had taken me in right after the funeral, an arrangement that was supposed to have been temporary. But here I was, all these years later, still in the same place, living on the same farm my mother had lived on, sleeping in the same room that had been hers, and spending time at the same pond that had drawn and captivated her. I had accepted my lot and the fact that my dad found a new life with a new wife—and even a new son—without me. I'd see them now and then, but for all intents and purposes *Mammi* and *Daadi* were more like parents than grandparents to me. For that matter, the aunt and uncles I'd grown up with—Sarah, Thom, Eli, and Peter—were more like sister and brothers. Even Jake, who was a mere six months older than I, was technically my uncle, even though we felt and acted like brothers.

That very first day I arrived, I had traded in the jerseys and jeans for broadfall trousers and plain white shirts and had been raised Amish from then on. My dad had remained peripherally involved in my life even after he remarried and became a father a second time, but I had now been living here, on this farm, for seventeen years. At twenty-three, I was on the verge of big decisions that would determine the rest of my life, my future, my path—whether *Englisch* or Amish.

And I'd never been more perplexed.

Before she left here for good, my mother had been confused as well. I knew that much from what I'd been told by her brother Thom, who had been sixteen at the time. As a child, I hadn't known much about my mother at all, or at least not the person she was when she lived in this world. She had never talked much about her years growing up Amish. I don't remember her telling me about the house, or the smell of the horses' tack, or the sounds the buggies made when their wheels rolled on pavement, or how quiet the dark was on winter nights.

Most of what I knew about my mother I had learned from my aunt and uncles and from *Daadi* and *Mammi*. They told me she loved peaches and jonquils and her horse, Nutmeg, and the first snowfall. That she liked surprises and twirling and laughter.

Even though she had never joined the church, they would always see her as Amish. I looked Amish too, but lately it seemed as though underneath the Plain clothes and the hat and the language, there was a different man. Rachel Hoeck, who was the closest friend I had besides Jake, said I was as Amish as any man born right here in Lancaster County. I grew up here. I went to school here. I'd worked in my grandfather's buggy shop since I could tighten a bolt. I was on the verge of church membership and baptism. At twenty-three I was more than old enough to take my vows as an Amish adult—vows of commitment to the Amish life and vows of marriage to an Amish bride. Those faraway years when I lived in the *Englisch* world were just that, Rachel would say—far away. But how could she know? I'd never brought her here at the crack of dawn. She'd never seen the man in the pond who stared back at me with questioning eyes. Then again, if she did see him, I knew what she would say to me.

That is just your reflection, Tyler. That's you. The Amish man I love.

And I would want to believe her.

But there would be this tugging inside me, as there was every time I came to the pond now, pulling at all that I knew to be true of me. As though a loose thread was in the grasp of something or someone who wanted to yank it free…

My thoughts were interrupted by the subtle sound of a hundred tiny bubbles breaking on the surface.

A beautiful sight. The diffuser was doing just what it should.

I rowed back to shore, returned the rowboat and oar to the tall grass, and whistled for my dog. Then I gathered my things and started up the path toward home, Timber trotting alongside. I knew I should have felt good. After all, the aerator was working again, it was a beautiful morning, and God's presence was everywhere. But up ahead, as the farmhouse came into view, I felt a surge of emotion I couldn't even name. Loss? Joy? Hope? Fear?

Maybe all of the above, simultaneously?

My mind again went to my mother and one of the few memories I had of her, the first time she ever told me about this pond. We'd been far from here—a world away, in fact—but the way she talked, that small body of water had come as alive as if I'd been standing on its banks myself.

I had been in my bed, crying because there was a thunderstorm outside and lightning was scissoring over the house as though it wanted to slice me in two. My mother was sitting on my bed, trying to convince me the storm couldn't hurt me. Then, to take my mind off what was happening outside the window, she began telling me all about the pond, her favorite place on the farm where she grew up. She went on and on, finally concluding her elaborate description with the words, "You can see a different world in the water. It's like there's always another place besides the one where you are."

I hadn't known what she meant by that, but I remember asking her if there was thunder and lightning at that other place too.

She chuckled softly. "Every place has something about it we would change if we were in charge."

Swallowing hard, I closed my eyes now as I walked, trying to picture my mother's pretty face from that night, her gentle hands as she smoothed the covers around me. But then a voice echoed across the silence and the image tumbled away, back to the unseen place where I kept all of my memories hidden—or at least my memories of her.

"Tyler!"

I opened my eyes to see Jake watching me from where he stood in the drive, arms crossed over his chest. He and I were supposed to have loaded some additional benches we'd made in the buggy shop into the wagon first thing so that right after breakfast we could deliver them over to the Bowmans' farm for Anna's wedding. But my task at the pond had taken longer than I'd expected, leaving him to do the loading all by himself. I felt guilty, as I knew my errand could have waited for a more appropriate day. To be honest, I had probably just used the diffuser replacement as an excuse to get down to the pond this morning and have a little time to myself.

I gave him an apologetic smile and a shrug, and though I could tell he was about to lay into me, when he saw that my shirt and pants were covered in dark, slimy mud, he hesitated and then simply grinned.

He and I both knew that whatever my *grossmammi* doled out once she saw what I'd done to my clean clothes would be payback enough.

Stepping inside, I tried to soften the blow by warning her first.

"Just so you know," I called out as Jake and I paused in the mudroom to remove our hats, jackets, and boots, "changing out the diffuser in the pond was a lot messier job than I'd expected."

"Oh, Tyler, no," she replied from the kitchen. "You didn't fall in, did you? Your *grossdaadi* told you not to trust that old rowboat."

"No, nothing like that."

I stepped around the corner to see her at the counter, spooning out scrambled eggs from the pan. The aroma of coffee and peach strudel wafted past my nose, and I realized I was starving. I'd fed Timber before going to the pond but hadn't eaten a thing yet myself.

She didn't even look up to see me, so Jake let out a low whistle as he pushed past to go to the table. "Wow, Tyler. Nice going on your clothes there! Did you leave any mud in the pond?" He whistled again, dramatically.

Of course, at that *Mammi*'s head snapped up. She took in the sight of me, her eyes narrowing.

"Just for that, no strudel," she said. When Jake burst out in a victorious laugh, she gave him a sharp, "I'm talking to *you*, young man. No strudel for troublemakers."

Lucky for me, she hated tattling even more than she hated extra work on laundry day. I grinned, though I didn't dare make a sound in return lest she come down on me as well.

"I'll rinse everything out as soon as I take it off," I told her.

"See that you do," she replied, returning her attention to the food preparations in front of her.

I flashed Jake a "gotcha" look. He snagged a corner of the strudel when *Mammi's* head was turned and tossed it into his mouth with a smirk that said "gotcha back."

Ten minutes later, I had returned to the kitchen, cleaned up and ready for the day, relieved that the mud had rinsed right out. I spotted *Mammi* still standing at the counter and Jake sitting at the table. He was sipping coffee but otherwise waiting to dig in until everyone else had convened here too. I heard *Daadi* come in the back door as I was taking my seat, and once he'd hung up his hat and jacket, he joined us in the kitchen and crossed the floor toward his wife.

Daadi always greeted my grandmother the same way when the morning's first chores were done and it was time for breakfast and devotions: kissing her cheek and speaking in the softest words, meant just for her, saying, *"Gud mariye, meiner Aldi."* Good morning, my wife.

Mammi smiled the way she always did. *"Gud mariye,* Joel."

I loved how tender my grandparents were with each other in these first few moments of the day. Like most Amish, *Daadi* didn't give *Mammi* kisses in front of people, or fuss over her in a personal kind of way, especially not in public. But their morning custom made me feel good about the start of the day, and it always had. It was strange and wonderful to think my mother probably saw them do this same thing every morning of her life too.

Daadi brought a mug of coffee to the table and took his seat at the end. "Beautiful sunrise over the pond this morning?" he asked, letting me know in his gentle way he'd seen me heading to the place I always went when there was much on my mind.

"Sure was," I replied, adding nothing else, not even about the diffuser repair. He knew as well as I did that that wasn't really why I'd gone out there.

I avoided his gaze, watching as *Mammi* brought a plate of sausages to the table. We bowed our heads for a silent prayer, and the topic of the pond was dropped. That was fine with me. I had always felt free to share even my most troubling thoughts with my grandfather. But I wasn't ready to have *that* conversation.

Not yet, anyway—and especially not with him.

Two

After breakfast Jake and I drove the wagon a short distance over to my aunt Sarah and uncle Jonah's farm to deliver the extra seating we'd constructed for the wedding. We'd helped to get everything set up the day before—clearing out some of the furniture from the main room of the house and filling the space with all of the benches from our district's bench wagon. The Bowmans still lacked a few more rows, though, and as none of our neighboring districts had benches to spare thanks to weddings of their own, last night Jake and I had ended up doing some quick carpentry work in the buggy shop, making the extra benches ourselves. Today we were back to deliver them, with just two and half hours to go before the festivities would start. When we arrived, we greeted Anna and then went right to work with the help of her brothers, Sam and Gideon, carrying the supplementary benches inside and setting them up.

This was one of the earliest weddings of the season, and intentionally so, according to Rachel. As the youngest of four children, Anna had grown tired of being the last of everything, so she wanted to be among the first of the courting couples to marry this year. Rachel was Anna's best friend and had been talking about this event for weeks.

At least she hadn't used it as an opportunity to put pressure on me, I thought as Jake and I lifted down another bench from the wagon, though she certainly had every right to. Rachel and I had been a couple for years, long enough for her—and everyone else, for that matter—to assume we, too, would end up married.

Though we hadn't begun courting until we were in our teens, we'd been friends long before that. I first met Rachel when I was ten and she was nine. She had come from Ohio after her grandfather died and her parents moved to Lancaster County to take over his dairy farm. Rachel was the youngest of three daughters—all honey-brunettes with a sprinkling of freckles—but she was by far the prettiest. Her eyes were a vivid blue, easily rivaling the bluest cornflower ever to sprout.

When she first moved here, she was just a new girl to tease—all in good fun, of course. Jake and I couldn't resist, and we told her all sorts of tall tales, the biggest being that he and I were twins. Though we looked almost nothing alike, she believed us until she learned that he was a Miller and I an Anderson.

"How can you be twins if you have different last names?" she'd asked one day during her second week there.

"That's so people can tell us apart," Jake replied with a perfect deadpan.

After a long moment, her eyes narrowed, and then she turned on her heel without a word and marched off to speak to the teacher, knowing we were pulling her leg and ready to settle the matter once and for all.

"Tyler?" For the second time today, Jake's voice pulled me out of a memory.

"Huh?" I asked, blinking.

He was lifting down his end of the final bench, waiting for me to do the same. "I said, 'What's going on?'"

"What do you mean?"

"You're a million miles away. What gives? You okay?"

"Of course. I'm fine." Or I would be if he would mind his own business.

We carried the last bench into the house together and slid it into place. After that, Sam and Gideon went out to handle some other chore, leaving Jake and me to finish up. We both looked around at the room, transformed now from a living area to a church, and began to shift things a bit to allow a little more leg room between rows.

Nearby, the large kitchen area was bustling with women, including Anna and her mother and various relatives, helping to prepare the wedding feast. If I'd been in there with them, I would have been stepping on people's toes, bumping into their backs, and generally making a big mess, but they worked together seamlessly, thanks to years of practice.

"I know what it is," Jake said suddenly, pausing to look my way as I was tugging a bench into place.

"What *what* is?"

He glanced toward the kitchen before lowering his voice so only I could hear. "Why you're so nervous and distracted today. It's because you know that this time next year we'll be slinging benches around for *your* wedding."

He laughed.

I didn't.

"Oh, come on, Tyler," he prodded in a soft voice. "I don't know why you're not *already* married. And neither does anyone else."

I glared at him, gesturing toward the kitchen and the women who might overhear his words.

"I'm serious!" he said, moving closer now so he could speak even more softly. "You're getting up in years, you know?"

"I'm twenty-three."

"Which is high time to take that next step. And you'll never find a better match for you than Rachel."

Now it was my turn to pause. Why didn't he get it? I spoke through gritted teeth, telling him I was not going to discuss it with him, but he kept talking as if he hadn't even heard me.

"You know she's perfect for you. *She* thinks you're wonderful." He put the emphasis on "she," meaning, of course, that Rachel thought it even if no one else did.

"Funny," I snapped.

Jake moved to the end of the row. "It's time to take that next step, buddy, just like Tobias will today with Anna. I know it and you know it. Most of all, Rachel knows it."

Unsure how to reply, I leaned down and made one final shift, intentionally pushing the bench at Jake's knees. He yelped as he tried to avoid the impact.

"Sorry," I said in a loud voice, glancing toward the kitchen and giving an "everything's okay here" wave to the two women who had turned to look. "Guess I didn't see your legs there, buddy. Must need to get my eyes checked."

"Get your brain checked, you mean." Jake sat down to rub his knee and whispered, "I'm only saying what you need to hear."

"No," I hissed, "you're only saying a bunch of stuff that's none of your business."

I was saved from further harassment by the appearance of Jonah Bowman—Anna's father and my uncle—who came in from outside. "We're all finished here," I said. "Anything else we can do for you?"

"*Ya.* Before you go, can you cut some more logs for cooking? We use propane in the house and in the wedding wagon, but I also borrowed three big cookstoves that we have going out back." Glancing toward the kitchen, he added, "I thought I had enough wood, but I may have underestimated the need."

We all shared a smile, knowing that the women in there would have an absolute fit if they ran short of fuel before they were finished roasting all the chickens this day would require.

"Happy to do it."

Jake and I went outside to the toolshed, grabbed some axes, and then made our way to the woodpile, where we pulled out logs of birch and oak and began breaking them down into smaller, stove-sized pieces. Across the driveway from us, the barn's big doors were open to the sun, and I could see people milling around inside, setting up for the reception.

We chopped for a while, quiet except for the thwack of our axes and the crisp splitting of wood.

"I guess I'll let you off the hook—for now," Jake said finally, pausing to wipe the sweat from his forehead. "But just let me say that I really am glad you have Rachel."

"Thank you," I replied, relieved he was willing to let it go.

Then he added, "After all, you'll need *someone* to fill the lonely hours once I leave tomorrow."

I couldn't help but smile as I reached for another log and placed it on the chopping block. "Oh, yeah? You think I'll be counting the days till you get back?" I slammed the ax down, splitting the log neatly in two.

"Absolutely. Mark my words. You're going to miss me while I'm gone more than you can imagine."

"Uh-huh," I said, leaning down to pick up the larger of the two pieces and placing it on the block to split it again. "More likely, I'll forget all about you. You'll come back in four months' time, and we'll have to be reintroduced. I'll be all, 'What's that? Jake who? I suppose you do look kind of familiar…'"

I grinned, he smirked, and together we continued working side by side, the only sounds our occasional grunts and the steady rhythm of our task. I was glad he had dropped the discussion of Rachel, but I would have liked to avoid this topic as well. We both knew that his teasing words held more than a little truth. I couldn't imagine what the next months were going to be like without Jake around. He was headed to Missouri for blacksmithing school, something he'd been looking forward to for a long time. Though Jake had always labored alongside me in *Daadi's* buggy shop, his first love was the horses that pulled those buggies. Shoeing took skill, craftsmanship, and a level of trust between animal and man that few people appreciated. I did, but only because Jake had been talking about it since we were kids.

Now that he was going to become a blacksmith, he'd be the first of the Millers to leave the buggy trade. His older brothers, Thom, Eli, and Peter, all worked in the buggy shop, as did some of their sons. On a busy day, there could be a dozen of us in there. Now it would be eleven.

"So I suppose you're all packed," I said, clearing my throat.

He smiled at me. "Just about."

"You probably won't want to come home," I said, pretending that wouldn't bother me in the least.

We both knew it would, though. Low-key guys like me didn't have a lot of close friends. But since the day I'd come to live here seventeen years ago, I'd had Jake, the best friend of all.

"Are you kidding? Of course I'm coming back. You might forget me, but the horses in Lancaster County won't. They need me."

"At least the horses, if not the ladies," I teased.

Before he could respond, we both heard the distinct clip-clop of hooves behind us. Turning, I spotted a familiar market wagon coming our way, a sight that always filled me with inexplicable warmth. I watched until it rolled to a stop nearby. My eyes met those of the driver, and then she softly said my name. Hers was the sweetest voice I knew beyond that of my mother's echoes.

Rachel.

She climbed down from the wagon, a casserole dish tucked under one arm.

"*Guder mariye*, Tyler. *Guder mariye*, Jake," she said. She smelled like a summer morning, like sweet pea blossoms. The ties of her *kapp* flitted in the slight breeze like butterflies.

We tipped our hats, and she and I shared a smile. As Anna's closest friend, Rachel was one of her two *newehockers*, or attendants, so I wasn't surprised that she had come early.

"*Mariye*, Rachel," I said. "You're looking pretty today."

Blushing, she was about to respond when Jake interrupted.

"Got a full load here?" he asked, moving to the back of the wagon and peeling up a corner of the tarp to peek underneath.

"*Ya*. The last of the dishes and table linens."

"Okay. We'll get them into the barn once we're done here."

"*Danke*, Jake."

He took over with the horse, leading it toward the hitching post nearest the barn as Rachel turned back to me and spoke in a softer voice.

"How's Anna?" she asked, her eyes sparkling. "Excited, I bet."

I glanced toward the house and admitted I didn't know, that we hadn't really taken the time to speak—other than a quick hello—since I'd arrived.

"*Ach*, well, she's probably busy in the kitchen. Guess I'd better get in there too."

"Guess you'd better," I said, but then neither of us made a move to go. Instead, we just stood there, our eyes locked. Rachel really did look especially beautiful today, her cheekbones a rosy pink, her skin perfect cream, her lips soft and full.

"What?" she whispered, giving me a sexy smile, as if she could read my mind.

"Nothing," I said, a twinkle in my own eye. She and I both knew that what I wanted more than anything in that moment was to give her a kiss.

"All right you two, enough with the googly-eyes," Jake said, returning to the woodpile. "Tyler, get over here. We're not done yet."

I tipped my hat again and Rachel gave me a wink before she turned and headed for the house.

Jake was right: Rachel really was the perfect woman for me. So why did I keep putting things off?

I returned to my work—lift, place, *thwack*, split—my mind racing despite the calming scent of fresh-cut wood that wafted up from every chop. Rachel had been so patient with me thus far, but how much longer would she wait before giving up on me—on us—for good?

Reaching for another log, I thought again of that time long ago, back when we were children in school. After the "twins" incident and our teacher told her that Jake was my uncle, not my brother, I had expected Rachel to be mad and to keep her distance.

Instead, it seemed our deception had only fueled her curiosity. That night she must have put two and two together and begun to wonder that if I was being raised by my grandparents, then where were my *real* parents?

She came to me in the schoolyard after lunch the very next day, concern etched into her face. "Do you not have a mother and father?" She was practically crying.

"Everybody has a mother and father," I said, pretending I was not moved by her concern for me. "You can't be born without parents."

She was unfazed. "Are they…are you an orphan?"

I frowned. "No, I'm not an orphan."

"So where are they?" Her eyes glistened.

Even then, I hadn't known how to explain. What could I say? My mother had died. She was gone for good, living now in a place very far away, as she had since the moment she'd passed. But what of my dad? I had seen him just twice in the past three years. At the time Rachel asked me that question, he was in Japan, by choice, on an extended tour that would keep him gone until I turned eleven. And even though I knew he was very much alive, most days he seemed just as far from me as my mother was.

"They're not here," was all I said. Then I'd walked off in search of someone to play with who already knew my story and didn't need to ask stupid questions.

But Rachel wasn't giving up that easily. The next day, she tried again, this time taking a seat on the swing beside mine and saying, "Tell me about your mother. What was she like?" Obviously, someone had filled her in, at least a little bit. Otherwise, she wouldn't have put it quite that way.

I wanted to rebuff her, but again, her question left me silent and confused. What *had* my mother been like? Did I even know anymore? I still had some memories of her, of course, but Rachel had asked me not for memories but for a description.

Sitting on the swing, my toes digging a rut into the dry, dusty ground at my feet, I tried to picture my mom. I could barely recall her face by that point, though I could still hear the faintest echoes of her voice, sometimes in English, sometimes in the Pennsylvania Dutch she'd grown up speaking.

What else?

I remembered her smile, from when we lived in Germany and I found three *pfennigs* in the street as she and I walked to the *backerei* to buy bread.

I remembered her eyes, from when she watched me blow out the candles on a cake she'd baked for my birthday—white frosting with sprinkles on top, just like I'd asked for.

I remembered her long brown hair, flowing out behind her as we ped-aled down the street together on our bicycles.

Of course, that had been back when we still lived in Germany. I couldn't remember moving out of our house in Heidelberg or the long airplane ride to the States, but I remembered my mother calling her parents once we were settled into our new home in Maryland to tell them we had returned from overseas at last. I remembered that conversation well, remembered hearing her say that we wanted to come for a visit. But then after she hung up the phone, she just cried for a long time. And that visit never happened. I never even met my grandparents, in fact, until the day of the funeral, the day they took me home and my old life came to an end and my new one began.

"My mother?" I said finally, turning to Rachel. "She was smart and funny and nice and everybody liked her." Glancing her way, I couldn't help but add, "She wasn't *Amish*, you know. Neither is my dad."

I could still see Rachel's face in that moment, the hurt in her big blue eyes. I could still feel the shame burning my cheeks, shame at the way I had said the word "Amish," as though it was something to be disdained, as though I wasn't wearing Amish clothes myself or living an Amish life, day after day, in my grandparents' Amish home.

Once again she had walked away without a word. That was on a Fri-day, and I felt bad all weekend long about what I'd said. When I saw her again that Monday at school, I was ready to apologize. But before I could, she simply came up to me and gestured across the playground toward the swings. We ran there together, and that time we didn't just hang still but instead tried to get ourselves going. By pushing off with our feet and pumping our legs, over and over—leaning back, stretching out, leaning forward, curling under—we eventually went so high we were nearly per-pendicular to the ground.

"We're going to swing to the moon!" she cried.

"We're going to swing to the sun!" I responded.

"We're going to swing all the way to heaven!" she said. "All the way up to your mother!"

I glanced at her, but she wasn't making fun. She wasn't even pretending, really. She was just trying to make me feel better, to say something kind. That was the first I became aware of Rachel's gift for compassion.

"All the way up to heaven," I agreed, and in the look we shared as we soared toward the sky, I knew all would be well between us from that moment forward.

THREE

After our tasks at the Bowmans' were done, Jake and I had just enough time to go home to get cleaned up and dressed before coming back for the wedding. In our district, weddings were always held on Tuesdays and Thursdays from October to December. That seemed like a lot of time to fit all of them in, but in densely populated Lancaster County, getting that many young couples married off in such a short amount of time was nearly impossible. Jake had pulled out a calendar once and done the math, and those Tuesdays and Thursdays each fall added up to a total of less than thirty possible days per year on which to hold a wedding. For the people in our district, that meant running like crazy for three months, attending at least one or two weddings per week and struggling to decide between the numerous options that inevitably popped up. Having been through seventeen such seasons myself since coming to live with my grandparents, I'd seen many a couple take their marriage vows. But I was definitely more aware of the details at Anna and Tobias's wedding ceremony than I had been at any of those in the past.

During the long service I sat with the men as usual, but my gaze kept wandering over to where Rachel sat on the women's side, in the front row. Looking at her, I pondered the notion that this was most likely my last wedding season as a bachelor. If she and I became engaged soon, as everyone expected us to, then Jake was right. Next fall, I *would* be a groom.

For that to happen, though, I would also need to be a baptized member of the Amish church. While I embraced that idea in theory, in reality I wasn't so sure. That would mean no more dawns spent gazing into my mother's pond and wondering what was on the other side, no more sunsets spent thinking of Rachel and wondering if this really was the life I wanted. The time for wondering would be over. The time for commitment would begin.

Rachel had been done with her wondering a few years ago, taking her baptismal vows when she was nineteen. She'd had her *rumspringa* like the rest of us, but over time she had worked through all her questions and doubts about becoming Amish and decided to make that commitment for life. While my period of *rumspringa* continued to drag on, she had slowly outgrown the youth gatherings and lost the itch to see movies or own a cell phone or wear *Englisch* clothing. When I was eighteen and wanted to get a driver's license, she helped me study for the written test, but she had no desire to get one of her own. She never made me feel silly or sinful for wanting it, but she did ask me what was the draw in having something that, as an Amish man, I would never use. I'd told her I wanted to see what it was like to drive a motor vehicle, not just sit in one while someone else drove.

What I hadn't added was that my dad was a collector of muscle cars—something that would have been foreign to her indeed. Though I didn't visit him often, when I did he would always ask if I wanted to take out his latest acquisition for a spin. If I had a license, I could be the one behind the wheel. Besides, if I really was going to become Amish someday, that meant I would never own a car of my own, and I wanted to know what it was I would be turning my back on.

Now, as the minister began the main sermon, I looked again at Rachel and it struck me that she was walking the path she'd been set on since the day she was born. From a young age, she'd been able to see herself living the life her parents lived and their parents before them and their parents before them. She'd been given an unbroken heritage that surely felt as solid as the earth beneath her feet.

My situation was more complicated than that. What I had was a mother who had left the Amish faith when she was just eighteen for reasons no one had ever been able to explain. I had an *Englisch* father who couldn't get rid of me fast enough once she died, suddenly and unexpectedly, of a brain aneurism. I had a pair of loving Amish grandparents who had taken me in and raised me as one of their own, even though I'd known nothing at all prior to that about them or what they believed or what their lives were like.

My heritage was about as broken as they come. Sometimes, I felt broken too.

Yet there sat Rachel on her side of the room, her attention rapt as Anna and Tobias spoke their promises to the bishop, the congregation, and each other. As they did, Rachel never once looked away from what was happening in front of her. Watching her watch them, I felt a sudden surge of emotion—guilt, pain, grief—so intense I could barely breathe.

How could I do this to her? How could I keep putting her off, making her wait? I loved Rachel more than life itself, I knew that. But to love her for the rest of her life *as her husband* meant loving the church as well.

And that was something I just didn't know if I could do.

What if, in the end, I simply couldn't bring myself to join the Amish faith? What would happen to us then? As a baptized member of the church, Rachel didn't have the freedom to walk away the way I did. If I left, my grandparents and other family members would be hurt and disappointed, of course, but we could always maintain a relationship. I would always be welcome in their home.

If Rachel left, she would probably be excommunicated. Not only would her loved ones be brokenhearted, but they would likely cut all ties with her, shunning her for the rest of her life—or at least until she repented and came back to the church. Bottom line, unless I joined the church too, she was caught in an either/or situation. She could have me, or she could have her Amish world, but she couldn't have both.

What kind of person was I to force a choice like that on the woman I loved?

My heart pounded at the thought, but I tried to swallow back a feeling of despair and focus on the situation at hand. None of this had to be decided today, I told myself. There was still plenty of time to figure things out.

I somehow managed to make it through the rest of the service. Once it ended, I found a welcome distraction in helping Jake and the rest of the cousins move the benches to the barn, where the feasting tables had been set up. By the time we were finished, my mind was no longer on questions about the future but instead was tuned in to the heaping platters and bowls of food that graced the tables of the reception.

The abundant display revealed how much we had all missed the wedding feasts during the long summer months. Spread out before us were pickled beets, cucumbers, and eggs; giant bowls of salads; five kinds of bread and a dozen varieties of jams and preserves; ham and beef; four kinds of chow-chow; baked lima beans, baked cabbage, and baked corn casserole; mashed sweet potatoes, boiled new potatoes and green beans, and potato dumplings; spicy carrots; and four kinds of roasted squash.

Unlike at other communal feasts, at weddings the young, single adults were allowed to eat first. Long tables were set up in a *V* shape, with the bride and groom sitting at the point of that *V*—or the *Eck*, as we called it. Then the rest of us divided out, the men sitting along the table on one side and the women on the other. Once seated, Anna and Tobias's aunts and uncles served as the *Ecktenders*, bringing the food to us while the other married adults stood and looked on from the fringes, chatting among themselves.

I sat beside Jake and proceeded to eat until I couldn't fit another bite in my stomach. But that wasn't the end of the celebration by any means. Once we were done eating, the adults took their turn eating as well, in shifts, and then finally the "going to the table" ritual began. Reserved for the younger, unmarried guests, it was a custom unique to our district and the part of the wedding day that those my age either dreaded or adored. The young single women filed out to wait in one of the larger upstairs bedrooms of Anna's house while the young single men stayed in the barn, most standing around pretending they weren't nervous as each one tried to get up the nerve to go to the room where the girls were waiting and ask one of them to "go to the table" with him. If the girl agreed, then the two of them would come downstairs together, sometimes holding hands, usually blushing, and make their way back to the tables in the barn, where this time the young men and women would sit together, rather than across from each other, and be served dessert and other special treats.

Next to Sunday evening singings, going to the table was the best way to see how you might fare with the young Amish girl who had caught your eye. It could also be the worst way, as there was nothing more awful than working up the courage to ask a girl to go to the table and then have her giggle to her friends in response and tell you no. Or so I had heard.

I hadn't ever had to worry about it, as Rachel and I had always gone to the table together.

"You *are* going to come upstairs and ask for me, aren't you?" she had said under her breath a cold November day nearly six years ago when Ruth Suderman and Wayne Yoder got married. Rachel had just turned sixteen and was allowed to participate. We were passing each other at the beverage table during the noon meal.

"You *are* going to say yes when I do, aren't you?" I had whispered back with a grin.

After the third or fourth wedding that year, Jake started complaining that I had it easy, that I had no idea what it was like to have to prove yourself worthy to someone you were dying to get to know.

These days, Rachel didn't really have to head upstairs with the other single girls because she had no need to find a suitable mate. She'd already found me, and I her, and it was a given that someday we would wed. But she went anyway to encourage her single friends, some of whom were from other districts.

Now, once the young women were gone, I realized I couldn't wait to go to the table with Rachel and have her all to myself. During the meal, I had been able to steal a few glances, but other than our brief exchange in the driveway much earlier, she and I had barely interacted all day.

I was suddenly so eager to be with her, in fact, that I was the first to head out of the barn door, much to the laughter of my envious friends. When I reached the house, I went upstairs to get her, and then Rachel and I came back down together, hand in hand, and crossed back over to the barn. Though we were supposed to sit where designated, I led her to the far end of the table, nearest the door, so that when the singing started, we could still hear each other talk. We sat there together, holding hands under the table, watching and laughing as one by one the guys headed off and then returned, hopefully victorious, with the woman of his choice.

Once everyone was seated—including the small group of girls who had not been asked or had said no to the asker—plates of candies, fruit, and little pieces of wedding cake were placed before us.

"Nice wedding," Rachel said, her dainty fingers reaching for a piece of fudge.

I looked over at Anna and Tobias at the *Eck*, enjoying their own plates of sweets. "They look happy."

Rachel poked me in the shoulder. "That's because they are."

I smiled at her, but my gaze was drawn back to Anna's new spouse. Tobias had been born in Lancaster County and lived here his whole life. He'd gone through the usual period of *rumspringa*, eventually even taking a month off to go and explore the outside on his own. That took him as far as Myrtle Beach on the coast, and then he'd come back home to the family furniture business, bowed his head in baptism, joined the church, and now had married an Amish girl. I doubted he'd ever spent a moment wondering who he was or where he belonged.

"Tyler."

I swung my head back around to face Rachel.

"Are you going to tell me what's bothering you?" Her kind face was sweetly marked with concern.

"I ate too much," I said, not wanting to mess with the festive mood around us.

"Nice try. What's up?"

I shrugged, but her compassionate gaze wouldn't allow me to say nothing at all. "Just thinking."

"About?"

Fueled by excitement and chocolate, the noise level was beginning to rise. Soon the singing would start. It would be hard to have a deep conversation.

"Just…life in general." I toyed with a candied walnut on the plate. But then out of nowhere I voiced what was somersaulting around in my head. "Sometimes it seems that something out there is calling to me. Like maybe I have missed doing something I am supposed to take care of. And then I come to an event like this, and that feeling grows so strong, it's nearly overwhelming."

I shut my mouth. I hadn't wanted to say all of that aloud, especially not at that moment. Yet it had spilled out of me anyway.

Pained uncertainty flickered across Rachel's eyes. "Something out *where* is calling to you?"

I shook my head. "We don't need to talk about this now. I don't know why I said anything."

Rachel stared at me, unwilling to drop it. "What is calling to you?"

I squeezed her hand. "Forget I said anything." Which was a dumb suggestion. She wasn't going to forget.

Besides, she knew me better than anyone. Better than Jake. Maybe even better than *Daadi* and *Mammi*.

She also knew the timetable for when the next membership classes were to begin—and that I wasn't sure yet if I was going to sign up for them. Membership preceded marriage. That's how it had always been, which meant if I didn't attend the next set of classes and take my vows of baptism and membership in the spring, I would not be able to marry her in the fall.

"Is this about God? About your faith?"

I shook my head. "No, of course not. I know what I believe. My faith is solid."

She nodded, quiet for a moment. "But this *is* about joining the church." Her voice sounded sad, and for good reason. We both knew that if my faith was solid and yet I was still reluctant to join the church, then my hesitation was about things other than theology. Things like living the Amish lifestyle. Things like being married to her.

"It's about a lot of stuff," I finally replied, though that wasn't the whole truth. It *was* about the church. But it was also about me. And the world outside. And her, too, which I realized at that moment I didn't want to add to the equation.

"Stuff," she echoed. "You mean *things*? Like the watch your father gave you? Your driver's license?"

My face grew warm. She was latching onto the few vestiges of the outside world I had yet to dispose of, but they had nothing to do with this. These days, except when I went out to visit my dad, the watch and the license remained tucked away in a drawer.

"No, it's not about things. It's about all of this," I said, gesturing toward the people and activities that surrounded us on every side. "It's about figuring out where I belong."

Understanding seemed to bloom in her eyes. "Ty, this is where you belong," she said emphatically. "With me. Everyone here loves you. I love you. This is your home."

"I'm not like Tobias." I looked at the happy new groom across the barn from us. He seemed a perfect fit in every way.

Rachel squeezed my hand. "Only Tobias is Tobias. You're you. And whatever it is you think is out there calling to you, don't you think you would have found it already? You've been outside, Tyler, more than most. You've seen the *Englisch* world every single time you've visited your dad."

"I know, but—"

"And every time you have visited your dad, you've always been ready to come home after just a few days. Doesn't that tell you anything?"

Her last comment took me by surprise. The world outside Lancaster County was a lot bigger than just California, where my father now lived. "This isn't about him," I muttered, releasing her hand.

Rachel's gaze wouldn't let me go. "How do you know it's not?"

I thought again of our schoolyard friendship so many years ago and how, not long after we'd made our peace on the swings, Rachel had responded when she learned my father was in the military. She'd been shocked, but not because of what my dad did for a living and how it conflicted with the Amish stance of nonresistance. She was upset because he'd handed me off to be raised by others once my mother was gone.

"What difference does it make what his *job* is? He's your *dad*. And he just *gave you away*."

Now, as she sat here next to me in a crisp, newly sewn dress, one strand of hair falling loose from the bun under her *kapp*, it was clear to me what her long-standing opinion of my father had led her to conclude, given my restless state. And she couldn't have been more wrong.

She glanced around and then leaned close as she whispered, "You know what I think, Tyler?"

I swallowed hard, wishing we'd never started this conversation in the first place.

"I think this has nothing to do with you and God *or* you and me. This is about you and your dad and the fact that you think he doesn't want you and never has."

She didn't mean her words to be unkind, just honest, as she and I had always been with each other. But they struck in a place so deep that I was shocked to find my eyes instantly rimmed with tears. I blinked them away, trying to decide whether to walk out of there right then or just stay and pretend she hadn't said that to me. To my dismay, however, she persisted, trying to be supportive but delivering a message that couldn't have been crueler.

"I think you still feel as rejected by him as you did the day you first came here," she said in an even softer whisper. "In a way, you're still that same six-year-old little boy who, more than anything, just wants his father to want him."

FOUR

When I look back now, it is no wonder that the part of me that held my earliest memories didn't know what to make of the first year I came to live in Lancaster County. My entire universe shifted when I was six years old.

First, my mother died of a medical condition that meant nothing to me. It wasn't as though she got sick or was hit by a car or fell off a high cliff. The word "aneurysm" had no context in my young world. She was simply alive one moment and gone the next.

Second, my father, who already had orders for a year-long remote assignment to Turkey, hadn't sought a hardship reassignment after she died—though he could have. Military members could always ask to be reassigned if a death in the family or a terminal illness or some other serious circumstance meant the member needed to be somewhere other than where he or she was scheduled to go. Instead, Dad asked my grieving grandparents to take me to Pennsylvania to live with them while he was gone and simply kept his orders as they were.

Thus, in the span of just a few days, I essentially lost both my parents and was thrust into an Amish life, where I had to learn a new language, a new way of living, a new way of thinking. It was like going through a doorway to another world where everything I knew and loved was gone and I had no choice but to start over.

At least my grandparents were kind, and they had a son my age, who didn't seem to mind at all that he would now have to share everything he had, including his bedroom, with the nephew he'd never even met before. For that matter, he hadn't met my mother, either—his own sister—because she'd left home before he was born.

Once I was settled, I'd made do the best I could, secretly marking off the days till my father's return on a calendar I kept hidden under my mattress, a free one that had come in the mail from a tractor company and my grandmother had thrown away.

When my dad's year in Turkey was up, he came back to see me, bringing along presents for everyone from overseas as well as some of my favorite toys from home and the cigar box containing my most treasured possessions that I'd always kept tucked away under my bed. I had already outgrown most of the toys by then, but I had been thrilled to get back the cigar box, which I'd missed at first but nearly forgotten about by then.

I'd been so happy to see him, and to have him there—until it was time to go and I learned to my astonishment that he wasn't taking me with him. Again. He told me he had accepted a follow-on assignment in Spain and would need me to stay right where I was until that was over too. I'd been devastated and spent many an hour once he was gone wondering what I'd done wrong to send him away.

Looking back now, of course, I realized that my father probably just couldn't handle being a single parent of a seven-year-old boy, especially while living overseas and being in the military. I tried to be patient, but it was while he was in Spain that he met an army nurse named Liz Brinkman. By the end of that tour, he married her and then they moved to Japan. I didn't even meet Liz—or see my dad again, for that matter—until a year after that, when she was pregnant with their son, Brady. That time, it was a quick visit, as they had only brief leave to come back to the States for her own mother's funeral.

After that they returned to Japan, and I didn't see my dad again for two more years.

All in all, I was eleven years old before my father was reassigned stateside, Liz got out of the military, and they came to Lancaster County to get me at last. Finally, he sat me down and asked me if I wanted to come live with him and his wife and their toddler in California.

It was the moment for which I'd been waiting for five years, yet all I could think about in that moment was that he was *asking* me. Not telling me. Asking me.

My father didn't say, "I want you to come, Tyler." He said, "Do you want to come?"

Even at eleven I could sense the difference. He and Liz and Brady and I had spent the afternoon with my grandparents at the farm. Then that night my dad took me to stay with the three of them at their hotel in Philadelphia, where he finally said those words.

Brady was almost two, and he was tired and cranky from the long day. Liz was busy entertaining him and didn't say much, though I knew she was listening to every word. She kept glancing at me, her eyes filled with an anxiousness that angered me. After Dad asked his question, he sat there, looking from me to her, and then he did something that sealed my decision. He reached for Liz and patted her shoulder. Brady let out a little wail and they both gently hushed him before lifting their gaze back to me and the question that hung in the air between us.

I told them I would stay with my grandparents.

Now I sat with Rachel, all these years later, telling myself I'd never regretted that decision, even as her words pounded inside my head like a drum. *You're still that same six-year-old little boy who, more than anything, just wants his father to want him.*

How on earth was I to respond to that? I couldn't. Instead, I excused myself and then simply rose and left, moving outside and around the corner of the barn to where it was quiet and empty and I could breathe. From there I could see the horses out in the field, lazily munching grass until they would be rounded up and reattached to the buggies they had brought here in the first place. My own horse seemed to sense my presence, and he sauntered in my direction. When he reached the fence, I walked over to greet him, absently patting his broad, muscular neck.

"I always miss your mother so much on special days like this one," a woman's voice said.

Startled, I turned to see my aunt Sarah, the mother of the bride, standing just a few feet behind me. I instantly thought she'd overheard what Rachel and I had been talking about and had come out here to see if I was okay. But when she stepped to the fence beside me and began cooing to my horse as well, I saw the sadness in her eyes, and I realized that she'd come out here for herself. Sarah didn't often mention my mother, her only sister. Those rare times she did, it was only with me.

"I can't imagine how hard it must be." I returned my gaze to the animal in front of us.

"*Ya*. It still hurts, even after all these years. I don't think most people know how much."

I didn't reply. I didn't need to. We'd always had this bond, this loss, even though Sarah wasn't one to bring it up often.

"She ran off the night before my birthday, did I ever tell you that?"

My eyes widened. "No."

"It was my twentieth birthday. We were supposed to have a family party, of course. But she and I also had plans for a fun time later that night, off on our own with Jonah and some of our other friends. We were all still on our *rumspringa*, and she and I were sort of known as the two sisters who were always raising a ruckus."

I smiled. "Somehow, I can't picture you as the ruckus-raising type."

Now it was her turn to smile. "*Ya*, well, you're probably right about that. Sadie was far more outgoing than I, far more energetic and alive. After she left, I refused to celebrate my birthday that year—at home or with my friends. I just stayed in my room and cried all night. At the time, I wondered if I would ever be happy again. She was my best friend. And she left me without even telling me why."

There was nothing I could say to that, so finally I just reached out, took her hand in mine, and gave it a squeeze. She squeezed back, her grip firm.

"Of course, time and forgiveness heal all wounds. And marrying Jonah two years later brought joy back to my life, but I have never been able to get over the fact that your mother isn't here, sharing special days like this with me. I had always imagined she would."

She released my hand to dab at her eyes, which had filled with tears.

"I'm sorry, Tyler. Here you are enjoying Anna and Tobias's special day, and I come along and start blubbering like an old fool."

I shook my head, wishing I had more comfort to offer her. All I could do was give her a hug and tell her what I always told myself, that at least we had our memories.

When I returned to the barn and my place at the table, Rachel seemed to sense she had crossed a line. Except for reaching over to give my hand a loving squeeze, she let me alone for a while, remaining silent and simply watching the others around the table. When she finally spoke, it was to point out the various treats, saying who made what, and how. The earlier topic was dropped and all serious conversation avoided, though I sensed we would both spend the rest of the time at the wedding pondering our exchange.

Later that night, when Anna and Tobias's long wedding day was over, the evening chores done, and I was alone in my bed, Rachel's words kept replaying in my mind. Truth be told, I didn't want to believe my current restlessness had anything to do with my dad's long-ago decision to leave me behind. But once she brought it up, I couldn't stop wondering if that was part of it, a leftover yearning from childhood.

I hadn't regretted the decision I'd made in my father's hotel room. I'd known where I stood with my *Englisch* family—as a distant fourth to their little group of three. There was no room for me in their world.

And I'd always been okay with the trajectory my life had taken after that—or at least I'd told myself I was. Certainly, I could see God's hand in it. Here on the farm, I had learned what it meant to be Christlike, to be part of a community, to live among people who put their beliefs into practice, day after hardworking day.

On the other hand, I admitted to myself now, I had also sacrificed much by staying here: the presence of my father in my life on a daily basis, any sort of a real relationship with my stepmother, quality time with my little brother, Brady. Once they moved to California when I was eleven, I started going to stay with them for several weeks each summer. But those visits had always been difficult for me. So many elements came into play. My deep affection for Brady. My jealousy over the life he'd been given, one that should have been mine too. My relationship with Liz, who always seemed so uncomfortable when I was around. My resentment toward my father, who acted oblivious to the fact that he'd basically abandoned me after my mother's death.

Worst of all, I would spend those times feeling like the odd man out, not just because I wasn't a true part of their family, but because I wasn't even a true part of the *Englisch* world. I was an Amish boy, and being at my dad's house only accentuated that.

Yet once I came home, it always took a little while for me to reenter my Amish life. Both worlds were mine, yet in truth neither was. I didn't really belong there. I didn't really belong here. I was caught somewhere in the middle, a man without any place at all.

I turned over in my bed and pushed the curtains away from the window above the headboard. Moonshine bathed me in pearly radiance. A patch of clouds hung low, and a single star glimmered in the open space between the heavens and the earth. The sky had looked just like this on my first night in this house. I didn't remember arriving or much of the long ride that had brought us here, but I did remember some of the events leading up to that. I remembered the afternoon my first life ended and my second one began.

Closing my eyes now, I could see myself in my *Englisch* funeral clothes—gray slacks, a new clip-on tie, a blue button-down shirt that was still wrinkled from its packaging. Just prior to the service, my father pointed out a couple I'd never met, saying they were my mom's mother and father, my grandparents. They were so oddly dressed, I wouldn't have believed it except that the woman looked like an older version of my mother. She had the same beautiful eyes, the same, though far more wrinkled, heart-shaped face.

After the service, I sat in the tire swing of the chapel playground while funeral-goers sipped punch and munched on tiny chicken salad sandwiches and talked softly among themselves. My dad, in his dress uniform, stood talking to the man he'd said was my grandfather. But this was not the grandfather I already knew, my dad's father, the one who walked with a cane and smelled like cigarettes. This other grandfather had a beard like Abraham Lincoln—whiskers with no moustache—and a broad-brimmed black hat.

The other grandmother was with them as well, but she didn't seem to be paying attention to their conversation. Instead, she just stood there in her dark dress and black bonnet, looking back at me, her face a strange mix of happy and sad.

I couldn't hear everything my father was saying to them, but I picked up snatches, such as "only for a year" and "just until I can figure out how to do this on my own," and "Sadie was the one who did everything."

Sadie.

Mommy.

And then my dad walked over to the swing and knelt down. He looked tired, and the rims of his eyes were red. He told me my grandparents had a farm in the country and they wanted me to come to see it. He said there were cows and horses and a big house and other kids my age.

"And a pond," I replied, remembering the night of the storm when we still lived in Germany and my mother was still alive.

"What?"

"There's a pond at the farm. Mommy told me."

"Uh, well, okay. A pond. You'll have a great time there. And you get to ride a train."

I asked when we were leaving, and his face took on an odd expression as he said, "No, Tyler, you don't understand. I'm not coming. It's just you and your grandparents."

My eyes widened.

He looked down at his hands. "I have to go far away to supervise all the people who take care of the helicopters."

"Are you going where Mommy is?"

"No." He shook his head.

"When are you coming back?" In my head I was attempting to keep the details straight. *Mommy is far away, not coming back. Daddy will be far away, so…*

"I'll be gone a while. It may seem like a long time, but I will come back."

"How will you know where to find me if you don't take me there yourself?"

He put a hand on my shoulder. "I know where your grandparents live, Ty. I've been there before."

"You have?"

He nodded. "When your mother and I were first married, right before we left for Germany. We drove out to the farm and I met her family and she got to tell them goodbye."

"Did I come too?"

"No. You weren't born yet. That was back when it was just your mom and me." His voice cracked at the word "mom" and then he looked away.

I was not as close to my dad as I had been to my mother. He was away from home more often than he was at it. But at that moment, he was all I had that felt safe. I didn't want to go on a train with people I didn't know.

"I want to stay with you."

He shook his head. "Families can't come to the place I'm going to, Tyler. It's not like Germany. I can't bring you with me."

"Then stay here." Tears, hot and wet, pooled in my six-year-old eyes.

"I can't, Tyler. I have to go. It's my job."

I wiped at my wet cheeks as he added, "You'll be happy there. Trust me. You really will."

"I don't want to go," I wailed. And across the playground, my grandmother wiped her eyes with a tissue. My grandfather was talking to her and stroking her back. She looked at me and tried to smile.

"Sometimes you have to go somewhere even when you don't want to. I'm sorry, Tyler, but I'm only doing what's best for you. I can't...I don't... you need someone like your grandma and your grandpa. They already love you. They always have, even though you've never met. And they have other kids. One is almost your exact age. You'll be happy there. You have to trust me on this."

"I want my mom," I sputtered.

"I know you do. I do too. But she's not coming back." Dad stood up and held out his hand. "Come on, son. Let's go meet your grandparents."

Reluctantly, I climbed off of the swing, took his hand, and let him lead me over to the people who were going to take me home with them to live.

After we were introduced, my grandfather shook my hand as he asked me to call him *Daadi*.

"That sounds like 'Daddy,'" I said softly.

He smiled. "*Ya*, it does. But it's spelled differently. And it's our word for grandfather."

"Call me *Mammi*," my grandmother said, kneeling down and opening her arms tentatively for a hug. I hesitated, but there was something so familiar about her kind face that I couldn't help but move into her embrace.

I couldn't remember anything about the rest of that day, not packing up or saying goodbye to my father or getting on the train.

I did remember waking up next to my grandmother a long time later, when the train blew its loud whistle. She helped me settle more comfortably across her lap, and she said something soft and gentle in another language. It sounded so familiar, like something my mother would say. Then I drifted back to sleep.

Jake and I hadn't had to share a bedroom for a number of years now, but we did back then, and I remembered my first night, lying in this bed and listening to his gentle snores from across the room. We were both six.

Mammi had turned out the light, a funny little lantern that sounded like it was breathing when it glowed with flame. And I began to cry because I was afraid of the dark and there were no outlets for my Power Rangers night-light.

Mammi returned quickly, and after I told her why I was crying, she pulled the curtain open above the bed. "Here is your night-light, Tyler. The same one your *mamm* had when this was her room."

Outside the window, near a diamond-bright star, sat the moon in a cushion of clouds, its light shining across my pillow in a broad streak of white.

"Can you show me the pond?" I whispered.

Mammi stroked my forehead. "*Ya, dire kinder.* Tomorrow."

In the morning, my grandparents walked me out to my mother's pond, and it was just as beautiful as she'd told me it was. Even better, there really was another me—another world—reflecting back from the glassy water, just as she'd said there would be.

Daadi and *Mammi* and the farm became my solid ground when my dad let me go. They gave me a home, a big family, a place to belong, and a faith in a heavenly Father on whom I could hang my every hope. Though my loss had been great, somehow over the years their steadfast love had helped to fill the empty, aching places inside. They hadn't just given me somewhere to live but, ultimately, a new life.

When I was eleven and my father asked me if I wanted to live with him and Liz and Brady—*asked*, not told—and I said no, my grandparents had been the ones to comfort my aching heart once they were gone.

When I was sixteen and about to jump into my *rumspringa* with abandon, *Daadi* had been the one to show me what godly manhood looked like through his own example, and then he guided me through the worst of it with lots of prayer and an enormous amount of patience.

When I was twenty and learned that Rachel would be joining the church, *Mammi* had been the one to encourage me to join as well, saying that this was where I belonged. My visits to California had stopped by then, the dividing line between my world and my father's more distinct than ever before.

Now it was three years later, and though I knew I would always have a home here, a big part of me still couldn't fully accept that fact. As I'd told Rachel earlier, something out there was calling to me. Something beyond myself. And that was what needled me as I lay unable to sleep. I wanted to believe God wanted me here, wanted me to be Amish. Yet it almost felt as though *He* was that something, that Someone, who was calling to me from outside.

Could this restlessness be of God?

If so, I couldn't begin to fathom why.

FIVE

Somewhere deep in the night, I finally managed to fall asleep, only to be awakened again at five by the clomp of Jake's heavy footsteps in the hallway moving past my door. As the house slowly came to life around me, I forced myself to yank the covers off. Sitting up, I placed my feet on the cool wood, hoping it would startle me fully awake.

Morning chores needed to be done before breakfast and devotions, and then after just an hour or two of work, I would be giving Jake a ride to the bus. After that, I would join in with the massive, post-wedding cleanup effort at the Bowman farm, which would likely last until sundown. It was going to be a tiring day, made worse by my lack of sleep the night before.

I came downstairs yawning. Jake, standing at the sink eating an apple, regarded me with comic concern. "You look terrible."

"Thanks. I'm going to miss hearing that." I snagged a mug, hoping to down a quick swallow of coffee before heading out to help him with the family horses.

"I mean it, Ty. You look terrible."

"Couldn't sleep."

Jake tossed his core in a bowl for the compost pile. "Aw, you miss me already." He laughed and headed for the mudroom. "Either that or you ate too many dumplings at the wedding."

I swallowed the hot liquid and winced at the burn at the back of my throat. "I'll be out shortly," I rasped.

"Okay. See you there."

I blew into the cup, listening as Jake paused in the mudroom to suit up and then headed outside into the last vestiges of night, the door slapping shut behind him. We usually went to the stable together each morning, laughing and joking all the way, but he was eager to wrap things up before it was time to go, and I was in no mood for socializing. Moving to the sink, I stood and watched through the window, spotting *Daadi* in the light of the henhouse just as Jake rounded the side of the barn.

Outside the window, a slender line of light was sneaking onto the horizon. I'd hoped for a few quiet minutes alone, but *Mammi* came into the kitchen just then to start making breakfast, and she shooed me away. I took one final sip and then gave her cheek a quick kiss before moving into the mudroom. She began humming a quiet tune as I pulled on my boots and then grabbed my hat and coat off their pegs and slipped into them. I swung the door open to see Timber there waiting for me, eagerly wagging his tail.

I greeted him warmly, and then the two of us walked side by side toward the stables. As we went, I couldn't help but wonder how different my growing-up years would have been if Jake hadn't been around. If I had gone to live with my dad and Liz when they asked me, the only brother figure in my life would have been little Brady, who was nine years younger than I, far too young to tease or knock around or share banter with.

Even after Brady was older, our lives were just so different that it was often hard to relate. I loved him, of course, and it was easy to see he looked up to me, but sometimes it took the first day or two of my visits there just to relax and grow comfortable together again. I knew he enjoyed having his big brother around, and it hit me with new clarity that my life had been made much richer by the aunt and uncles I'd grown up with, all of whom had been like siblings to me.

Since coming here to live, I'd always been surrounded by other kids, but what of Brady? Except when I visited, he was the only child living in their home, which had to be a lonely state indeed—especially given that our father was not one to show emotion unless it involved the acquisition of a new muscle car, the only thing Dad had a passion for outside his former military life. And Liz? She was polite and hospitable, but she always seemed to be on her guard, as if she were hesitant to be her true self. I didn't know if she was that way all the time or just around me, but if it was the former, then it was no wonder Brady looked forward to having me in the house for a few weeks each summer. There was much he had that I didn't, but I saw now that that was true in the reverse as well.

When Timber and I reached the stables, I paused at the supply closet to serve up some dog chow and then used the hose to rinse out his water bowl and refill it. After that, I moved the rest of the way inside and turned my attention to Jake, who had obviously been going through his duties at record speed. I was feeling a little more up to conversation by that point, but he was so antsy that we barely spoke. Instead, he finished picking each horse's hooves while I drained the watering trough, scrubbed it out, and filled it back up again.

Jake had already dumped the grain into the feeding trough before I got there, so as the horses had their fill of water, I opened the broad double doors to the pasture. The animals were usually eager to get outside, but this time several of them hung back, as if they knew Jake was leaving today. The stalls needed mucking out, however, so finally I insisted on taking over, telling Jake to go on back to the house, that he and his mopey animals were in my way.

"Thanks, Tyler," he said without a hint of his usual sarcasm. He tried to shoo the animals out, but as he patted down the one who lingered, he called out to me a laundry list of things I was not to forget about caring for his beloved horses while he was gone—from keeping an eye on the pasture for a particular invasive clover that was toxic to horses if ingested to checking them daily for bites and sores and rashes. None of it was news to me.

Finally, he headed out, pausing at the doorway to turn back. "You'll take good care of them for me?" he asked. He'd been a good farrier, and I knew he would become a great blacksmith as well.

"They'll never even know you're gone," I replied, though he and I were both well aware that wasn't true. He had a way with horses I would never master, no matter how hard I tried.

I managed to finish the rest of the chores by myself, and then I returned to the house for a delicious breakfast of fresh sausage and banana pancakes. That was followed by the reading of a psalm and prayers for the day, and then I headed to the shop.

My morning was spent on finish work to a buggy that was nearly complete. When the detailing was done, I straightened up my work area and then went in search of Jake. I found him in the driveway, beside the family buggy, his backpack slung over one shoulder and a large duffel bag at his feet.

I grabbed the duffel and threw it onto the rear seat of the vehicle as he stepped toward *Mammi* to give her a hug. *Daadi* tightened the harness on the horse as the animal lazily chewed on the bit in his mouth.

"There are two sandwiches in the bag for when you get hungry and a slice of coconut cake leftover from the wedding," *Mammi* said as she pulled Jake in and squeezed him tight.

"*Danke, Mamm.*"

Daadi came around to where Jake and *Mammi* stood, placed a hand on Jake's shoulder, and bowed his head. "'Be of good comfort, be of one mind, live in peace; and the God of love and peace shall be with you,'" he said, quoting from the book of Second Corinthians. Then he clasped Jake to his chest.

"*Danke, Daed.*" Jake returned his father's embrace.

I climbed onto the driver's seat as Jake said his final farewells.

He stepped aboard, resting his backpack on the floor, and gave his parents a final wave as we moved down the driveway and set off at an easy canter along the main road. A few other buggies were also out and about, some no doubt headed over to the Bowman farm. Only a few cars passed us at first, but the closer to town we got, the more the automobile traffic increased.

I was bringing Jake to a stop on the New Holland line, where he would catch the local to Lancaster then switch over to Greyhound for the day-and-a-half ride to Missouri.

We talked about nothing in particular as we made our way, but when we were just a few blocks from the bus station, his voice took on a more serious tone. "Tyler, are you okay with my leaving the buggy business? I never asked you. And things will be different when I get back."

"Of course I am. I know how much you want to do this, Jake. We all do."

He regarded me for a moment. "You don't have to stay with the buggies either, you know. *Daed* would understand if there was something else you wanted to do."

I had been trained on nearly every facet of the buggy-making process, from welding the axles to upholstering the seats to installing the hydraulics for the brakes. I had been working alongside *Daadi* every weekday, all day, since my schooling ended when I was fourteen. It was the most familiar thing in the world to me.

"What else would I do?"

Jake laughed, but gently. "What do you *want* to do?"

I turned my head to look at him before swinging my attention back to the road in front of me. "Why are we talking about this?"

He shrugged. "I know you've had a lot on your mind lately. I thought maybe it had something to do with my leaving the buggy shop."

"Oh. No."

"Okay. Good." He was quiet for a moment. "Do you and Rachel have a problem?"

I shook my head. "No."

"You want to tell me what it is, then?"

I did and I didn't. I wasn't sure I could articulate what was on my mind, especially after yesterday's mishandled conversation with Rachel. But I knew I couldn't keep it in much longer, so finally I gave it a try.

"I don't know what it is exactly, but I've been feeling restless lately. Like there's something out here I am supposed to be doing or looking for." He knew I meant out in the non-Amish world. The world outside.

"And you don't have any idea what that might be?" He didn't seem shocked or surprised, and I was glad.

"I don't. But I can feel something tugging at me, Jake. And I think… this is going to sound crazy, but I think it might be God. Pulling me to the outside."

"That doesn't sound crazy at all."

He couldn't have understood what I meant. "I'm talking about feeling that God wants me *out there*!"

He nodded. "I get it, Tyler. Like I said, not crazy."

I signaled for a turn and eased the buggy into the left lane. "Well, it feels crazy."

"What are you going to do about it?"

"I don't know. But I can't go to the bishop and tell him I want to become a church member when I'm feeling this way." I made the left turn and the car behind me zoomed past as soon as it could.

"No. Of course you can't."

"And that means I can't ask Rachel to…I can't…"

"I know what it means. And you're right. You need to settle this first."

I looked over at my uncle, envious for a moment that he had already made his membership vows and was now headed out to learn a trade he'd been longing to pursue for years.

"But I don't even know where to start." I motioned to the busy streets, the cars, the people on the sidewalks with their cell phones in hand, the humming buzz of activity that was everything the Amish world was not. "I get out here and I sense no direction. And I just can't see how God would be drawing me to look for something when I don't know what it is or where I should begin. That's not like Him at all."

"I wouldn't say that."

We were just half a block from the bus stop and Jake reached for his backpack. He slung it over his shoulder.

"God calls people out of the familiar all the time when He wants to teach them something new."

"Okay, maybe He does. But the problem is that when I'm here, I feel a restlessness to be out there. But when I'm out there, all I want to do is get back here. It's like I don't belong in either place."

I pulled on the reins and my horse obeyed. We slowed to a stop.

"You know you need to talk to *Daed* about this." Jake stepped down and reached into the back to retrieve his duffel.

I sighed heavily. "I know. I've been putting it off. I don't want him to think I'm like…that I'm just like my mother. That I want to leave. I'm afraid I'll hurt him the way she did."

He shook his head. "That was different, Tyler. She was raised Amish, but they have always known that the outside world was a part of…" He gestured blindly, trying to state the obvious without putting it in a way that would sound mean. I knew what he was saying, that the outside world had been a part of my past—and a potential for my future—since the day I was born.

Jake leaned forward across the passenger seat to clasp my hand, meeting my eyes with a firm gaze as we shook. "Talk to *Daed*. He's a very wise man."

"I know. You're right. Have a great time in Missouri."

Releasing his grip, he stood up straight, shifting the weight of his pack. "Tell *Mamm* I'll call the shop phone when I get settled."

"*Ya.*"

"See you in February?"

I nodded. I very much hoped he would see me in February. He stepped out onto the street and then turned back to face me.

"So you'll talk to him?" His eyes were filled with brotherly concern.

"I'll talk to him."

Jake shut the buggy door, patted the horse goodbye, and turned to wave as he walked off. I watched until he joined the handful of people already at the bus stop, some chatting on cell phones, a few smoking, the rest simply staring off into the distance.

Turning my eyes from the scene and swallowing hard, I waited for a lull in the traffic and in my racing thoughts before signaling and easing the buggy back on the road.

I spent the rest of the day at the Bowmans', silently beseeching God to help me find the right words to tell *Daadi* I was struggling with something I hardly knew how to describe. I was also praying He would show me the right time for that conversation to happen. God answered my second prayer first. Actually, He answered only that prayer.

The next afternoon, back at the buggy shop, everyone was either done for the day or working outside in the covered bay, and *Daadi* and I ended up inside alone. It was obviously a great time to have a quiet conversation with him, but I had no ready words at my disposal.

His final task of the day was to mount a new set of tires on a courting buggy. As he did that, I worked in the space next to his, adding extra suspension to the rear axle of a new top wagon. *Daadi* slid the first tire on the back axle and then pulled out a wrench and began tightening the nuts. Glancing his way, I could almost feel God whispering over my shoulder.

This is the time you prayed for.

Pausing in my work, I cleared my throat. "*Daadi*, I need to talk to you for a minute."

"Oh?" He looked relaxed and unfazed, his eyes on the task at hand.

"I'm struggling with something, and I don't even know how to put it into words."

He stopped turning the wrench and gave me his full attention. "Have you done something you regret, son?"

"No. No, it's nothing like that."

He began to turn the wrench again, perhaps sensing it would be easier for me if we kept working while I stumbled through what I needed to say. "Tell me what's on your mind."

And so I told him, as near as I could, what I had admitted to Rachel and Jake, what I had been sensing lately when I went to the pond on early mornings, and how I had begun to feel that God Himself was beckoning me from beyond Lancaster County—though for whatever reason I couldn't imagine. *Daadi* continued to mount the tires as I talked, pausing now and then as I spoke but saying nothing.

As soon as I was done, I felt a crushing weight, not a lifted burden. Despite what Jake had said about my situation being different from my mother's, I knew this conversation had to be nearly as hurtful to *Daadi* as when she ran away from the Amish life almost twenty-five years before.

"I'm sorry if this is hard for you to hear," I concluded. "It's hard for me to say. But it's been even harder to keep locked up inside me. I had to tell you."

"Yes, you did." *Daadi* set the wrench down. "And I'm glad you did, Tyler."

"I don't want to leave. I don't want to be anywhere else but here, but I can't ignore this restlessness inside me."

He nodded. I could tell he was thinking. Maybe praying. Trying to form the right response.

"Rachel thinks this has to do with my dad and the fact that he essentially abandoned me here all those years ago," I added.

"Hmm," *Daadi* said, but nothing else. He was deep in thought.

"But I forgave him for that. It's not like I lie awake wondering why he didn't want me. I've been happy here. You and *Mammi* and Jake and the aunts and uncles—you're my family. And I had my chance to go back with my father."

"Yes, you did. A long time ago."

"But I've never regretted staying, *Daadi*. Not once. This is my home. This is my life."

"And yet you have not gone to the bishop to seek your vows of membership."

I opened my mouth and then shut it again. What could I say to that? My mind spinning, I returned to my own work. Outside in the work bay, I could hear various strains of conversation as one by one the other workers called it a day and began to head home. Inside, *Daadi* and I were quiet save for the clink and clank of our tools, both of us lost in contemplation.

Finally, I turned to my beloved grandfather and said, "It can't really be God calling me from outside, can it?"

He tightened a bolt. "God is everywhere. You know this, Tyler. If He can call Father Abraham out, He can call you."

"Yes, but why would He? What is out there that is better than what I have here?"

Daadi finished putting on the tire, and then he went over to the bench behind us, sat down, and patted the seat next to him. I set my screwdriver aside and joined him there.

"Your life is not one to be spent in pursuit of what is better or best. Your life is to be spent in surrender, Tyler. Surrender and service to God."

"But I am to be separate," I countered, hearing the words of the *Ordnung* in my head.

"You are to be obedient."

Another span of seconds passed. I let my gaze travel around the shop, taking in the familiar tools and products of the trade. Over near the window, the late afternoon sunshine splayed across the sewing area, where the upholstery was made. Beyond that, in the painting bay, sat the half shell of a new spring wagon, ready for its electrical work to be started as soon as the final coat was dry.

I sucked in a deep breath, relishing the buggy shop's familiar scent of oil and paint and new fabric and metal and fresh-cut wood. The work here could be tedious at times, but I loved it just the same. Why would I ever want to turn my back on this?

Then it came to me. What if God was just testing me? What if He was allowing me to feel the lure of the world outside so that I could firmly renounce it? What if I had only to state my intentions, fulfill the class requirements, bow my head in baptism, and make my vows to prove I could forsake that which I had been born into?

My heart raced. If that were the case, then maybe I really could silence forever this beckoning voice that confused me. I could train myself to see only the Amish Tyler when I gazed into the pond. I could marry Rachel and be done with wondering.

If this was a test, I was ready to pass it.

Eyes wide, I turned to *Daadi* and spoke, surprising both myself and him with the urgency in my tone. "I want to be obedient. I want to become a member."

Daadi nodded slowly, but his mind was far away.

"Did you hear what I said, *Daadi*? I want to become a member."

My grandfather placed a hand on my arm. "I heard you, Tyler," he said, his voice heavy. "We shall pray about this. And I will speak to the bishop."

I couldn't believe it. Here I was finally saying the words he'd longed for, and he was putting me off?

"You don't think I should take my vows?" My voice sounded harsh, demanding, even in my own ears.

He was quiet for a long moment.

"Vows are never for the purpose of silencing what you don't want to hear." He stood, moved slowly to the tool rack, and set the wrench in its place. "But I will pray. And I will consult the bishop."

With that, he turned and walked out of the shop, leaving me alone with my thoughts, even more confused now than I had been before.

Six

The days following were strange for me. Morning chores without Jake took longer, and his empty place beside me in the buggy shop was keenly felt. Worse, more than once I caught my grandparents staring at me in concern when they thought I wouldn't notice.

Daadi had obviously confided in *Mammi* about our conversation because I could see that she knew and it was bothering her. The fact that he'd shared it with her didn't surprise or annoy me. I wanted her to know, but I also didn't want her to worry. And it was obvious to me she *was* worried, even though she never brought it up.

At least I was doing this honorably, I told myself, thinking of how my mother had simply packed her things and left in the dark of night without a word to anyone. I didn't remember her being unkind or uncaring. I felt certain she left the way she did because she didn't want a tearful scene peppered by harsh words everyone would regret having said. Such a departure would have been easier for me too, but I refused to repeat the past that way.

It wasn't just that I knew well the pain such an action would cause. It was also a matter of age and maturity. I was in my twenties, but at the time my mother left the farm for Philadelphia, she'd been all of eighteen and far less experienced with the world than I. She did not have another home and family on the outside where she could visit each summer and try the *Englisch* life on for size.

My aunt Sarah had been closer to my mother than anyone, and I had asked her once why she thought my mother left. I was twelve and wanting to know more than the little my grandparents had told me, but I hadn't felt comfortable asking them about it.

"I've never understood why," Sarah had responded, and it was obvious not knowing still pained her. "Perhaps she just wanted things the Amish life didn't give her. Fancy things. She liked the city and dancing and television and movies and riding in cars. I guess it reached the point where the Plain life just wasn't enough for her."

"Enough for her," I echoed.

She nodded. "Jonah believes so as well. We were all good friends back then, you know, and I think he saw the situation even more clearly than I did. He tried mightily to comfort me in those early days after she left. He kept reminding me of all the times she would push for more even as I would insist on holding back. My sister and I were the best of friends, but there was a wild streak in her that I never had—not wild like *bad*, just wild as in she couldn't be tamed. She had too much energy. Too much curiosity. Too much desire for the things of this world."

I had accepted Sarah's explanation then, but now that I looked back, I had to wonder if there had been more to it than that. Could it have been a crisis of faith that drove my mother away? A need to seek something in the broader world? A tugging from outside that she, too, had attributed to God?

Sadly, there was no way I could ever know.

What I did know were the basic facts that my father had told me over the years, how she left her family's farm in Lancaster County in the middle of the night and caught a bus to Philadelphia. How she moved into a tiny apartment there and took a job as a waitress. How not long after that, my dad just happened to go into the restaurant where she worked, spotted her behind the counter, and fell in love.

He'd been a first lieutenant back then, on leave before heading oversees to an army base in Heidelburg, Germany. He had come to Philadelphia to visit with his old West Point roommate and best buddy, and when the two of them came into the restaurant that night, they both flirted with the pretty girl working the counter. She flirted back only with my father, however, as if it had been love at first sight on her side too. At the end of the evening, half joking, he had asked her if she'd like to come to Maryland and take a ride in his '67 Charger convertible. To his surprise and delight, she had said yes. And she hadn't been half joking.

Three weeks later—and just a month before his deployment to Germany—they had driven down to Maryland to tie the knot and spent their honeymoon at the Jersey Shore. At some point fairly soon after that, they went to Lancaster County to tell her family about their marriage—and their upcoming move—in person.

I knew that was one of the few times my dad had ever been to the farm. And I also knew the visit hadn't gone well. Years ago, I had asked Sarah if she remembered that day, and she'd nodded as a heavy sadness fell across her face.

"That was the last time any of us saw her. She was so happy, and she wanted all of us to be happy for her too, but how could we? First, she ran away without a word. Then when she finally came back it was to announce that not only was she married—to an Englischer—but that her husband was in the military—and that they were bound for Germany for three years. I think it was just too much for my parents to take in all at once. Too much for all of us. I was so upset I couldn't even talk to her."

"Did any of you stay in touch? Maybe write to her over there?"

She shook her head sadly. "In the beginning she didn't send us an address, Tyler. I think she needed some space."

I nodded, knowing the fault was hers, not theirs.

"I think she wrote *Mamm* once, and then we didn't hear from her again until after you were born. One day out of the blue she called the buggy shop from the Philly airport, saying that she and her husband had a child now and that the three of you were back in the States while he attended some special training or something in Maryland."

"Maryland? That's not far. Did they come out for another visit?"

"No."

"So did any of you go down to see her—see us—in Maryland?" I was careful not to sound accusatory.

"No." Sarah grew quiet for a long moment. "But I think *Mamm* and *Daed* would have done things differently if they had realized what was going to happen. I know I would have."

I could see the truth of that statement in her eyes. I could also see the infinite pain behind it.

"Only God knows the future, Tyler. Sometimes you learn how to handle things by making mistakes the first time around."

That Sunday, the worship service was held at Rachel's farm, and though I was glad to see her, she and I did not speak of what I had mentioned at the wedding. Not directly, anyway. Chatting after lunch, she asked me about Jake—if we had heard from him and how he was liking farrier school so far—but there was a veiled concern there, as if her question really didn't have much to do with his absence at all. We were surrounded by other people, so I wasn't free to tell her that I had talked to both Jake and *Daadi* about what I was wrestling with, and that *Daadi* would be asking the bishop what I should do. I could only tell her that Jake had left a message on the buggy shop phone, assuring us he had arrived safely in Missouri, and that I missed him but appreciated not having to fight him for the last pork chop at dinner.

Back home that afternoon, as I put away the buggy and began to brush down my horse, *Daadi* joined me in the stable. I could tell something was on his mind.

"I spoke to the bishop," he said, taking the harness from me and hanging it on its hook.

"Yes?" My heart was pounding, but I focused on running the brush over the mare's brown flank.

"He feels as I do, Tyler. We will join you in praying for wisdom and clarity for you to hear from God. If He is speaking to you, you must listen."

"But how will I know if this is actually *God* speaking to me or if it's just my own thoughts made to seem that way?"

"Discernment is a discipline. That is why you must fast and pray and ask God to show you His way. Bishop Ott is praying for you even now. As am I. And your grandmother. We are already praying for you to hear from God. Like the prophets of old, if you ask Him for wisdom, He will answer with wisdom."

I didn't doubt for a moment that Bishop Ott's counsel was wise, but I didn't know what that meant for the here and now. "And what do I do in the meantime?"

My grandfather reached out a strong arm to touch my shoulder. "That is all you do, Tyler. You pray and ask for wisdom. Do not rest until you have it."

I spent the following week in a concerted effort to hear from God—fasting for the first twenty-four hours, rising each day earlier than usual to pray on my knees at my bedside, returning again and again to the quiet of the pond because that was where I first felt that flickering summons of unrest.

Mammi still said nothing to me about what we were all quietly praying for, though several times that week she reached out her hand to touch my face or my arm when she served me at the table, and her eyes spoke encouragement mixed with apprehension.

During the day, I kept my mind on the work I had at the buggy shop. We had a new hydraulic brake we were putting into all of our buggies, and I had a week's worth of retrofits to keep my hands busy while I listened for an answer from God.

By that Friday, I was getting weary of the diligence this sort of prayer required. I knew God did not always answer prayers in a swift manner, but I felt a growing sense of urgency as the week ended. Everything that related to the rest of my life—baptism, church membership, marriage to Rachel—hinged on God's answers to these prayers.

On Sunday morning, I woke well before the sun. It was not a worship Sunday, so I crept downstairs, grabbed my jacket, and quietly opened the mudroom door. I could feel the change in the air the moment I stepped outside. It was early yet for snow, but overnight a heavy frost had fallen, and I was greeted by a rousing chill. My breath came out in puffy clouds as I whistled softly for Timber.

Once he joined me, we walked across the pasture to the windmill and then took the well-worn path down to the pond, icy grass crunching under my boots. The surface of the water was lightly frozen around the edges, and I was tempted to break the thin layer of ice so that I could see my reflection, so I could search for the me on the other side. I didn't, though. Somehow it didn't seem right to disturb what the finger of God had done overnight.

As Timber made his usual sniffing tour of the shoreline, I knelt there at the bank, closed my eyes, and prayed with renewed vigor.

Lord, You know all things. You know what has been keeping me awake at night and dropping me to my knees in the morning. I don't want to feel restless and unsettled anymore. I humbly ask that You would reveal to me whether You are testing me or tugging me. Show me what to do. Show me...

I stayed there until after the sun rose, long after Timber had trotted back to the house. My limbs were stiff and cold when I finally stood and left the pond, but my vision was no clearer than it had been when I had arrived. Back at the stables, after I fed a hungry dog and tended to the horses, the morning passed slowly. I shared a quiet breakfast with my grandparents but otherwise kept to myself. No answer came the rest of that day, or the next few days after that.

It wasn't until the following Thursday, in fact, that my answer seemed to come. I was in the buggy shop finishing up a brake job when the phone rang. My cousin Harley answered it.

"It's for you, Ty," he said after a moment, turning toward me.

I put down my tools and took the receiver from him, a bit puzzled. The phone was primarily for staying in contact with our suppliers on the outside. I hardly ever used it and wasn't expecting a call from anyone.

"Hello?"

"Hey, Tyler."

The voice on the other end of the line was my father's.

SEVEN

It took me a few moments to grasp the notion that my dad had called me on an ordinary Thursday in October. We usually only talked to each other on special occasions, never just to chat. In fact, the last time we'd spoken had been when he'd called me on my birthday, seven months earlier.

My first thought was that something terrible had happened, but his voice didn't sound upset.

"Dad, how are you?" I asked, the only question I could think of as I moved away from the noise of the shop's interior and closer to the outside door.

"I'm doing well. And you?"

"Um…I'm good. Is something wrong? Is everybody okay?"

"Everything's fine. I'm calling because I need to ask a favor."

A favor? For a second, I was speechless. I couldn't imagine one thing I could do for him from almost three thousand miles away. "Oh?"

"It's kind of a big one. But I wouldn't ask if it wasn't important."

"What is it?"

"What are you doing for the next month? Say, through the end of November?"

I blinked, not sure I understood the question. For the next month I would be working here in the buggy shop, as always. He should know that.

He didn't wait for an answer before he continued. "The thing is, I need you to come out here to California. I need you to come and stay with Brady."

"Stay with Brady?"

He cleared his throat. "Yeah. It's kind of complicated. We've never had this happen before, but it turns out that Liz and I are both going to be out of the country at the same time."

"Out of the country?" I asked, starting to feel like a parrot.

"She's about to leave for Central America for a humanitarian project, which wasn't going to be an issue. I was all set to handle things here on the home front. But now I've had something come up too, important contract work in the Middle East, and I don't know what else to do."

"I see," was all I could manage.

"I'll be gone for three or four weeks—and Liz for five. Ordinarily, Brady could just stay with a friend, or we could have Liz's aunt come to the house for a visit, but this is too long a time for either solution. We couldn't impose like that on a friend, and Liz's aunt can't be away from her job for more than a few days."

I closed my eyes and pinched the bridge of my nose, trying to sort this out. Liz was going away, my father was going away, and there was no one else on earth left to stay with their son except for me?

"Why don't you just take Brady with you?" I asked.

Dad let out a half chuckle. "It's the middle of the semester, son. Just because *you* didn't go to high school doesn't mean *he* can get out of it."

He hadn't meant his words to sound cruel, but they were. I had always been sensitive about what my father perceived as my lack of education, and nothing I had ever said could convince him that my learning had continued even after my years in formal schooling were done.

My silence must have made him realize how his words had sounded, because he switched to a different tact and tried again, his voice softening.

"Actually, Tyler, Brady has been going through a bit of a tough time lately. He could really use his big brother right now. It would be a huge help, and it would mean a lot to Liz and me if you could come spend the month we'll be gone at our home. I can't even tell you how much it would mean."

"What does Brady have to say about this?"

"Are you kidding? He's the one who thought of asking you."

Again, his words hurt my feelings, albeit unintentionally. Here they were in a bind, and it had been Brady, not our father, who had first thought to bring me into the mix.

"I think he could benefit from your influence right now," Dad continued, oblivious. "He made the varsity football team at school. Did I tell you that? As a *freshman*. He has a bright future ahead of him in sports, but there's a lot of pressure on him. He's feeling it. I don't want him to quit the team while we're gone. It would kill his chances, and I know he would regret it. I really need you to come and help him stay strong, help him stay on the team."

I stood there, wordless, my mind racing.

"Tyler?"

"I'm still here."

"I wouldn't ask if I didn't think it was crucial. He's always looked up to you."

"I…uh, I don't know what to say. I have a job here, Dad. Responsibilities."

"Surely your grandfather can get along without you for a month. He has all those sons and grandsons working for him. But Brady only has one big brother. You're it."

I could hardly believe my father was asking me to drop everything and come to California for a month. Could hardly believe it.

Unless…

Unless God was at work here, and this was part of His answer to my prayer.

This is not what I had in mind, Lord, I prayed inwardly.

"We're worried about him, Tyler. He seems to be withdrawing from us. I have friends who tell me that's normal for a fourteen-year-old, but I don't care if it supposedly is normal. You didn't do this to your grandparents. You didn't shut them out when you were this age. You didn't shut me out, either. You've always had your head on straight. I don't want Brady to blow this opportunity he has to make a name for himself in prep football. It's pretty important here. If you want to play in college, you can't mess with your high school years."

While I appreciated hearing my dad tell me I had my head on straight, I didn't think it was fair for him to compare me to Brady. Our lives were completely different. Besides, my dad had seen me for what had been a total of ten days at the most the year I was fourteen. What did he know?

I'd done my share of stupid things, teenage things. It was just that the Amish in our district handled it differently. Parents, or in my case grandparents, tended to look the other way. As long as we weren't causing problems or being disrespectful at home, what we did was our own business, within reason. It was part of *rumspringa*, the chance to stretch our wings, find footing of our own, learn the truth about the outside world and what it really had to offer. Of course I had looked like the perfect child to my father, because he didn't get that I'd had far more privacy during my teenage years than Brady ever would.

"I don't know, Dad. I haven't spent more than a couple days in a row with Brady in four years. I'm afraid he wouldn't care what I had to say about anything."

"But you're wrong! He respects you. You're his big brother, Tyler. Please. We really need you to come."

I took a deep breath and blew it out slowly. "Maybe what you really need to do is stay, Dad. Maybe this isn't the best time for both you and Liz to be gone." It was out of my mouth before I could consider how disrespectful that might come across. But apparently he had not been offended.

"That's just not an option. I have to go. And Liz has had this trip on her calendar for a year. Besides, I think Brady might need for Liz and me to be away for a little while. The distance might help us all out. Say you'll come. Just for one month. Please, Tyler?"

I leaned my forehead against the wall and closed my eyes. This was not the answer I had been praying for, not at all. A month in Orange County, babysitting my little brother? How on earth could something like that ever help bring clarity to my muddled mind?

Worse, what if that's not even what this was? What if the timing of my father's request was purely coincidental, not an answer to prayer at all, and I was just misreading things?

Show me, God. Show me if this is from You, if this is what You want me to do.

I turned away from the wall to pace the entrance. I knew I needed to say something to my father, who was still waiting for an answer from me.

Glancing up, I spotted *Daadi* standing nearby, and I knew from the way he looked at me that he had been there a while. Our eyes met, though I couldn't read what his were saying. Then he turned and walked away to give me some privacy.

"This is a really busy time for me, Dad. I have a lot going on in my life."

"Seriously? Come on, Ty. You lead as uncomplicated a life as anybody I know. Besides, I can't believe you of all people would say no to family. Not you."

My father never had understood that being Plain didn't mean I led a carefree, easy life. I was as busy as any *Englischer* with a full-time job, land and farm buildings to maintain, and animals to care for. Still, my father's other indictment hit home. I wasn't one to say no to family. That was not the way I had been brought up.

Besides, he had never needed anything from me before. Not once. Now, for the first time ever, I had the power to do something for him that he could not do for himself. To be needed this way was astonishing—and, at some level, deeply pleasing.

"When would you want me to come?"

"I'm thinking you should aim to get here by next Tuesday at the latest, if you can. Liz will already be gone, and my flight to Qatar is the next day."

My mind raced as I glanced toward the calendar on the shop wall. "But this is already Thursday. That means I'd have just this one weekend to prepare for being away for a whole month."

"So? That should be more than enough time. I mean, it's not like you've got a bunch of Halloween parties to go to this weekend or anything, is it?"

I closed my eyes, pinching the bridge of my nose. "Of course not." In the Amish world, as he well knew, Halloween was a non issue.

"Well, then, here's the deal. I've already checked the flights, and there are still a couple of good options available. Just give me the word, and I'll lock one in for you. Why don't we try and plan for you to come out on Tuesday?"

I took a deep breath, held it in, and then opened my eyes as I slowly let it out. "Look, Dad, even if I come, I'm not sure I will travel by plane. I need to talk this over with *Daadi* before—"

"No, you don't. You're an adult. And you're not a church member yet. I know how this Amish stuff works."

"*Daadi* is also my employer, Dad. I *do* need to talk to him first. Can I call you back?"

"So you'll come?"

"I need to talk to *Daadi* first."

But in my heart I already knew how my grandfather would respond. He would consider the timing of my father's call and the prayers everyone had been saying on my behalf, and he would conclude God was showing me what He wanted me to do. If the bishop and the district elders felt the same way, then it would be doubly wrong of me to tell my father no.

"I'll get back to you as soon as I can," I said.

"Thanks, Tyler," my dad replied, obviously sure that *Daadi* would never allow me to decline a family need as great as this one. "I'll pay for the flight, of course, and I'll match whatever you make at the buggy place for the whole time you're here."

"That won't be necessary."

"I insist. Brady will be so glad you're coming. He's missed you."

"It will be nice to see him too." I *had* missed my brother. The last time we'd been together had been almost two years ago when he and Dad had come to Philadelphia for an Eagles game and to spend a weekend with me.

"I can't thank you enough, Tyler. Really."

"Well, let me call you back before we say it's a done deal."

We said our goodbyes, and then I went in search of my grandfather.

It took the bishop, elders, and my grandfather only one day to decide that I should do as my father asked and go to California for the month. I was brought to Bishop Ott's house on Friday morning to hear their decision, so that they could personally admonish me to use my time away wisely, fully seeking God's call on my life.

I could see in the eyes of every man in the room that they had always known I would someday need to do this. I was born *Englisch*. I lived for six years in the *Englisch* world. I had an *Englisch* father and an *Englisch* half brother. I was different from everyone else in my district in this way. I could take vows to become one of them, but I wasn't like them yet. Bishop Ott and the other ministers and deacons were convinced that my restlessness was God's way of calling me out to lay to rest any lingering affection for the world I had been born into.

When I returned in December, I would be expected to tell them if I was ready to seek membership and baptism or not. The elders said it was time for me to figure out who I was. Was I Tyler the *Englischer*, man of the world, the son of a retired army colonel? If so, then I knew nothing about what my life would become except that I could then do whatever I wanted, be whatever I wanted, learn whatever I wanted.

Or was I Tyler the Amish buggy maker and future husband to an Amish bride? If so, then I knew exactly what my life would look like. My choices were fairly limited, but I would have my church, my community.

I would have Rachel.

The men laid their hands on my shoulders and prayed for me. As they did, I asked God to remove any desire in my life that hadn't been given to me by Him. Before I left, Bishop Ott gave me permission to fly out to California rather than take the train. I'd been allowed to travel to my dad's by air when I was young as it was the quickest and safest mode of transportation for a child. But I wasn't a child any longer, so I was surprised that air travel had received the okay this time. No other Amish person in my district had ever been given permission to travel by airplane that I could remember.

Then again, I wasn't like any other Amish person in my district. I knew it and the leaders of my district knew it.

My grandfather and I were quiet as we rode home from Bishop Ott's, each of us lost in our thoughts. I knew *Daadi* didn't want me to leave. He loved me like a son. But I think he and *Mammi* had always believed I was theirs for a season. What happened beyond that was up to God, not them.

I straddled two worlds, and I had to figure out which was the one I belonged in.

The scariest part about it was that Rachel didn't stand with me in the middle. She was already firmly planted on the Amish side.

EIGHT

Rachel needed to hear about my father's request and the elders' decision, so Friday evening I took her out to the pond where we could talk. She knew what a comfort this place had been to me over the years, but this was the first time I had ever invited her to see it for herself. In the past I'd always treated the pond as my own private place, a sanctuary for me alone. Now, however, I knew I needed to give her this, to open up to her this way. I also wanted her to be reminded of what I'd been through in my life and of what I'd lost when I was six. Somehow, I hoped, maybe that would help her understand, at least a little bit, about my imminent departure and what it would involve and why it was important.

The air was crisp and cool and hinting of the winter to come as we moved down the path in Timber's wake. We reached the clearing and came to a stop at the water's edge, the sun low on the horizon, the sky a vivid orange. Standing there, I pointed out the cluster of rocks and my favorite weeping willow and the old boat I'd taken out in the water just two and a half weeks before. Then, taking her hand in mine, I began to describe that long-ago morning when my grandparents had brought me out here so I could see for myself the pond my mother had told me about.

I had no gift for painting pictures with words, but I tried as best I could to describe the scene for her, focusing on the sadness and fear and confusion of that lost little boy.

From there, I moved into all that had been happening recently. I reminded her of the restlessness I'd been feeling, and then I told her about my prayers for guidance, my father's phone call, and the meeting at Bishop Ott's. I told her everything, ending with the news that the elders expected me to use the time I was gone to discover who I was—Amish or *Englisch*—once and for all.

Rachel was quiet as she listened, the pensive expression on her face slowly turning to dismay.

"You're telling me the bishop *wants* you to go?" she asked when I was done, pulling her hand away from mine. "And your *daadi*. And the elders? They all *want* you to go?"

"It's not that they want me to go. They think I *should*. They think God is answering the prayer we've been asking, that He would show me who I am."

"I can tell you who you are!" Her raised voice sent a burst of starlings in the tall grass flinging to the air. "You've lived the Amish way for seventeen years, Tyler, with people who have loved you from the minute you got here. God brought you to us when you needed us most, when your father—"

Her voice cut off mid-sentence, one hand flying to her mouth. Then she turned her back to me, leaving the unspoken to hang there in the air between us, ringing out loud and clear.

When your father…abandoned you.

When your father…didn't want you anymore.

When your father…found it easier to dump you on someone else and just walk away.

I closed my eyes, feeling more alone in that moment than I ever had in my life.

When I felt Rachel's hand on my arm, I opened my eyes to see that she was again facing me, only now her cheeks were glistening with tears.

"I shouldn't have said that," she whispered, eyes liquid with regret. "I never should have said that. I'm so sorry."

I hesitated only a moment, and then I pulled her to me and wrapped her in my arms. We stood that way for a long while without saying anything.

"Please forgive me," she whispered. "Please, please forgive me."

"Shhh. Of course I forgive you."

"I'm just so afraid you won't come back."

"I love you, Rachel. I want to come back. I really do."

She raised her head to look at me. "But you and I both know you can't become Amish just for me. What if you get out there and you find the answer you're looking for…and that answer is that you are *not* Amish? What then? What then, Tyler?"

I couldn't even begin to imagine what that would mean. I ran my thumb across her cheek to brush away a trail of tears. "So you would have me stay and always wonder?"

"I would have you stay and know that love means you do not have to wonder."

I let my hand fall away as I looked beyond her to the pond, where a slight mist had gathered above the surface and was hovering there. Was that what loving Rachel really meant? That I didn't have to wonder which man I was?

"I'm sorry, Rachel, but it's more complicated than that. When I think about my mother and what happened with her…" My voice trailed off. How could I explain my feelings to anyone else if I didn't even understand them myself?

"What happened with her? You mean her death?"

I shook my head. "No. When she was younger. When she ran away from the Amish life. When I think about that, I just…" Again, words failed me.

But she wasn't going to make this easy for me. She eased herself out of my embrace. Folding her arms across her chest, she just stood there and waited for me to continue.

"Nobody knows why she did that," I said finally. "Not really. No one has ever been able to explain the thoughts and feelings that sent her away from here."

Rachel frowned, her delicate brow furrowing. "But Tyler—"

"Don't you get it?" Now it was my turn to take a step back. "How do I know what happened to her won't happen to me? *Something* convinced her to walk away. Now that I've been feeling so unsettled lately, I have to wonder if that's what happened to her too. Maybe this same feeling of restlessness just rose up in her, and it got worse and worse until it eventually took over. Maybe *that's* what finally drove her away from the home and family and community she loved—for good."

I could tell by the expression on Rachel's face that she didn't really understand what I was saying. How could she? Her own mother was an open book to her, a constant presence throughout her life. Mine had gone to the grave when I was only a child, leaving me with questions that could never, ever be answered by anyone else.

"Because your mother left," Rachel said slowly, trying to understand, "you fear you will leave too?"

I took in a deep breath and looked into her eyes. "What I fear is that whatever drove my mother away will take root in me as well."

"Maybe it already has."

"Maybe it has," I agreed. "But if so, I will not do as she did and slip away in the dead of night. If I leave, I will leave honorably."

Fresh tears were now rimming Rachel's eyes, which were wide with surprise and dread. She didn't say what she had every right to, that there was nothing honorable about leading a girl on for years, implying marriage, only to desert her when it finally came time to take that next step.

I swallowed back the guilt that surged in my throat.

"So you are saying a life here with me, and our children, Lord willing, would not be enough for you?" Her voice was tender but trembling. "That *I* would not be enough?"

If I could have set a match to the warring thoughts in my head, I would have done it right then. But I couldn't.

I saw in her eyes every meaningful time she and I had ever shared.

Ten thousand conversations, ten thousand laughs, ten thousand common moments. I had never wanted any other woman besides her. I didn't even know when it was I fell in love with her because I hadn't fallen at all. She had been my constant, my one true love, from the very beginning.

"I want it to be enough," I whispered. "I do." Even as I spoke, I was reminded suddenly of that long-ago conversation with Sarah, when she told me that the Amish life had not been "enough" for my mother. Was that really why she had left?

Was that what would end up keeping me away as well?

Rachel studied my face, searching to reconnect with the boy she had grown up with, loved, and with whom she wanted to spend her life. Then she turned and walked to the cluster of large rocks and sat, her expression bereft, her big blue eyes filled with the hurt my actions were causing. My heart nearly crushing under the weight of my own remorse, I hesitated only a moment before I went to her, took a seat at her side, and wrapped my arm around her shoulders. We sat there together that way for a long time, both of us quiet, until the sky was a deep purple and the first evening star appeared above the shadows of the horizon.

"I want you to be sure," she said finally, her voice soft but resolute. "I want you to regret nothing. Ever. Go to your father's, Tyler. Do what you need to do. Follow God's will, not mine."

Nor mine, I prayed, drawing her into an embrace and holding on as tightly as I could.

Monday afternoon, I set my nearly packed duffel bag on the floor and then surveyed my bedroom, which suddenly seemed small and bland and devoid of the life—the lives—that had been lived here over the years. The Amish way, of course, was to keep possessions to a minimum, to avoid ornate decorations or mementoes or photographs. Usually, such simplicity gave me a feeling of peace. On this day, however, it brought only one word to mind: Empty. Like a flashing neon sign. *Empty.* As if my time here had never existed at all.

Needing to feel grounded somehow, I went to the bureau, slid open the bottom drawer, and reached under a sweater to pull out my old cigar box, the one I had used to hold my treasures when I was young. I carried it over to the bed and sat, placing it atop the covers in front of me. Though not exactly a secret, I had always kept this container and its contents to myself. I'd added a few things to it since coming here to live, but the box mostly held mementoes of my former life, the one that had been mine for only six years before it was taken away from me for good.

Opening the lid, I sat back against the pillows and looked inside, taking a quick inventory of all the box contained. Though Jake had nothing like this among his possessions—nor did anyone else I knew, for that matter—I felt sure that many an *Englisch* boy did. It seemed to be the *Englisch* way of things, to hang on to items for sentimental reasons, as if the things themselves had value.

Inside the box were the treasures of my youth: baseball cards, a tiger's eye marble, a shark's tooth, some foreign coins, a piece of petrified wood, a rock with a hole in it, a ticket stub from a ball game, a long-dead mini-flashlight, a small key, and two photographs.

I took out the pictures and studied them. The first was of Brady and me, taken when I was about the age he was now. My dad kept a copy of this same photo prominently displayed in his home, and I liked it so much that Liz had made a copy of it for me too. In the picture, my little brother and I were at the beach with the dancing surf behind us, sitting in the sand, our hair wet from having been in the water. I had my arm around him, and we were both smiling at the camera, brown from the sun.

Gazing at it now made me smile, as it always did.

Setting that one aside, I picked up the second photo and looked at it, something I'd done countless times in my life. When I was a child, in fact, I would often lie here at night, waiting for Jake's soft, even breathing from across the room before I would pull out my little flashlight and this picture of my mother. Then I would stare at it, sometimes in a vague way, sometimes sucking in every last detail, trying to memorize her beautiful face before it was gone from my recollection entirely.

The snapshot had been taken when she was about sixteen years old. In it, she was wearing Amish clothing and sitting on the top rail of the wooden fence that still fronted the pasture of her parents' farm. She was looking off to the side, not just smiling but laughing, her face filled with delight. She'd shown me the photo herself, a year or so before she died, when she was trying to explain about the Amish clothing she'd worn back on the farm. I had wanted to keep it—not because of the clothes, but because such moments of glee were so rare for her. To my mind, she had almost always been somber, sometimes smiling a little but hardly ever lighting up like this with such joy.

I realized now how lucky I'd been to have a picture of her at all. The Amish frowned on photos for several reasons, mostly because they were seen as a graven image, something the Bible warned against. The fact that she'd allowed herself to be photographed while she was still living at home said a lot about her propensity to defy Amish convention.

Feeling an odd sadness, I returned both photos to the box and then picked up the only other memento of my mother it held, one that evoked a distinct memory. I'd been just six years old, watching cartoons in the living room one day, when I decided I wanted a snack. I called out to my mother but she didn't answer, so I went to the kitchen to get something for myself.

That's when I found her there, lying on the floor near the sink, unconscious.

I tried everything I could to wake her, first shouting out her name, then shaking her by the shoulders, then throwing a cup of cold water on her face, just like on TV. When none of that worked, I climbed up on a kitchen stool, grabbed the phone, and called the only number I knew by heart, that of my best friend and next-door neighbor.

While I waited for his parents to come over and help, I returned to my mother's side, curling up on the floor next to her and trying to pull her lifeless arms around me. When that didn't work, I decided to hold her hand—and that's when I discovered in her right fist a small key, perhaps an inch long, that I didn't recognize. At the time I'd slipped it into my pocket and returned my attention to interlacing her limp fingers with my own until help arrived.

It wasn't until hours later, that night when my father finally picked me up from next door, brought me home, and made me get ready for bed even though my mother wasn't there to tuck me in, that I discovered that key in the pocket of my jeans and remembered where I'd found it. Fearing my dad might take it away from me if he knew about it, I kept the key to myself and slept with it under my pillow.

Stuck at home with a sitter most of the next day, I spent much of the time going around the house and trying the key on various doorknobs, hoping to figure out what it unlocked. I had no luck, so finally I tucked it away in the cigar box for safekeeping until I could make sense of it. But I never did.

And as it turned out, that was the night my dad came home and gave me the news that mommy had gone far away and wasn't ever coming back.

Holding the key in my hand now, I realized afresh that I would never know what it unlocked or why she'd been holding it when she died. The thought overwhelmed me with such grief that finally I put the key back in the box and put the box back in the drawer, where it belonged. My little stroll down memory lane had only made me feel more agitated and confused.

I decided to call Jake, who always knew how to cheer me up. Using the phone in the shop, I dialed the number for the bunkhouse and waited as someone retrieved him for me. As we talked, he surprised me by being positive about the task ahead of me. He said he'd always known I would have to come to terms with who I was before I could take my membership vows, and that he'd had a feeling I could only do that by making a trip into the outside world.

After our call, I squeezed in a quick trip to my aunt Sarah's house, feeling the need to reassure her that history wasn't repeating itself. Over coffee in the kitchen with her and Jonah, I assured them that if I chose not to return to the Amish life, I would do so in the light of day, with the full knowledge of my loved ones.

"I would never just disappear without warning," I told her, looking into the eyes of my sweet aunt and offering her the most encouraging smile I could give.

I had hoped my words would bring her comfort, but instead they just sent her to her room in tears, leaving me there in the kitchen alone with my uncle Jonah.

"She'll get through it in time," he told me in his deep, gravelly voice, "just as she got through the loss of her sister."

I hadn't known how to reply to that, as I was well aware that Sarah had never really gotten over the loss of her sister—neither her leaving, nor her death.

Later that night, I went over to Rachel's to tell her goodbye. It was difficult enough as it was, but she made it even more so by insisting that we keep things short. She didn't want to take a walk or go for a buggy ride or do anything with me that would allow us to have more than five minutes alone together. It pained me to think she was already starting to prepare herself for the worst.

Standing on her parents' front porch, I told her I loved her and that I would write, and that she could call me anytime she wanted. She and her family shared a phone shanty with the farm next door. I gave her my dad's home phone number and assured her I wanted to hear from her while I was away.

She allowed me to kiss her goodbye, but in that kiss I could already sense that she was pulling away, like a helium balloon tugging itself from the hand of the one holding it.

My flight was the next day, at eight thirty in the morning. *Daadi* had offered to hire a car to drive me all the way to the Philadelphia airport, but I hadn't wanted him to go to that expense. The train was cheaper, so I'd arranged for the driver to just take me to the Lancaster train station instead.

In the predawn darkness, saying goodbye to my grandparents was even more difficult than I had expected it to be. *Mammi* hugged me longer than she ever had, and even *Daadi* seemed on the verge of tears. It scared me a little to think how tenuous they saw my hold on the Amish life in which they had raised me.

Even my farewell to Timber had been tough. He was a good dog, and though I knew *Daadi* would take excellent care of him in my stead, I sure would miss having him around.

I took just one small duffel bag, filled mostly with clothes, and a backpack that held my Bible, notepaper to write letters to Rachel and Jake, a wallet with a few hundred dollars in it, the watch my father had once given me for Christmas, and my Pennsylvania driver's license. I hadn't used the license in a couple of years, but I knew I would need it while taking care of my brother, not to mention for getting on the airplane.

When I was finally on the train, I settled in beside the window and watched as the rolling fields and farms of Lancaster County slowly gave way to the more densely packed houses and shops of suburban Philadelphia. I took Amtrak all the way to 30th Street Station in the heart of the city and then changed over to a SEPTA line for the twenty-minute ride from there to the airport.

It wasn't until I stepped off the SEPTA train a few minutes after seven that the magnitude of what I was doing began to hit me. Thanks to a single phone call from my father and a gathering of my church elders, I was about to fly across the country in pursuit of some understanding, some truth, that I couldn't even begin to comprehend.

I sure hope You really are in this, Lord, I prayed as I fell in with the crowd walking inside.

The airport was busy, far busier than I remember it being the last time I flew, when I was seventeen. I made my way through airport security, past the staring and pointing people—it wasn't terribly common to see an Amish man in an airport—and then to my gate to wait for my plane to board. I took a seat near the door to the jetway and picked up a newspaper that someone had left to give myself something to do while I waited.

A mom with two young girls, maybe eight and ten, sat down next to me, and the children proceeded to whisper to their mother, and she back to them. I heard the word "Amish," though I pretended I didn't.

I heard the mother murmur, "Girls! It's not polite to stare."

I raised my head to smile at them and wordlessly assure the mother I wasn't offended. Sometimes when I was out in the big world, people stared. I was used to it.

"I'm so sorry!" the mother said when our eyes met.

"It's quite all right."

"They've just never seen an Amish person before. Well, except for on TV."

I smiled and nodded. I had no ready comeback for that comment.

"Actually, I haven't either," the mother added. "We live in Los Angeles, so…"

"I see."

"I didn't think you could fly."

"He can *fly?*" the younger of the girls asked, wide eyed.

The mother laughed. So did I.

"Where's your buggy?" the older one said, quite serious.

"Back at the farm."

"How about your horse?" said the other.

I sat up straight and feigned looking around. "I'm not sure. Last I saw, he was having a little trouble getting through security."

She hesitated and then giggled, not quite sure if I was kidding or not.

The older one rolled her eyes at the naïveté of her little sister. "Do you want to see my iPad?"

"Uh, sure."

While we waited to board, she showed me photos of her family and friends, a word game, an interactive map of Hershey Park, and a sketch pad where I could draw with my finger. The girl seemed intent on introducing me to every technologically wonderful thing the device could do, as if my spaceship had crash-landed here and she were welcoming me to her planet.

When we finally boarded, my row was way past that of the little girls, but they knelt on their seats, facing backward, to look at me and wave before it was time to buckle in.

Everyone on the plane seemed to be looking at me.

The man in the Amish clothes.

The Amish man.

NINE

The moment I stepped off the plane at John Wayne International, all that was home to me seemed far more distant than the thousands of miles that now lay between us. I was keenly aware of how I stood out in my Amish clothes, even after I took off my hat and carried it under my arm. At least the pace of the hundreds of people all around me was harried and hurried, which meant that most of them were too busy getting somewhere or staring at their cell phones to actually pay me much notice.

The last time I had been to California, my dad was stationed at Camp Pendleton near San Diego, on loan to the Marines as a helicopter maintenance instructor. He and Liz and Brady were living on base, which in a way seemed as secluded and protective an environment as the community back home. The only people who lived on base or had any business being there were other military members and their families. And because the base was located in a sprawling stretch of wilderness between San Diego and Los Angeles, it had been easy to forget I was smack-dab in the middle of the metropolitan universe of Southern California—though day trips to Disneyland and SeaWorld and crowded beaches quickly reminded me of where I was. My dad had since retired a full colonel after twenty-five years and now worked for a Los Angeles-based defense contractor. Dad and Liz had bought a house in Newport Beach—a beach community in the suburbs south of Los Angeles—two years ago and, from what I could gather from our infrequent phone calls, he had slowly adjusted to his new life as a civilian.

I hadn't had to check a bag, but because I was to meet my father at baggage claim, I followed the signs there, searching for him in the sea of faces as I made my way. I stood near the carousel to wait, where I met up again with the woman and her daughters. I helped them retrieve their heavy luggage as it came around, and when the mother thanked me, she asked if I needed a ride somewhere. I thanked her in return but assured her my father lived in Orange County and was coming to meet me. That seemed to take her by surprise. She probably assumed that an Amish man like me surely had an Amish father, so how was it that he lived in Orange County?

They said goodbye, the mother's eyes still full of questions as they walked away, pulling their suitcases like wagons. I could tell she was worried for me. I smiled at her and then gave a confident wave to assure her I would be fine.

That's when I spotted my father. Our eyes met through the milling throng, and he came toward me, looking almost annoyed.

"There you are!" He reached for my hand and pulled me toward him for a manly, one-armed embrace. "First thing we need to do is get you a cell phone, Tyler. That was crazy."

"Hi, Dad."

"So. Good flight, then?"

"Sure. It was fine."

He sized me up and then smiled. "You look older."

I laughed lightly. "Time passes at the same rate in Pennsylvania, Dad. You look older too."

He laughed in return. Actually, he didn't look older. But he did look different. He had always kept his hair at regulation length, which for the army was very nearly a buzz cut. His hair was now almost long enough to comb. He might have put on a few pounds since he got out of the military, but only a few. He was still fit and trim, a good weight for his six-foot-one-inch frame. He was also sporting a moustache for the first time that I could remember.

"No, I mean it," he continued. "You're taller. And you've filled out since I last saw you. How long has it been? A year? Two?

"Something like that."

"Making buggies must be a more physical job than I thought. Either that, or you've joined a gym."

"*Ya*, an Amish gym." I cracked a smile.

He laughed and clapped me on the back. "Let's get out of here."

We began to walk, and as we made our way toward the exit for the parking lot, I was again aware how my broadcloth pants, white hand-made cotton shirt, and suspenders were out of place. Even with my hat still tucked under my arm, I stood out like a stalk of corn in the middle of a hay field.

My father had said the airport was about a fifteen-minute drive from his new house, so I didn't think he would mind if I asked to take a detour on the way to a used clothing store so that I could pick up a few things to help me blend in better. The last thing I needed was to draw attention to myself. I didn't want to come off as an Amish man trying to fit into the non-Amish world. I just wanted to be a man, Amish or not.

"Say, Dad. Would you mind if we stopped somewhere so that I could get some jeans and a couple different shirts?"

"Sure, we can swing by the mall." He smiled at me. "Liz already bought you a few new things, just like she used to when you were a kid. But we can still stop."

"We don't need to go to a mall. I'm fine with a used clothing—"

"No, no. New is better. And actually, now that I look at you, I'm thinking you and I are about the same size. You can probably wear most of my stuff too. I'll pull out some things for you when we get home."

We stepped outside the terminal and a brilliant sun greeted me. The icy Pennsylvania morning I had awakened to seemed ages ago under the seventy-two-degree sunshine here. Moments later we were in Dad's car and pulling out into traffic.

While he drove, he filled me in on his civilian job, his life as an army retiree, Liz's trip to Honduras, and her regular work as an RN at a local hospital.

I was interested in what he had to say but also intrigued with my surroundings, the sheer amount of cars on the roads, and how everyone drove with their windows closed even though the day was beautiful. When he began to talk about Brady, I forced myself to pay attention to everything he said. Brady was the reason I was here—or half the reason, at least.

"He's been playing Pop Warner all these years, so we knew he was a shoe-in to play JV as a freshman. But we never dreamed he'd make regular varsity in ninth grade. He knocked the coach's socks off when he tried out. He's an amazing kicker. He can send that ball flying dead center through the uprights, on the worst snap ever, on the poorest placement ever, from practically midfield. I'm telling you, Ty, he's headed for the Pac Twelve."

"Pac Twelve?"

Dad seemed surprised I didn't know what he was talking about. "Oh. That's the conference name for all the great universities here in the West, you know, the Pacific side of the country. It's all the big ones, Ty. The ones that matter. UCLA, USC, OSU, U of O. He has the talent to be picked up by one of them. That's what I'm saying."

He glanced at me as he drove to make sure I was getting all this.

"That's why it's so important that he not blow it right now. He's on the varsity team, Ty," he continued. "As a *freshman.*"

That part I got.

"I know what you're saying, Dad. I just hadn't heard of the Pac Twelve before."

Dad seemed to need a moment to absorb this. Apparently, my lack of football expertise was something he hadn't thought of when he called me with his desperate request. Now he was probably wondering if I realized how important this really was.

I did, of course. I knew what it meant to feel that something important to you was at stake. "You don't want him to do something now that he will regret later, maybe for the rest of his life," I said.

My father visibly relaxed as he returned his gaze to the road ahead. "Exactly. He has the talent. He could go all the way with it."

"All the way?"

"The NFL, of course," Dad laughed. Surely I knew that.

I was beginning to understand why, as my dad had said when he first called me, Brady was feeling the pressure of being in such a highly visible, high-stakes place as a freshman. Dad was probably doubling whatever pressure Brady was reacting to. No wonder there was tension between the two of them.

"But he's fourteen. There are a lot of years between now and the NFL," I said casually, as if it were something my dad could have said just as easily but feeling pretty sure he wouldn't have.

"That's my point, Tyler. These are the years that will decide how far he will go."

"So how far does he *want* to go?"

"He loves playing football. He's loved it since he was little. It's always been what he's wanted to do." Dad tossed these sentences back to me a bit defensively, as if he'd said them before to someone else. I wondered if maybe he and Liz—or maybe even he and Brady—didn't see eye to eye on Brady's future as a football player.

I decided I would wait to see if my dad was right about that. Until I could talk to my brother, I wouldn't know for sure, so for now I just said something I thought Dad would enjoy hearing but was still true.

"I'm looking forward to seeing him play."

"He's crazy good, Tyler. Phenomenal."

The pride in my dad's voice was almost painful for me to hear. Almost.

Our first stop was at an electronics store where Dad bought a pay-as-you-go cell phone. I was fine with him wanting me to have a phone while I was in California. It actually made sense. I knew Brady lived and breathed for his cell. When I'd called him from the shop on his last birthday, Brady told me how much he wished I had a cell phone so that he could talk to me whenever he wanted.

"You Amish are totally wrong about technology putting distance between people," he had said. "If you had a cell, I could talk to you all the time."

"Except you wouldn't want to talk. You'd want to text."

"It's the same thing," he shot back. "If you had a cell it would be like you're just on the other side of town instead of the other side of the country. And with as often as I see you, it may as well be the other side of the universe."

I had tried to explain that in Lancaster County, when you wanted to talk to someone, you went to them in person and talked to them. It kept the sense of community between you and your friends and neighbors and family strong and solid.

"Yeah, but I don't live in Lancaster County."

He had just made the case for why Amish families stay in their communities, but I didn't point that out. Instead, I told him to call the shop phone as often as he liked, but he hardly ever did. He wanted to be able to text me now and then, and the shop phone wasn't set up for that.

"Texting is how people my age communicate," he had told me, more than once.

As it was after four o'clock my time, Dad suggested we eat first and then shop. We went to a Cheesecake Factory, and in between bites of flatbread pizza, something I had never had before, I programmed into the new cell phone the few numbers I would need as Dad dictated them to me: my dad's and Liz's numbers, Brady's, the physician they used, the high school, a couple of neighbors, and the closest pizza place to their house that delivered.

Eight numbers.

Dad shook his head when I was done.

"Must be nice to just need eight telephone numbers to get by in life."

"Ten, actually," I corrected, adding in the numbers for Rachel and *Daadi*'s shop as well.

"Same difference."

"Why? How many numbers do you have in yours?"

"Too many. I probably have more than a hundred in my contacts."

I slipped the phone in my pocket without comment. I had never considered that a hundred phone numbers was the norm for the average cell phone user. Because my goal was to figure out where I belonged,

I realized I needed to start making a list of things that were distinctive of ordinary life in the outside world. I mentally began the list so that later I could transfer it to the notebook.

People drive with their windows rolled up, no matter what the weather.

Used clothes are undesirable.

Young people text to communicate.

The number of contacts in your cell phone is too numerous to keep in your memory.

When we finished eating, we headed to Macy's, where Dad bought me two pairs of jeans, a belt, and a package of colored T-shirts. I tried to use my own money, but he wouldn't hear of it.

Before we left the store, I went back into the dressing room and changed, folding my Amish clothes and stuffing them into the Macy's bag. When I turned and regarded myself in the long mirror, I decided I looked pretty normal in the new clothes. The vibrant green in the shirt—a hue I hadn't worn in years—brought out the same shade in my eyes.

But then I looked at my chestnut brown hair and realized that there was still one big problem. My clothes may be *Englisch* now, but my hairstyle was definitely still Amish. I pushed my bangs away from my face as best I could, telling myself that at least I worked primarily indoors in the buggy shop rather than out in the fields, so I didn't have the telltale white forehead of an Amish farmer who labored all day in the sun with his hat on. I thought about asking my dad if we could go for a quick haircut too, but something about that seemed almost traitorous—not so much getting the cut as telling him I wanted one. I decided to wait and go myself in a few days, once he was out of town.

The clothes smelled new and their fabric was stiff on my skin, but I was relieved to be blending in better now. As Dad and I walked back to the car, people were no longer turning and staring at me—though one gaggle of teenage girls seemed to take an interest. I flashed them a friendly smile as we walked past, and the flirty looks they gave me in return nearly made me blush. A few of the Amish girls back home were known to be flirty too, but never to someone they didn't already know and like. Add one more observation to the book.

Young women flirt with complete strangers.

We got back into the car for the final leg of my journey and headed down I-405 to Newport Beach. From the highway, it looked just like the city before it, and the one before that, a phenomenon Dad called "the urban sprawl of Orange County." I expected to see the ocean as we got closer, but Dad said Newport Beach was the name of the city.

"That's the name of the beach too, of course, but it's a city first. Our house is a few miles inland, where the real estate is newer and not so expensive. And where the beachgoers and surfers don't park their cars. It's crazy here in the summer."

We took an exit that ascended into a hilly area filled with row after row after row of large but lookalike houses.

"The ocean is back that way," Dad said, motioning with his head to what lay in the rearview mirror. "Brady can show you where if you care to see it while you're here. The water's too cold to swim in right now, even for an Easterner like you, but at least the crowds are gone, so it won't take you hours on end just to get down there or to find a parking place."

After a few turns on residential streets, we pulled up to a cream-stucco, two-story house with white trim and a red tile roof. It looked really nice. Skinny palms in the front yard swayed on their impossibly slender trunks. Flowering shrubs and sand-colored boulders edged the manicured lawn. He turned into the driveway and pulled to a stop on the left, just outside the garage.

I got out of the car and followed Dad on a tiled walkway that led from the driveway to a covered entrance and a heavy wooden door. I could hear the yips of an agitated little dog inside.

"Well, here we are." He put his key in the lock and swung open the door.

TEN

I expected Liz and Brady to be home to greet me and was actually relieved that we arrived to an empty house. I had forgotten for a moment that Liz was already away on her humanitarian trip and Brady was still at school. It was after three o'clock, but my brother had football practice every day.

The sole welcome I received was from a wiry gray terrier. The little dog seemed happy enough that I was there. It was hard to tell. He ran around barking fiercely, but his little stub of a tail wiggled the entire time.

"That's Frisco," Dad said. "I forgot to mention we have a dog now. He's not too much trouble, though. He likes walks. And there's a dog park not too far from here. Liz says he likes playing with the other dogs."

"Sounds good."

"Brady can help take care of him too."

I bent down to pat the dog. Frisco licked my hands and then spun around me, barking and jumping. He was nothing like Timber, either in size or temperament. I had a hard time imagining myself walking the yapping little thing. I'd never walked a dog on a leash. Timber had free rein on our farm and never left it.

"Okay, so let me show you the house," Dad continued.

"Looks like a really nice place."

"Thanks. We like it. And Liz has a way with decorating, especially now that our income has gone up a few notches." He must have realized how prideful his words sounded, because he seemed to blush as he added, "Now that I'm in the private sector, I'm earning a good income on top of my military retirement pay, which is also quite generous."

"I see," I told him, not knowing what else to say.

We moved past the flagstone entry and into the main part of the house. The living room on our right boasted high ceilings, a white leather sectional couch positioned at an angle, a massive stone fireplace, glass-topped tables, and brown accent rugs on the tiled floor. It looked like a room no one spent much time in. We then turned left into an expansive kitchen lit by fist-sized, recessed lights in the ceiling. Forest-green granite counter tops and mahogany cabinetry with pewter hardware gleamed. The kitchen was twice the size of *Mammi*'s and sparkling clean, as though no one had ever cooked or eaten in there. Dad dropped his keys and cell phone on a counter-height table of sturdy wood and led me to the open formal dining room containing a long table and high-backed chairs. Add that one to the notebook.

Homes with just three people can have a dining table large enough to seat more than ten.

White-trimmed French doors revealed a patio and pool in the backyard. Off the dining room was a family room dominated by a wall unit and a TV screen the size of a picture window. A second fireplace, this one framed in wood, was accented by a huge portrait of my dad, Liz, and Brady. They were dressed in white shirts and denim, and they posed in the midst of a grove of oaks, the three of them looking relaxed and at ease with each other and the beautiful setting. Other photos of the three of them were placed among the shelves of the wall unit: Brady in his football uniform, Liz in her nursing clothes in a sea of ebony faces, my dad in his army uniform in front of one of his helicopter crews, and a few other family shots of them by the ocean, and on a sailboat, and one of the three of them with the dog.

What I didn't see was the picture of Brady and me that was my favorite, the one of us on the beach that I kept a copy of in my cigar box back home. It had been framed and on display in my dad's last house, but for some reason he had opted not to put it out here.

He continued with the tour, apparently unaware that I noticed that picture's absence. "The cleaning people come Tuesdays and Fridays, so they were just here today."

"They?"

"Liz found a service that sends out three maids at once. They can get in and out in less time. They have the key, and they know the alarm code and all that. So you don't have to be here when they come. We never are."

It struck me that I might need a bigger notebook.

Dad moved on to a hallway that branched off the kitchen. "Here's the laundry room. Brady can show you how to use the washer and dryer. Garage is right through here. Oh, and look what I found since the last time I saw you."

We walked through the laundry room. Dad opened the door into the attached garage, which was big enough for three cars.

"Here's what I want you to see," Dad said as he moved past a silver Honda and the red 1973 Dodge Challenger he'd had the last time I had visited, to the far side of the garage. There sat a midnight blue sedan with lots of chrome and a long front end.

"It's a 1969 Pontiac GTO." Dad was smiling from ear to ear. He looked up at me, awaiting my response to his newest acquisition. He always did this whenever he got a new muscle car, but as automobiles weren't a regular part of my world, I usually had to feign my excitement.

"Wow. That's a nice-looking car."

"I've been wanting one of these for years. This one's in great shape. The best I've seen without taking me to the cleaners, if you know what I mean."

I was pretty sure I did.

I didn't know what to say beyond another comment that it was a nice car. Whatever I was looking for out here, I knew it had nothing to do with a vehicle.

"I'm glad you finally found it then," I said.

He ran his hand across the car's smooth side. "It needs a little fixing up, and a good detailing on the inside. But not much else." He paused for a moment. "Sometimes I wish…"

I waited, not sure where he had been headed with that.

"Maybe when I get back from Qatar, I can take you out in it," he finally said.

"Sure."

An awkward silence followed that wordlessly reminded us both that the life I had lived up to this point had not included cars.

He abruptly turned from the vehicle. "Well, let me show you the rest of the house."

As we moved back across the garage, Dad gestured to the silver, small-ish sport utility vehicle that was parked closest to the laundry room door.

"That's Liz's. It's a Honda CRV. You can use it while you're here. Or mine." He turned to me. "Been a long time since you've driven?" He said it with a small measure of what I could only describe as trepidation.

"*Ya.*"

He patted my shoulder. "It's like riding a bike, Ty. It'll come back to you the minute you get behind the wheel. Just take it slow. And stay in Newport Beach and surface roads if you can. Brady can get a ride to school with the neighbor kid while I'm gone and another kid's parents will bring him home after football practice every day, so you won't have to worry about that unless you want to."

"All right. Whatever Brady wants. He and I will figure it out."

Retracing our steps, we went back through the kitchen, the little dog following us, excited to be on the move again. Dad pointed to a closed door on the farthest family room wall as we walked past.

"That's my den. There's another door to the patio in there, and my desktop computer if…if you care to use a computer. Brady can show you, uh, how to find your way around on it."

"I use a computer at the library, Dad. We order parts from our suppliers off the Internet."

He seemed pleased. "Oh! Good to know. I guess I haven't been to your grandfather's shop in a while."

"Twelve years. Brady was two the last time you came."

"Really? Has it been that long since I was there?"

"Last couple times you came to Philly, we stayed in the city. I came out on the train, remember?"

He nodded. "Right, right. Anyway, Brady can show you the password for the computer. He has his own laptop."

We headed back to the entryway, where I grabbed my duffel and backpack, and then we ascended the staircase.

Three bedrooms were located on the second floor: a master bedroom, Brady's room, and a guest room where I would sleep, each with its own bathroom. My room was decorated in an African theme. Oversized photos-on-canvas of giraffes, elephants, and zebras hung on the toasty brown walls. The photos of the animals intrigued me.

"Liz went on a medical mission trip to Kenya last year," Dad said, noticing my interest. "She took these pictures on one of her days off there."

"They're very…compelling."

My dad was quiet for a moment, and I could sense him studying me. "Are you into photography?" he finally asked. "Because your mother was, you know."

She was? I blinked, some memory stirring, an image of her with a camera in her hand. I could see her quite clearly, standing on the shoulder of the road, feet planted on each side of her bike, her camera aimed toward the beautiful countryside ahead of us. She and I frequently went bike riding when I was little, and now that I thought about it, I remembered her bringing that camera along many times. Funny that it hadn't occurred to me for years.

"I was away a lot, so it gave her something to do," he continued. "She was good too."

"Really?"

"Yeah. I found a box of her old photos during this last move. I think they're in our storage unit. When I get back from the Middle East, I'll see if I can find them for you."

"I'd really like that." I sensed a stirring inside me, the first since I left Lancaster County hours before. The pace of life in Orange County hadn't drawn me, nor had my father's muscle cars, but as I stood there looking at these beautiful photos of Africa and thought about my mother and her camera and her picture-taking, I knew here was something that evoked a hunger in me similar to what I had been feeling in recent days at the pond. I didn't own a camera, of course, but at that moment I suddenly and surprisingly wished I did. Even more strongly, I wanted to see the photos that my mother had saved.

Dad stepped past me and opened one of the double closet doors. "There's plenty of room to hang up your clothes. And here are the things Liz got for you. If they're too small, just leave the tags on. The next time she and I talk, I'll find out where she put the receipts, and you can exchange these things for ones that fit."

I peered inside. Tags still hung from the shirts, which included collared, colorful plaid shirts with buttons and beach-themed T-shirts.

"They're great. Thanks."

We went back downstairs and headed out back so that Frisco could relieve himself. Like the house, the yard was clean, free of clutter and expertly landscaped. The filter on the pool hummed, and the sapphire-blue water sparkled in the sun.

"The pool guy comes on Thursdays and the gardener on Mondays. They don't need keys or anything; they'll just show up. And the sprinklers are on a timer, so unless we have a heat wave, you won't have to water anything."

Maids. Pool guy. Gardener. Automatic sprinklers. I had never noticed before how little my dad did to make his house a home.

"You don't have to have all those people coming to take care of the house," I said. "I'm happy to do it."

"Oh, it's no trouble. I've already paid for the month," he said, as if I merely wanted to relieve him of the expense. "In fact, it would be more bother to cancel everything now and reinstate it later than it would just to leave it alone."

I nodded, suddenly seeing the hours of my days here stretch out endlessly, with nothing useful to do other than keep an eye on Brady. I would definitely need to find something constructive to occupy my free time.

"The gas grill is right over there by the hot tub," my father continued. "You can grill just about anything on it. Other than that, Liz has a bunch of casseroles in the freezer for you and other stuff she bought at Costco, and you can always eat out a couple nights a week."

"I'm sure we'll manage just fine." I knew it would be easy enough to throw some food together for dinner every night.

I was going to have a lot of empty time if the only thing I needed to do when Brady was at school was walk a ten-pound dog. At the same moment I realized this, something else occurred to me. God already knew how my days here were going to unfold. Was this His intention, for me to have the time I would need to explore my interests so that I could find out in which world I belonged? Somehow it felt like it, and I silently thanked Him.

Dad looked at his watch. "About time to go get Brady. You want to drive? Might as well get back on that bike."

He opened the door to the laundry room, grabbed a key ring off a decorative hook, stepped into the garage, and then pressed a button on the wall. One of the garage doors began to rise. He tossed the keys to the Honda to me.

I told myself as I got behind the wheel and oriented myself to the Honda's pedals and gears that the vehicle was nothing more than a buggy with a well-trained, invisible, very powerful horse. I backed out slowly, feeling especially nervous as I eased alongside my dad's car, which was still parked there in the driveway.

The fifteen-minute ride to the high school was unremarkable. Dad sat beside me giving me directions and pointers. I didn't break any laws or run into another car or cut anyone off, though one guy did honk at me for driving too slow. Dad just laughed and told me to take as much time as I needed.

When we arrived at the school, we got out of the car and stood by it while the football team members dispersed onto the parking lot by the gym. Brady was soon walking toward us with another teammate. Both had freshly showered hair and gym bags slung over their shoulders. The friend said goodbye when he arrived at his own car. Brady hiked up his gym bag and continued on toward us, one of the few, I realized, who had no car of his own.

I don't know what I was expecting exactly by way of welcome. I hadn't seen Brady in two years, and though I figured he wouldn't come running to me with arms outstretched, especially not in front of the other guys, I did think he would at least pick up the pace, maybe drop his bag when he reached the car to give me an enthusiastic hug or two-handed shake. Yet, if anything, his paced slowed when he saw me. As he closed the distance between us, I could see that he had grown more than I had imagined. He was nearly as tall as I was, and he looked much older than fourteen.

"Hey, Tyler," he said casually, when he was a few feet away, as though he had just seen me the day before. He made no move to embrace me, which was fine, but he didn't stretch out his hand to me either. So I stretched out mine.

"Hey, Brady." When he took it for a shake, I pulled him close to give him the same kind of half hug our father had given me.

But he stiffened at my touch and pulled away quickly. When his eyes met mine, I saw traces of disappointment. Or maybe annoyance. Anger, even?

"How's it going?" I asked, pretending I hadn't noticed.

"Great." He answered quickly and politely, but with no enthusiasm.

We got into the car and exchanged a few more pleasantries, and the tone of my brother's voice and demeanor didn't change. As we drove out of the parking lot I was sure of two things.

First, Dad had greatly exaggerated Brady's enthusiasm that I be the one who stayed with him while he and Liz were out of the country.

Second, something had changed between Brady and me since the last time we had talked.

He was definitely not pleased to see me. And I had no idea why.

ELEVEN

Dad took us out to dinner at one of his favorite seafood restaurants. It was a noisy place, full of people enjoying buckets of crab legs, beer, and a basketball game on big screens scattered throughout the restaurant.

It was hard to have a meaningful conversation, though maybe that's what Dad wanted. Surely he had sensed Brady's less-than-genial attitude toward me, not just in the school parking lot, but after we got home and in the hour or so before we left to go out to eat. The raucous vibe of the restaurant didn't lend itself to intimacy, so we didn't need to feel awkward about our lack of it.

I tried to engage Brady in conversation anyway, but his one-word replies to whatever I said stifled any true dialogue. He wasn't rude. He answered every question, but he didn't elaborate and he didn't ask me anything in return. Dad was the one who brought up my grandparents and Jake, and he asked whether I was still seeing Rachel.

When we arrived at the house again, Brady excused himself to go upstairs and do homework. Dad invited me out on the patio, tossing me a UCLA hoodie to wear because it was chilly enough for a jacket but not so cold that I would need the coat I had worn when I left Philly that morning. He grabbed a beer from the fridge and offered me a drink. I spotted a tall, skinny bottle of Italian orange soda, which looked interesting, so I decided on that.

As we settled onto chairs, he turned on the fire pit. I had to smile at how effortless it was for him to start a fire. Another for the book.

Fires are worked by remote control.

I waited to see if he would bring up Brady's attitude toward me. When he didn't, I knew I had to.

"So what's up with Brady? Does he not want me here?"

Dad took a swig from his bottle. "I honestly don't know why he wasn't happier to see you. I told you on the phone he's going through a phase of some kind. This must be part of it."

"But you also told me he wanted me to come."

"He did. Before I called you, he did."

"What happened between then and now?" It had only been a week. Something had to have transpired since then.

Dad shook his head. "I have no idea. I didn't know he was going to be that way around you. I'm as surprised as you are." He paused for a moment and then sensed how uneasy that must have made me feel, considering he was leaving the next day for a month. "I'm sure he still wants you to be here. He's just...he's mixed up right now."

"Mixed up about what?"

Dad shrugged, as if the answer was a no-brainer. "He's a teenager living on the edge of the adult world. It's that way when you're fourteen and you're half in one place and half in another. I'm sure it was the same even for you. When you were done with school at Brady's age and went to work for your grandfather, you felt the same way. Mixed up. I remember it."

It had been a long time since my dad had mentioned the year that school ended for me and my adult life began. It was always such a sensitive topic for me, I was surprised to hear now that I had somehow communicated to him my true feelings about the matter.

"What do you mean?"

"You came to visit us that summer. I could tell you were sad that school was over for you. I know I wasn't happy about it, but what could I do? That's the way things are back there."

I nodded, waiting to see where he was going with this.

"It took you a while to figure it all out. I called you that Christmas and asked if you were happy, and you told me you were. You even sounded happy. So obviously you weren't feeling mixed up about it anymore. That's what I mean. Brady is no different than you were. He's doing what he loves, but that doesn't mean it's easy."

As I considered this, it occurred to me that maybe Brady had decided I was only there to enforce our father's will. That I had become Dad's ally, not his.

"Maybe he thinks I'm here just to keep him from quitting the team," I ventured.

"That's not the only reason," Dad shot back quickly. "You're his brother, Ty. Who better than you to stay with him while Liz and I are gone?"

"But it is a reason."

"So?"

"So if this is a source of conflict between you two, then it will seem that I am not here as his brother but for your sake, to keep him on the team whether he wants to be there or not."

Dad shook his head. "That is not a source of conflict between Brady and me. He loves football. He loves being on the team. He's just feeling the pressure of being in such a visible spot. It's scary to have so many eyes watching him all the time. He just needs to settle in to being in the spotlight. You settled in when your teenage life took an abrupt turn. That's what he needs to see."

I took a drink of the soda. It was tangy and sweet at the same time. And highly carbonated. "I'll do my best, but I'm only human, Dad."

"That's all anyone can do, Ty. I just want Brady to give this his best. I don't want him to look back ten, twenty years from now and wish he'd made different choices."

We were silent as his words settled over us.

"So. Think you'll end up marrying Rachel?" he asked, after a long thoughtful pause.

"Maybe. Probably."

"How long have you been dating? Five years?"

I smiled. "Six, actually."

"Six. Wow. I envy your long courtship. Isn't that what you call it? Courtship? I married your mother less than a month after meeting her." He laughed. "Craziest thing I've ever done."

I smiled and said nothing, wanting him to continue and hoping he would. He hardly ever talked about my mother.

"I'm not saying I have any regrets. She was drop-dead beautiful and the kindest person I'd ever met. And she was so ready to see the world. I guess we both were. She proposed to *me*, did I ever tell you that?"

I shook my head.

"We'd seen each other every night for three weeks and I was getting ready to head back to New York. I was just in Philly visiting a friend." Dad raised his gaze to the starry horizon, almost as if he were looking through a glass back to the time before I was born. "I would be heading out to Germany soon, and we were both wondering if we would ever see each other again. I had fallen pretty fast for her, that's for sure. She wasn't like any of the girls I'd ever had my eye on. She was fun to be around, but she was innocent too. Everything was new and amazing to her. There wasn't a jaded bone in her body. I was kind of awkward around girls, but never around her. With her, I felt wise and clever and experienced in the ways of the world."

He glanced at me, a tad embarrassed. "I've never been a very affectionate guy," he admitted, "and Liz says I'm still not. But your mother... she didn't seem to mind that the only thing I knew how to talk about in romantic terms was my '67 Mustang back home." He laughed. "Anyway, it was my last night in Philly. We were at a club, dancing, which your mother loved, and I said something like, 'What am I going to do without you,' and she said, 'Take me with you.' I laughed but she didn't. She just smiled and said, 'Let's get married.'"

Dad grinned at the memory and I continued to listen in spellbound silence.

"I wasn't sure if she was serious, so I said something like, 'And what would your Amish father say if I told him I wanted to marry you?' And she said, 'We won't tell him, Duke. Not until after the fact, anyway.' And you know what? The minute she said it, I knew that was what I wanted to do. There wasn't one person in her family who would approve, and the only one left on my side by that point was my dad, who wouldn't care either way. No one would be happy for us, but we'd be happy for ourselves."

He flashed me a sheepish grin.

"Everybody knows you get married in Maryland if you're in a hurry," he continued, "so that's what we did. Drove right down to Elkton and found us an available chapel. She wore a blue dress and carried some kind of flowers. Daisies, maybe. Anyway, after that, it was just two hours over to Cape May for our honeymoon. That was the first time she ever went in the ocean—first time she'd ever even seen the ocean, actually. I can't tell you how much fun it was to be there with her on that beach, to see how excited she got. Just ran right into the water, blue dress and all."

He lowered his gaze to the fire that danced before us, his grin fading to a more somber expression. "The next few weeks weren't nearly as fun, though, I'll tell you that. I was still stuck in bachelors' quarters back at my post, so your mom had to stay with one of her friends in Philly for a couple of weeks since she'd already given up her sublet. While I finished things at the base, filling out the paperwork and such so she could come with me to Germany, she spent her time wrapping up her own affairs and trying to get a passport for herself."

He grew silent, lost in thought, so I prodded him by asking if she was successful.

He seemed to snap back to attention. "Sure was. Now that was an act of God, I'll tell you. She prayed every day that the passport would show up before we had to leave, and, to my astonishment, it did." With a grunt, he added, "In fact, it was her getting that passport in time that made me think maybe someday I could have as much faith in the good Lord as she did, you know? She just *believed*, to her very core."

He glanced at me, adding, "I know you've probably been told by your grandparents that she turned her back on God when she married me. I can tell you that she did not."

Though that knowledge was deeply comforting to me, I said nothing. I wanted him to keep talking.

After a moment, he did. "We went to see her family before we left for Germany, to tell them we were married and to say goodbye. It was a disaster. You would have thought your mother had married a mafia warlord. Her sister Sarah wouldn't even talk to her. And your grandparents? They wouldn't look at me. Did you know that?"

I shrugged. The way Sarah had described it, that day hadn't gone well for any of them.

Dad turned to face the fire again. "Your grandfather pulled me aside before we left and told me to be good to your mother, but he wouldn't look me in the eye when he said it. At least what he did next was...well, he put a hand on my shoulder and mumbled out something about God protecting us. Your mother told me later he was reciting a Bible verse, but at the time it felt totally personal, you know? Like it was just to me."

I nodded. How sad my father didn't know that the Bible could speak personally to him all the time if he would bother to read it.

"It was really touching, in spite of the cold welcome. I still remember it. Nicest thing anyone had ever said to me, besides your mother, of course."

"That sounds like *Daadi*."

"It was doubly meaningful because I knew what he really wanted to do at that moment was wring my neck, not pray a blessing over me."

We both chuckled. That definitely did *not* sound like *Daadi*, the gentlest person I'd ever known.

"They never forgave me for taking their daughter away."

I glanced at him. "Not true."

He raised his eyebrows at me.

"I mean, that's not the Amish way. We always forgive. If we don't forgive others, then God in turn will not forgive us. The Bible says so."

He took a long sip of his drink, draining the bottle.

"Yeah, well, all I know is, they about broke her heart that day."

"That wasn't about forgiveness, Dad. That was..." My voice trailed off. How could I explain it to an outsider? She hadn't been shunned, but they had sort of treated her that way when she ran off. It wasn't meant to be hurtful. It was meant to be biblical, a way to bring a wandering sheep back into the fold. I doubted that was a concept my father could understand, much less appreciate, so instead I just told him about my long-ago conversation with her sister Sarah, how she'd described it as a day none of them had been ready for.

"Clearly," my father said, shaking his head.

"She also said that if they had known what was going to happen, they would have handled things differently."

"Yeah? Well, hindsight is twenty-twenty and all that. But I guess I'm glad to hear it. Trust me, I can relate."

We were both quiet for a moment.

"I will say this about your grandparents. They sure came to my rescue when your mother died. I don't know what I would have done if they hadn't taken you in."

I hesitated, grappling for a response. How different my life would have played out had he done back then what a great many widowed fathers managed to do: find a way to carry on as a single parent. At the very least, I wouldn't be as torn as I was now, because there would be no question about which world I truly belonged in.

"They are good people," I finally managed to say.

Dad nodded. "Yes. Yes, they are."

A few minutes of silence stretched between us as we stared into the fire.

"If you love Rachel, you should marry her, Ty."

"It's not…it's not that simple."

"Of course it's that simple. It's love. Love isn't complicated. You just ask her, son. I know you're still young and all, but not in Amish years."

I smiled in spite of myself. "Amish years? Is that like dog years?"

He chuckled. "Sorry. You know what I mean. From what I understand, at your age, you should be married and a member of the church by now."

I was surprised to hear him put it so bluntly. I was tempted to tell him the truth, but I wasn't sure if I wanted him to know the internal burden I had brought with me or not. Would he be happy or surprised or alarmed that I didn't know where I belonged? In his mind, he probably thought I had settled on that long ago.

I gathered my courage and then opened my mouth to tell him that Rachel was a member of the Amish church already and that *that's* what made proposing to her complicated—because I wasn't yet and didn't know if I ever would be.

But he stood and clicked off the fire pit. "I need to finish packing, and we have to go over the last of the details. The airport shuttle is coming at the crack of dawn."

The conversation about Rachel fizzled away.

We went inside.

I saw Brady for a few minutes before I turned in for the night. His attitude toward me was the same. Polite but reserved. I knew one of the first things I had to do after Dad left was have a heart-to-heart with my brother so that I could let him know I was on his side.

Back in the guest room, I hung up the pants and shirts from my suitcase, though I wondered why I had brought them. I probably wasn't going to wear any of my Amish clothes while I was there. I set my hat on the shelf above and then laid my suspenders and the empty duffel next to it. Dad had told me to hang on to the UCLA hoodie to wear while I was here, and though he hadn't had time to pull together any clothes for me from his closet, he said I was welcome to help myself once he was gone.

After I'd put my things away, I got the notebook out of my backpack and settled into the armchair that was positioned in a corner of the room. I began writing down the list of observations I had mentally made about living the non-Amish life. Then I added a few more:

Houses can be kept by little work on your part.

One man can own three cars.

A house can have rooms that are never even used.

I got ready for bed and knelt at the chair to say my prayers. I thanked God for getting me safely to California, and I asked Him to watch over *Daadi, Mammi,* Jake, and Rachel while I was gone. I asked that He give safe travel for my father the next day and safety for Liz, wherever she was in Honduras, and that He would show me how to reach out to my little brother.

And I asked for wisdom and clarity to see His path for me. At this point it felt foggier than ever.

TWELVE

I was awake when I heard my dad getting ready to go to the airport. It was about five in the morning, which was eight back in Pennsylvania. Given that I was usually up before sunrise at home, sleeping in this late felt almost decadent.

I dressed for the day in my new *Englisch* clothes and slipped on my watch, though I had to loosen the strap first. It had been a few years since I'd worn it. When I opened my bedroom door, Frisco was there to greet me. He had apparently heard me moving around and assumed I'd be coming out. He danced at my feet, and I leaned down to pet him before heading to the stairs. I had yet to warm up to the odd little creature, though his presence made me miss Timber all the more.

The house was bathed in darkness, and out of the large window in the living room I could see that the street lights still shone and stars had only just started to wink out. I found my dad in the kitchen, sipping a tall glass of orange juice as he stood at the counter-height table, tapping his finger on an iPad.

He looked up when he sensed he wasn't alone. "Tyler. Hey. Did I wake you?"

"No. It's just way after sunrise back on the East Coast."

"Ah. Of course. Farm life and all that." He powered down the iPad and slipped it into a black leather case slung over one of the tall chairs. "Any last-minute questions for me?"

We had already gone over a lot, from how to use the Keurig coffeemaker to where the dog park was located to what day and time Liz needed to be picked up from the airport. The minor details I had down. The things I wasn't sure about, he couldn't address.

"Can't think of anything at the moment."

"You know you can email me whenever you want. I'll be checking it often during the day. Do you still have email?"

I nodded. I had a Gmail account I had opened a few years back that I used only for the buggy business. It had been a year since I had used it for anything personal. I really didn't have anyone to email except for my dad and Brady. Dad wasn't one for email small talk, and Brady had barely used email since he had gotten his iPhone and could text instead.

"You can call me if there's an emergency. And make sure you give Brady the number to that cell phone we got yesterday."

"Will do."

Dad grabbed the leather case off the chair. We walked toward the front door, where his bag was already waiting. From inside a coat closet he pulled out a leather jacket.

"I tried talking to Brady last night after you went to bed," Dad said, a sigh in his voice. "I asked him why he didn't seem too happy you were here. He acted as though he didn't know what I was talking about. I didn't press it. I'm on thin ice with him already. I know you probably don't want to hear this, but I feel that you're my last hope. If you can't reach him, I don't know who could."

"God could, Dad."

He smiled wistfully. "Sure. God could." As an afterthought he added, "So maybe you'll put in a word with the Big Guy on our behalf?"

"I already have," I said with a smile.

He opened the front door, and the warming night sky was tinged with dawn. Dad inhaled deeply and then turned to me. "I feel like I didn't do right by you, Ty. I've felt it for a long time. I can't change what's in the past, but I can try to do better with Brady."

In my entire life, I had never once heard my dad speak of regret when it came to me. I didn't know what to make of it now.

"I don't feel that you didn't do right by me," I said quickly.

He nodded, but not by way of agreement. It was as if he already knew that's what I would say. "I kind of wish you did," he said softly, almost so soft that I didn't hear it.

A white van pulled up to the curb, its side painted with an airport shuttle logo and a navy blue jet.

He thrust out his hand to shake mine in farewell. "Thanks for being here, Tyler. It really means a lot to me."

Our eyes met, and for some reason my father suddenly looked different to me. He was only fifty, but he seemed older than that and… defeated somehow. My heart went out to him. With a sigh, he stepped onto the tiled walkway, pulling his black suitcase behind him. Frisco was at my ankles, watching him go and barking the whole time. I scooped up the dog to shush him before he woke up the entire street.

My dad got into the van, slid the door shut, and the vehicle pulled away.

I went back inside the quiet house, set the dog down, and headed to the kitchen to have a cup of coffee, read my Bible, and contemplate what had just happened here.

I feel like I didn't do right by you, Tyler. I've felt it for a long time.

I had to admit, just hearing those words filled some need inside of me, one I couldn't explain and didn't even realize I'd had until now.

I was showered and dressed and already on my second K-cup, as Dad had called it, when Brady came down the stairs a few minutes after six. He looked half awake and irritable.

"Hey," he said to me as he crossed the kitchen floor and grabbed a clean coffee mug and a K-cup for himself. As I watched him use the machine, I mentally added another one to my list.

Individual cups of hot coffee can be made in a wide variety of flavors with the push of a button.

I almost made a comment to Brady about him starting the day with coffee at his age, but thought better of it. I was drinking coffee at fifteen. "Morning," I said instead.

He shuffled over to the fridge and pulled out a tall container of flavored creamer. "Dad get off okay?"

"Yes." At last, a question instead of just an answer. "Can I take you to school today?"

"Nah. I got a ride." The coffeemaker sputtered and spewed as it filled my brother's mug, ending the cycle with an odd mechanical whir.

"I'm happy to take you. And pick you up after football."

"Yeah, I know. I got a ride, though."

Brady poured the cream in his cup and stirred it lazily. He turned to leave the kitchen.

"Brady, can you hold on a second?"

He stopped.

"Look, I just want you to know that I'm really glad I can be here with you while Dad and Liz are gone. And I'm looking forward to finding out what you've been up to since the last time we talked."

"Okay." His tone was cordial but void of warmth.

"Can we catch up at dinner tonight? I think I can figure out the grill. I could make us some hamburgers. Would that be okay?"

He blinked. "Sure."

Again, he started to leave.

"Wait, Brady."

Again he stopped. This time, I detected a sigh of annoyance.

"What?"

I moved closer to him so that just a few feet separated us instead of the entire kitchen. "Have I done or said something to offend you?"

"What do you mean?" There was no questioning lilt to his voice.

"You've barely said a whole sentence to me since we picked you up from school yesterday."

"What would you like me to say?"

Was he serious?

"I guess I'd like you to tell me what it is that I have done wrong so we can clear the air."

Brady took a sip of his coffee, but his eyes never left mine until he lowered the cup. "How could you have done something? You don't even live here, man."

He turned from me to head back up the stairs, but I called out after him, asking if he wanted eggs.

"Okay," he mumbled, not even glancing my way as he went.

As a child, I had helped *Mammi* in the kitchen often enough to know how to prepare eggs. I sprinkled a bit of paprika on them as they were finishing, just like she did, and popped bread into the toaster. When Brady came back downstairs, he grabbed the plate I made for him, grunted his thanks, and took it over to the family room. He clicked the remote for the TV to an ESPN station and ate while he alternately watched the TV and fiddled with his phone.

I brought my plate into the family room too. I took a seat on the other side of the couch, set my plate down on the coffee table, and pulled out the phone Dad had bought me the day before.

"I have a cell phone to use while I'm here."

"Yeah, Dad told me." Brady didn't look up from his own phone.

"Can I give you the number so you'll have it?"

"Just text me. I'll have it then. Dad said he gave you my number." Again, no eye contact.

"Sure." I found Brady's name in the short list of contacts and tapped out a message.

How are the eggs?

I sent it and waited. Almost instantly, Brady's phone made a trilling sound. He grinned ever so slightly and tapped a message back to me.

Not bad. Add some grated cheddar next time.

I responded with, *Will do.*

And then I quickly followed up with, *Is there a camera in the house I could use?*

He looked up at me when he got the message. "What do you want a camera for?"

"I don't know. To use as a doorstop?" I smiled, but he didn't exactly appreciate my attempt at humor.

"Well, duh, you know what I mean. What do you want pictures for? You can't take them back with you."

I shrugged. "I was thinking I might sign up for a photography class or something."

Brady stared at me. "A photography class."

"Yes."

A few seconds passed before he responded. "You're kidding me, right?"

"No. No, I'm not. Do you have one? A camera, I mean?"

"I use the one in my phone. Dad uses his phone. My mom has a real one, but I'm sure she has it with her in Honduras."

"Ah." My heart sank. I hated the thought of having to buy one when I didn't even know yet if I was going to like it or not.

"There might be a couple old ones in a cabinet in Dad's study. I think I saw one or two in there when I was looking for an HDMI cable."

I didn't know what an HDMI cable was, but I supposed it didn't matter. "Great. Thanks."

"You're only here for a month, though," Brady said. "How much can one person learn in that amount of time anyway?"

"I don't know, but time is the one thing I do have. From what I can tell, there's not one unfinished project to complete or broken appliance to fix or even flower bed to weed around here. You're gone all day. I might as well put those hours to use somehow."

"Uh-huh. Like with photography?" My brother over-enunciated the last word just in case I hadn't recognized the sarcasm.

I ignored it. "That's right. You know of a place where I could take a few classes while I'm here?"

Brady still seemed to be waiting for the punch line. An Amish man learning to use a camera? I supposed that made *me* the punch line.

"Well, my mom took a community ed class on tai chi last year in Irvine. It only lasted six weeks. You could maybe look into something like that if you're serious. But I don't think you're going to find a class that only lasts a month and that starts, like, this week. Maybe you could hire a professional to tutor you."

"Great idea."

"Though that could get pretty expensive."

I thought for a moment. "What about, instead of a professional, a gifted amateur? Aren't there people like that who will just teach me one-on-one for a few lessons?"

"Well, you could look on Craigslist or the classifieds, but…" He made a face.

"But what?"

"You just need to be careful, Tyler. You're not in Amishland here. Not everybody who says they have something to offer can be trusted. Know what I mean?"

I did. His concern for me trumped his Amishland comment. He may have been mad for some reason, but he still cared about my welfare.

"Here's a thought," he continued. "My friend Aaron has a sister who goes to Orange Coast College. I think she's majoring in photography. Maybe she can recommend someone. I'll ask him at school today."

"Orange Coast College? Is that local?"

"Yeah. She lives at home and commutes to school."

"Okay. Thanks. That would be great."

"So, you won't go contacting people you don't know, right?"

I laughed. "I promise I won't contact people I don't know."

"Good. And if you need something to do while I'm gone, here's a suggestion. Find out everything you can about the Vikings. And I don't mean the football team. I have a paper about them due on Friday, and I haven't even begun thinking about it."

Brady rose from the couch and headed toward the kitchen, so I clicked off the TV and followed him there, telling him I'd be happy to round up some resource materials if he thought that would help get him started.

"Where's the public library?"

Brady set his plate in the sink. "I don't know. Except for in school, I haven't been to a library since I was a kid. Why?"

"To help with your research?"

"Dude, just use the computer in Dad's office."

I felt my face grow warm. Since when had my little brother become so mean spirited? "I know that," I said, trying to recover from my embarrassment. "I just thought it would be good to get out of the house at some point today."

Brady rinsed out his coffee cup and set it next to the plate. "So get out of the house. Walk the dog. Go to Starbucks. Relax a little. Life isn't just making buggies, you know."

On that note he left the kitchen to finish getting ready for school. Good grief. This kid was too much. Dad had been right about one thing. Brady had definitely changed.

Putting him out of my mind for now, I made a plan for my day as I rinsed my own plate.

I would walk the dog.

Then I would call the buggy shop to let *Daadi* know I had arrived safely.

Then I would write a letter to Rachel.

Then I would head to the nearest library.

Then I just might stop in at a barbershop. It was time to make my temporary transformation complete.

THIRTEEN

By twenty after seven, Brady was gone and the house again became very quiet. I washed our breakfast dishes, fed Frisco, and checked the fridge and pantry for what I would need for our hamburger dinner. After making my bed and resisting the urge to make Brady's as well, I programmed the number for the buggy shop into my cell phone and then called.

Thom answered.

When I said hello, my uncle began speaking to me in Pennsylvania Dutch, and I realized I hadn't heard one word of my everyday language in more than twenty-four hours. I couldn't remember the last time that had happened.

"*Daed* is out making a delivery," Thom said. "But *Mamm* is here. Hold on."

A second later I heard my grandmother's gentle voice. "Tyler. *Wie bischt?*"

"I'm fine. My dad left for the Middle East this morning. It's just me and Brady at the house now."

"Your little brother must be very happy you are there."

I laughed uneasily. "Maybe. It's hard to tell. He's changed a lot since the last time I saw him."

"It has been a while. At that age, change comes more quickly."

"That's true, I suppose."

"So are you glad you decided to go?"

I wasn't sure how to answer that. I had barely even begun the quest that had brought me here. It wasn't a matter of being glad, but of listening to God. "I think I'm supposed to be here right now, *Mammi*," I finally said.

"All right. Then we shall pray all the more that God shows you why."

"*Danke*. If you see Rachel, tell her to call me on Saturday. She can use this number. It's a cell phone Dad bought me to use. Or the landline. She has that number already."

"Oh. All right."

"Say hi to *Daadi* for me. I love you."

"We love you too, Tyler. *Farrywell.*"

With that call taken care of, I wrote a letter to Rachel telling her about the airplane flight, this new house that seemed to do everything itself, my dad's opening up to me about my mother, and Brady's strange attitude toward me.

After that, I put the letter in the mailbox and took Frisco for a walk. Dad had said to bring along a plastic bag, as it was considered littering to leave your dog's mess on the sidewalk or in someone else's yard. Two more for the list.

Dog mess must be picked up.

There are special plastic bags manufactured just for that purpose.

Out on the sidewalk, I noticed I was not the only one walking a dog and clutching a little plastic bag. I said "Good morning" to several others who also came prepared to take their dogs' waste home with them. Most responded with just a nod, polite but cool.

Back at the house, I made a lunch to take with me for the day, dug around for a phone book to look up libraries, and then headed out in Liz's Honda to go to the nearest one. I got lost twice but finally made it. By eleven, I was inside the Newport Beach Public Library, roaming the shelves. It had been a while since I had immersed myself in researching something that didn't have to do with buggies.

I consulted many books on Viking history, getting my fill of the seafaring warriors' knack for raiding and piracy and taking things that didn't belong to them. I read as much as I could stomach for Brady's sake and then decided to move on to something else more benign, just to clear my head.

After stacking to one side the books I would check out for Brady, I returned to the shelves in search of the photography section. Once I found it, I was surprised to see how big it was. I perused the offerings, and though some of the books looked too dry and technical and boring to slog through, others seemed quite intriguing. I gathered together the most promising ones, carried them back to my table, and dug in.

My intention was to familiarize myself with the basic mechanics of picture-taking, but I was soon immersed in the history of photography instead. Except for the problem of nosy, camera-snapping tourists, the topic never came up much in the Amish community, so my knowledge base was pretty much nil. Now I realized how fascinating photography was, especially when I saw how long it had been around. The first photographic image was captured in 1825, but the story of pictures on film actually began in ancient times, with the creation of a primitive device known as a "camera obscura." Variations on that device persisted for centuries and were eventually coupled with photo-sensitive compounds, which allowed the images seen through the camera obscura to be captured not just with the eye but on paper. I followed along the timeline step by step and was up to 1837 and the invention of the daguerreotype when I realized my stomach was growling. Glancing up at the clock, I was surprised to see that between my Viking research and these photography books, I had been reading for four hours straight. Time to go. There was a bagged lunch waiting in the car, calling my name.

I stacked my top choices, both Viking- and photography-related, and carried them up to the counter. I asked the librarian for a card, intending to use my father's address. She said they couldn't do that without proof I lived there and suggested I get a temporary, out-of-state card instead.

Thanking her for her help, I handed over my driver's license so she could take care of it.

"Pennsylvania, huh?" she said as she typed in my information.

"*Ya*. Have you ever been there?"

"No, but I understand it's beautiful."

I smiled, assuring her that it definitely was.

Our conversation continued as she kept typing, and soon she was urging me to visit the ocean while I was here.

"You can't come this far west and not see it at least once," she said, softly but enthusiastically.

I agreed, asking how to get there and saying that I knew it wasn't far, not just because I'd checked on a map, but because I could smell the salt in the air.

She handed back my license and my new card, and then she gave me directions to the "beach" of Newport Beach. I thanked her for the help and headed out, deciding I would go there now.

Despite my growling stomach, I managed to wait on eating my bag lunch until I had driven all the way, parked, and taken a seat at a picnic table at the edge of a wide expanse of sand. Beyond that was the glistening expanse of the Pacific Ocean. People in workout clothes were running on the beach and a few surfers were clad in black wet suits. The sound of the waves was rhythmic and soothing, like an oscillating fan on a hot summer day.

I needed to get back to the house, but for some reason it was hard to tear myself away from the beautiful scenery. At least I knew Frisco would be okay, as my father had assured me the little dog could spend a whole day inside, if need be, without any backyard breaks.

Thus, feeling just a little indulgent, once I'd finished my lunch, I kicked off my shoes and locked them in the car, and then I allowed myself the pleasure of a walk along the hardpacked sand of the surf. As I did, I found myself moving into a state of quiet prayer. How could I not? All of the magnificence that surrounded me had been created by God. To not praise Him for that would be like dining on the most amazing meal ever and not thanking the chef who cooked it.

Finally, I managed to tear myself away, though I got lost trying to get back home. Dad had told me there was a GPS unit in Liz's car, but I had convinced myself I didn't need it as long as I had a map or verbal directions. I pulled into a gas station, asked God to please help me figure out how to use it, and gave it a shot. Fortunately, it wasn't nearly as difficult as I'd feared. It helped too that Liz already had the home address programmed in.

Once I was oriented, I made two stops on the way, first at a hair salon with a sign out front that said, "Men's Cuts a Specialty." Inside, the place was subdued and elegant, with a trickling fountain, slate floors, and at least a dozen hairdressers. I would rather have gone to a plain old barbershop, but I hadn't seen one along the way.

I asked for something stylish but neat, and the woman who took on the challenge was very young, with a rather bizarre hairdo herself—a mix of long and short and even shaved portions, dyed in various colors of the rainbow. Her own appearance made me nervous at first, but as she snipped away at the bowl-shaped cut I'd worn my whole life, or at least my whole Amish life, I could tell she knew what she was doing. Sure enough, once she was finished with me and I saw my own image in the mirror, I felt utterly transformed. I no longer looked Amish at all.

Whether I was still Amish or not on the inside was the more important question—and one I hoped I would find the answer to soon.

Stop number two was at a grocery store for hamburger patties, buns, a carton of potato salad, and a yellow onion. It was a good thing Brady hadn't taken me up on my offer to pick him up from school. It was after six by the time I pulled into the garage, and he was already home.

I entered the kitchen carrying the grocery bags and the books. Brady was sitting at the table, drinking a protein shake and looking at a magazine.

"Where have you been?" he said, almost the way a parent would.

"I don't know. Errands."

"Errands," he repeated. Irritation shone clearly on his face, but when our eyes met, he did a sort of double take. "What did you do?"

"What do you mean?"

"You look…different."

"Different bad or different good?"

He shrugged. "Different better, I guess. Not so Amish anymore."

"Ah," I said, moving further into the room. "Haircut." Feeling suddenly self-conscious, I set the books down next to him on the table and changed the subject. "I also found the library."

The pile spilled over. Brady picked up one of the books, shaking his head. "Seriously, Tyler? You think a history of photography is going to teach you how to take pictures?"

I took the grocery bags over to the counter by the fridge. "Of course not. I just needed to clear my mind with something interesting and uplifting after reading about the Vikings. They weren't very admirable people. At least not the ones I read about."

Brady pulled the two Viking-related books from the pile. "Hey, thanks." He flipped through them both, pausing at several of the goriest pictures. "These look cool." Finally, he set them aside in their own pile. "Are you really going to read all these others?"

I opened the fridge and set the potato salad inside. "Maybe. The history of photography really is fascinating, all the inventions and discoveries and developments and things. Do you know that the first photosensitive compound was created by accident? If the guy hadn't realized what he'd done, who knows how much longer it would've taken to come up with the chemistry for preserving images on film?"

"Captivating," Brady said dryly.

Ignoring his sarcasm, I continued. "I guess I'd just forgotten how much I liked learning new things. I didn't get to go to college, so—"

"Or high school."

He said it in an almost condescending way.

"Learning the family trade *was* my high school." I pulled out the package of hamburger and set it on the counter. "It's no different than a vocational high school. I know about those. And it's never seemed to bother you before that I finished school at eighth grade."

"I just think it's weird, that's all. I've always thought it was weird."

My patience with his attitude was reaching its limit. I needed to know what was up with him. "So why the attitude with me?"

"Why your attitude with me?" Again, the disrespectful tone.

"You know, Brady, when Dad first called me, he said you *wanted* me to come."

"So?"

I had the onion in my hand and I tossed it on the counter. It rolled into the sink.

"So why are you acting like you wish I weren't here? Is it because you think the reason is for me to keep you from quitting the team?"

He didn't answer, so I continued. "Because I have news for you, little brother. I'm not Dad. I don't care what you do about football."

Brady's eyes flashed anger and then went steely cool. "You told Dad you'd do your best to make sure I didn't quit."

"No. I told him I would do my best to make sure you didn't make a decision you would later regret. That happens, you know. If you want to be on the team, then I want you on the team. If you don't want to be on the team, then that's fine too. All I ask is that you think it over carefully before you make a decision that big. "

He narrowed his eyes and glared at me with suspicion. We were getting nowhere. If anything, the vibe between us now was worse than it had been the day before.

"Believe it or not," I continued, "I want whatever you want. I want you to be happy and to make of your life what will bring you the most joy and to God the most honor."

I could almost hear *Daadi's* voice through my words, though when he spoke this way it felt comforting and wise. Out of my mouth, it just seemed to agitate Brady even further. He wouldn't respond or even look at me.

"Do you think I'm lying to you?"

He shrugged, his lips pinched tightly together.

"You do. Why? When have I ever lied to you before?"

Brady picked up one of the library books. "Apparently, never."

I blinked. "What does that mean, 'Apparently, never'? You think I've been less than honest with you in the past?"

He opened the book and began to thumb through the pages. It took supreme effort not to pull it from his hands and send him to bed without dinner. That's what *Daadi* would have done. And maybe even our own father. But I wasn't Brady's grandfather or his father. I was his brother.

Half brother.

I prayed silently for wisdom to know what was eating away at him and how to draw it out so we could settle this once and for all.

"First of all," I said, trying to keep the anger and frustration from my voice, "I have never, nor will I ever, lie to you. Second, if you want to quit the team, that's fine. I'll stand with you. It's your life and your future."

He put the book down. "I never told Dad I wanted to quit the team."

"But he said—"

"Maybe you should ask me what *I* said."

He had me there. It hadn't been my intention to begin this conversation in this way. "You're right. I was going to ask you tonight over dinner how you were feeling about being on the team. I did this all wrong. Can we start over?"

Brady shook his head and laughed as though I still didn't get it. "Not that it's truly any of your business, Tyler, but I happen to like football. What I don't like is Dad needing to cram his dreams for greatness down my throat. And if my playing football is going to bring out the worst in him, then I am going to take up marching band. Because I am telling you right now, I will not spend the next three years and then the next four years and then who knows how many years after that in the NFL, should I get lucky enough to play for them, being Dad's...never mind."

And there it was. As I'd suspected, Dad really was coming down way too hard on his younger son. Before I could think of how to respond, Brady continued.

"Just forget it. Look, I have no plans to quit the team. At least not while you're here. But if I do, it's *my* decision to make. And mine to regret, for that matter. See, I do understand the consequences and I do take them seriously. Okay?"

"Okay." I was quiet for a moment. "But even if you stay on the team, you really need to talk to Dad about this when he gets home."

Brady rolled his eyes. "I already have. He doesn't get it."

"What if you and I talked to him together?"

He barked out a laugh.

"I'm serious, Brady. Once he returns, I think the three of us should sit down and discuss this whole issue. Calmly and respectfully. Trust me. He already knows you're not happy with him right now. And I'll be there beside you to back you up."

My brother sighed. "Right." He stood, picked up his glass, and brought it to the sink. "Just like you've always been there before."

I had no idea what he was implying. All I knew was that he didn't respect me anymore—nor did he trust me, for that matter. Had I let him down somehow? Certainly, I had lost credibility in his eyes. I couldn't imagine how that might have happened, but I hoped I would find out soon. The chip on his shoulder was huge, far too big to be knocked off in a single conversation.

I decided to leave it alone for now.

"Okay, maybe now's not the time to talk about this. I'm hungry, and I'm sure you are too."

He seemed relieved that we were dropping the subject for now. I asked him to turn on the grill, and he walked to the door, pausing before he went out.

"Oh, yeah," he said, turning back. "Lark picked up Aaron after practice today. I asked her about the photography thing. She said she might have a few suggestions for you."

"Pardon?"

"Aaron's sister. The photographer, remember? Her name is Lark. She couldn't think of anyone who might be willing to teach you offhand, but she offered to ask around. She wants to talk to you first, though, hear what you have in mind."

"No problem. Should I call her?"

"She said she'd just meet you after the football game Friday night. You're coming, right?"

"I'll be there."

Fourteen

The rest of the evening passed without further conflict. Something was still between Brady and me at the dinner table, something we would need to get back to soon, but we managed to bury the hatchet, temporarily at least, and share an uncomplicated evening. That would have to be good enough for now.

Later, before getting in bed, I updated my list.

The Pacific Ocean shines like glass.

Some young women tint their hair with colors not found in nature.

Reading and researching simply for knowledge is uncommon, at least once one is no longer in school.

Sitting back in my chair, I thought of the various things I wanted to explore while I was here, including photography and bike riding.

I hadn't gone bicycling in many years—not since my mother died, in fact. But I'd seen some bicycles in the garage, and for some reason I had been feeling the urge to hop on one and take it for a spin ever since. Maybe I just wanted to experience that old sensation of flying down the street, like a plane about to take to the sky.

Or maybe I just wanted to feel closer to my mother, doing something I had memories of us having happily shared together.

The next day, Thursday, when Brady came downstairs for breakfast—just cereal and a banana this time—he seemed to be in a much better mood than he had when I'd arrived home the night before.

He poured cornflakes into a bowl. One flake spilled onto the counter and he tossed it to Frisco. "So what's up for today? More fascinating journeys into the world of research and libraries and history?" He was being sarcastic again, but this time it felt a little less mean spirited and more like simple teasing between brothers.

I smiled. "You never know." I didn't feel like sharing with him my plans for the biking. "Maybe I'll find some things to do around the house. Something useful. Any ideas?"

With a shrug, he dug into his cereal, thought for a moment, and then said, "You know how to make a container garden?"

"A what garden?"

"A container garden. My mom wants one on the south side of the backyard so she can grow her own herbs and lettuce and stuff. That's what people do in the suburbs, I guess. Dad was going to hire somebody to do it, but he hasn't yet."

"I could probably build that," I said, eager to have a project at last.

"You'll have to take out the bushes that are there first. They're right where she wants it."

"No problem. Great, actually."

He regarded me with a lopsided smile. "Nice to know I've made your day." He picked up his bowl and took it to the table. "You know where to go to find out what a container garden looks like, right?"

I smiled back at him. "Internet?"

He gave me a thumbs-up. Another one for my list.

The first—and often only—step in any quest for knowledge is to search the Internet.

When Brady left for school and the dishes were done, I headed into the backyard to check out the south side of the house. I found a loose pebble walkway that led to a small garden shed. It was neat and orderly, likely used by the hired gardener and no one else. Walking along a leafy hedge, I could see the area Brady had been talking about. It was about eight feet deep and twenty feet long, give or take. Frisco seemed particularly enthused about my interest in the backyard, and when I tried to head back to the door, he dropped a red rubber ball at my feet. Wishing I had a farm for the little guy to explore, I took pity on him and threw the toy for him to fetch ten or eleven times, much to the dog's delight. As I did, I had to admit that he was growing on me.

"You're no Timber," I told him as we headed back inside, "but you'll do for now."

I made another cup of coffee to sip while I used Dad's computer to find out what a typical Southern California container garden looked like.

I hadn't really been in the study until that moment. As soon as I stepped inside, I was hyperaware that the room was my dad's and no one else's. Two tall, potted palms stood by French doors that opened to the fire pit in the backyard. Built-in bookshelves lined one entire wall, though my dad didn't appear to own a lot of reading material. The shelves were sparsely populated with books, leaving the remaining space for models of military helicopters, a wedding portrait of him and Liz, and pictures of muscle cars. The few books Dad had were mostly related to collectible cars, his military career, and the places he had lived while he was in the army. As I scanned the titles, I saw that he had a pictorial guide to Germany, where he'd been stationed when I was born. I ran my finger along the spine, knowing I would want to take a look at it later.

I walked to the desk, put my coffee mug down on a leather coaster, and rolled back the office chair. As I settled into the seat and scooted forward, I was startled to see my own face staring back at me. On Dad's desk, next to the computer and facing the chair, was the framed photo of Brady and me at the beach, the one I had looked for in the living room. Several seconds passed before I was able to move on mentally from the knowledge that he kept my picture, one of perhaps only a few that he had, sitting on his desk, in the one room of the house that was solely his.

I powered on the computer and checked my email account to see if Dad had sent a note to let us know he arrived safely in Qatar. I also wanted to write to him about the container garden—to let him know I could make it and wanted to make it while he was away. There was indeed an email to me from my father, letting me know his flight had been trouble-free and that he would be in and out of communication while he was over there working. I typed back a quick message about the container garden idea, asking if he or Liz had a preference on what shape it took. I also told him Brady and I were settling in just fine.

I then spent the next hour hopping around how-to websites for container gardening. I had mistakenly believed that a container garden was one thing, like a 1967 Camaro. But I found dozens of plans for gardens made of contained spaces, from using barrels, to giant terracotta pots, to wood-framed beds raised off the ground and situated in rows.

These seemed to be the best way to use the long and narrow space and to give Liz distance between whatever things she decided to grow, like maybe one row for lettuce, fennel, and chives and another for basil, oregano, and thyme. I found a set of free plans on one how-to site, which I downloaded and printed. The instructions, labeled "Easy to Moderate," were for one rectangular box, measuring four feet long by two feet wide by three feet tall. With the space on the south side of the house, I could make four of them, either out of cedar or maybe Douglas fir. I was pretty sure Dad didn't have a table saw in his garage, so I would need to rent one. The rest of the supplies would be easy to get my hands on: painter's caulk, lamp holder, electrical covers to use for drainage, some PVC pipe, sandpaper, wood screws, wood stain, and polyurethane.

I also saw that there were several options for watering the containers, from an automated bubbler system to a soaker hose. It took me all of two minutes to decide I wanted my California family to experience the singular joy of doing something for themselves. I wouldn't install the automated bubbler. Somehow, I would convince Dad and Liz and even Brady that caring for this garden would awaken something inside of them that appeared to me to be dormant: gratitude for the simple things in life. Caring and tending what God has given you made you more thankful for it. My Amish family had taught me that.

I tallied up the things I needed and came up with a rough estimate of what it would cost. Dad had left a credit card for me to use for entertainment, groceries, gas, eating out, and emergencies. I wasn't sure that this qualified as any of those, except maybe entertainment for me.

I was excited to go to the nearest builders store and get the supplies, but I figured the first order of business was to hack down and dig up the hedge, which, after doing more Google sleuthing, appeared to be a Japanese wax leaf privet. That would likely take a whole day. And then I'd need to figure out how to get rid of the bushes once I dug them up.

I wouldn't do any of it, though, until I heard back from Dad. Brady had been acting so odd that for all I knew he was trying to set me up, like maybe that particular hedge was Liz's favorite thing in the whole yard and he had lied just to make me do something stupid and look bad. I hated to be paranoid, but I'd hate even more to cause some sort of problem. I'd wait for an email from Dad before I would proceed.

I also knew that while all of this planning was well and good, I'd been at it for too long now. I shut down the computer, returned my mug to the kitchen, and headed upstairs to look for a pair of shorts among my father's clothes with one specific challenge in mind.

It was time to get back on a bicycle.

Whoever invented the expression "It's like riding a bike" to indicate something one never forgets how to do had clearly never gone without riding a bike for seventeen years. In the next fifteen minutes, I came to understand that this was, indeed, a skill that would need to be relearned.

I was pretty sure I was doing everything correctly—pedaling, sitting, steering—and I was going as slowly as I could, yet the bike kept falling over. I managed to thrust out a leg and catch myself each time, but after three such incidents, I was getting really frustrated, not to mention embarrassed. Finally, I decided that the next time it happened I would just keep pedaling regardless—which was how I ended up flat on the sidewalk a block from the house, in pain and feeling like an idiot.

"You're going too slow."

I sat up and twisted around to see who had spoken. A boy of about ten or eleven was sitting on the front stoop of the nearest house, tightening the wheels on a skateboard.

"Excuse me?" I said, trying to recover some dignity as I brushed myself off.

"You keep falling 'cause you're not pedaling fast enough. Pick up the speed and you'll be fine."

I stared at him for a long moment, realizing he was right.

"Thanks," I said, standing up and checking myself for damages. An elbow and knee were both throbbing, and I saw that they had been scraped up a bit. "What are you doing home at this hour anyway? Shouldn't you be in school?"

"In-service day," he replied with a shrug, as if I would know what that meant.

"Oh, okay then. Thanks again."

"You're bleeding."

I glanced his way and then back at my wounds. "I'll be all right." The scrapes weren't that bad.

"I'd offer to get you a Band-Aid, but I'm not supposed to talk to strangers."

I smiled, not stating the obvious. "I understand. No problem."

Despite the increasing sting from my scrapes, I swung a leg over the bike, thanked him again, and took off. He was right. The key really was to pick up the speed. By the end of the next block, I was sailing along as if I'd been doing this every day for years.

I rode around for at least an hour, exploring the neighborhood in full and just allowing myself to have fun. It was a beautiful morning, the sun warm on my arms, the sky cloudless and blue. Even my knee and elbow stopped hurting after a while. I felt so free—and so carefree. The experience was glorious, and I knew I would be doing this again while I was here.

Eventually, I decided to head back, and I was glad to see that it was far easier to find my way home via bicycle than it had been by car. As I retraced my path, turn by turn, I realized why. It was because this was the pace I was used to, the pace of a horse and buggy.

I was getting close when I passed the big Spanish-looking house with the front courtyard. Then it was a simple right at the home with the rock garden instead of grass, left at the street light, and straight on from there, just two blocks more.

I slowed a bit as I neared the house where I'd fallen earlier, hoping the boy was still outside so I could thank him again for the tip. I could see movement on the stoop as I drew closer, but as I passed by, he didn't even look up. He was muttering to himself, obviously frustrated with his skateboard, whacking at one of the wheels now with a wrench.

He seemed to be having trouble with some sort of repair. I would have loved to stop and help, but I had to remind myself that I wasn't in Lancaster County anymore. What would be seen as neighborly there might come across as downright creepy around here.

Instead, I just called out a loud, "Thanks again! You were right!" as I rode past.

When he glanced up, it looked as though there were tears of frustration in his eyes. Embarrassed, he gave me a wave and then quickly returned to the task at hand. Poor kid. I said a quick prayer for him, that he would find a way to solve his problem or at least find someone to solve it for him.

When I got back to the house, I made myself a sandwich and polished it off with a glass of milk. For a moment, I felt a little homesick, thinking how much I already missed *Mammi*'s delicious noon meals.

As I washed my dish and neatened the kitchen, I calculated the time difference between California and Qatar then decided to check my email for a response from my dad. It had only been a few hours since I wrote, but the timing was good. If he'd gone online prior to turning in for the night over there, he would have seen it.

Sure enough, he had responded. His message was brief and to the point and exactly what I wanted to hear.

Great idea on the container garden! Put the supplies on the card. Don't work too hard.

Smiling, I shut down the computer and then headed out to the backyard, Frisco yapping excitedly at my heels. I was happy to find work gloves, hedge trimmers, and a spade in the garden shed.

Then I got to work, thankful to have something constructive to do at last.

By the time the sun was setting, I had the remains of the hedge in neat piles on the patio. I had dug out two of the four stumps, which meant I could start on the containers the next afternoon. Brady came outside to see what I'd accomplished, and then I showed him the plans I had found on the Internet. I was relieved when he told me the boxes looked very much like what Liz had described to our dad when she first mentioned the idea.

While a frozen lasagna baked in the oven, Brady helped me put the pieces of the hedge into big yard waste bags. I liked working side by side with him, even for just a few minutes. When we were done, he said a yard waste truck followed the garbage truck on Friday mornings, which would be tomorrow. We pulled the eight bags out to the curb and then went inside to eat.

After dinner, Brady brought his laptop into the family room to work on his paper. I asked him if there was anything I could do to help.

"Not unless you know what MLA is."

"Should I?"

He just laughed, but it was void of mirth.

I was beginning to see a pattern with him. Whenever a conversation veered toward me as a person or the life I had known as an Amish man, his tone took on a condescending edge. Brady had never been this way around me before. Prior to this, he had always seemed interested, maybe even intrigued, by the kind of life I lived as a Plain man. But not anymore.

"What *is* MLA?" I pressed.

"It's the format I have to follow for writing this paper. They use it in college. Forget I asked."

He flipped open his laptop, letting me know he expected no further help from me. Just as I had felt God's prompting that morning at breakfast, I sensed I should not let this conversation drop.

I went into Dad's study, searched for "MLA," and within a few minutes found an easy-to-follow example of a research paper written in the Modern Language Association's standards. I printed out the example to take back to the family room, and as I passed my father's bookshelves, I grabbed the pictorial guide to Germany to look at while Brady worked.

Back in the family room, I placed the example on the couch next to him. He glanced down at it.

"Hey!" He picked up the pages. "Where did you get this?"

"Internet," I said as nonchalantly as I could as I sat back down on the other couch.

He cracked a smile, the first genuine one I had seen in what seemed like hours on hours. "It's a better example than what my teacher gave me. Way better." He looked up at me. "Thanks."

"Sure. Anything else I can do?"

"Maybe you could read it over when I'm done?"

"Be happy to."

Brady slipped white ear buds into his ears and disappeared for all intents and purposes. I didn't know how he could write a research paper while listening to music on his computer, but it seemed to work for him.

Settling into a wide leather easy chair, I opened the book on Germany. The first page nearly stole the breath right out of my lungs.

The inside cover had been signed to my dad by its giver.

To my dearest Duke,

So we will always remember the sweet years of our just-new marriage!

Love always,
Your Sadie

I turned the page, and the emotional tug I was feeling intensified. My mother had not only given the book to my dad, but she had written little notes on many of the photographs inside, in a curly, swirly script that begged to be touched.

On a full-page photo of a verdant green snapshot in the Black Forest, she'd written: *Remember the picnic we had at that park in Triberg? And how it rained? You carried me to the car so my new shoes wouldn't get muddy.*

On a photo of a sparkling snow scene in Garmisch-Partenkirchen: *"I told you I couldn't ski! Ha!"*

On a photo of a cobbled street in Berchtesgaden: *"Do you remember eating ice cream on this street? And then I said I wanted to go into that little children's clothing store so I could buy some lederhosen in case it was a boy. That's how I told you we were going to have a baby. You nearly fainted in the street. And we did have a boy! We should have gone into the store and bought the lederhosen."*

Page after page, message after message.

When I felt tears pooling in my eyes, I rose from the couch to take the book upstairs to my bedroom.

I would read the rest of it when I was alone.

Fifteen

On Friday I began my morning devotions an hour before Brady's alarm went off. It was growing more clear to me that my coming to California was layered with purposes that were not just my own or my dad's. To start with, something had wedged itself between my brother and me, and I likely would not have picked up on it had I not come. Second, I was still prayerfully contemplating my dad's parting words when he left on Wednesday, that perhaps he wished he had done things differently with me. This was not something I had ever detected from him before. Third, and the most compelling, I was feeling my mother's presence here in a way I never had before, which was odd considering she'd never stepped foot in this house nor even been to California, as far as I knew.

This was not a trip just to discover who I was. It was also a trip to discover who my mother was out in the world, beyond the farm and my Amish family's recollections. Perhaps, I realized now, what God had been doing the last few restless months was not so much preparing me to figure out where I truly belonged, but to confront once and for all the reasons why my mother left the Amish faith. I was her son. Those reasons mattered.

Especially if I ended up following in her footsteps.

In my prayers I asked God to keep guiding me to the truths He wanted me to find. If I really was here to learn more about my mother, I wasn't sure why He had ordained I come at the exact time when the one person who had known her best—my father—was out of the country, but I trusted He had things under control.

As for me, all I had to go on thus far was the one conversation between me and my dad before he left, the new knowledge that my mother loved photography, and the messages she had written to him in the pictorial book on Germany. I desperately wanted that box of my mother's photos my dad had mentioned. It was no good to me locked away in a storage unit somewhere.

When my prayer time ended, I headed to the study and emailed my dad, asking him if he would mind if I went to the storage unit myself to find that box of photos.

After that, I made blueberry pancakes for Brady and me, using *Mammi's* recipe with a little nutmeg and cinnamon. They turned out pretty good, and as he wolfed down his share, he told me that his friend's sister, the photographer, Lark, would meet me at the snack bar tonight as soon as the game was over.

"Thanks for setting it up," I told him. "Any idea what she's hoping to accomplish when we meet?"

He took one final bite and then carried his plate to the sink. "I dunno. You said you wanted to learn stuff about photography. She told me she knows a few other students who might be willing to help. Not for free, but it'll still be cheaper than hiring some professional. Isn't that what you wanted? A cheap tutor?" His tone was still sharp, his attitude defiant.

"Um, yeah. Sure. Thanks, Brady."

"Yep." He rinsed his dish and set it in the sink. He hesitated for a moment, as if he wanted to say something else, and then he seemed to think better of it and held his tongue. He walked back to the table and began gathering up his papers and books.

"What about you, though?" I asked. "You don't mind waiting around after the game while she and I chat?"

He paused to look up at me, the now-familiar disdain fully return-ing to his expression. "The players can't leave right away, Tyler. I'll be in the locker room, at least for a while."

"Ah," I said, my voice even. "Thanks for clarifying."

He asked what I would be wearing so that he could text Lark a description and she could find me. I told him probably Dad's UCLA Bruins hoodie.

"Good choice," Brady said, with no hint of whether he was being sar-castic or not.

Once he was gone, I took Frisco for a morning walk, trying to put my little brother's contentiousness out of my mind. It was trash day but the trucks hadn't come through yet, which unfortunately meant stopping at nearly every set of cans in the neighborhood for a good sniff.

At least we had another beautiful day, I told myself as I tugged on the dog's leash to get him moving again. And again. I was looking forward to the time I would spend working on my container garden project. I hoped I could finish clearing out all of the bushes this morning and then finally get to a store for all of the supplies this afternoon.

Frisco and I walked our usual three-block by three-block square, the last leg bringing us past the house where I had fallen off the bike the day before. I wouldn't have given it a second thought except that when we paused at their trash cans, I spotted a familiar sight crammed into the pile: the little boy's skateboard.

I glanced toward the house, amazed that he would simply throw it out, especially after spending all that time on it. The poor kid really had needed my help, and all I'd done was ride on by.

I felt terrible. I considered knocking on the door, introducing myself to his parents, and offering to fix whatever was wrong if I could. But, again, I had no idea how something like that might be received. Behind me, I heard the telltale beep-beep-beep of the garbage truck slowly work-ing its way along, so I knew I needed to make a decision.

Impulsively, I removed the skateboard from the can and tucked it under my arm. Then I carried it home, deciding I would fix it here, on my own, and then bring it back. For now, though, I was itching to get to my big project, so I set the skateboard aside in a corner of the garage to work on later.

I spent the rest of the morning and early afternoon out back, removing the last of the bushes on the south side of the house and decreasing the amount of space taken up by the pebbled walkway. I found an empty heavy-duty storage tub in the garage to put the extra pebbles in. When I was finished, I would use them for ground cover in between the boxes to make access for planting, watering, and harvesting easier.

Brady had told me where the nearest builders' store was, so in the midafternoon I made the trip to get the supplies and rent a table saw and sawhorses, and this time I used Liz's GPS to get there and home again. Some conveniences sure made life easier.

Back at the house, I eased Dad's car out of the garage and parked it next to Liz's so that I would have the space to set up my work area inside. Once I got organized, I dove right in. I was relieved that it didn't take long to get the hang of using the saw, which was similar to one I used back home—though mine was retrofitted to run on compressed air while this one simply plugged into an outlet in the wall.

Dad didn't have a sander, but I actually preferred using elbow grease to get the shorn ends smooth. The heady smell of pine as I rubbed the planks reminded me of home, and the exercise felt good.

I stopped at six, made myself a couple of grilled cheese sandwiches, and checked my email to see if there was a message from Dad about the box of photos. There wasn't. I shut down the computer and went upstairs for a shower. After cleaning up, feeding the dog, and bringing in the mail, I secured the house to go to Brady's football game.

The last time I had seen him play had been four years earlier when he was on a Pop Warner team and I happened to visit at a time when the season had just started. I didn't remember much of that game, only that Brady had a solid kick for a ten-year-old.

Watching him now, it was easy to see that he was incredibly gifted—and that the pressure on him must be tremendous. On three different fourth-down situations there was no hope for points unless Brady kicked a field goal. Anybody on the field could make a touchdown, even a defensive player if he caught an interception or recovered a fumble. But only one person could do the job Brady had. He did it beautifully.

And he was only fourteen years old.

Making the stakes even higher was the fact that most of the other players were seniors whose post–high school plans would be shaped by how the team fared overall this season. Brady's points made the better players shine all the more. Add to that the load our father was heaping on him, and it was no wonder he was bucking against it.

By the end of the game, not only had my empathy for Brady greatly increased, but I was surprised to find myself empathizing with my father as well. Just like Dad, I began to swell with satisfaction over the way Brady handled himself on the field. When the last points on the scoreboard, which were his, sealed the win for his team, I nearly turned to the family sitting next to me and said, "That's *my* brother!" in a very non-Amish display of pride.

Afterward, as the crowd began moving from the stands and the team jogged off the field to head to the locker room, I said a quick prayer, asking forgiveness for my attitude, strength and guidance for Brady, and the right words to speak to my father on his behalf.

The night was chilly, even for Southern California, and as I made my way to the snack bar to meet Aaron's sister Lark, I wished I had worn something heavier than Dad's hoodie. Most people were headed out of the stadium and away from the concessions, so I found myself going against the tide as I walked.

I had no idea what this Lark person looked like, so I positioned myself near the first window, within easy view of the departing spectators, and waited for her to find me. After a few minutes my phone vibrated with a message from Brady. He was finished in the locker room and some teammates were going to "In and Out," whatever that was, for hamburgers and shakes. He didn't need a ride home. And he didn't invite me to join them.

I texted him back. *These friends are ones Dad and Liz are okay with?*

Yes was his short answer.

I replied with, *Have fun and be careful.*

His *Yep* seemed shorter still.

After about five more minutes, a young woman approached. She had reddish-blond hair with hints of blue, a diamond stud sparkling on her left nostril, and a daisy tattoo gracing one side of her neck. A few inches shorter than me, she was rail thin, wearing a colorful scarf, leather jacket, black leggings, and fat suede boots that to me seemed better suited to the tundra than Southern California.

"Tyler? I'm Lark Parrish."

I thrust out my hand. "Hi. Nice to meet you."

"Nice to meet you too. Sorry it took so long to get over here."

"No problem. I appreciate your help."

She cocked her head slightly as she released my hand. "You have an accent." Before I could respond, she added, "I thought you were from Pennsylvania."

"I am."

"You don't sound like it. You sound like you're from another country or something."

I shrugged, concerned at how things were starting out. Had Brady not told her that I'd been raised Amish? If not, why not? Had it simply not come up? Or was it because he was ashamed of that fact?

Pushing those questions from my mind for now, I ignored her comments and shifted the conversation over to the task at hand, explaining that I'd never had anything to do with cameras or photography before, but that I had taken an interest of late and wanted to find someone knowledgeable to teach me a few basics over the next month while I was in town. The crowd continued to thin out as we stood there and talked, me answering her questions and the two of us discussing what I was looking for and what might be involved. To my dismay, though, once Lark and I had hammered out the details, she hopped right back to the topic of my accent.

"I just can't place it," she said, looking me over closely as if my face or hair or clothes might give her a clue. "I've met your parents, so I know you didn't get it from them."

Startled, I hesitated for a moment before understanding her confusion.

"Oh, Liz is my stepmother. Brady and I are just half brothers, not full."

"Ah," she replied, stretching it out. "So that explains it. I didn't realize Liz was your dad's second wife. Is your mom foreign? I know he was in the military, right? So he's probably lived all over the world."

I could tell she wasn't going to let this go. I glanced away to see that the playing field was nearly empty and the concession stand workers had begun to close up shop.

"Actually, I was raised Amish. The accent is from Pennsylvania Dutch, the language we speak among ourselves." I didn't add that my mother had passed away seventeen years ago.

"Whoa," she said, eyes wide. "Seriously? You're *Amish*?"

I shrugged, feeling as though she expected me to whip out a straw hat and a pair of suspenders at any moment.

"It's not that big of a deal," I told her, feeling self-conscious. "I mean, I'm still just a regular person. All Amish are. Just regular people."

She seemed to realize her behavior had been bordering on rude. "I'm sorry. I guess it just took me by surprise. You're the first Amish person I've ever met."

"Then we're even," I replied with a smile. "You're the first photographer I've ever met."

She tossed back her head and laughed. "Holy cow. You're cute and funny. Want to give me a ride home? I think I just might end up deciding to tutor you myself." She started to walk away.

"What?"

Lark turned back. "Give me a ride home and we can talk about it some more. You came here tonight in a car, right?"

"Yes, but—"

"So where is it? Come on. Let's go."

She turned and continued on toward the parking lot. I hesitated and then had to run a few steps to catch up with her.

"You always ask rides of people you've just met? Isn't that kind of dangerous?"

Lark laughed and quickened her pace. "First of all, you're not some random stranger. Our little brothers are best friends."

"True."

"Besides, you're *Amish*. That means you're probably the most decent man in all of Orange County."

As we neared the parking lot, I could see that it was more than half empty now.

"I kinda wish you had your horse and buggy here, though. That would have been a cool ride home. The only buggy rides around here are at Disneyland."

I wasn't sure whether to be offended or not. Was she really comparing a centuries-old way of life, a treasured heritage, an honored tradition, a symbol of separation and submission and simplicity with a ride at an amusement park?

She must have seen the consternation on my face because she added, "You have a horse and buggy back in Pennsylvania, don't you?"

"Uh, yeah. Several of each. Listen, how did you get to the football game in the first place?"

We reached the lot and continued on past the first row.

"I came with my parents. My car's not working right now."

"Won't they be expecting you to go home with them?"

"Nah. I told them to go ahead, that I'd catch a ride with somebody."

I was quiet for a moment, gesturing over toward Liz's car, which was now sitting by itself in the next-to-the-last row. In my head, I added one more observation to the list.

Young women ask for rides from near strangers.

"I still live at home, unfortunately," she added as we moved toward it. "It's too expensive out here to get an apartment unless I work full time, even if I went in on a place with friends. And I'm trying to save up for a new camera too. So, there you go. At least their house isn't far from my school, and there's a stop for the city bus just a block away."

When we arrived at the car, I opened the passenger side door so that she could get in.

"See? You *are* the most decent man in all of Orange County. I can't remember the last time a guy opened my car door for me."

"Really?"

"Really."

I pondered that as she climbed inside and then said, "Maybe you're just not hanging around with the right kind of guy."

The words slipped out of my mouth before I could stop them, and though I was afraid I may have insulted her, she just laughed.

"Maybe not."

I closed the door, went around to the driver's side, and got in. As I put the key into the ignition, she placed a hand on my arm.

"I wasn't kidding when I said I will tutor you myself. When would you want to meet?"

I wasn't so sure she was the right tutor for me, but I couldn't exactly say that to her. I decided to go with it for now, hoping that once we spent a little time together, she would calm down and stop making me feel so flustered.

"My schedule is pretty open," I said, starting up the car and putting it into gear. "You name a time and I can probably make it work."

"Tomorrow at two?"

"Sure. Tomorrow at two sounds good."

I maneuvered us out of the parking lot but had no idea where to go. "Which way? I assume you don't live too far from here?"

"You want to go get something to eat first? I'm starving. Want some sushi?"

I had heard of sushi but I wasn't entirely sure what it was. "I've never had that before."

"Whoa! You have to try some!"

I hesitated, looking her way. "Doesn't sushi have something to do with...raw fish?"

She shrugged. "Technically, *sashimi* is raw fish. *Sushi* just means 'vinegared rice.' But most people mean raw fish when they say sushi. Pull over."

"What?"

"Pull over here and let me drive."

"Why?"

"Because you drive like my grandma. No offense. It's just easier this way."

I didn't know how Dad would feel about me letting someone else behind the wheel of Liz's car, but Lark didn't give me time to consider it.

"C'mon. Seriously. Pull over. You're going to get us into an accident."

"I am not."

"Yes, you are. You're too slow. And I'm totally starving. Pull over."

Her impatience was making me nervous. I indicated and obeyed. A minute later we had switched seats and Lark was zooming off down the street as if we were late for the last meal on earth.

SIXTEEN

I'd been in a number of cars as a passenger before, but I'd never been in the kind of traffic Lark was zipping in and out of with not a care in the world. For her, the crowded Friday night streets of Newport Beach were apparently nothing short of ordinary, and the speed with which she took them even less remarkable.

As we drove to the sushi bar, she chattered away, volunteering that she was a junior in college, would turn twenty-one in February, was the oldest in her family, and that she had just broken up with her boyfriend, Matt, after she found out he'd been going out with other girls behind her back. I thought of my list.

People volunteer all sorts of personal information without provocation or invitation.

"He could have just told me he wanted to see other people," she said. "That he lied about it was the worst. I asked him point-blank if he was cheating on me and he said no. I hate dishonesty in people. I really do. Don't you?"

I had my hand on the door handle for no reason that made sense to me because a quick evacuation would have been disastrous. "Yes," I said, my knuckles turning white.

"I mean, what's the point in being with someone if they aren't going to be truthful with you? I just think that's a waste of time."

"*Ya*," I said, pressing my foot to the floor of the car to hit a brake that wasn't there.

She turned to me. "What'd you say?"

"What?"

"You said, '*Ya*.'"

"*Ya*. Sorry, that's yes. In Pennsylvania Dutch."

Lark had her eyes fully off the road as she grinned my way. "What else?"

"Excuse me?"

"Say something else."

"*Less mich's Rawd nemme.*"

"That's great! What does it mean?"

"It means, 'Let me take the wheel.'"

Lark seemed not to have heard me. Returning her eyes to the road, she yelped and then crossed two lanes in a mad dash to get into a left turn lane while the light was still green.

"You're lucky you're bilingual, Tyler. Most Americans can only speak English. We're useless when we travel abroad. I went to Paris in between my freshman and sophomore year in college, and it was pathetic. And even though I had two years of Spanish in high school, when I went to Mexico City a couple of years ago, I could barely ask for directions, and when I did, I couldn't understand the answer I was given."

The mere mention of her travels intrigued me enough to distract me from her driving. "You've been to France and Mexico?"

"Yep. I absolutely love to travel. Love it. I am going to Thailand next summer on an internship. I can't wait. It's going to be so cool. I am going to take a million pictures."

We pulled into a conglomeration of buildings that included the sushi bar, a coffee shop, clothing stores, and other specialty shops.

Lark parked by the sushi bar, which appeared to be quite busy. When we stepped inside, she instructed me to "snag a table" while she ordered for us at the bar, adding that it would be her treat.

"That's not necessary."

"Hush. You can get the next one. Hurry up and grab that empty table before someone else takes it, would you?"

She shooed me in the direction of a table for two in the corner. I sat down and took in my surroundings. The place was filled with people of every age and ethnicity. Though I was at the back of the restaurant, I could see the chefs up front in their white hats and stern faces, working behind a bar with speed and precision. The energy in the room was accented by dozens of conversations, some in languages I had never heard before.

Lark returned to our table with a little bowl of pudgy peas in their pods, tiny plates of pink shavings and a greenish paste, some smaller dishes, and two sets of chopsticks.

She set the dishes down and I took a closer look, recognizing the beans as edamame but otherwise clueless as to the various foods she was expecting me to eat.

"Okay," she said, as though I had asked her a question. "We'll start with this as our appetizer, and then for your meal, I ordered you a California roll because you're new at this and it's pretty tame. You'll like it. You can be more daring next time."

"A roll?" I was picturing one of *Mammi*'s yeast rolls, slathered with butter and her plum preserves, yet I saw no one in the restaurant with anything resembling bread at all.

"They make sushi in rolls. Long and skinny. And then they cut them into pieces so that you can pick them up with your chopsticks."

She withdrew wooden chopsticks from a paper sleeve and broke them apart. I took the second set and followed suit. Next, she pulled one of the doll-sized dishes toward her and used her chopstick to put some of the green paste in it. Then she took a container of soy sauce sitting on our table like a ketchup bottle back home and spilled some drops into the paste. She mixed the two together.

"The green stuff is wasabi and it's super hot. You're not going to want to lick it off your chopstick. The pink stuff is ginger. It cleanses your palate in between bites. Here. Watch me."

Lark opened the edamame pod and emptied the beans onto a tiny plate. She picked up a single bean with her chopsticks, dipped it into the sauce she had made, and placed it in her mouth. "Mmm. Delish. Now you try."

I tried to mimic her seemingly simple actions, but it took me several minutes to get the sticks to obey me. I was able to make the sauce with the wasabi and soy, but three beans skittered off to who knows where when I tried to pick them up. On the fourth try I managed to douse the bean into the sauce and then place it in my mouth. The taste was pleasant, even for all the work.

"Do you like it?" Lark asked

I nodded. "Pretty good."

"Pretty good? C'mon. What do you have back on the farm that's as good as this?"

I smiled, and when she smiled in return, I realized she was actually quite pretty under the strange hair and nose ring and tattoo. "*Mammi's* succotash is tasty."

"Succo*what?*"

"Succotash. Lima beans and corn mixed together. With butter, salt, and pepper."

Lark made a face. "Ick. I hate lima beans. They're disgusting."

I pointed a chopstick at her. "This said by a woman who enjoys raw fish."

She smiled.

"Nothing my *mammi* makes is disgusting," I added.

"Your mommy?"

"*Mammi.* She's my grandmother. I call her *Mammi* the way you might call your grandmother Granny."

Lark popped a bean in her mouth as she regarded me, chewing thoughtfully. "So where's the beard and the Amish clothes? Can't you get shunned for dressing like this, even on vacation?"

I hesitated, wondering how to sum things up for her in the easiest possible way. "First of all, I'm not on vacation. I'm here to stay with Brady while Dad and Liz are out of town."

"Oh. Okay."

"Second, I can dress like this when I'm away from home because I haven't yet officially joined the church. Once I do, the jeans and things will have to be put away for good."

"I see."

"Third, no Amish man starts growing a beard until the day he gets married."

"Seriously?"

"Yes. Then he doesn't shave it off, ever."

Her eyes widened. "Get out of town." She seemed delighted by that notion, though I wasn't sure why until she continued. "If only a wedding ring were so hard to ditch! I mean, it's not like a philandering Amish man can slip off his beard for a night out on the town and then put it back on before he goes home to his wife."

We both laughed. "I guess not."

"So I assume your mom is Amish?" she asked, popping another bean into her mouth.

"She was raised Amish, yes. She passed away when I was six."

Lark froze for a moment, looking shocked. Mortified, even.

"My father was just about to ship off to Turkey when she died," I explained, "so he sent me to live with my mother's parents. My grandparents. I've been there ever since."

Lark sat back in her chair, shaking her head thoughtfully. "I'm really sorry, Tyler. I shouldn't have been so nosy."

Her eyes were so genuinely repentant that for a moment she reminded me of Rachel.

Rachel. My girlfriend. The woman I hoped to marry.

Clearing my throat, I sat back as well, my face flushing with heat. What would Rachel think if she could get a look at me right now? Truly, I didn't want to know.

To my relief, our number was called then and Lark left the table to get our food. I had managed to recover by the time she returned, bearing our plates and two iced teas. As she set the food down in front of me, I saw that my "roll" was six round slices of rice-wrapped clumps of pale pink, yellow green, and verdant emerald.

"So what is this exactly?" I said, poking one of the pieces with a chopstick.

"Crab, avocado, cucumber, and nori wrapped in rice and sesame seed."

"What is a nori?" I plied the sticks to attempt to lift a piece to my mouth with no success.

"Nori is seaweed. And no yucky faces. It's good for you. Lots of vitamins."

I spun one of the slices around on my plate for a couple more seconds before I set the sticks down, picked up the piece of sushi in my fingers, and popped it into my mouth.

"Fingers? Really?" Lark exclaimed.

The piece was bigger than a normal bite, and I couldn't immediately respond to her friendly indignation. I chewed and found the taste to be agreeable but not amazing.

"Well?" Her eyes sparkled with anticipation.

I swallowed and reached for the iced tea. "Pretty good."

"Pretty good. That's it?"

I took a drink and swished away the strange, lingering flavor of seaweed. "It's a nice snack. I can't see making a whole meal of it."

She shook her head. "There's more to life than meat and potatoes, Amish boy. Here. Try one of mine." Lark wrangled a piece from her plate, where something brownish gray peeked out of her sushi roll.

"What's that?" I asked.

"Eat it and then I'll tell you."

I used my fingers to pick it up from where she'd placed it on my plate. I smelled a distinctly fishy fragrance. I took a small bite. It was rubbery, earthy, and mushroomy, as if I had eaten some of the reeds in my mother's pond back home. A very strange taste.

"Like it?"

"What is it?"

"Raw eel."

I reached for my drink again. "And you think lima beans are disgusting."

Lark laughed in mock exasperation. "Fine! You can pick the next place."

I didn't know how to move on from that remark. Would there be a next time? Again, our impromptu stop for food suddenly felt a little too much like a date. Lark was just someone who knew something about photography and was willing to share it with me. We weren't on a date. There would be no next time.

"So, what made you want to major in photography?" I said, as much to remind her as myself why we had met.

"I've always loved it. Always been drawn to it. You must like it too or you wouldn't want to spend the month you're here with your brother learning about it."

I took another bite of my own roll. "Not exactly. I just found out a few days ago that my mother was into photography when I was younger. I want to learn so I can see what she saw in it, what she liked about it."

"That's sweet. What kind of photography did she do? Portraits? Landscapes? Architecture?"

I shrugged. "I don't know. My dad has a box of her pictures in a storage unit, but I won't be able to see them until he gets back from his trip and he can go over there and get them for me." As an afterthought, I added, "My memories of her with a camera are fleeting, but if I had to guess, I'd say landscapes. She was always drawn to the countryside."

"How about you? What kind of photography interests you?"

"I don't know that, either."

Lark cocked her head in amusement. "You must have some general idea."

"No, I really don't. I have been reading up on the history of the subject, which is quite interesting. But I haven't gotten to the part yet where it talks about different kinds of photography. How many are there?"

"Besides the ones I already said?" She held out a hand and began counting off on her fingers. "Gosh, there's aerial, wildlife, sports, fashion, weddings—"

"Okay, well I think we can definitely rule out those last two."

She stopped short, with a grin.

"Bottom line," I told her, smiling in return, "I have no experience whatsoever with taking pictures. But I'd like to learn."

She gazed at me for a long moment and then her eyes widened.

"Wait a minute. You people don't believe in taking pictures," she said, seeming to remember a peculiarity about the Amish faith she had perhaps heard once and forgotten about. "You think it will steal your soul or something..." Her voice drifted away, as if she knew that wasn't the real reason, but what else was she to assume?

"That's not it," I said, shaking my head. "My soul belongs to God."

"Well, why not, then?"

"A few reasons." I recited the verse in Exodus 20 about not making graven images and then added, "Besides, posing for pictures doesn't help us live lives of humility. Quite the opposite. We would think too much about ourselves. We'd rather be concerned with living in obedience than with worrying about our outward appearance."

She grinned. "I bet they pay you to say that."

I laughed and took another bite of my sushi.

"Are you going to get in trouble for taking photography lessons?"

"I told you, I'm not a member of the church yet. That's why I want to do it before I go back."

If I go back...

"How about your mom? Did she get in trouble when she took up photography?"

I shook my head. "She left home at eighteen, without ever joining the church. They weren't happy about her leaving, but there wasn't much they could do about it. Except pray."

"Did she ever go back before she..."

I shook my head. "To visit—once—but not to stay."

Lark tugged on the straw in her drink. "I'd go plum crazy living without cars and electricity and, heaven forbid, my camera. But that's me. Do you think it's possible your mom ever wished she had remained Amish instead of leaving?"

I was surprised by the question. More times than I could count, I had wondered why she left in the first place. But never once had it occurred to me to consider whether she'd ever regretted that decision and wanted to go back home again. Of course, if she had, the family and community would have taken her in with open arms, her sins forgiven and forgotten. But once she was married to my dad, returning to the Amish life and joining the church at last wouldn't have been an option for her. Not unless he was willing to become Amish as well.

Which was about as likely as Timber walking on two legs and speaking Pennsylvania Dutch.

"That's…I don't know," I said, meeting Lark's eyes. "I never thought about it before. Up till now, my biggest questions have been about why she left."

The words were out of my mouth before I could rein them in. I had known Lark Parrish for less than an hour, and I was already telling her my deepest, most secret ponderings.

But she seemed to understand perfectly what was weighing on me. "I'd want to know that too."

We were quiet for a moment as we each ate a piece of our sushi. Then she asked more about my childhood, including how long I lived with my grandparents before my dad's tour ended and he came back and got me. I explained how things progressed, one tour following another, until finally, by the time he was ready, he was remarried with a two-year-old child.

"I had seen him twice in three years. I didn't know Liz at all, and they seemed pretty complete with Brady. So I decided to stay where I was, and he didn't force me to leave."

Lark was staring at me, wide eyed. "Wow. That's crazy."

"Is it?"

"Uh. Yeah."

"Why do you think it's crazy?"

"Because it totally is. Holy cow, no wonder."

She mumbled the last two words, almost as if she hadn't meant to say them out loud.

No wonder what? I thought but did not say. I had a feeling I already knew.

No wonder you seem so lost.

SEVENTEEN

When I arrived at the house a little after ten, I found Brady in the family room watching TV with Frisco in his lap.

He swung his head around when I stepped into the open kitchen behind him. "Where were you?" He sounded perturbed.

"Lark needed a ride home, but she insisted on taking me out for sushi first."

Brady's eyes widened. "You went on a date with her?"

"It wasn't a date."

"Sounds like a date."

"Not a date."

Brady turned back to his TV show. I grabbed a bottle of water from the fridge and joined him on the L-shaped couch. "Hey. Great game tonight."

"Thanks."

A few seconds of silence. My eyes were drawn to the TV screen. A parade of humanoid monsters were stalking a man whose only weapon was a baseball bat. I turned from what promised to be a gruesome spectacle.

"Want to help me stain the wood for the container garden boxes in the morning?" I asked.

Brady shifted on the couch. "Uh, not really. That's your deal, Ty. I'm glad you're doing it, and I think my mom's really going to like them. But tomorrow morning I'm sleeping in. And I have plans in the afternoon."

A chorus of wails and screeches erupted from the TV, along with harried music and sounds I couldn't even begin to describe. "Oh? What kind of plans?"

"Mom already said I could go."

"You talked to your mother?"

"She called me this morning to say hi and I asked her. She said I could go."

More crunching and wailings and screaming. I winced at the sound of it. "Go where?"

Brady picked up the remote and clicked off the TV.

"Wow. Um, you don't have to turn it off because of me," I said, but I was glad he did.

"I can tell zombies aren't your thing. It's streaming. I can watch it on my computer in my room." He stood and so did I. Frisco jumped to the floor.

I had the distinct impression Brady was leaving the room because I was in it.

"You don't have to go. I can find something else to do."

"It's cool. I'm tired anyway." Brady tossed the remote onto the couch and started to walk away.

"Would you tell me where you're going tomorrow? I'm sure Dad and your mom expect me to know."

"Because you're in charge?"

"Because we're brothers. And yes, they did leave me in charge."

He spun around to look at me. "Paintball. I'm going with some friends to play paintball."

Our eyes locked. So many unspoken words lay hidden behind Brady's stare.

"Need any money for it?" I asked.

He kept his eyes on mine. "Nope. Dad left me some."

My brother walked past me, Frisco trailing.

"Good night," I called after him.

"Yep."

"I meant what I said about the game tonight. You did great."

I heard him sigh quietly before he responded, as if hearing my praise annoyed him.

"Thanks," he said and then he was gone from view.

If that was the way Brady responded to admiration regarding his football-playing, no wonder Dad assumed he wasn't happy about being on the team. I tossed up another prayer for wisdom when it came to my brother and then headed into the study to see if my dad had emailed me back.

He had, but there was no mention of my request to go down to the storage unit and hunt for the box of my mother's photos. Instead his email just talked about the hot and humid weather, the dust storms, the food. He wanted to know how the game went, so I typed a quick update, electing not to tell him about Brady's continued strange attitude. I was still hopeful that I could figure out why my little brother was mad at me before my dad returned.

I said nothing more about the photos, though suddenly they were all I could think about. I had a feeling the omission in my father's email was intentional, which really irritated me. As I closed down the first floor of the house and headed up the stairs to my room, I felt myself growing even more agitated until my heart began to pound with anger. Didn't he understand how important this was? My request had not been made lightly. What right did he have simply to ignore it and pretend I'd never said a word? Truly, if I had a key to the unit and the knowledge of where it was located, I just might march over there and dig up those pictures myself.

My bedtime prayers were brief and rote, and as I lay in bed afterwards, trying to calm my frustration, Lark's comment about how I came to be raised Amish kept repeating itself in my head.

Crazy.

I knew she didn't mean insane. She meant it didn't make any sense.

Thinking about that now, I realized her reaction hadn't been all that different from Rachel's when we were kids.

"He's your *dad*," she had cried. "And he just *gave you away*."

Maybe they were right to be so appalled.

Maybe a part of me still found it appalling as well, even though I had forgiven my father years ago.

I tried to sleep in the next morning so that I could identify more closely with Brady's desire to do so, but by eight o'clock I could stand it no longer. I got out of bed, dressed, and took Frisco outside.

After my morning devotions, coffee, and two bowls of Cheerios, I headed for Dad's study to go in search of the cameras Brady had told me were in there. My first lesson was later today, and I wanted to be prepared. Sure enough, after poking through several cabinets, I finally found what he'd been talking about. Three different cameras shared space with neatly labeled electronics cables and small computer components. I had no idea if they would even function, but I knew Lark could tell me, so I grabbed all three and set them on the counter in the kitchen.

After that I headed out to the garage. I opened the doors to let in plenty of fresh air and then got to work on staining the wood for the container boxes. I had plenty to think about as I did, so the morning passed quickly.

I was still confused about my time with Lark and the questions our conversation raised. I was also feeling guilty about the depth of my anger toward my father the night before. He obviously had his reasons for ignoring my request to retrieve my mother's photos myself, and for now I had no choice but to respect that. Patience was an important virtue to the Amish, but in this situation, my own patience had been in short supply.

At least there was nothing like a good ol' hands-on, sweat-it-up project to help me sort things out. Before long my mood had improved considerably, especially when I saw so many other people outside enjoying their day, walking dogs or jogging or riding bikes, soaking up the

California sunshine. Of course, it wasn't as though any of them stopped and spoke. But for a while a least, they made me feel not quite so alone.

They also made me realize how very much I missed my community.

At noon I went inside for a sandwich. Brady had just arisen and was eating waffles he had heated in the toaster. He seemed in a better mood than he had been in last night, or maybe it was just that I hadn't had the opportunity yet to say anything that irked him. I decided to make two peanut butter, banana, and honey sandwiches, a favorite since my childhood.

"What time are your friends coming for you?" I asked, trying to sound merely curious, not parental.

"Three. I won't be here for dinner, by the way. One of the guy's moms is making ribs."

"Sounds good. I hope you have a great time."

"Yeah. Thanks."

Brady reached for the syrup and squirted some onto his plate. "So does Lark think she'll be able to find you a tutor?"

I made a concerted effort not to congratulate him for asking *me* a question for a change.

"Sort of. She decided to tutor me herself. We're starting today."

He raised his eyebrows. "Oh?"

"It's not like that. I have a girlfriend back home, remember."

"Yeah, and I'm sure she'd be totally cool with you taking private lessons from a hottie like Lark Parrish, right?"

This time, it was my turn to raise my eyebrows.

He laughed, but mirthlessly. "Fine, whatever you say. It's just about learning photography, nothing more."

"Nothing more."

Brady shoved the last piece of waffle in his mouth as he walked with his plate to the sink. "I still can't figure out why you're interested in learning about something you're not allowed to do. That seems like a waste of time to me."

"I don't think it's ever a waste of time to learn something," I said, not adding that he would probably come to realize this once he was older and out of school and learning was no longer mandatory for him.

I finished making my sandwiches and he headed back to his room. After I ate, I went upstairs as well, showered and changed, and then left for Lark's house.

She lived just eight miles away, but with traffic and my cautionary driving it took me twenty minutes to get there, even with Liz's GPS talking to me the whole way.

The Parrishes lived in a subdivision not unlike the housing tract of Dad and Liz and Brady. The stucco-and-red-tile-roofed houses were similar to each other in what seemed to be a repeating pattern of fives.

Lark was waiting for me on the front stoop, a polka-dotted camera bag slung over her shoulder. Today she was wearing red high top sneakers, tattered jeans, a black T-shirt, and enormous hoop earrings. Her hair was swept up on top of her head and held in place with an odd clip that looked painful to wear. She jumped up when I pulled to the curb. I stepped out of the Honda. As Lark walked toward me she pointed with her thumb to a turquoise, older-model VW Beetle in the driveway.

"My sad car," she said.

I pulled open the passenger side door. "Sorry it's not working. If it were a buggy I could fix it for you."

"No buggy, just a Bug." She laughed at her own joke. "Hey. Can I drive?"

"I don't mind driving," I said, as politely as I could.

"I'm sure you don't, but your driving makes me nervous."

I laughed. "*My* driving makes *you* nervous?"

"It's your inexperience out on the roads, Tyler. You're killing me."

"Hey, I'm out on the roads at home all the time."

"Yeah, in a buggy."

"So?"

She shook her head, the hoops dancing on her shoulders. "Totally not the same. This is Orange County—practically L.A. I'm sure you've heard our streets aren't for wimps. Not that you're a wimp. You're just too…nice. Let me drive."

I huffed my reluctant agreement and folded myself into the passenger seat.

"Awesome." Lark flitted over to the driver's side and got in, tossing her camera bag gently onto the backseat next to my backpack

"Where are we going?" I asked, not that it truly mattered.

"Balboa Island. You're going to love it."

"Like I loved sushi?" I pulled the seat belt across my chest and clicked it into place.

"Oh, be quiet," Lark said, but with a smile. "It's way cool, as expensive as Manhattan to live there, but so cute. Lots of photo ops."

"Ops?"

"Opportunities. The water, the sailboats, the houses, people on the streets. Lots of things to take pictures of. And it's only fifteen minutes away."

She pulled from the curb and took off down the street. "I googled you last night."

"You what?"

"I googled you. I looked up the Amish on the Internet."

"Great." I could only imagine what "facts" she might have discovered about the Amish there.

"You guys aren't some wacky cult or something. You're Christians. Like, born again and all of that, huh?"

Okay, so at least that one was true. I nodded.

"Cool. Me too."

"Me too what?"

"I'm a Christian."

"Oh." I knew my voice sounded a little too surprised, but I couldn't help it. God's grace was extended to all, of course, but I didn't think that those who responded to His call usually had nose rings and tattoos.

"Is that so hard to believe?" she asked, seeming genuinely offended for the first time since we'd met.

I thought for a moment and then decided to be honest. "Yes, actually, though that's a reflection on me, not you. I guess my world does get a little small sometimes. I know plenty of non-Amish Christians, but they're generally more...they generally don't..." I floundered.

"It's okay, Ty. I know what you're trying to say."

"You do?"

"Yeah. Most Christians don't eat sushi."

I inhaled, ready to respond, when I glanced her way and saw that her eyes were twinkling. She was teasing me.

"Touché," I replied with a grin, echoing one of my dad's expressions as I turned to look out the window.

Lark was silent for a moment as she drove us south toward the bridge that would take us to the island.

"The world is a lot more than buggies and bonnets, Tyler. You can't imagine the things that are out here to see and do and learn and discover. There's just so much to know."

I nodded, glancing at her and then again turning away. Truly, my desire was not to know the world.

I just wanted to know my place in it.

EIGHTEEN

When we finally crossed the bridge onto Balboa Island, Lark asked what kind of camera I had. "You have one, right? I can't believe I didn't think to ask you that before."

I smiled. "I don't have one of my own, no, but I did bring along several I found at my dad's house. I figured you could tell me which one I should be using."

"Sure. No prob. I'll take a look before we get started."

As we searched for a parking place, Lark told me about Balboa Island, saying it was actually two man-made islands in Newport Harbor, a larger island and a smaller one separated by a canal and accessible by a bridge. We were on the smaller of the two, which boasted quaint buildings, restaurants, waterfront properties, and lots of tourists. Parking appeared to be scarce. We finally found a spot on a quiet residential street.

I unzipped my backpack and was about to produce the cameras for her inspection when she hopped from the car.

"Wait," I said. "What about—"

"Coffee, then cameras. That's lesson one, to get the two C's in the right order. Coffee first, always."

She grabbed her bag, closed the door, and took off walking down the street. After a moment, I managed to follow, though once again I found myself trotting to catch up with her. When I did, she tossed me the keys with a smile.

We found a little outdoor café on the next corner, and soon the two of us were about to be doing the one thing I had wanted to avoid, dining together in a restaurant. Still, it clearly wasn't a date this time. I was paying her for the session, after all, and the moment she had a caramel macchiato in her hand and a seat in the shade at a little wrought iron table, she was all business.

"Okay, Farmer John, let's see what you got."

Setting aside my own cup of black coffee, I pulled the first camera from my bag and set it down in front of her.

"Good grief, where did you get this?" she asked as she picked it up to inspect it. "The world's worst yard sale?"

"I told you. I found some cameras at my father's house."

"Right. Well, if you can call this piece of junk a camera. Next?"

She gave it back and kept her hand held out for another. I produced the second one from my bag, though it didn't fare much better. At least she looked at it for a little longer, but in the end it was a reject as well.

"It's just a cheap little point-and-shoot," she said, handing it back to me. "And it needs charging. I guess you could use it for practice when you're on your own, but not for our lesson time, okay? I'd rather let you use my camera than bother with that thing."

Nodding, I returned it to the bag and pulled out the final choice, which was bigger and heavier—and much older and more banged up—than the first two. I thought it would get the biggest scorn of all, but instead, the moment I pulled it from its worn leather case, Lark nearly spit out her coffee.

With a gasp, she put down her cup and grabbed the camera from my hand.

"What the heck, Ty?" she practically screamed. "Where did you get this?"

I sat back, startled. "A cabinet in my dad's study. Why?"

"Good grief, man, it's a Leica. A *classic* Leica."

She spoke as if I would know what that meant. I waited for an explanation, but she grew silent after that, every speck of her attention focused on the instrument in her hand.

Cradling it carefully, she examined the thing on every side, her fingers testing out each moving part, and then she held it to her eye and fiddled with it some more. Though I was eager to know what on earth she was so excited about, I was content to wait until she was ready to tell me. I just sipped my coffee and watched her put the device through its paces. When she was finally finished, the look she gave me was one of pure joy.

"You have no idea how awesome this is. I mean, it looks pretty banged up on the outside, but on the inside…Aw, man, I'm so jealous."

"I take it this one is not a piece a junk?"

"Are you kidding? A lot of photographers consider this particular model to be one of the best cameras ever made. The thing's a *tank*, man. I mean, sure, if it were mine and I had the money, I might get the prism resilvered, and maybe do a whole cosmetic makeover. But even without all of that, this is a true find. A real treasure. I can't believe your dad had it tucked away in a cabinet."

"Is it valuable?"

"Uh, yeah. Are you kidding me?"

"Then I have a feeling it belongs to Liz. She's into photography too."

Of course, the thought crossed my mind that this camera could have belonged to my mother—it certainly seemed old enough—but then I doubted that conclusion for several reasons. First, my parents probably wouldn't have bought anything so expensive back then, no matter how much my mom enjoyed photography. Liz, on the other hand, had come from money, so that seemed far more likely. Second, my father would have had no reason to hang on to a camera of my mother's after she died. He would have discarded it—along with everything else of hers that he didn't need—because he had to move around so much. As a military man, he was meticulous about his possessions, super organized, and quick to get rid of anything once it was no longer necessary.

Just like he'd gotten rid of me.

Startled at the thought and how it had just popped into my mind like that, I looked away. For some things, I reminded myself, forgiveness was not a one-time deal. I had forgiven him years ago, but clearly it was time to do so yet again. As Lark returned her attention to the camera, I said a quick prayer, asking God to purge my heart of any resentment and to forgive me, just as I was determined to again forgive my father.

She continued to study the camera and then finally asked if she could keep it.

"Excuse me?"

"I'd like to take it home with me, give it a good cleaning, and load it up with film and batteries."

"Oh. Sure. Just don't forget to add the cost to my bill."

She nodded, tucking the battered old classic into her own camera bag.

"We can both share my camera today. I was planning to focus on digital photography anyway, rather than film, so you could learn about composition."

"Composition?"

She shrugged. "With some people, I might start elsewhere, like teaching the various camera settings and what they mean—exposure, depth of field, shutter speed—stuff like that. But for you, I think composition is the best place to begin. If you've never even held a camera before, you need to get a feel for the fun part first, the creative part. The technical stuff can follow later."

"Okay. Sounds good."

"Great. So let's cover the basics, and then we can roll."

Lark leaned forward and placed her camera in my hands. I held it awkwardly, so after a pause she positioned my fingers where they should go, lingering in a way that made me feel uneasy. I couldn't exactly pull my hands away, at least not without dropping the camera, so I was relieved when she finally finished and sat back in her chair.

After that, she gave me a quick tour of her camera, showing me how it worked and teaching me the terms for its various parts, such as the viewfinder and the lens. Once I felt confident enough to give it a try, she had me snap a picture of her there at the table, and then she brought it back up onto the little screen and used it to point out the "basics of composition," as she called it. It was a lot to take in, but she was a surprisingly good teacher, leading me down the path of knowledge in just the right order.

"Let's go," she said finally. "I'll talk as we walk."

I paid the bill, insisting it was my turn this time, and we set out.

"The easiest way to compose a photo is to use the rule of thirds," she said as we made our way down the sidewalk. "Think of your image as a rectangle divided into nine equal-sized segments. You know, mentally draw two vertical and two horizontal lines across it so that you have nine squares total."

"Okay. I can see that."

"Good. The most important elements in your scene should either fall along these lines or, better yet, at the points where they intersect. When we look at a picture, our eyes are naturally drawn there, so if you use them in your composition, you can pull us into the picture. You know how some pics are awesome and some are boring? The awesome ones are almost always composed along those lines. Here."

Lark reached for the camera and knelt down on the sidewalk. She pointed the lens toward a flowering vine on a white picket fence. She snapped two photos and then got back to her feet, pressing a button on the camera and then handing it to me.

"See? First look at this one," she said, showing me an image of the flower at the middle of the screen. It looked okay to me until she pressed a button to show the next picture, where the flower was instead located a little to the left, its bloom tilting vaguely toward the center.

"Which image is better? The first or the second?"

"I don't know enough yet to say."

"Just in your gut, Ty. Which one do you find more pleasing?"

"Okay, the second one," I admitted. "But I don't know why."

She grinned. "The rule of thirds is why."

She pointed out the placement of the stem and the bloom, and I nodded as understanding slowly began to dawn.

"Got it? Okay. Now, look how I used the invisible horizontal lines to draw your eye to what is keeping the flower tethered. The fence. See? The vine wants to venture out on its own, but it needs the fence to hold it up. And the fence isn't going anywhere."

I pulled my gaze from the little image on the screen to look at her face. "You saw all that when you took that photo?"

"You have to train your eye to see past the obvious. Here. You try. Look at that house across the street. What is your eye drawn to?"

I turned to look at the blue-and-white house across the narrow street from us. It was well-kept and festooned with half a dozen hanging geraniums. Lacy curtains hung in all the windows, and a striped cat sat in one of the sills.

"The cat, I guess."

"You *guess*?"

"The cat."

"Zoom in on the cat and then pull out. Imagine those nine squares."

I tried to obey. But I couldn't see the nine squares or anything else remarkable.

"See them?"

"Not really."

She took the camera from me, fiddled with it, and then handed it back. Now on the little screen was a nine-square grid overlay.

"Cool."

"Don't get overly dependent on it."

I tried again. I zoomed in on the cat so that he filled the right-hand side and pressed the shutter. I handed the camera to Lark and she pulled up the image.

"Okay. So what is this?"

I shrugged. "It's a picture of a cat."

"What else?"

"Nothing else. It's just a picture of a cat."

"That's my point. Look at the house again. What do you see?"

I sighed. "Blue and white paint, a door, geraniums, windows, lacy curtains, and a cat."

"How many windows?"

I counted them. Five on the first floor. Four on the second. "Nine that we can see."

"And how many cats?"

"One. What are you getting at?"

"Try the photo again. This time include the two other windows closest to the cat. Match the symmetry of the empty windows with the symmetry of the horizontal and vertical lines."

I did as I was told and snapped the shutter. When I looked at the picture I had taken, I was amazed at the difference. The first two thirds of the image contained two perfectly symmetrical windows, and then the last third contained a window just like the other two, but also not like them. Because this one held a cat. And my eye was drawn to it.

"Wow," I said.

"This photo tells us a story. Several stories maybe."

"That's pretty cool."

Lark smiled. "Yes. It is. Now let's do some more."

We continued walking toward Grand Canal and Beacon Bay, stopping along the way so I could take pictures of boats in their slips, footprints in the sand, and the wooden docks. Then we took a side street leading away from the water, where I tried a few more shots of buildings, trees, and people—when I could do it without drawing attention to myself.

Every few shots, Lark would offer some pointers so that I gradually began to feel more confident about the proper way to compose a photo, how to minimize shadows, and how to take advantage of the sun's unique lighting. She also took the camera off its automatic setting so that I could experiment with manual focus and shutter speed. I took a number of duds, but Lark just deleted them and told me to try again.

By three fifteen, my mind was tired and I was ready for a break. Lark suggested more coffee, with cinnamon rolls this time.

"My kind of food," I said, and I told her to lead the way.

We walked to yet another outdoor coffee shop. We settled at a table outside, this time choosing a spot in the sun rather than in the shade because the air was growing cooler.

"Are you having fun?" she asked.

"It's more mentally exhausting than I thought it would be. There's so much to consider. I had no idea."

"When it becomes second nature to you, it won't seem like work. Anything new is difficult until you get past the learning curve. You're doing well."

"Am I?"

She smiled. "Yes. Especially for someone who has never owned a camera before. Your mother would be proud."

I smiled back. "I wish I could know what drew her to photography, but that's not something anyone else could ever tell me. My Amish family wouldn't know, of course. I doubt my dad would either." I took a sip of my coffee.

"It's probably not some complicated reason. In fact, I'm sure it's not."

"Why do you say that?"

"Because I know why I love it. Photography enables me to capture moments that would otherwise just blend into all the other moments that have passed. My photos are a reflection of me—what I see and how I see it. Just think about it, Tyler. We can freeze time and be able to look back at it years later, maybe seeing something new or different because even though the image hasn't changed, we have."

I took a bite of my cinnamon roll and used the moments my mouth was full to consider her words and wonder what my mother would have wanted to look back on over time. What moments might she have yearned to capture on film that would have otherwise just blended into all the other forgotten moments?

"Do you remember her?"

"I remember little things about her. Certain things she said to me. Or the way she said them. And my grandparents and other family members have told me a little."

"And your dad?"

"He's never been one to talk much about her. Plus, I didn't see him for the first few years after she died."

Lark shook her head. "I don't get that at all."

"What? That I lived with my grandparents?"

"That he just left you there."

"My dad thought I would have a more stable life with them. Then, by the time he came back, I'd been there so long it just seemed more logical to stay."

Lark tore off a piece of her cinnamon roll and tossed it into her mouth. "But really, Tyler, did you *want* to stay with your grandparents after your dad finally came back for you? Or did you stay because maybe you were scared of the unknown?"

I was about to say yes, I wanted to stay, but I couldn't get the words to come out of my mouth. Instead, I asked, "Is that so odd? My Amish family was the only family I knew. And I had a really great life there. Surrounded by loved ones, animals, lots of fun work to do and plenty of hands to do it…" My voice trailed off when I realized I was protesting too much.

"So when did you and your dad ever see each other? Or did you?"

"Of course we saw each other. I flew out to visit every summer until I was sixteen. Sometimes Dad and Brady came out to Philly to see me. We made it work."

Lark shrugged and tore off another piece of her roll. "If you say so."

"We made it work," I repeated, as much to convince her as to convince myself. We *had* made it work. It wasn't the most conventional of arrangements, but what's conventional about a child's mother dying? Nothing.

"But you're an adult now," Lark said. "Do you still have to stay there? How old are you anyway?"

"I'm twenty-three. And no one raised Amish has to stay if they haven't taken vows of church membership yet. I could leave if I wanted to without repercussions."

Except that I would break the heart of my grandparents and lose the love of my life forever.

"Are you going to? Leave, I mean?"

The question that had brought me out to California in the first place now hung between us, and I found myself instantly defending the Amish life I'd known for the last seventeen years. "I have a place there, Lark. A job, a home, a family, and someone I care about."

"A girl?"

"Yes, a girl!"

"Whoa. You don't have to get all defensive about it. I was just asking."

I hadn't realized I'd been steadily raising my voice until I noticed a few people were looking our way. "Sorry. I'm sorry. It's just…I've had a lot on my mind lately."

"What's her name?"

I was about to say "Rachel" when a thundering truth clobbered me. It was Saturday. Rachel was going to call me today. I looked down at my watch. It was already after four, which meant it was after seven back home. I pulled my cell phone out of my pocket to see if she had tried the number I'd given Thom. But clearly I wasn't used to owning a cell phone. The battery was dead. In all likelihood Rachel had tried both my cell and the landline at the house—and I had missed them both.

"I should get you back," I said quickly, rising to my feet.

"Just like that? You're not even going to tell me her name?"

"It's Rachel. Let's go."

Lark stood. "Fine. We'll go. What's the matter anyway?"

"Nothing. I just…I just forgot something important."

We paid, Dutch treat this time, then we walked back to the car at a quick pace. Lark pumped me for information the whole way, asking what Rachel looked like, about her personality, how long we'd been dating. I finally had to change the subject. I asked her to tell me about her upcoming trip to Thailand, which she was only too eager to talk about.

I was in such a hurry that I actually told her to drive before she even asked if she could. After another nail-biting trip, we reached her house around four thirty. She was tied up with schoolwork tomorrow and classes on Monday and Tuesday, but she had Wednesdays off, so we made plans to get together then. With a quick thanks, I drove as fast I could manage all the way home.

It still took me fifteen minutes. When I got there, Frisco was ecstatic to see me and began running around the house looking for a ball or a toy for me to throw. Ignoring his antics, I came into the kitchen to check the answering machine and saw with a measure of relief that it wasn't blinking. Maybe Rachel hadn't called yet. But then I saw that Brady had left me a note. My heart sank as I read it.

Your girlfriend called from Pennsylvania. I told her you were out and I didn't know when you were getting back. Don't worry. I didn't say you were with another woman.

Nineteen

The hardest part of knowing Rachel had called was the fact that I couldn't call her back. She was not going to be hanging around the phone shanty waiting to hear from me. Plus, it was already dark in Lancaster County. It had been stupid of me not to arrange a time for us to talk. I had been home all morning.

Perhaps she had tried my cell and I'd missed it because the battery was already dead by then. I hooked up the phone to the charger and then put a leash on Frisco to walk off my frustration.

An hour later, twilight had fallen and Frisco and I returned to a dark and quiet house. The phone wasn't fully charged yet, but it had enough power to show that a message was waiting for me, from the number of the Hoecks' phone shanty. It had been left at 12:30, when I was still home. Oh, why hadn't I thought to charge my stupid phone?

I pressed the button to listen to the messages, recognizing Rachel's voice the minute she said my name.

> "Hi, Tyler. It's Rachel. It's about three thirty here. I stopped
> over to visit with your grandmother, and Thom gave me this
> number for your cell phone. Hope it's all right that I use it. I

might try your dad's regular phone line later if I don't hear from you. Hope it's going well. I miss you. Okay. Bye."

It had only been five days since I'd seen her, but it seemed so much longer. Hearing her voice reminded me of how far away I was, not just from her but from everything that was familiar to me. I wanted so badly to speak with her!

I needed to tell her about Brady, to ask her advice about how to fix what was broken between us. I wanted to tell her I was learning photography, and how I hoped taking pictures might give me some insight into my mother. Mostly, I just wanted to have a conversation with someone who was the embodiment of the life that waited for me in Lancaster County, should I return to it to stay.

But all I could do was to plug the phone back in, feed Frisco his dinner, and open a can of soup for myself. As it heated, I went into my dad's study to return one camera to the cabinet and find the charger for the other.

I found it easily. As I was leaving the room, charger in hand, I noticed the beautiful potted palms over by the French doors and wondered if they needed watering or if that was something the housecleaners did. Moving to the kitchen, I plugged the camera into the charger, checked on my soup, and then filled up a big glass of water and carried it back to the study, figuring I was better safe than sorry.

It wasn't until I had already poured out half the glass that I realized the plants were fake. The water pooled at the base of the "trunk" then spilled over onto the floor. My face burning with embarrassment even though no one else had been here to see, I ran to get a towel and cleaned up the mess as best I could.

After that, I just sat in the kitchen and ate my soup in silence, feeling utterly homesick. I longed for the place where I was loved, where I was surrounded by family. Where potted plants were made of real leaves and grew in actual dirt.

When I was done, I still felt the need to do something active to work out my frustration, so I went into the garage and grabbed the skateboard that had been propped up against the wall since I'd pulled it from the neighbor's trash yesterday morning. I didn't know anything about skateboards, but I knew wheels and I knew movement, and I had a feeling I would be able to figure things out.

Fifteen minutes later, I gave up. The problem wasn't that I couldn't fix the thing. It was that I couldn't figure out what was wrong with it in the first place. It seemed fine to me. I even climbed onto it myself, gave a little push off, and went rolling across the garage. Fearing I might slip and put a nick or a dent into one of my dad's beloved cars, I finally stepped back off of the skateboard and put it away. Maybe Brady had some experience with these things and could take a look at it later and give me a little insight. It surely hadn't ended up in the trash for no reason.

Back inside, I fiddled around with the camera, taking pictures of Frisco and trying to imagine those nine squares. The pictures looked terrible and his eyes were a demonic red in all of them. I read for a while, looked at all the images in the German pictorial where my mother had written something, and then scooped some ice cream into a dish. I turned on the TV for company but had a hard time finding something to watch that interested me, even among the hundreds of channels at my fingertips.

I settled on a documentary about sled dog racing. While I ate my ice cream, Lark texted me.

Hey. Wanna come to church with me tomorrow? It's at 11.

Lark had said she was a Christian, but I had no idea what kind of church she attended, and that alone interested me. I decided to go, and if Brady didn't sleep in on Sundays, I thought maybe he could come too. Dad and Liz had a church of their own but attended only sporadically, partly because of his travel schedule and her weekend hours as a nurse. But also because, as my dad stated some time ago, he'd outgrown the need for church attendance, preferring a quieter, more private approach to faith. When I tried to counter that, he had cut me off, saying he didn't think he needed to discuss his decision with anyone, especially me.

Looking down at my phone, I tried to text Lark back to say that I would like to go and that I was going to ask Brady if he wanted to come, but I was making so many mistakes and getting so many words wrong that finally I just called her instead.

"Don't like texting?" she answered.

"It takes too long. And it doesn't seem necessary when I can just talk to you. I wanted to say yes, I'd like to go. Do you mind if I invite Brady along too?"

"Sure, though it's mostly geared for twentysomethings. You know, people our age."

People our age. I realized that was one for the list.

The generations are all so divided, even in church.

"Tyler?"

"*Ya*, I'm here. Your church sounds like our singings."

"Your what?"

"We have singings every other Sunday night for young people. Our twentysomethings. And teensomethings."

Lark laughed. "Well, we do more than just sing. The messages are relevant to our age and what matters to us. The people at this church care about orphans and poverty and the oppressed and the exploited. That's why I like it. The leadership actually puts actions behind their words. You can't just pray for the hungry when it's in your power to do more. Know what I mean?"

I definitely knew what she meant. No one in my district back home went without food or shelter or medicine or clothing when the need arose. We also helped those outside of the faith—sorting canned goods for a local hunger-relief mission, rebuilding homes after disasters, things like that.

If I belonged in the non-Amish world, I would still need to be a part of a congregation of some kind. It made sense to attend Lark's church and see what it was like to worship God without the *Ausbund* and the High German and the Pennsylvania Dutch.

"I'll ask Brady anyway."

"Do you want to drive? My mom will let me borrow her car if I must, but if you drive I won't have to ask her."

"Sure. What time should I come for you?"

"Around ten thirty. It's not far but the parking lot fills up fast. And I want you to be able to get a good seat."

Now that was a new concept. "A good seat?"

"So you can see the band and the worship leader and the pastor instead of having to watch them on the screens. It's better when you can see the real people."

"I've always believed that," I quipped, but she didn't get that it was a joke.

"Do you have a Bible? One that's in English, I mean. If you don't, it's not that big of a deal. They put the verses on the screen, but I like bringing my Bible with me anyway."

"Me too," I said, trying again with the humor. "The screen alone never feels like enough for me."

She still didn't catch on. "So I'll see you at ten thirty?"

"Ten thirty."

We hung up.

Talking to Lark had lightened my mood, which both cheered and irked me. I wished I could punch in a few numbers and talk to Rachel the way I had just talked to Lark. I tossed the phone onto the couch beside me and let the TV lull me into a half stupor.

Brady showed up at ten. He seemed to have had a good time with his friends, but he didn't elaborate and I didn't push him. I asked him if he'd like to come to Lark's church with me in the morning.

He kind of laughed. "I don't think so. I have homework, and there are two football games I need to watch."

"Oh. Okay."

"But you go ahead."

I let his reasons for not wanting to come fall away. I hadn't really expected him to join me, but I sensed I should continue the conversation. It had been a long time since I had gone to church with Brady, probably the summer I was fifteen. He would have only just turned six. That suddenly seemed like a million years ago. And even though I'd always tried to be an example of my faith when I was with him, it was clear to me that he hadn't applied any of it to himself. In the Amish culture, there was always an awareness that the younger boys looked up to the older ones. Emulated them. Wanted to be a part of their group. In church, we sat in prescribed sections—males on one side, females on the other, children with their mothers—but it was a known fact that every little boy yearned for that right of passage when he would be allowed to enter the service not with his mother but with the big boys and sit with them instead.

As such, we men were always taught to live as an example, ever mindful that younger eyes were watching. I had taken that responsibility seriously since I was sixteen or seventeen and had become part of the older crowd. Yet here I stood now, realizing with piercing clarity that the most important young eyes of all had been watching yet hadn't been influenced by me in this way one bit. If anything, he had a blatant disrespect for everything I stood for.

I prayed, asking God to open Brady's eyes to a closer relationship with Him—and to show me what part I could play in that. I thought it might help to get him involved in a good youth group out here, so when Brady stepped into the kitchen, I followed and asked if he'd ever been to Lark's church before.

"No."

"It sounds like a great place. You should try it sometime."

Brady opened the fridge and withdrew a can of Dr Pepper. "So you guys are, like, spending a lot of time together."

"What?"

He popped open the can, took a sip of the soda, and then turned to me. "Whatever, man. She's pretty. She's available."

Words failed me for a couple seconds. "It's not like that. Not at all."

Brady took another drink. "Okay. Like I said, it makes no difference to me."

"No, seriously. It's not like that. I'm not...I have a girl back home."

He moved past me. "Whatever." His tone was relaxed and nonchalant. As though he really didn't care who I saw or who I might possibly hurt in the process.

I gently reached for his arm. "There is no 'whatever.' I am not interested in Lark in that way. I simply want to see what her church is like. I thought you might want to see it too."

Brady looked down at my hand on his arm and he slowly lifted it out of my grasp. "It's none of my business what you do, Tyler. You don't owe me any explanations."

He started to walk away, but I could not let him go. Perhaps I should have prayed about it or thought about it or just waited to say something. But that's not what I did.

"Hey, I'm your brother," I called after him. "I'm not just some person your parents hired to look after you while they're gone. I came here because Dad said you wanted me to come."

Brady swung around. The nonchalance was gone. He was mad. "Well, I'm real sorry you feel that you're wasting your time with me. I'm sure I can stay with a friend until my parents return. If you want to go on back to your Amish people and your Amish life and your Amish girlfriend, no one's stopping you."

He turned from me and I followed him.

"That's not what I meant. I'm not wasting my time here. I just want to know what you're so angry about."

"Who says I'm angry about anything?" he said as he continued on toward the stairs, Frisco following him.

I went after them.

"Who says? Well, let's see. You've been distant with me since the first day I got here. You barely talk to me, you don't want to do anything with me, you resent my asking you any questions. What else am I supposed to think? Did you tell Dad you wanted me to come?"

There on the stairs, poised between the floors, Brady's gaze met mine. He was two steps ahead, looking down on me as if I were a grubby beggar pleading for money.

"I did," he finally said. "My mistake."

With that, he turned and continued up the stairs to his room, quietly pulling the door shut behind him.

TWENTY

Sleep eluded me after I went to bed and turned out the light. I prayed for the better part of the hours I spent tossing and turning, asking God to show me what had come between my brother and me.

I felt God's peace and presence calming me and encouraging me, but the lightning bolt of clarity I pleaded for didn't come. I awoke late, at least for me, and had no new insights on why Brady was acting the way he was.

Frisco was scratching on the other side of Brady's door when I walked out into the hallway. I opened the door as quietly as I could to let the dog out, but I couldn't help but peek inside. My brother was soundly asleep, his face turned the other way. I closed the door softly and Frisco and I went downstairs.

I hoped that Brady would get up before I left for church so that I could at least tell him good morning. But when it came time to leave, his bedroom door was still closed and there was no sound coming from behind it.

Lark was in a happy mood when I came for her, and she talked the whole way, for which I was thankful. She also didn't insist on driving, which meant I had the distraction of the road to keep me from dwelling too much on my predicament with my brother.

Her church looked more like an auditorium for a play than a place to meet with God, but as I settled into the strange environment, I began to see that the people around me definitely were happy to be there and eager to worship. Everyone sat wherever they wanted and laughed and talked before the service began, as if they were at a social event. But when the service started, the social atmosphere grew more worshipful. The music was loud, which I didn't mind, but it seemed to be aimed at sounding good to the listener instead of pleasing to God. At least that's how it came across to me. The songs were also incredibly short, with lights to change the mood for each one and animated projections of the lyrics on the giant screens on either side of the stage. I couldn't sing any of the songs, and I had a hard time concentrating on God with such contemporary-sounding phrases that often seemed like words we were speaking to each other about God instead of to God.

But the pastor's message, taken from Psalm 103, was thoughtful and inspiring. After the message, another pastor came on stage and the screens began to detail how many ministry and growth opportunities were available. Homeless outreach, life groups, couples night, financial freedom classes, recovery support groups, midweek Bible studies, an upcoming trip to Haiti, and more. I thought of my list.

Opportunities for service and involvement abound.

The question was whether everything else was as loud and frenetic as the worship hour had been. By the end of the service, in fact, I felt an odd fatigue. I longed for just a quiet moment without any kind of directed appeal to my senses, just to refocus on God and God alone.

But there was no quiet moment. As we walked back out to the main foyer, conversations and laughter erupted all around us. Lark saw some people she knew from her life group, the meaning of which I hadn't quite figured out yet, and we stopped so that she could introduce me to them.

I was glad she didn't say, "This is Tyler Anderson. He's Amish." She just told them I was someone visiting family in Newport Beach and that I lived in Pennsylvania. Her friends were kind and seemed genuinely interested in me. They even invited me to their midweek get-together that coming Wednesday night. As we walked back to the car, Lark asked me what I thought of the service.

"It was…" I searched for the right word. "It was busy."

"Busy?" she asked, laughing. That was apparently not the word she was expecting.

"There was so much happening. So much for the eye and ear to take in. I'm not used to that."

"Well, what is your worship service like?"

"Not so busy," I said. And she laughed again.

"For starters, we sing a cappella, and each hymn lasts about twenty minutes."

"Get out!"

I nodded. "It calms the heart and quiets the mind. Brings you to a far more worshipful place." I went on to explain what the rest of our services were like, with Scriptures and prayers and three sermons.

"*Three* sermons? No way!"

I smiled. "Yep. And we don't have fancy church buildings. We take turns meeting in our homes—living rooms or basements or barns. Then, when the service is over, we share a light meal together."

"That part sounds really nice."

"It is," I said, surprising myself with how much I believed that to be true.

We reached the car, but Lark suggested we wait for a few minutes for the lot to clear some. The day was warm and beautiful. We leaned against the Honda as a steady stream of other vehicles inched past us.

"Does that mean you didn't like the service?" she asked.

"I wouldn't say that. It was just so different from how I have always worshipped. It seems to me that life here in Southern California is so very busy. Complex. The one place you might opt for simplicity is in your worship."

"I haven't ever thought of it that way before." She was quiet for a moment. "I suppose there are churches out here that are like that. You know, less busy and all. But I don't think I would be happy at it. I love the artistic approach at my church. I'm afraid I'd get bored at a service where there was so little happening. I guess it's all about what brings you closer to God."

It seemed strange to me that a hectic approach to worship would draw someone closer to the Lord, but I didn't say this. What seemed hectic to me was obviously meaningful to Lark and everyone else who attended her church.

In my search to figure out where I belonged, I knew I had stumbled on a major discovery. I would probably always want to worship God in the most simple of ways. But did that make me Amish?

Did my preference for an uncomplicated life make me Amish?

Did my view on nonresistance make me Amish?

Did my love for Rachel make me Amish?

If those things didn't make me Amish, and I found that I instead belonged in the non-Amish world, where in its vastness was my place in it? I didn't think it was in Southern California, where the pace of life didn't appeal to me. And yet that's where my family was. Where else could I possibly go?

With this as my only viable option, it was clear to me that I didn't belong to either world. I was still a man without a place.

And even if I thought my place might be here, Brady certainly did not agree.

"Tyler?"

I turned to Lark. "What?"

"You were a million miles away. Did you hear what I just said?"

"I...I don't know."

"I said do you want to grab something to eat?"

I was in desperate need of advice and completely disconnected from the people I trusted most to give it to me. *Daadi*, *Mammi*, Jake, and Rachel. It wasn't that I wanted to share yet another meal with Lark, but she was the only friend I had at the moment.

We went to a burger joint, and I was thrilled to order a hamburger with grilled onions, a side of French fries, and a chocolate shake. No chopsticks, no seaweed, no raw fish. The place was crowded inside, so we sat on the covered patio at a stone table with kidney-bean shaped benches made of pebble rock and cement.

In between bites of my hamburger I told Lark about what I was experiencing with Brady.

"He's definitely mad at you about something," she said when I was finished.

"Yeah, I figured that. But he won't tell me what."

"That's not so weird."

"Uh, yes it is. It is weird. He's never been afraid to talk to me before. Why won't he tell me what's wrong now?"

Lark dipped a long, slender French fry into a tiny pleated cup of ketchup. "Something you did or said hurt his feelings. He may sound like he's mad, but I bet you ten bucks he's more hurt than angry."

"Why? What could I have done to hurt him? I've asked him to tell me and he won't. I want to make it right and he won't let me."

Lark folded her arms on the table. "Tyler." Her tone was a bit condescending, as though I had missed something glaringly obvious.

"What?"

"If he has to tell you, that means you don't know. And if you don't know, that means it wasn't that big of a deal to you. So you can't possibly make it right. You would only be saying you were sorry his feelings got hurt, not that you were the one who did it."

"But I *am* sorry I'm the one who did it!"

"Did what?"

I tossed my crumpled napkin onto the table. "Are you trying to be funny? How am I supposed to know what I did?"

Lark tugged on the straw on her milkshake. "It's not supposed to be funny at all. Sounds to me like you want it to be easy. I mean, you want to make it right, but you want to do that the easy way."

"No, I don't."

"Yes, you do. You're going to have to figure out what you did that has him so upset. Not everything is easy and simple and plain."

I didn't appreciate her veiled jab at my Plain way of life. "I never said it was. But I am not a mind reader. There were just five days between the moment my father called me and the moment I got here. Five days. How could I possibly have done anything to Brady during that time? First he wanted me here, and then he didn't. So what happened to change his mind?"

She took a drink from her shake. "Okay, I admit it's going to be a challenge. But think about it. It's obviously something you did before you came."

"Within those five days?" That made absolutely no sense. "How is that possible? Brady and I never even spoke."

Lark shrugged. "Your guess is as good as mine. But whatever it is, you can show him how much this rift matters to you by how hard you work to figure it out. Asking him to tell you is the easy way. I might not tell you either."

She pulled her straw out of her empty shake and licked it clean.

I knew there was wisdom in what she was saying. I knew it because I could hear Rachel telling me the exact same thing.

I pondered her words for a few moments. "I don't know where to begin."

"I would write down everything he has said to you about this."

"Okay, that will take two seconds."

She tossed a French fry at me. "Have you been listening to me? Stop looking for the easy way out. Write down everything he has told you about this problem between the two of you."

I tossed the fry back. "He hasn't told me *anything*. Have you been listening to *me*?"

"For a nice guy you sure are thickheaded. What was it he said to you last night? Something about how you're 'wasting your time' here? If he really believes you feel that way, well, that sounds significant to me."

I was beginning to sense a light dawning. There was substance to what Brady was saying, vague as it was.

"Everything he doesn't tell you is something he's telling you, Tyler. You're not listening. No wonder you don't get it." She tossed the fry back, and this time I let it hit me in the chest and fall to the table unchecked.

"All right. I see your point. I'll do it. But I don't know what I'm looking for."

Lark smiled. "You're looking for truth, just like the rest of us. And one more thing."

"What?" I sighed. Audibly.

"Sometimes the things that hurt the people we love aren't the things we've done. They're the things we haven't done and should have."

"Like what?"

"Well, you came here for your dad, right? Maybe Brady wishes you had come for him."

Sitting there in a pool of brilliant sunlight, I was overcome by the weight of a fresh realization. From the time I was six I had been taught to live a life of selfless service, thinking of others before myself, as Jesus had taught us.

But I had come to California for really just one reason—and that reason was not Brady. That reason was not even my dad, as Lark assumed.

I had come here for myself. For me and only for me. It was the most un-Amish thing I had ever done.

TWENTY-ONE

After I dropped Lark off at her house, I prayed the whole way home that God would give me wisdom and patience to make things right with my brother. I knew it was up to me to discern what I had done or not done that had somehow convinced him that I could not be trusted. For now at least, I needed my relationship with Brady to be my top priority.

The moment I turned into the driveway and pulled to a stop, I felt God whispering an answer to that prayer with just four simple words. They were words that were familiar, as I'd been taught them since the moment I arrived in Lancaster County as a child.

Honor others before yourself.

I turned off the car and closed my eyes. Why would God bring to mind this important truth at this moment? Why now, when I was already on this intense search for truth and for the place I belonged? Was I to put that aside entirely?

Honor others before yourself, Tyler.

Breathing in deeply, I allowed His truth to roll around in my mind over and over. My eyes snapped open. God was not asking me to give up my quest. He was assuring me that in making things right with Brady, He would take care of the rest. He would make it clear where I belonged. I didn't have to give up one pursuit to have the other. They were one and the same. I didn't have to run around Southern California experimenting with every *Englisch* thing that interested me to figure out if underneath my Amish upbringing I was an *Englisch* man. I needed only to repair what was broken and then I would know.

"Thank You," I whispered as relief coursed through me. I was amazed and grateful God was going to work out my dilemma in such an incredible way. A moment later, with my hand on the door handle to get out of the car, I again sensed God prompting me, nudging me to look deeper because I had missed something.

Honor others before yourself.
Honor others.
Honor others.
Others.

My mouth dropped open as I realized what God was trying to get through to me. This wasn't just about Brady. It was about my dad too. And the way in which my mother had left things with *Daadi* and *Mammi*.

I was there to do more than just restore my relationship with Brady. The words Dad had said to me the morning he left came echoing back to me now. That conversation had shown me that he had misgivings about the decisions he had made concerning me, perhaps huge ones. But I hadn't wanted to think about those regrets, because that would mean I would also have to dredge up emotions I had long since buried. Clearly, restoration was needed there, on both his side and mine.

And then there was my mother's relationship with *Daadi* and *Mammi*. My mother could not fix what she had broken, but could I? If I learned what had driven her away, would I be able to use that knowledge not just for myself but also for others, to help heal the hurts she'd left behind?

Such a thought nearly took my breath away.

There in the car, I closed my eyes. *Lord, please forgive me for not trusting that You had this all in Your capable hands from the very beginning. Thank You for Your patience, for showing me the way, for being generous with Your insights. Help me as I go about mending my relationship with my brother. Help me to be patient, kind, compassionate, and wise. Show me where I have failed him. Help me to make it right. And watch over my dad in the Middle East. Bring him home safely and prepare us both for the conversations that need to take place. Show me why my mother left her Amish life and what that means, if anything, for me and for her parents. Watch over my Amish family and Rachel too. She deserves a man who can give her his whole heart. Help me to know if that man is me or if I need to let her go. I want what You want, for both of us, and nothing less.*

Many minutes passed before I emerged from the car, deeply at peace for the first time in not just days or weeks but months. I had a lot of work to do, but now I truly knew I wasn't in this alone.

Up in my room, after changing into more casual clothes, I took a moment to update my list.

I spent the rest of Sunday doing what I hoped God would have me do. I tried to be highly attentive to Brady. I wanted to say I was sorry for the words that had passed between us the day before, but I knew that was not the apology he deserved or wanted. Instead, I would simply be present and nonjudgmental and open to whatever may unfold between us.

He sat down to watch a football game, so I made a point of watching it with him. The entire time, I worked hard not to say anything that sounded parental or nosy or fake. Though he seemed irritated by my presence at first, he gradually warmed to my being in the room. By the fourth quarter, he was commenting on the two teams' kickers, telling me things about their style I would have missed.

For dinner, I put a pan of Liz's baked macaroni and cheese into the oven and tossed a salad. Brady wanted to sit in front of the TV while we ate, which wasn't my preference, but I could see how eating this way protected him from having to endure another conversation with me like the one we'd had the day before. He was clearly not interested in more demands for an answer about the rift between us. I silently thanked God for showing me that.

After dinner, I offered to make us some brownies, and while I did that Brady turned on his Xbox, started up a football-based game, and pulled out a controller. Just the one. After I had put the brownies in the oven, I came and stood just behind the couch, watching him. Suddenly, I wanted very much to ask if I could play too. Not that I had any idea how, of course, but still.

Standing there, I waited to see if he would ask me. He didn't, so finally I brought it up myself.

"Does this game work for two players?"

His eyes still glued to the screen, he replied easily, "Sure. Just grab the other controller. It's right there next to the console."

Stifling a smile, I did as he said, and after he gave me a brief tutorial I found myself engaged in an onscreen battle of wits and reflexes with my little brother. Of course, he destroyed me. Repeatedly. But I did get better as we went on, and eventually it felt like I was holding my own. Somewhat.

To my surprise, the game wasn't just fun but downright addictive. Games about killers or mutants or soldiers or whatever had never held any appeal for me. But somehow, sitting there on the couch and using my thumbs to run around a football field with a bunch of digital teammates was a blast. Despite being in good shape, I knew Brady would always outplay me in real football—he was just so talented. But on this field, at least, I had a fighting chance. We played until the brownies were done, laughing and yelling at each other and generally sounding like two regular brothers hanging out. Not one Amish brother and one *Englisch* brother, just two brothers. It was wonderful.

In my mind, I added this new realization to the list.

Sometimes, technology really can bring people closer together instead of driving them apart.

We wrapped things up, shut down the game, and went into the kitchen. While I took out the brownies and grabbed some plates, he gathered ice cream, fudge sauce, and whipped topping. We each assembled our own dessert, creating two disgustingly decadent mountains of chocolate delight.

We sat and ate there at the kitchen table, chatting easily, as if there had been no contention between us lately. I found myself telling him about Lark's upcoming trip to Thailand, and then I asked him if there was anywhere he had always wanted to go.

Brady slid a gooey piece of ice-cream slathered brownie into his mouth. "I don't know," he said after he swallowed. "Maybe backpacking in New Zealand."

"I've seen pictures. That place is really something."

He nodded. "Remote too. Be nice to just get away from everything. School. Teachers. Homework. Papers. Even other people." Brady took another bite. "It will never happen, though. It's too far away, too expensive."

He had apparently thought about it before and had seen only obstacles. "Nice to think about, though."

"Yeah, I guess."

I waited to see if he would ask me where I would go. When he didn't, I pretended that he had. "I'd like to go Germany to find the place where I lived when I was a kid."

"But you don't travel. You never go anywhere." Brady slipped his spoon in his mouth.

My first response was to rise to my own defenses, but I held my tongue and tried to do what Lark had told me to do: Listen.

Brady was right in a way. My life in Lancaster County revolved around the life of my community. Traveling to faraway places did nothing to bolster that community and, in fact, could even serve to help break it down. And so we made that sacrifice, trading the freedom to travel far and wide for the peace and security of preserving our communities.

While I might envy Brady's ability to go wherever he wanted, I realized that he might envy what I had too, the tight family bonds of my Amish life, if he understood what that was truly like. In fact, the longer I ruminated on it, the more it made sense. Whether he knew it or not, deep inside he probably longed for those kinds of bonds as well.

"I'd still like to do that, though," I said. "I like thinking about going to Germany, even though it's also far away and probably too expensive."

He scraped the last of the dessert from his bowl. "Europe looks cool. I would go there."

"Hey. That really would be fun. You and me. Backpacking or whatever."

Brady tossed his spoon into his bowl and carried it to the sink. "Yeah. You'd have to do all the talking, though. The only German I know is *gesundheit*."

I laughed as I rose to join him at the sink. "Deal," I said, not telling him that I might not fare much better. I'd been taught High German in school, and we always read from a High German Bible as part of our worship services, but I wasn't so hot at speaking the language myself. We said nothing more as we rinsed our dishes and put them in the dishwasher, a wordless and ordinary action shared by ordinary siblings everywhere.

It was late, but we were both still pretty wired from the video game, so before we headed off to bed for the night, I took a chance and asked Brady if he would mind helping me with something out in the garage.

He groaned, but not in a hurtful way, just in the way every fourteen-year-old who hated extra work might groan. "Not the container garden boxes again."

"No, not those. It's something else."

I led the way to the garage, flipped on the light, and then picked up the skateboard from where I had propped it against the wall. I handed it to him.

"You know anything about these things?" I asked.

"About skateboards?"

"Yeah. You're a California kid. Ever use one before?"

He shrugged. "Sure."

"Perfect. Then maybe you can take a look at this one and tell me what's wrong with it."

He looked at me. "Is this a joke? Or a trick?"

"Not at all. I'm trying to fix it for someone…it's a long story. But I'm so clueless that I don't even know why it needs fixing. I was hoping you might tell me what's wrong with it."

I thought he would ask for more details than that, but instead he just hit the button to open the first garage door and set it down on the ground in front of him. "If you say so."

With that, he placed one foot on the board and pushed off with the other, squatting to sail under the still-opening door and down the slope of the driveway beyond.

Smiling, I moved forward out into the driveway myself to watch. Brady had so awed me at the football game, I half expected him to take off down the street doing loops and flips and pipes or whatever they called those crazy stunts skateboarders did. Instead, he just took it up and down the sidewalk in front of the house a couple of times, shifting his weight and the placement of his feet here and there, hopping off and then back on, and weaving left and then right. Finally, he rolled back over to where I was standing, hopped off the board, and kicked down the tip of it with his foot. As he did, the other side flipped upward and he caught it.

"The problem is with the pivot cup," he said, handing me the skateboard. "Did you see how it keeps veering to the side after I jump off? That can be bad news when you're doing certain tricks, like a pop shove it or a kick flip."

He tried to explain what each of those tricks involved, speaking animatedly and demonstrating with his hands.

"So you think the pivot cup is broken," I reiterated when he was done.

"Probably not broken, more likely it's just too tight and needs loosening up."

As we walked back into the garage together, he went on to explain how I might go about doing that. It sounded simple enough, especially as it would require nothing more than sandpaper, a cloth, and some oil. I would have to take apart the whole front wheel assembly first, but that didn't look too difficult. If I could dismantle and reassemble an entire buggy, piece by piece, then surely I could handle a couple of wheels and a single slab of wood covered in polyurethane.

"If you get in there and see that the pivot cup actually *is* broken," he continued, "it's not a hard fix, and a new one will only run you a couple of bucks. But let me know how it goes either way, because there's always a chance I'm wrong and it's a problem with the kingpin nut assembly instead, or maybe a bent hanger. Those get a little more expensive to replace, probably somewhere around twenty bucks."

"Thanks. I'll keep you posted."

"No prob, bro."

I stifled a smile as I the carried the skateboard over to its place against the wall. Even though I knew "bro" could be a slang term used with anyone, I chose to believe that in this case he really did mean *brother*.

Brady pressed the button to close the garage door again, then together we went inside, shut things down, and headed upstairs.

"You know, Brady, if this NFL thing doesn't pan out, it seems as if you're pretty mechanical," I joked as we reached the top. "I could always put in a good word for you at the buggy shop."

"Or maybe we could ditch the buggies and the NFL. That backpacking Europe thing is sounding better all the time."

We shared a smile, and our parting "Good night" was by far the most amiable of this entire trip. As I moved into my bedroom and closed the door behind me, I knew I had not fixed anything between us, but I had begun the careful work of regaining Brady's trust. And I was sure I had stumbled on an insight I needed to pay attention to.

Brady was restless. Just like me.

The next day, Monday, right after morning devotions, I calculated the time difference back home and decided to call the buggy shop.

Daadi answered. It was so good to hear his voice. I was overcome with how comfortable it felt to speak the everyday language of my childhood.

He asked me how I was, and I spent the first few minutes of our conversation telling him about the container gardens I was building for my stepmother, the sushi I had tried, and the worship service I had attended, leaving out spending the afternoon on Balboa Island with Lark and her camera. I did however, tell him about the trouble I was having with Brady. I knew *Daadi* would pray for me about this.

He then asked if God had revealed anything to me about what had brought me to Southern California in the first place. It felt good to tell him about the tender words I had sensed God speaking to me the day before, especially as I was now keenly aware that my motivations for coming had been centered too much on me alone. I didn't tell him that I also believed I was in California to understand why my mother left Lancaster County. Whatever I discovered about that I would share with *Daadi* and *Mammi* in person, regardless of where my destiny lay.

As much as talking to my grandfather had comforted me, it had conversely troubled him. He sounded concerned for me, afraid perhaps that everything was about to change.

I didn't want to think about that right now. "I missed Rachel's call on Saturday," I said quickly. "Do you know when you might see her again? I really did want to talk to her."

"She told Thom she would try again Wednesday. In the late afternoon here. Will that work for you?"

I assured him I would make it work. Lark and I would be going out in the morning for another photography session, but I would be home before one o'clock. I told him Rachel could call the landline at the house at four their time, and I would be sure not to miss it.

Before I hung up, I said hello to a few of my cousins and uncles, which quickly reminded me how much I wished Jake was still at the buggy shop so that I could talk to him too.

I missed my family back home. Hearing their voices reminded me just how much.

Twenty-Two

After my phone call with *Daadi*, there was still some time left before Brady would go to school, so I headed into the garage in the hopes I could fix the skateboard and get him to test it out for me. Sure enough, it ended up being a simple repair, and my brother's quick test run resulted in a solid thumbs-up.

Once he was gone, I took the board back inside and spent another fifteen minutes or so with a rag and some spray cleaner, just shining it up and making it look nice. I propped it back in the corner after I was finished, thinking it might be best to deliver it to the boy's house in the afternoon, shortly before he got home from school. I would just leave it on the front porch with a note that it was all fixed.

During the rest of the morning and early afternoon, I worked diligently on the containers. Around one thirty I applied the last coat of sealant and then downed a quick ham and cheese sandwich. As the sealant dried, I took Frisco for a walk, skateboard in hand. We headed straight up the street to the little boy's house and paused there, Frisco happily sniffing at a terra-cotta planter filled with succulents while I propped the gleaming board on the porch next to the front door. It really did look good now, and the Post-it Note I had stuck on the front seemed just right:

All fixed. I hope you enjoy it.

A neighbor.

When I returned to the house, I headed out to the south side to ready the ground for the placement of the containers.

I lost track of time as I scraped at the hard, unrelenting earth. Southern California's blond, rock-hard dirt was nothing like Pennsylvania's rich and giving soil. It took a long while to break down the groundcover and level it. I was hard at work when Brady appeared at my side. I hadn't even heard him come into the backyard.

"Looks different back here," he said.

I wiped my sweaty forehead. "In a good way, I hope."

"Yeah. I guess."

I stood and surveyed the newly prepared area. "I think I'm ready to bring out the boxes. Want to give me a hand?"

He shrugged. "Sure."

We walked to the other side of the house where the gate was located and propped it open with one of the trash cans. Then we made our way to the garage, where I'd left the containers to dry.

I tested one edge to make sure they were okay to move. The sealant wouldn't be completely dry for two more days, but we'd be able to move them into place at least. "Looks good," I said. "Want to walk forward or backward?"

But Brady was staring at the four long, wooden boxes, shining golden in the late afternoon sun, and he didn't answer me. He reached out a hand and stroked one of the corners. I couldn't read the look on his face. My heart did a stutter step.

"You don't think she will like them?" I asked when he said nothing.

Brady lifted his head to look at me. "These are really nice, Ty. I can't believe you made them with just some instructions you found on the Internet."

Relief filled the spot where worry had just been. "So she *will* like them."

He nodded. "Oh, yeah. She's going to like them. She's going to love them."

His gaze was again on the containers. "They all look so perfectly the same. Professional, I mean. I wouldn't have guessed somebody who didn't…who hadn't…I mean, they look *really* good."

A tiny smile spread across my face—not from pride, but from relief. Brady had just paid me a compliment, albeit in as awkward a way as possible. But that was good enough for me. "Thanks."

My brother lifted his head again to face me. "I don't mind walking backward."

I said nothing else. I wanted his affirmation to echo around in my head for a little while. We wordlessly moved the containers into place. I couldn't have been more pleased with how well they filled the space and yet still left room for Liz to move in between them.

When we were done we stood back to admire the new look of the south side.

"You need help getting the potting soil for these?" Brady asked.

"That would be great." I tried hard not to sound surprised that he offered.

We went to the nearest garden center and filled the back of the Honda with eight forty-pound bags of potting soil. When we returned to the house, we hauled the bags to the backyard, where they would be stowed until the sealant had dried completely.

Brady was quiet as we ate supper, but this time I didn't mind. It seemed like he was mentally working through something, and because I was pretty sure it had to do with me, I gave him the space to do so.

A knock came at our door the next morning while he and I were in the kitchen and he was eating his breakfast.

Wiping my hands on a towel, I went to answer it and was surprised to see two people standing on the front step, the skateboarding boy from down the street and a woman dressed in a business suit.

"Is this him?" she asked, looking to the boy.

He nodded.

"Can I help you?" I asked.

"I think you already did," she replied, and then to my relief she smiled. "I assume you know something about a broken skateboard that was magically repaired?"

I hesitated and then smiled in return. "That was supposed to be anonymous."

"Yes, well, Christopher saw you taking it out of our trash can the other morning. He thought you wanted it for yourself, but then it showed up again at our house yesterday, so we had a feeling it was you who repaired it. Now he has something he wants to tell you."

He didn't speak or even look up, so finally she placed a hand on his back and gave him a nudge.

"Thanks for fixing my skateboard," he mumbled, eyes on the ground.

"You're welcome. I'm Tyler, by the way."

"Chris," he replied, glancing up at me.

I thrust out a hand, and he had no choice but to give it a shake.

"And I'm Rosemary. Christopher's mother," the woman said, her grip far stronger than her son's. "I'm afraid skateboard repair doesn't exactly fall under my skill set. And his father...well, that's not an option."

An awkward silence followed, so I put my hands into my pockets and spoke again to the painfully shy kid standing in front of me, trying to make my voice as warm and friendly as I could.

"So, Chris, how's the board working for you now?"

He nodded. "Good."

"My brother's the skateboarder around here," I continued. "I showed it to him and he thought the problem was likely the pivot cup. I loosened it up some. Did that do the trick?"

Again the kid nodded. Behind me, I felt the presence of Brady, and I turned to see him standing there, watching with interest.

"What's going on?" he asked.

I glanced at Rosemary, who explained. As she did, Chris looked up once and then again at Brady, his eyes growing wide by the time she was done.

"You're Brady Anderson." He turned to his mother. "He's the new kicker over at the high school."

The woman looked at Brady, taking him in. "Of course. I thought you looked familiar. You're really something, you know that?"

"Thanks."

"I mean really, all the parents are so excited about you."

"Appreciate it," Brady said, and it struck me that with his talent, he was in for a lifetime of such praise. Some might see that as a good thing, but I knew it could become a real snare, one filled with pride and arrogance and inflated self-worth. Self-indulgence as well. Brady had a difficult road ahead indeed, thanks to the mixed blessing of such an outstanding talent.

"My daughter is Tiffany Ward," Rosemary said to him, interrupting my thoughts. "She's a cheerleader there."

"Sure, I know Tiff," Brady replied. He stepped forward to stand beside me. "But I didn't realize she lived in the neighborhood."

"Been there for about ten years."

"You're a skater too?" Chris asked, looking up at Brady.

"Not in a while. But I used to be."

"Good thing you're not anymore," Rosemary said. "You have to protect that kicking leg. Can't let down the Mighty Sailors." Looking to me, she added, "We need to run, but we wanted to stop by to thank you. That was a very kind thing you did."

I shrugged, waving off her words. "It was my pleasure. I'm here visiting from Pennsylvania, so I had the time."

"Well, Christopher appreciates it very much. So do I. It hasn't been easy for him since his dad left. And I'm useless with a screwdriver."

Chris rolled his eyes as if to say, *You have no idea.*

After one last thanks, they turned and walked away.

"Well, that was bizarre," Brady said as soon as I closed the door.

"What do you mean?"

"You did some random skateboard repair for someone you didn't even know?"

I laughed, moving back toward the kitchen. "I'd seen the kid trying to fix it himself. I felt sorry for him."

I returned to the counter and the cantaloupe that was waiting for me on the cutting board. I thought Brady would go back to his breakfast, but instead he just stood there, staring at me. I grabbed the knife and began slicing.

"Sometimes, Tyler…" He shook his head.

"What?"

"I don't know. Sometimes I can't figure out what to make of you. Must be your Amishness, I guess."

I stopped cutting and looked at him, not sure if he'd meant it as a compliment or an insult. Either way, I decided to seize the moment. "Hey, can I give you a tip, one that comes out of that Amishness?"

Brady shrugged, moved back to the table, and picked up his spoon. "What is it?"

"That kid was looking at you like you were some kind of superhero."

Another shrug. Brady took a bite of cereal and looked my way, waiting for me to continue.

"Just always remember that if you act a certain way, and someone like Chris sees you, then he's going to act that way too."

"What do you mean?"

"I mean, it's sort of a known thing where I come from. The younger boys are always watching the older boys, trying to be just like them. For someone like Chris, you're a living, breathing example—in every little thing you do. It all makes an impression, more than you can imagine."

Brady scowled. "Why are you telling me this? I haven't done anything wrong."

I set the knife in the sink, rinsed my hands, and carried the bowl of cantaloupe slices over to the table.

"I know that. I just want you to be aware. Younger eyes are watching. The bigger and more important you get in the world of sports, the heavier that responsibility will become."

He laughed. "Great. Now you sound like Coach."

"Well, how about that?" I replied, snagging a slice of the juicy orange melon for myself. "Guess I'm not the only one around here with Amishness."

That day, while Brady was at school, I laid out the pea rock in between the gardens, took a long bike ride, and returned the books to the library. Brady was still in a contemplative mood when he got home from football practice. I made a point of listening intently to whatever he had to say the rest of the evening, which wasn't a lot, and I prayed for wisdom to know how to talk to my father when he returned.

On Wednesday morning I filled the containers with the soil Brady helped me haul home. Then, just before I left to get Lark, she texted that I should bring flip-flops because we were going to the beach. I had none, but I grabbed a pair of men's sandals I had seen in the garage, assuming they were either my father's or Brady's, and headed out, arriving at her house a few minutes before nine. Once again we followed the rule of the two C's and went to a coffee shop first, settling down at a table with our hot beverages before beginning our next lesson.

She started things out with a "Ta-da!" as she pulled my newly cleaned and lubricated Leica camera from her bag with a flourish. She seemed very excited by what she had done, though I couldn't see much difference. It still looked like an old banged up piece of junk to me, but what did I know?

She launched into our next lesson, starting with the difference between digital photography, which was what we had done last time, and film photography, which was what we'd be doing today.

"The word 'photography' is Greek in origin," Lark said as I sipped my coffee. "It means 'painting with light.' That's what you're doing when you're taking a picture. You're using light like a box of crayons, and the film is your canvas."

She showed me how to load a roll of film into the Leica and then explained the difference between an SLR camera and a point-and-shoot. From there she went into much detail about F-stops and film speed and light meters, most of which I was able to understand. In fact, I was amazed at how scientific the art of photography was. I had never considered that the rules of God's created world were the backbone of every picture that a film camera took.

After about twenty minutes of teaching time, Lark pulled out a small album of her own photos and used them to show me some of the principles she'd been talking about. As I flipped through the pages, I couldn't believe how perfectly composed the pictures were, with just the right amount of light and focus. Some were photos of animals and landscapes, some of people, and some of buildings or parts of structures, such as a curve in the length of a wrought iron fence. Each one did what she said a photo should: It drew me in. It was odd being so enchanted by frozen bits of time like that. Each was a real moment, but one that had long since passed. It seemed photography only ever made you think of the past. Was that its purpose? To let you have a hold on what was?

If so, was that one reason why my mother had been so interested in it?

We wrapped things up and headed out to Corona Del Mar State Beach so that I could try my hand at taking pictures the old-fashioned way, on film, the way my mother would have done. Lark gave me a notepad and told me to write down how I composed each picture. She also told me to take several photos of the same thing using different amounts of light, saying that we would compare them after they were printed.

"That's how you learn which way is best," she said.

It was slow going, writing down the information each time I took a picture and trying to remember the artistic approach she had told me about on Saturday along with the scientific approach I was paying attention to now. I took photos of cliffs, rock formations, shells on the beach, the pier, gulls, palm trees, and even a few of Lark, which was a little bit awkward. After the third roll of film, it was getting close to eleven thirty and time to stop. As we walked back to the parking lot, she asked me how things were going with Brady. I told her I had taken her advice about spending more time listening and had noticed a slight improvement in our communication. That made her happy. She asked if I wanted to stop for fish tacos on the way back to her house.

"I can't. I need to get home. I'm expecting a phone call from back East." I added that a taco with a fish inside it seemed like a bad idea all the way around.

We arrived at Liz's car and took off our flip-flops to bang the sand out of them.

"I bet you're expecting to hear from your girlfriend."

"As a matter of fact, yes. I missed her call on Saturday, so she's trying again today. At one o'clock my time."

We got into the car, which was warm inside from being closed up.

"What's she like?" Lark asked as she clicked her seat belt.

I followed suit and started the car. "She's smart and pretty and isn't afraid to speak her mind. We've been friends since we were kids."

"How long have you been *more* than friends?"

I started to pull out of the parking lot. "I don't know. Probably since I was about seventeen."

"Holy cow. That's, what, six years? You guys have been dating for six years?"

"I guess we have."

"So why is she still just your girlfriend? Why don't you marry her?"

"It's complicated," I said, repeating the word I'd used with my dad. Except unlike the conversation I had with him, Lark didn't interrupt as I continued. "Rachel is already a member of the church. I'm not yet."

"You can't marry her unless you're a member?"

"It's more that she can't marry me unless I'm a member."

"And you're not," she said, echoing my words. "How come?"

"Membership isn't a decision to be made lightly, especially for me."

"Why especially for you?"

"Because I'm not like anyone else in my district. Every other Amish person I know was born into an Amish family and has an Amish mother and father. It's different for me."

"I see." She was thoughtful for a moment. "So how long can you wait to decide?"

I pulled into a lane of fast-moving cars and someone honked at me. "Most Amish people my age have already decided. I really can't put it off much longer."

"What are you going to do?"

"I am here hoping to figure that out. I need to know which world I belong in. I am either Amish all the way to my core or I'm not."

"But if…if you find you belong to this world out here, that means you and Rachel can't…" Lark didn't finish her thought.

"Yes. It means I can't marry her."

We were quiet for a moment as I drove.

"That's why you are so interested in your mother, isn't it? She didn't become a member."

"No, she didn't."

"Instead she married your dad, who wasn't Amish." Lark sat back in her seat. "Wow. Do you think you will figure this out before you have to go back?"

"I'm counting on it."

Fifteen minutes later I was pulling up to the curb at her house. I thanked her again for the lesson, and she tried to make plans for when we would meet again, but with her complicated schedule it was taking too long, so I told her I had to go and she could just text me once she'd figured it out.

The main road to home had been reduced to one lane because of some construction, and it took me twice as long to get back as I was expecting. I watched the clock the whole way, though, and ended up with fifteen minutes to spare as I turned onto my dad's street.

Nearing the house, I spotted a vehicle I didn't recognize in the driveway. It wasn't the day for the cleaning service; they had already come this week. I parked next to the car, noting that no one was standing on the doorstep, ringing the bell.

When I got close to the front door, I heard voices on the other side of it. I had set the security system before I left, so whoever was in there had to know how to disarm it. I had a feeling it was some other sort of service personnel to take care of yet another thing this family owned that they didn't take care of themselves.

Steeling myself for the possibility that I was wrong and the voices I heard were those of thieves or murderers, I quietly opened the door and listened more closely for a moment. What I picked up on was the sound of Frisco's toenails clattering excitedly on the tiles in the kitchen and what I realized now were the voices of two women.

Stepping inside, I closed the door behind me and strode across the entryway to the open kitchen and family room. On the couch sat Liz.

My stepmother. The woman who was supposed to be in Central America.

Another woman, dressed in nurse's scrubs, was walking toward Liz with a bottle of water, Frisco at her heels.

At the sound of my gasp, they both turned to look at me.

"Oh, Tyler, there you are," Liz said, giving me a wave. "I'm sorry. I hope we didn't scare you."

"Of course not. I'm just surprised. What's going on? What are you doing here?" I stood frozen for a long moment, feeling…what? Surly. Irritated. Maybe even downright angry.

What was she doing here? Didn't she realize this would ruin everything?

Reminding myself that this was her home, I moved through the open kitchen and into the living room area, intending to give her a perfunctory hello hug. It wasn't until I got around to the other side of the couch that I realized she'd been injured. Her left leg was in a cast, her right arm was in a sling, and there were bruises and scrapes along both sides of her face.

"Liz! You're hurt!" I stepped forward and lowered myself onto the coffee table in front of her, feeling terrible about my attitude. This changed everything. "What happened? Are you okay?"

Forgive me, Father. Forgive me for being so selfish.

With her good hand, Liz waved away my concerns, as if half her body wasn't covered in bandages.

"I'll be fine." She gingerly repositioned herself, stuffing a second pillow under her injured leg. I noticed that she had cut her hair short since the last time I'd seen her, three years ago. Other than that, and except for her injuries, she hadn't changed much. She was still petite and golden brown from the sun, still attractive in a neat, "mom" sort of way.

"Tyler, this is a friend and coworker from the hospital, Nancy," Liz said, gesturing toward the other woman. "Nancy, this is my stepson, Tyler."

"Nice to meet you, Tyler. Sorry we startled you. Liz didn't want to make a big fuss and call ahead." Nancy tossed this comment back to my stepmother.

"Don't be dramatic." Liz winced as she sat back and repositioned the arm that was in the sling. Frisco jumped into her lap, causing her to gasp, though whether from pain or surprise I wasn't sure. Oblivious, he licked her face, and she responded by putting her good arm around him and snuggling him close.

"What happened?" I said again.

"It's so stupid. I was in the wrong place at the wrong time."

"She was in a dilapidated house in Honduras and it fell in on her," Nancy said. "She's lucky to still be alive."

"Oh, Nancy," Liz scoffed. "You weren't even there. The whole house didn't collapse."

"Yeah, well, the part you were in did. That's what matters."

"Does Dad know?" I asked.

"Not yet. I was waiting to call him until I got home. He would have been a basket case if he had found out while I was still out of the country."

I still couldn't quite believe she was here. "How did it happen? When did it happen?"

"Yesterday morning, while I was on a home visit. It had been raining a lot, and the house where the family lived was very old and rickety. Without a solid foundation, one of the walls just collapsed in the saturated soil."

I shook my head, trying not to picture it.

"At least there were people right outside who helped us get out from under the mess."

"Wow."

"No one in the house was seriously hurt. One of my team members patched me up at the local hospital, but I'll need to go in tomorrow for a proper cast on my ankle. We think it's fractured. My shoulder's not broken, just badly bruised. I got the first flight out of Tegucigalpa this morning."

"And Brady doesn't know either?"

She shook her head and then asked almost wistfully, "How is Brady? We've spoken on the phone a few times, and he sounds good, but I've missed him. Has everything been working out okay here without your dad and me around?"

"We're fine, though he's going to be upset when he finds out you didn't call to tell him about any of this."

Liz rolled her eyes. "I didn't want people freaking out. It's easier this way. I contacted Nancy and asked her if she could get off a little early and pick me up at the airport. It's done now. I'm home. I'll go to the hospital tomorrow and get a new cast. It's as simple as that."

The knowledge that Liz had called a coworker to pick her up instead of her stepson was hurtful somehow, and it reminded me of the distance that had always been between us. Pushing those thoughts aside, I asked what I could do now to help. Again, Liz waved away the question.

"Make sure you're here for her," Nancy said. "For whatever reason she needs. Keep her pills handy. Keep her off her feet. You'll also have to give her a ride to the hospital tomorrow for that cast."

"Not a problem," I said, looking from Nancy back to Liz. "On any of it."

"Liz, how are you going to get up and down the stairs?" Nancy asked.

Liz shrugged. "I'll figure something out."

"What about meals?"

"I put all kinds of stuff in the freezer for these guys before I left. I'm sure a lot of it is still there."

I seconded Liz's words, assuring Nancy that we would take good care of her.

"Well, okay," she said doubtfully. "I guess I'll leave you to it then. Call me if you need anything." She gave my stepmother a hug and then asked me to walk her out so I could retrieve Liz's suitcase from the car. As we headed for the door, Liz called after us, "Don't talk about me out in the driveway, you two. I'm *fine*. I really am."

We both chuckled—and obeyed, to a point. As I lifted out the navy blue bag, closed the trunk, and gave Nancy a final thanks, she said softly,

"You have to be tough with her, Tyler. She's in full 'carry on, soldier' mode, you know."

"I can see that. And I sure will."

"Good."

Back inside, I asked Liz where she wanted the suitcase.

"Up in my room, but can you bring me an ice pack first?"

"Of course."

Setting the bag at the foot of the stairs, I went to the kitchen, pulled out one of Brady's ice packs from the freezer, and carried it over to her at the couch.

"Thanks," she said, taking it from me and placing it behind her shoulder.

With a nod I grabbed the bag and headed up. When I was halfway there, the phone rang. I checked my watch. It was five minutes to one.

Rachel.

I charged back down the stairs.

"Just let it go to the answering machine," Liz called from the couch when she saw me.

It rang a second time.

"I can't," I replied as I set the suitcase on its wheels and dashed across the tiled entry toward the open kitchen. "I'm expecting a call."

It rang a third time.

I scrambled for the handset and answered at the end of the ring, practically shouting my hello.

"Tyler?" Rachel's gentle voice met my ears.

"Rachel! Yes, it's me. Hi. I was afraid your call was going to go to the answering machine."

"Oh. Your *daadi* said this was a good time…" Her voice fell away.

"It is, Rachel. Well, it was. But something's come up." I glanced over at Liz.

"Do you not want to talk?"

"No, no," I assured her. "I do. It's not that. It's just that I just need to call you back. Five minutes. Ten at the most. I'll explain everything then."

"Okay." By the tone of Rachel's voice, I couldn't tell if she was hurt or merely confused. Either way, explanations would have to wait until I called her back.

"Just one thing," she said as I was about to hang up. "I'm not at the shanty. I'm in your *daadi's* buggy shop. He said I should call from here so I don't have to pay my parents back for the long-distance charges."

"That was nice of him," I told her, and I meant it, but a part of me was sorry. What kind of privacy could she and I have if people were everywhere and machines and noise and commotion were in the background? Every word of our conversation—or at least her end of it—would be overheard by *Daadi* and the others, even if they tried not to listen. My grandfather's offer to allow her to use the shop phone had been generous but not very well thought out.

Still, I would take what I could get. Promising her I would call her back in just a bit from my cell phone, I hung up and returned my attention to Liz.

"That your girlfriend?"

"Yes. Rachel. It's the first time we've spoken since I got here."

Liz's eyes widened. "Oh, then by all means call the poor girl back. Take your time. I'm okay here on the couch. If you could just open this bottle of Advil and hand me the phone, that's all I need. You make your phone call and I'll make mine."

"To Dad?" I asked, trying not to wince at the thought. He wasn't going to be happy about this news, that his beloved wife had been injured. I carried the house phone over to her.

"Might as well get it over with."

We traded the phone for the Advil and I pushed down the lid, twisting it open.

"Do you think he'll insist on coming home?" I asked, handing it back to her and feeling a sudden surge of apprehension at the thought. Not that I didn't want to spend more time with him—that would be great, actually. But if he returned, then I wouldn't be needed after all, and I wasn't ready for my time here to be over. Not even close.

"I'm sure he'll want to," Liz said, shaking her head, "but no way am I going to let him do that. Coming home now would be ridiculous."

I tried not to breathe an audible sigh of relief.

"As long as you don't mind playing nursemaid as well as babysitter, we'll be fine here without him."

"Hey," I said with a smile, "I'm happy to be that and more. Nursemaid, babysitter, gardener, pool boy, soufflé maker, taxi driver, valet, caddie—"

"You can probably scratch caddie for now," she interjected, and we laughed.

"Well, whatever you need, I'm happy to do it."

Her eyes took on a grateful expression, and then, to my surprise, they suddenly filled with tears.

"Oh, for heaven's sake," she said, using her good hand to wipe the tears away. "I'm sorry, Tyler. It's just everything hitting all at once, you know? I've kept it together since this happened, telling myself *Just wait until you get home, just wait until you get home.* Now I am home, and I'm getting stupid."

My heart swelled with a surge of compassion, an emotion I doubted I'd ever felt for my stepmother before.

"You military types," I scolded softly. "Always so tough, always ready to soldier on no matter what. Give yourself a break, Liz. You've been through a lot."

That made her smile. Which made her cry again. With a groan, she once more wiped away her tears, laughed, and said, "Please get on out of here and call that girlfriend of yours."

"Yes, ma'am."

"Just be sure to come back when you're done," she added, her voice sounding almost vulnerable, something Liz had never, ever been with me before.

Twenty-Three

The weather was still so beautiful that I decided to call Rachel back from outside rather than in my room. Settling onto a patio chair next to the pool, I pulled the cell phone from my pocket and pressed the speed dial for the buggy shop. Thom answered and we spoke for a few moments, and then he handed the phone to Rachel.

"What's going on?" she asked as soon as she came on the line. "Are you okay?"

Despite all the background noise—the whir of a pneumatic drill, the pounding of a mallet, the lilting cadence of the men speaking Pennsylvania Dutch—the sound of her sweet voice came through loud and clear. How wonderful to connect with her at last.

I assured her that I was fine. "It's Liz," I added. "She was injured down in Central America and had to cut her trip short and come home."

"What?" Rachel exclaimed. "She's there?"

"Yeah, can you believe it? I didn't even know. I was out most of the day and just came home so I would be here in time for your call. To my surprise, when I walked inside, there was Liz, lying on the couch, all bruised and banged up and bandaged. A friend had brought her home from the airport."

Of course, compassionate Rachel immediately began peppering me with questions about Liz's injuries, her condition, her prognosis. I answered them all and assured her that things were fine on this end for now, that Liz was currently nestled into the couch pillows with an ice pack, waiting for her Advil to kick in.

"I don't know, Tyler," Rachel insisted. "Why don't we plan to talk some other time so you can get back to her?"

I smiled. Despite all that she and I had both gone through to make this phone call happen at last, she didn't think twice about giving it up for the sake of one in need.

"Actually, Liz doesn't even want me in there at the moment. She's on the phone with dad, breaking the news to him."

"Ah. Okay. I can see why she might need a little privacy."

Having convinced her at last, I settled more comfortably in my chair, took in a deep breath, and let it out slowly. "So how are you? Gosh, it's good to hear your voice."

"Yours too," she said. Her tone was so formal that for a moment I feared there was something wrong, that her feelings for me had somehow begun to cool. But then I realized she was just self conscious.

"Hey," I said, smiling to myself as I pictured her there on the phone, in the buggy shop. "You're surrounded by a bunch of guys all pretending not to listen, aren't you?"

"*Ya. Exactly.*"

"So you're not free to say all the things you'd like to say. Like how much you miss me. How much you love me."

"*Ya. Exactly.*"

"This could be fun," I teased, "especially because I've got all the privacy in the world out here. Right now, it's just me and you and this phone. I can say whatever I want."

"I'm listening," she replied, and I could hear the smile in her voice as well.

"I miss you so much. Do you miss me?"

"*Ya.*"

"I love you so much," I told her. "Do you love me?"

"*Ya.*"

"I'd give anything to kiss you right now. Would you like to kiss me?"

"*Ya.*"

"How much?"

She was quiet for a long moment. "Think of a horse in the morning, once the stable door is unlocked and opened, and how eager it is to run out into the field. About like that."

I laughed aloud. "I hear you. Okay, I'll stop teasing."

"*Danke.*"

I leaned forward, my voice growing somber. "Listen, I'm really sorry I missed your call on Saturday. You've no idea how sorry."

"I understand, Tyler," she replied. "These things happen."

"I know, but I wanted to talk so badly. I really did. I needed to know how you are, if you're okay, what you've been doing. And I wanted to hear the sound of your voice. A recording wasn't enough. I wanted to hear *you.*"

"*Ya.* That's how it was here, too."

"And there are so many things I want to tell you, Rachel, so many things I've been discovering."

"Like what?"

"Not yet," I replied, watching as a squirrel darted out from behind the shed, ran to an empty birdfeeder, and began picking around on the ground underneath for seeds. "First things first. Tell me about you. How are you? What's been going on there since I left?"

"Do you even have to ask?" she said, and I could just picture her on the other end of the line, lips curled into a pretty smile, blue eyes sparkling. "It's that time of year, remember."

"*Ach.* Right. Weddings. Have you been to many?"

"Been to them, cooked for them, served at them. I think we may set a record this year for marriages in Lancaster County. I'm so tired of roasted chicken! I told my mother we should do a ham for Thanksgiving this year. Two weddings later, she has finally agreed with me."

Rachel went on, her voice growing more relaxed as she talked about various friends and relatives, catching me up on all the news I'd missed since leaving home. As she chattered on, I watched the squirrel exhaust the supply of seeds on the ground and make his way up the pole, seeking more. Unfortunately for him, the birds had beaten him to it.

"But you don't want to hear all of this," Rachel said finally, just as the squirrel gave up, skittered back down the pole, and ran off into the trees. "I'm sure things are much more exciting out there in California. Have you seen any movie stars? Gone in the ocean? Started drinking fancy coffees with long, complicated names?"

She was being silly, but I was eager to move on to more serious topics. "Nah. It hasn't been all fun and games out here, you know."

When she replied, her voice was soft, her tone gentle and kind. "Of course not. Talk to me, Tyler. Tell me what's been happening with you."

Relieved to have her listening ear at last, I launched right in, describing the unexplained hostility Brady had toward me, my dad's parting comment, and how God had shown me that as I sought to honor both my brother and my father, I would find what I was looking for.

"Don't be so hard on yourself. You have always shown them honor."

"That's not what I mean. I'm saying I came here with my own agenda. I hadn't stopped to think that how I live the rest of my life affects my dad and Brady too. I've only been thinking about myself. And…and you, of course."

"Me," she said, suddenly sounding wary.

I hastened to explain further. "Yes. Look, I know what it means to my *Amish* family—and to you—if I become a church member or if I don't. I've always known that. But what I haven't ever thought about before is what it will mean to my family here. My *Englisch* family."

She did not respond, so I added, "And we both have to consider that I *do* have an *Englisch* family, Rachel."

Still silence on the other end, and more than anything I wished we weren't having this conversation under everyone's nose, with her right there in the middle of the buggy shop.

"We can talk about this later," I suggested. "Considering the situation on your end, I know this isn't exactly the time or the place."

"That would be an understatement," she replied, her voice now completely devoid of warmth.

I stood and began to pace there beside the pool, simply refusing to let our long-awaited call end this way, with the two of us so disconnected.

"I know you're not about to speak freely," I said, "so just listen, okay?"

"Okay." Her answer was small. Afraid.

"It's just that I realized I have to honor this family too. I have to. God expects me to. And I know that in your heart you would want me to."

I heard her sigh deeply on the other end of the line. "What exactly are you trying to tell me?"

"I'm saying I have never felt closer to finding out who I really am. I think my figuring it out is tied up with a couple of tasks." I began to list those tasks out loud. "I need make things right with Brady. I need to assure my father and myself that I don't feel abandoned by him. And I need to find out why my mother left the Amish faith." I didn't add the final element of that list, which was that I needed to help my grandparents find healing from what my mother had done to them by leaving.

"Your mother left because she moved to Philadelphia and fell in love with an *Englisch* man."

"She left because she wasn't happy in Lancaster County. She wanted something she felt the Amish life couldn't offer her. I want to know what that was."

Another sigh. "What do you think it was?" she asked, but she sounded as if she didn't really want to hear.

"I'm not sure yet, but I'm trying hard to figure it out."

I went on to tell her about my mother's interest in photography, how a box of her photos was waiting for me in a storage unit, how I was learning about photography from someone who was studying it in college. I wanted Rachel to know about Lark. To not tell her would seem as though I were trying to hide something from her.

"I don't understand. What has learning about photography got to do with any of this? Who is this person?"

"She's the sister of one of Brady's friends."

"And *why* are you doing this?"

"Because I want to know why my mother was interested in photography. Don't you find it odd that she was? She didn't grow up around cameras or photographs. Don't you think that says something about her, that this was the hobby she picked up once she was no longer living an Amish life?"

Again, Rachel hesitated before answering. "I don't know. I suppose…" Her voice trailed off, and at that moment my phone beeped in my ear.

I pulled it away to check the screen and saw a message.

Low battery.

Unbelievable. In the week I had been in California, I still had not gotten used to the idea of thinking of my phone as something that required constant surveillance from me. Brady always had his phone with him. He probably stayed aware of what his phone needed at all times.

"My phone battery is dying, Rachel. I don't know how much longer we have." There was so much more I wanted to tell her. I hadn't even shared with her about the container gardens, visiting Lark's church, and eating sushi. "When can we talk again?"

"Do you even want to talk again?"

Her question startled me. "Of course I do. I want to keep talking right now. I just can't."

"I see."

"Can we try for Saturday?" I suggested. "Same time?"

"I guess. But we're supposed to get our first snowfall on Friday, so if the roads are bad, I'll need to call from the shanty instead of from here."

I barely remembered as I sat there in a short-sleeved shirt that it was the second week of November—still early for snow in our part of Pennsylvania, but not unheard of.

"That would be better anyway," I said. "We need to talk more privately."

"*Ya.* You can say that again."

"Next Saturday, whatever time works for you, why don't you phone me once you're in the shanty, then we can hang up and I'll dial you back so the charges are on my end. Use the cell so I can take the call anywhere. Okay?"

"All right."

The phone beeped again.

"I need to go, Rachel."

I started to say goodbye and to tell her just how very much I loved her, but the line went dead and she was gone.

I sat for a moment with the phone in my hands, pain surging in my chest. I could tell she was disturbed about the distance that lay between us and perhaps even how I was approaching my quest for direction. I didn't blame her. She didn't have all the facts.

I decided I would write to her and post the letter today. I would fill her in on the details I hadn't had time to share over the phone. God willing, she would get it on Friday, before the weekend and the coming snowstorm. Once she read it, surely she would understand.

As I went back inside the house, I was struck by the thought that I could have simply come inside while Rachel and I were talking, plugged in the phone, and finished our call that way.

Oh, well. It hadn't been the best situation for talking anyway.

Liz was still on the phone with my dad, though it sounded as if they were wrapping up their conversation. She motioned for me to come toward her.

"I love you too," I heard her say. "I will. Okay. Here's Tyler."

She handed me the phone. "He wants to talk to you."

"Hello, Dad."

"So she's really okay? Is she telling me the truth?"

Liz could hear his questions even though I had the phone to my ear. She rolled her eyes.

"Tell him I've come home with a third eyeball," she said loudly so that he could hear it.

"I think she's going to be fine, Dad."

"She needs a new cast tomorrow, did she tell you that?"

"She did. I can take her."

"He needs to go to bed," Liz said, uncapping her water bottle and taking a drink. "It's almost midnight there."

"Liz says—"

"I heard her. Look, I am going to try to cut out of here early. No way am I staying the full month."

"He doesn't have to do that," Liz huffed.

"I'm going to shoot for getting home by the end of next week," he continued. "With a fractured ankle and a hurt shoulder, she will need more help than you can give her."

I glanced at Liz, sorry he was coming back sooner than planned but glad at least that I still had another week here before he did.

"And hey," he added. "If I get home early, we can actually spend a little time together before you have to go back."

"I'd like that," I said, and once again I realized I'd been thinking about myself rather than others. God had already told me that part of my time here was about restoring my relationship with my father. Of course he was coming back early. This had to be a part of God's greater plan, one I had to stop trying to orchestrate myself.

"All right. I probably should hit the sack. We're on the road at six a.m. tomorrow. You sure she's okay?"

Liz smiled wearily at me.

"She's fine," I said.

"Okay. I'll stay in touch. Take it easy, Ty."

"You too, Dad."

I clicked off the phone and returned it to its base.

"He already worries too much when I travel on these trips." Liz winced as she sat up and swung her legs around to the floor. "Now he'll never want me to go on another one again. Drives me crazy."

I hadn't ever thought of my dad as much of a worrier, and I said so as I walked back to the family room and perched on the far end of the couch. She turned to me, a half grin on her face. She thought I had been joking. "Seriously?"

"*Ya.* I mean, yes."

"He's always been this way with me."

"Really?"

"He pretends he doesn't worry until the tiniest little thing happens, and then he's like Eeyore, always thinking the worst will happen. Or has already happened."

I shook my head. "How odd. He's never done that with me at all. It's hard to imagine that's even in his nature."

"If I had to guess, I'd say it's not so much in his nature as it is something he picked up once your mother died." Liz looked toward the family portraits scattered on the shelves of the entertainment unit. "I know he loves me and that I've been married to him twice as long as she was, but sometimes I think she's still right there in his heart, hovering like a ghost. It's as though he never got over losing her, so he's that much more afraid he'll lose me."

She turned abruptly back to me. "I'm so sorry, Tyler. I took a pain-killer earlier. I'm really sorry I said that."

"It's okay," I told her, even though I was taken aback. I had never heard Liz talk that way. Ever. In fact, I doubted that she and I had ever had a conversation between just the two of us and no one else, not in all the years I had known her.

We both seemed to realize this at the same time, and we looked at each other for a long moment.

"Your dad doesn't talk about your mother around you, does he?"

"No. Not really."

"Docs anyone?"

"My grandparents and aunts and uncles will tell me things when I ask. But it's hard for them too."

Liz thought on this for a moment. "I knew your mother. Were you aware of that?"

Surprise rendered me wordless. I just gaped at her.

"In between your dad's two tours in Germany, they lived in Texas for a while. I was stationed at the same base. Our base housing units were near each other. You were just a toddler."

I cleared my throat and tried to speak. "I thought you met my dad while you were both stationed in Spain."

She shrugged. "Spain is where we got to know each other beyond a casual hello as neighbors who hardly ever saw each other."

"Were…were you and my mother friends? When they were still in Texas?"

"Not intimately. We'd talk sometimes in the front yard while you played. Your dad was gone a lot. I think your mom was lonely, even though she had you."

"What did you talk about?"

Liz pondered my question for a moment, and then she seemed to shake off the answer she had been composing in her head. It was as if it suddenly occurred to her that we had strayed into off-limits territory.

"That was twenty years ago."

I didn't want the conversation to end, but I could tell she was trying to wind it down. Before she did, I had to ask her the one question she might know the answer to.

"Was my mother happy?"

Liz regarded me, studying my face. "What makes you ask that?"

"My grandparents don't know, and I've never known how to ask Dad a question like that. But I need to know."

"*Need* to?"

Though Liz had opened up to me more than ever before, I wasn't ready to lay my soul bare and tell her everything about my own current issues, about the crossroads I was facing in my life. In a way, I hardly knew her. She had always kept me at a distance.

Instead, I just said, "If your mother had died when you were young, wouldn't you wonder that? She gave up a lot when she left her Amish roots. I'd like to know if she was happy."

Liz held my gaze, contemplating my words. "She loved you and she loved your dad. Very much. I know that."

A moment of silence crept between us. It was if we each were aware the other had laid a hedge around what we were really thinking. I wasn't saying everything—and neither was she, I was pretty certain of that.

"So, not to change the subject or anything, but I'm going to need a little assistance getting to the bathroom," she finally said. "This was a lot easier at the airport when I had a wheelchair. I don't need you following me in, but I do need some help walking over there."

"Oh. Sure." I stood and closed the distance between us, put my arm around her waist, and helped her to her good foot. She leaned into me as she started to hop to the half bath just off the entryway.

"This is ridiculous," she said as we went. "Brady has crutches from when he injured his knee last year. I think they're in the garage. Maybe while I'm in the bathroom you can get them. Or get one, rather. With this shoulder, I can't use both."

"Okay."

I waited until I was sure she wasn't going to topple over inside the bathroom, and then I headed to the garage. There wasn't that much in there now that the containers had been placed in the backyard. And I was pretty sure crutches weren't that easy to miss. But I searched every cabinet, rafter, and corner. I didn't see them.

I'd been gone so long looking for them that when I came inside the house, Liz was making her way back along the wall to the family room by herself. I rushed to help her.

"I didn't see them," I said as I eased her back onto the couch.

"Well, maybe they're in the storage unit. I might have you go over there and see, if you don't mind."

The storage unit.

"Do you guys have just the one storage unit?"

"Yes. It's not far." Liz raised her leg gingerly to the pillows that were waiting on the couch. "The GPS in my car will take you right to it, and our unit is on the ground floor. You know how to use the GPS, don't you?"

"I do, actually."

I thought about asking her if she knew where I might find the photos once I got there, and if she minded my retrieving them as well.

But then I thought of her earlier words, *It's as though he never got over losing her.* What if my father had never told Liz about the pictures, had never told her that he'd saved mementoes of his first, late wife? If I brought them up now and she didn't know anything about them, she wasn't going to be very pleased with him, nor he with me.

I decided to keep my mouth shut for the time being.

Liz reached into the carry-on bag that was leaning against the leg of the coffee table. She pulled out a slim notepad, wrote something down, and then stretched out her arm. "Here. That's the address and the gate code."

I took the notepad from her. "Don't I need a key or something?"

"You've been driving my car this week using the spare key ring, right?"

"*Ya.* Yes."

"Then you've been carrying the key around since you got here."

Twenty-Four

I made sure Liz was comfortable and had everything she needed before I left the house for the storage unit. But just as I was pulling the door shut behind me, I heard her calling me back.

I returned to the living room, where I expected her to ask for one more thing she might need before she was on her own. Instead, she had an exasperated expression as she said, "I don't know what I was thinking, Tyler. Those crutches aren't at the storage unit. They're in the attic with the skis and ski poles and the other off-season equipment."

I stood there, so disappointed. There was no need to go to the storage unit after all. No justification for letting myself in and rooting around until I found my mother's pictures.

Hiding my dismay, I asked where I would find the access stairs to the attic and then left her. But before retrieving the crutches, I took a moment to slip into my room to collect myself.

I would not be going to the storage unit. The storage unit that held my mother's pictures. The storage unit who's key and combination were both in my pocket.

When I came back to the living room, Liz was sitting on the edge of the couch waiting for me.

"Oh, I am so glad you found them. I'm already feeling like a caged animal."

I set one crutch against the wall and then looked at the other one before handing it to her. "Want me to clean it first?"

"I couldn't care less about cobwebs right now. I just want to get up off of this couch."

I helped her to her feet and then slid the crutch under her good arm, thankful for her sake that the injury to her leg was on the opposite side of the one to her shoulder. It still wasn't easy, but after some difficult maneuvering, she seemed to get the hang of it.

"One leg and one crutch," she said with a laugh. "Good thing I'm a nurse or I might never have figured this out."

I smiled, still standing close with my arms outstretched, just in case she might fall.

"What do we have here to eat?" she asked. "Any fruit or veggies or anything?"

"There are some baby carrots and snap peas. Ranch dressing for dipping. I'd be happy to pull something together for you."

"Sold." Liz carefully made her way to the table while I stayed close at her side. When she was safely there, I went to the fridge to gather the items for her snack.

"How's it been going here? Have you and Brady had any time to do anything together?"

I had no idea what to tell her. If I told her that Brady was mad at me and wouldn't say why, he'd get home and that would be the first thing she'd ask him. That would not help my cause at all.

"Uh, it's going fine. He's really busy." I opened the bottle of ranch dressing and poured a generous amount into a small bowl. "I went to his game last Friday night. That was really something. And I helped him with a paper on the Vikings. Not the football team." I laughed lightly and she merely smiled. I brought the bowl to her and the bags of ready-to-eat baby carrots and snap peas.

"Thanks. Are you two getting along okay?"

The way she said it suggested to me that she already knew we weren't.

She and Brady had talked on the phone the day he played paintball with his friends. Liz had probably asked him the same thing and picked up on the vibes he was putting out.

I could not lie to her. "It's been a little different. He's older than the last time I was here. And I wasn't in a caretaking role then."

She frowned as she crunched a dipped carrot, dissatisfied with my answer, so after a moment, I added, "He knows one big reason Dad asked me out here was to make sure he didn't quit the team while you guys were gone. That has kind of had him on his guard."

She nodded, still quiet.

"For what it's worth," I added, "he doesn't actually have any plans to do that. At least that's what he told me." Now I was just babbling.

"What did he tell you?" Liz said, emotionless.

"Uh, that he doesn't have any plans to quit the team. He likes playing football. But he doesn't like Dad pressuring him about it all the time. I told him he should tell Dad that."

"What else did he say?"

"About what?"

Liz dipped a snap pea in the dressing and swirled it around. "Nothing. Never mind."

But I knew she was holding back—though whether Brady had said something to her directly or she'd just figured out stuff on her own, I wasn't sure.

"Say," she blurted, and I could see we were done talking about Brady. "Duke told me you've been working on a surprise for me in the backyard."

"I have."

"Can I see it?"

"Sure. I think it's visible through the dining room window."

"That wouldn't be the same. I want to see it from outside."

I looked down at her ankle. "Are you sure you want to try? Looking out through a window would be a lot easier than walking across pebbles using a crutch."

She just waved away my concerns. "I'd rather do it now before the painkiller wears off."

"If you say so."

We finished our snack, and while I put her dish in the sink, Liz made her way slowly to the patio doors. Frisco began to happily bark, as if the only reason we were going into the backyard was to play with him.

I unlocked the door and swung it wide so that Liz could pass easily through.

"I wanted to do something while I was here, especially during the hours Brady was in school," I said as we slowly crossed the patio. "So I asked him if he knew of any projects around the house that you guys hadn't gotten to yet. He mentioned you've been wanting a container garden."

When we rounded the corner and the containers came into full view, Liz sucked in her breath.

For a moment I thought she hated them. But when she turned to face me, I could see that amazement, not disappointment, shone on her face.

"They're perfect! This is exactly what I wanted. How did you figure out how to do it?"

With relief I told her about the plans I had found on the Internet and of my decision not to put the containers on an automatic watering system.

"I thought you would enjoy the experience more if you didn't have a timer stealing away the tending of your garden."

She turned to me and grinned. "Nicely put. But Duke will probably want to automate it."

"Don't let him."

Liz laughed.

"I'm serious. Part of the reward of being a steward of something is the joy of taking care of it."

"A *steward*?"

"*Ya*. A *steward*. God is the one who gives us the things we enjoy while we're here. We're stewards of those blessings. You know, like managers."

"Is that the Amish way of looking at it?"

I smiled. "Well, it's my way. And the way of every Amish person I know."

"Okay. I won't let him change it." Liz moved a little closer to the empty containers.

"I suppose you'll have to wait until March to really use them to their fullest, although I've been reading that you can grow lots of herbs here year-round. You'll have to watch out for frost. And the angle of the sun will be different in the winter months than it is in the spring, so you might need to stick an old umbrella in the dirt from time to time."

Liz turned to me. "Thanks, Tyler. This is such a nice surprise. Really. It was so sweet of you."

"You're welcome. It was my pleasure."

She continued to look at me as though there was more she wanted to say. It was a little awkward. I finally had to look away.

"Do you ever think about…about being not-Amish?" she finally said.

I turned back around to face her. She definitely had my attention again. "That's an interesting way of stating it." A nervous laugh escaped me.

"You know what I mean, though. Do you?"

"You mean do I think about leaving home?"

"I mean do you think about living your life where it began. Outside Lancaster County."

"Uh…" I cleared my throat for no reason other than to collect my thoughts. "I do think about it. In fact, the time has come for me to make a decision."

"And?"

"And it's not that easy. There's a lot to consider."

"You mean Rachel?"

"*Ya*. She's part of it."

Liz breathed in deeply, filled her lungs, and then let the air out. She looked past the container, past the fence, to the sky above us. "I would imagine you probably have to decide pretty soon."

"I need to figure out where I truly belong, yes."

"I don't think your dad knows you haven't already decided, Tyler."

"Sure he does. He knows I haven't been baptized into the church yet. "

She continued staring into the distance. "I don't mean literally. I mean…" Her voice trailed off. I waited. "He believes he made that decision for you, essentially, a long time ago, before you had any choice in the matter. And I think there are days when he wishes he hadn't."

I didn't know what to say to this.

Liz turned to me. Her gaze was intent. "Will you promise me something?"

"If I can."

"Will you promise to talk with your dad about this when he gets home?"

"I had already planned to."

"Good. I'm glad. I think he might like to weigh in. Even though you're an adult now and it's obviously your life, I think he would appreciate getting the chance to share his thoughts on the matter before you do anything…permanent, you know?"

Again we were quiet. Again it felt awkward, so gently I took her by the elbow and began leading her off of the pebbles and back toward the patio.

"When you told me earlier that you needed to know if your mother was happy, it was because of this, wasn't it? You wanted to know if she was happy she left her Amish life because you want to know if you would be too."

"Yes, that's part of it."

Once more she breathed in deeply, as if the oxygen in her lungs carried the weight of heavy thoughts. I expected her to come out with some grand revelation then, but instead she just changed the subject. "Thanks again for building the boxes, Tyler. They really are just what I wanted."

I gave her a nod. "You're welcome."

I helped her inside and then went to the garden shed to retrieve Frisco's bucket of rubber balls. I spent the next twenty minutes tossing them across the lawn and watching him pursue each one like a hunting dog after a rabbit. As I did, I reviewed the conversation my stepmother and I had just shared. I wasn't sure if it was the injury or the pain pills, but she had been less guarded than usual, less "on," since the moment she'd arrived home. I couldn't help but hope she would stay this down-to-earth and approachable for the remainder of my visit.

Later that evening, after I'd made a burrito run and Liz had shared with Brady and me photographs and stories of the two weeks she had been in Honduras—including the harrowing minutes when the house caved in—I realized with a horrible jab to my gut that I had forgotten to write Rachel the letter I'd promised her.

For hours, in fact, I hadn't thought about Rachel at all.

TWENTY-FIVE

Things were definitely going to be different with Liz in the house, I could tell. With his mother there, my role toward Brady instantly downgraded to visiting older brother, although he was less cynical around me now that Liz was a spectator to practically every conversation we had.

Brady was the one who helped Liz up the stairs to her bedroom that night, who listened outside her door to make sure she didn't fall in the bathroom, and who brought her up a cup of tea and her pain medication before she turned in for the night.

As I knelt to offer my prayers before I also went to bed, I asked God to help orchestrate meaningful conversations between my brother and me so that I could continue to fix what was broken between us. It seemed to me that with Liz there, the likelihood of having those conversations had been greatly diminished. If God didn't intercede, I didn't see how I could change anything.

Then again, I realized, perhaps Liz, too, was among the list of people with whom God wanted me to find peace and reconciliation. If so, then I prayed He would give me clarity when dealing with her—and when it came time to talk to my father as well. The hunch that my dad was wrestling with regret after all these years had been confirmed by Liz. I searched my heart for pockets of bitterness or lingering resentment toward him, but I didn't find any. What I sensed instead was something closer to what I was already feeling. Restlessness. My inner being was not at peace. I was dangling between two worlds, and the plain truth was that nobody could be at peace if their feet were not planted on solid ground.

Finally, I prayed that God would watch over Rachel and not let me destroy something meant to last. If it was meant to last.

I was the first one awake the next morning, Liz's first full day home. After my devotions, I took Frisco out for a daybreak walk and then returned to the house to find Brady helping Liz maneuver down the stairs. She appeared to be in greater pain today. We had decided to leave one crutch upstairs and one crutch down, so at the bottom of the staircase, Brady handed her the downstairs crutch and helped tuck it safely under her arm.

"Want any coffee, Liz?" I asked as I watched her grimace.

"Yes, please." She made her way slowly to the couch, Brady trailing her with her iPad and cell phone. I followed them and turned into the kitchen.

"Can I make you some breakfast, Brady?" I poured coffee for Liz and turned to my brother. "Scrambled eggs or an omelet? My omelets aren't pretty but they are tasty."

"Nah, I'm good," he answered without looking at me.

"I'll take an omelet," Liz said. "What have you got to put in one?"

I opened the fridge. "Mushrooms, asparagus, and some kind of cheese."

"Sounds wonderful to me," Liz called out.

Brady turned to face me. "I guess I'll have one, then."

"Coming right up."

While I made breakfast, Brady took a chair at the kitchen table and tapped at the screen on his cell phone. Liz turned on the morning news, which seemed to be one story of conflict and chaos after another.

It was a beautiful November morning, unseasonably warm, even for just a few minutes after seven. When the omelets were ready—they actually didn't look too bad—I suggested we eat breakfast on the patio. It was my way of unplugging from the TV and its doom and Brady's cell phone. But Brady said he didn't have enough time before his ride came, and Liz said it was too chilly to eat outside.

We remained where we were and ate, each one of us in relative solitude.

Liz's appointment for her new cast was at ten. On the drive there, I asked her how she became interested in overseas humanitarian work.

"How could I not be? There is so much need out there. So many hurting and sick people, especially children. Thousands die needlessly every day. Nothing will change for them if people like us don't step in. I'm lucky I can take time off from work to do it. I would have done it long before this if we weren't always moving."

"So what do you do when you go?"

"Everything. On this trip we were conducting immunization clinics and diabetes management training. Last year when I went to Guatemala, I assisted two doctors who performed clef palate repairs to fifteen kids who had literally no future without surgery. The year before that we were in Haiti. And before that, in the Dominican Republic removing benign-but-life-threatening tumors and growths."

"Must be hard to see so much suffering."

"Oh, it would be far more difficult to look away from it, I think. I couldn't live with myself if I did nothing in spite of having the means and opportunity to do something."

Liz began to share with me some of the amazing stories from her past trips, and I found my admiration and respect for her growing. In all the years she had been my stepmother, I hadn't known that she, like Rachel, was very much moved by compassion to do something when a need arose.

"I feel like I am just beginning to know you, Liz, after all these years," I said as I turned into the parking lot of the hospital where she worked. "I'm sorry if I've kept you at arm's length. I didn't mean to."

This seemed to surprise her. "You don't owe me any apologies, Tyler. I'm the one who didn't know what to do about how you were raised. I've never known. It just seemed such an unfixable situation. And I'm a fixer. It frustrated me."

I pulled into a spot with my brow furrowed. Lark had said the way I was raised was crazy. Liz just now called it an unfixable situation. But for me, it was simply the way my life had unfurled as I had lived it. I didn't like the idea that to other people my life to that point seemed crazy and unfixable.

When I said nothing, Liz touched my arm. "I don't mean that you're unfixable, that you're somehow the problem. It's your dad and me. We're the ones who let what happened, happen."

"But there is no problem." I turned off the ignition.

"Well, maybe not for you," she said as she unclicked her seat belt, so softly that I wondered if she had said it at all.

"What was that?"

She had her hand on the door handle, but she paused. "Hey. Do you want to have lunch after this?"

She said it casually, but I could tell there was a purpose to her question, and that it had to do with why she hadn't really answered mine.

"Sure. If you're up for it."

"I'll be due for another pain pill when they're done with the new cast. If I'm not hallucinating or near comatose, I'd like to take you to lunch."

"Sounds great."

It was tough waiting for Liz to be seen and then tougher still waiting for her to emerge with a new cast. I was eager to continue our conversation.

Lark texted me as I sat in the outpatient waiting room to see if we could meet the next day instead of Saturday. The reception in the hospital was terrible, so I stepped outside to text her I was fairly certain I could make the switch, but that Liz had returned early from Central America with an injured ankle and shoulder and everything was now a little different.

That text prompted her to ask me what had happened.

I texted back: *Can I just call you?*

Her answer back to me: *No. I'm in class. Just tell me.*

She was in a house that collapsed while she was inside it.

No way! Really? Is she okay?

Like I said, she has some injuries. But overall she was lucky. Could've been worse.

Is it weird having her home?

You could say that. She's seeing the doctor now and then we're going to lunch. I have a feeling there's something she needs to tell me.

You want to call me later?

I really didn't know what I wanted—except for the hundredth time I wished I could call Rachel.

I'm sure it's not that bad.

Okay, but holler if you want to talk about it.

Will do. See you tomorrow.

I went back inside the hospital. Fifteen minutes later Liz emerged from the casting room with her injured leg bent at the knee and resting on a scooter-type contraption that she operated with her other foot. She was surrounded by colleagues who were wishing her well and offering sympathetic goodbyes until she returned to work. At least the sling was now gone from her arm.

As we headed back out to the car she told me the fracture wasn't as bad as she thought but it was still going to keep her off of her leg for at least six weeks.

"I have a few bruised ribs too, and a few contusions on my back that are blossoming into a hideous, purple road map. But I'll live. And it's nice to lose the stupid sling, which they said wasn't really needed anyway."

"Are you feeling okay?"

"I just took another pain pill, so by the time we get to a restaurant, I'll be able to be pleasant to people."

I helped her into her car and then we headed for a Mexican place she liked. Once we were seated, I noted with a quiet laugh that the Baja fish tacos were a house favorite. I opted for cheese enchiladas. Liz ordered flautas. When the waitress walked away with our menus, I could see that Liz was still in pain.

"Would you like me to change our order to go?"

She shook her head. "I'll be okay." She took a long sip of her water.

The feeling that she'd brought me here to tell me something was even stronger now, so I waited for her to begin the conversation. After a second or two, she did.

"I've been thinking about what you told me last night. You know, about your wanting to know if your mother was happy."

"*Ya?*"

"It's not like we were best friends. She was just my neighbor for a few months."

I waited.

"But I do know she wanted something she couldn't have."

"What? What did she want?"

Liz swirled a finger on the condensation sparkling on her glass. "She wanted both."

"Both what?"

"Both lives." Liz met my eyes. "She wanted to have the life she had *and* an Amish life. She wanted to return to Lancaster County, but she wanted to stay with your father. But she couldn't have both. Having one meant not having the other."

I sat, stunned, speechless, wondering how Liz could know this.

"I was working the night shift, so I was home during the day. One afternoon your mother was sitting on the steps of our duplex watching you play in your wading pool, and I had come out to wash my car. It was a blistering hot day. She asked me over for some lemonade, and we got to talking. I already knew she had been raised Amish because we had spoken before. But for some reason, on that particular day, she was feeling especially talkative—or maybe just homesick. She talked about the farm where she grew up and her family and how sad it was that her own son would never know the joy of an Amish life. She said she wished there was some cosmic way she could have both worlds."

I still could not speak.

"I didn't know much about the Amish, and I asked her why she couldn't just have both, like a cousin of mine who had a Korean husband. They lived in Korea, but she managed to be a Westerner while still embracing his culture."

Liz looked to me as if I would agree that these were valid suggestions. I just stared back at her, waiting for her to continue.

"Anyway, your mother told me it was different with the Amish. That that was impossible. That the two cultures were mutually exclusive. She said that living an Amish life meant giving up all other ways, not merging them." Liz took another long sip of her water. "Your mom told me your dad was on one side and the Amish life was on the other. And that those two sides would never meet. Ever. It was one or the other, but not both."

I looked away, out the window next to our table, where the busyness of life rushed past, trying to absorb what she was telling me.

"It wasn't that she was unhappy, Tyler. She didn't want to go back there if that meant leaving your father behind. But she wished there was a way she could go back and keep him too. And she knew that wish would never come true."

I slowly turned my head to look at her as she added, "I'm telling you now because I think she would want you to know."

We were both quiet for a minute, each lost in our thoughts.

"I honestly didn't think I would ever run into your father again," Liz said, breaking the silence. "I hardly ever saw him in those eight months they—you and your parents—were at the base in Texas. Then, five years later, when I was stationed in Spain, he came into the hospital one day with a burn from some equipment he'd been working on. I was his nurse. He barely remembered me, but I remembered him. I asked him how his wife was. And when he told me what had happened, I started crying, right there in the exam room. I don't know why. For some reason, I had hoped Sadie had finally come to peace with the choices she'd made. With her passing so young, though, I figured she probably hadn't. And that thought was just heartbreaking to me."

Our food arrived and we began to eat. I suppose it was cooked perfectly and I might have enjoyed it had my head not been brimming with new thoughts.

"Why did you say you thought my situation was unfixable?" I asked a few minutes later. "Earlier, in the car. That was the word you used, unfixable."

"Because it was. Duke waited too long to come back for you. And then *we* waited too long to come back for you. I should have insisted the minute we were married to come to Pennsylvania and get you. You had just turned eight. It had only been two years since you'd been there. But I got pregnant pretty soon after we were married and we just kept putting it off. By the time we got our act together, it had been five years since your grandparents had taken you. And we had Brady. And you... well, it was too late."

Too late.

She was right. For all intents and purposes, by that time, I was fully ensconced in the Amish world, fully a part of my grandparents' household. But had that been a good thing or a bad thing? I wondered. Then I realized that it didn't matter either way.

All that mattered was that it had been a God thing. Growing up Amish had been His will for me.

"I've had a good life, Liz. I'm not bitter about the way things turned out."

"I know you're not. And I'm really glad you're not. But you need to know that there's nothing keeping you there now but you."

"Are you telling me you think I shouldn't go back?"

"I'm telling you that right now, you have what your mother didn't have. The ability to choose."

I processed this for a long moment. Then another thought occurred to me.

"Can I ask you something?"

She nodded, waiting.

"When you were stationed in Spain and my father came into your hospital that day and you asked him about my mother..." My voice trailed off, unsure of how to say it.

"Yes?"

"Did he mention me at all? Did he say where I was or what had happened to me?"

Her eyes narrowed, and I knew she was wondering why I wanted to know.

Why *did* I want to know? To find out how he'd said it, if he'd been embarrassed or remorseful about leaving me behind? To find out if the situation really had been "crazy"?

"He told me you were living with your Amish grandparents until his next tour was over."

"How did you respond to that?"

She thought for a long moment. "I suppose I should have thought to ask why he hadn't brought you with him. But at the time the only thing that came to mind was, well, at least Sadie's son made it back, even if she never did."

Twenty-Six

I awoke Friday morning before dawn, wondering if snow was falling on Lancaster County as predicted. I wanted to be able to picture where Rachel was, what she was doing. I crept downstairs to my dad's study, turned on his computer, and opened an Internet browser so that I could check the Weather Channel's website.

Indeed, it said they had already received several inches and more was to come. A travel advisory had been issued for practically all of Eastern Pennsylvania. It was difficult to imagine that I wasn't on another planet. The forecast for Orange County was sunny skies and a high of seventy-three degrees.

I turned the computer off and closed my eyes, picturing Rachel in her wool cape and heavier bonnet, walking from her house to the dairy barns in the blue-white of morning snow. The cows would raise their big heads when she walked inside the milking parlor and slowly blink their long-lashed eyes. The breath coming out of their nostrils would look like wisps of gauze. They would be anxious to be milked, ready for break-fast, waiting for the human contact that would bring both. But Rachel would walk past the milking stanchions into the nursery to feed the new calves, change their bedding, and rub the little nubs of growing horns before they were removed. She might be humming a song as she did these chores. Was she thinking of me? Was she missing me?

This was the hardest part of my ponderings. Imagining the flip side of those musings: a morning without Rachel in it.

It was wrong to join the church solely for the love of a girl. I wouldn't do it. But Rachel was a part of the equation, just as my dad had been a part of my mother's equation when she was seeking peace for her situation.

"Rachel deserves to be happy," I said aloud to God. "I want her to be happy."

When she and I talked tomorrow, I would assure her I wanted this more than anything else, even more than my own happiness.

After lunch, I borrowed Liz's car and headed to my next photography lesson. Before I was halfway there, however, Lark called to see if we could postpone for an hour. One of her professors had offered a special study session after class and it was running a little long.

I assured her that was no problem, though after I hung up, I pulled over into the nearest gas station while I tried to figure out what to do with myself between now and then. I could always turn around and go back to the house, but I didn't want to. An hour to kill, the car at my disposal, nobody else aware of where I was or what I was doing...

What I really wanted was to go to my father's storage unit and dig around inside until I found the box of my mother's photographs, the ones I hadn't stopped thinking about since the moment he'd first mentioned them.

I had the key on my key ring. I had the security code on a piece of paper in my wallet. I could easily find my way there, get inside, and more than likely dig up those photos. Of course, that would mean rooting around through my father's private things without his permission, but was that really such a big deal?

For that matter, would he even have to know about it? After all, they weren't really his pictures to give. They were hers. And she was my mother. Maybe that really did give me the right to seek them out on my own.

A sensation of unease swept over me.

More than unease. Guilt. Shame.

I couldn't do it. I couldn't go over there and rifle through my dad's possessions, much less do so and then keep it a secret afterward. Before he left, he said I could have the pictures; they were practically mine already. But they weren't mine yet. Not until he handed them to me himself.

Outside the car, movement at a nearby dumpster caught my eye, and I turned to see a trio of seagulls fighting over a discarded sandwich. Their presence reminded me of the ocean not too far away and of God's magnificent handiwork on display there.

The moment my thoughts turned to Him, I could hear His words to me from earlier in the week. Like notes on a breeze, they came floating back now.

Honor others before yourself.

This would not be honoring my dad, jumping into his privacy to find something he had already said he would give me when he returned. This was just me jumping ahead and doing what pleased me without concern for how he would feel.

I made my decision. I would honor my father and wait to be given the pictures in his time, not mine.

Feeling frustrated but resolute, I knew what I needed most in that moment was a place to think and pray, somewhere quiet that I could disengage from everything that pulled at my affections and concentrate solely on God. I put the car in gear and pulled back onto the road to go in search of just that. The beach would have been a good choice, but traffic was so heavy that I knew an hour wasn't enough time.

Needing somewhere closer, I continued down the road, eyes open for other possibilities. When I was nearly to Lark's house and still hadn't found any place to retreat, I turned into a shopping center I'd noticed before, one that had a coffee shop with a large outdoor patio landscaped with trees, flowers, and a bubbling fountain. It wasn't secluded, but at least it looked peacefully busy. People were scattered about the tables, most talking quietly or tapping away at laptops.

I bought a large cup of black coffee and settled into a chair by the fountain, hoping that the sound of water rushing over stone would help me be still. Sprinklings of conversations and the songs of the birds that never had to fly south for the winter filled the air. Across from me, a woman and her two young children sat next to a playpen of puppies they were hoping to give away. On the other side of the fountain was a frozen yogurt shop, and every time someone opened the door, a few bars of reggae music floated onto the patio.

I found it difficult to pray there, so finally I turned my intentions to thinking instead. Sitting there among the busyness, I thought about my father first. Then Liz. Brady. Rachel. My mother. I thought about this *thing*, whatever it was, that pulled at me from the outside when I was home—yet pulled me home when I was out. I wondered, yet again, which man I was and in which place I truly belonged. If only God would show me soon!

I sipped my coffee and watched people stop to pat, hold, and cuddle the frolicking puppies. When I was done, I tossed out my empty cup and walked over to see them for myself, nodding at the older of the two children.

"Want to hold one?" he asked.

I held out my hands and the boy gave me a wriggling, spotted dog.

The pup smelled of wood shavings, energy, and confident trust. It had been a while since Timber had been a puppy, and longer still since we'd had much livestock. These days our attention was almost solely on the buggy shop. But holding that little dog reminded me of younger years when I was given a piglet to raise, or chickens to care for, or when one of our horses foaled. New life always reminded me of God's purposes being renewed in the most basic of ways.

I held the dog close to my face and he licked my cheek with his tiny pick tongue.

"You want him?" the boy asked.

"I'm just visiting," I said, shaking my head as I handed the puppy back. It wasn't until I turned to go that I realized what I'd just said.

It was true. I felt like a visitor. No matter where I was, I felt like a visitor.

It was as if when I turned six, that's what I became. A visitor.

I made it to Lark's house at two o'clock sharp. She thanked me again for being flexible with the time and then led me to the dining room, where she had spread out on the table prints of the pictures I'd taken with both the digital and the film camera. We looked over the digitals first, reviewing my composition, and then she made me go through the film shots one by one, comparing each against the notes I'd taken while shooting them.

Overall, I decided, a few were rather nice, most were okay, and a number were just plain terrible. We studied them together for a while, but finally I sat back in my chair, defeated.

"Well, I think one thing has been made very clear," I said, taking in the pictures in their entirety. "I do not have an eye for photography."

"Why would you say that?"

"These are just ho-hum. They're nowhere near as good as anything you've taken. Even your early stuff."

"Don't be so hard on yourself. They're not that bad."

"Don't be so easy on me. They're not that good."

Lark picked up a photo I had taken of a Corvette that had been parked at the beach lot. I'd thought my dad might like it. "This one's pretty good." She handed it to me.

"It's okay."

She picked up another, of a gull walking the fine line between wet sand and dry. "I like this one."

"It's not bad. I just don't see a story in any of these the way I saw in yours."

"Well, it's only your second try at it, Ty. You'll get better. It's like anything that requires practice. The more you do it, the easier it will become and the better your results will be. I'm sure the first buggy you made had its problems."

I laughed and tossed the photo of the Corvette onto the table. "Not this many problems."

Sitting back in my chair, I met the eyes of my tutor and friend and told her, reluctantly, that I had a feeling we were about done.

She blinked. "What do you mean?"

"I mean, the point wasn't to become some expert photographer. It was to learn enough about how it's done to get inside the mind of my mother, to figure out what the draw was for her."

"And?"

"And I'm realizing now that I'm never going to figure that out. Not from this."

Lark just stared at me, waiting, so I continued, understanding flowing into me even as the words came out of my mouth.

"Photography is too singular of an experience, I think. The way I feel when I'm taking pictures is completely different from the way you feel—and from the way my mother would have felt. It's not one size fits all, even though I had hoped it could be."

Lark pulled in a breath through pursed lips, held it, and then blew it out again before she spoke. "I hear what you're saying, but just because that's why you got into this in the first place doesn't mean you should stop. Whether it helps you understand your mother or not, you should be doing photography for your own sake."

I shook my head. "Yeah, *if* I enjoyed it. But I don't."

Her eyes filled with surprise and then hurt.

"I've enjoyed spending time with you, of course," I added quickly, "but the picture-taking itself really hasn't done anything for me. Mostly, it's felt tedious, you know?"

Lark sat back, the hurt in her eyes lingering. "So all of this was for nothing."

I felt bad for her, and I realized I should have reminded her along the way of my motivation. Somehow, she had managed to forget the one reason I was doing this at all. "Seriously, Lark, I'm really grateful for everything you showed me. More grateful than you know. It wasn't a waste of your time. Okay? I learned a lot."

"But we're done. You don't want me to show you anything else." She met my eyes. "Do you?"

I hesitated. "I don't know. I don't think so. I have a lot of other things on my mind."

"I see."

She grew silent, hurt clearly evident on her face, so finally I leaned toward her, searching for the words that would make her feel better.

"That first night over sushi," I said softly, "I told you why I wanted to learn photography, so I could understand what my mother saw in it, what she liked about it. Do you remember that?"

After hesitating a moment, she nodded.

"I've been honest with you from the start. That's all I wanted from it, but now I can tell that it's not going to pan out. And believe me, I'm even more disappointed than you are."

She seemed to take that in, and then her expression softened. "You really thought that learning to take pictures would help you understand why your mother took pictures?"

I nodded.

"And that if you knew that, you might know *her* a little better? Understand her a little better?"

"Yes."

"And that if you could understand her, you might understand yourself? That you might even know what she would want you to do now?"

I laughed lightly. "Yeah, I guess I did. Pretty big leaps, I suppose. Dumb, huh?"

Lark reached for my hand and squeezed it. "No, not dumb. I can't imagine making important choices without asking my mom's advice. Of course you want to know what your mother would say to you now. I really do wish you could ask her. I wish you could just say, 'Mom, what would you do if you were me?'"

"But she *was* me," I said, and my voice seemed to break a little. I looked down, willing myself not to tear up.

"Then it makes even more sense."

I stared at Lark's hand on mine, liking the sensation. It was warm and soft, far softer than any hand I had ever touched. Even Rachel, who was so beautiful and delicate in other ways, had the rough hands of an Amish woman, of someone who had spent years hand-washing dishes and scrubbing clothes and working the garden and tending animals and more. Rachel's hand in mine always felt solid and caring, but Lark's hand in mine felt gentle and tender and silkier than anything I could ever have imagined.

"I just don't know where I belong, where I fit," I said. "I am not truly Amish, and I'm not truly *Englisch*. Which means, I suppose, that I'm… nothing at all."

With her other hand, Lark reached up to my face and cupped my jaw, turning my head toward hers. "Oh, Tyler. Don't say that. I'll tell you exactly where you belong, where each of us belongs. With the people we love and who love us. Everything else is secondary."

I considered that for a moment. "There are people back in Lancaster County who love me, that's for sure."

Her eyes narrowed. "There are people here who love you too, you know."

Again, I nodded. "Of course."

"So it's no wonder you're torn. But you know what this means, don't you? It means you can't make a wrong choice. You have love in either place."

She smiled at me. The thought that she might possibly be right made the sudden weight in my chest lift a little, and I returned her smile without speaking.

"Look, I know there are pros and cons for both places, but…" her voice trailed off, but I knew what she meant.

"Yeah, I think—"

"I want you to stay."

I heard her but I couldn't quite wrap my head around what she had said.

I met her eyes. "What?"

Her hand was still holding on to mine, and now she gripped it even harder. "Stay, Tyler. You finally have the power to come home. You should be with your dad and brother. And besides all of that, I want you to stay. I like you. A lot."

As I sat there undone by her words, she leaned forward, bringing her lips to mine. She kissed me, and before I was even aware of it, I found myself responding. I kissed her back, the power of physical attraction and emotional affirmation surging inside of me, creating a force beyond my control. My Amish life seemed in that moment like a dream I had awakened from. I was just an ordinary man in ordinary clothes kissing a beautiful girl in an ordinary house in a sunny Southern California suburb.

My hand went to Lark's cheek, brushing across the delicate bones of her face, learning them, continuing on to her hair. I ran my fingers through its softness, both hands now gripping her head, pressing my mouth even more fiercely against hers. In that moment, I was the man in my mother's pond, the one who stared back at me on crisp autumn mornings when I looked into the water of the world beyond Lancaster County. I was an everyday man who drove a car and had a cell phone and texted the girl he liked and went to his brother's football games and ate sushi and had clothes with buttons and wore a watch on his arm. I was a man who took pictures with a camera. Looked up the weather on the Internet. Made coffee with K-cups.

I was the man I would have been if my father had kept me. If my mother had not died.

I felt Lark's arms sliding around my back, pulling me closer, and I did the same. As we clung to each other, our mouths melded together, everything about the last seventeen years suddenly began floating away from me. Floating away. Any moment, I realized, it could all disappear.

And then, with sudden and shocking clarity, I realized I didn't want it to.

I didn't want to be this man.

I pulled away, breaking off our kiss even as I stifled a gasp.

"What?" Lark's eyes were half closed. Glistening.

I swallowed hard, took my hands from around her slender shoulders. Shook my head. Tried to speak but could not.

I didn't want to be this man.

I saw it now, all too clearly. I wanted to be that other man. The Amish one.

The one I truly was.

Twenty-Seven

"I have to go."

I got to my feet, nearly knocking over my chair, and headed for Lark's front door.

"Tyler!" she called after me.

"I'm sorry, Lark. I really have to go." I couldn't look at her. I had to get out of that house and away from any physical remnant of the kiss I would have taken back had it not revealed to me who I was.

"Tyler, please! Wait!"

But I could not wait. I called out to her over my shoulder, saying I would contact her later once I figured things out.

The thing was, I already *had* figured things out. And I couldn't wait to tell Rachel what I'd discovered. I felt so close to an answer, a final knowledge of who I was and where I belonged. I finally understood that the world I treasured most, the world I would always consider my home, was the Amish one.

It's not that I wasn't drawn to Lark in a powerful way, because I was. Spending time with her had been one of the highlights of my days here. And kissing her had been…well, it had been amazing. Lark's kiss—and all that it spoke of—was enchanting, nearly intoxicating. Complex.

I had only ever kissed one other person, Rachel, and those kisses had been stolen in courting buggies when no one was looking or at singings when a walk outside under a sky of stars made us think we were on the threshold of heaven. Every kiss I had ever shared with her whispered to me that here was a taste of what it would be like to be married. But the kiss I had shared with Lark shouted to me that here was a taste of what it would be like to be *Englisch*.

And as much as I'd thought that might be what I wanted, I knew now that it wasn't. Lark was a lovely girl, but she wasn't for me—because this life wasn't for me. Finally, I understood.

The man in the pond was merely a reflection of my options, not an indication of my destiny.

That night Brady's team lost by a touchdown but not due to any mistakes or missed opportunities on his part. They were just outplayed. By the time the game was over, Liz was clearly in pain and ready to be home. Brady would be riding the team bus back to the school, with a friend giving him a lift from there.

"I think I did a little too much today," she said to me as we took our time walking to the car. "I just want my pain medication and sleep."

Once we were home, Liz dressed for bed and then called me in to help. Sitting on the edge of her mattress in sleep shorts and an oversized T-shirt, she let me tend to her, retrieving an extra blanket and a glass of water and her pills.

"I guess pain is the great equalizer, huh?" she mused, uncapping the bottle and tapping out one round white pill into her palm. "Let me tell you, it's not easy for an independent, headstrong woman to be so vulnerable. So needy. It's making me crazy."

"And yet it is often in need that God's voice can most easily be heard," I said.

She tossed the pill into her mouth and then reached for the glass of water.

"Oh, yeah?" she asked after she'd swallowed. "And what might God be saying to me now, if you don't mind my asking?"

I shrugged, wishing I could help her understand. "Maybe that independence is overrated. That need creates community. That by allowing others to help you, you are actually giving them a gift in return."

She handed back the glass of water and then leaned against the pillows, shifting to raise her injured leg onto the bed. "I was with you till you got to that 'gift' part."

I set the water on the nightstand and then grabbed an extra pillow from the side chair. She held her leg up while I propped the pillow under it.

"Really? But you're a nurse, Liz. And you do mission work. You more than anyone should know how good it feels to help others."

Her eyes widened as she seemed to connect the dots.

"The way I see it, the needier you are right now, the more blessed I am to be able to care for you. It's really that simple. And in the caring, the bonds we share are strengthened and renewed. That's how community works."

Her eyelids were looking heavy. I pulled the covers over her and then asked if she needed anything else. She said no, she was fine, so I wished her a good night and headed for the door.

"Hey, Ty?" she said as I reached for the light switch.

I turned to look back at her. "*Ya?*"

"How did you get so wise?"

The question touched me deeply even as it brought heat to my cheeks.

I smiled. "It's God's Word that is wise, not me," I replied, not knowing what else to say. She didn't respond, so I shut off the light and was just pulling the door closed when she spoke again.

"You're a good son," she uttered in a voice so soft I wasn't even sure if she'd meant to say it aloud.

The next day, Saturday, I checked my cell phone the moment I awoke to make sure it was fully charged. It was, but I left it plugged in anyway, just to be safe. My last call with Rachel had ended so badly that I would do whatever it took to make this one okay.

I served Liz some oatmeal with nuts and raisins and then told her I thought I'd spend the morning detailing the inside of my dad's new muscle car if she didn't think he would mind.

"I think he'd like that very much. He's calling me later this morning. I could ask him, but I think we should keep it a surprise."

"Sounds good to me."

Having the car to work on made the morning hours fly by. I knew very little about what was under the hood, but the leather upholstery was something I could clean, mend, and fix like a pro. After all, I'd been doing the same thing on buggies for years.

Out in the garage, I opened the doors to let in some air and light and set to work on the backseat. When I came in at lunchtime, Liz was on the couch with her leg on its bed of pillows and Brady, still in his pajamas, was watching TV.

I offered to make grilled cheese sandwiches, and then Liz told me my dad was hoping to get home by Wednesday. The TV was on during lunch and everyone did their own thing while they ate. Rachel and I were supposed to talk at one o'clock, so at ten minutes till I finished up the dishes and told Liz and Brady that I would be unavailable for the next half hour or so and why. Then I retrieved my phone and headed out into the backyard.

The device trilled right on time, and I answered it by blurting out the first thing that came to my mind. "Rachel? I'm so glad you called!"

The line was silent in response, and after a moment I feared she wasn't the one on the other end after all. I pulled the phone from my face to check the number on the screen before putting it back to my ear. "Hello? Rach?"

"Hi, Tyler, I'm here," she replied, her voice lilting and familiar. "You just startled me, is all. I wasn't prepared for…It's just that our last phone call…"

"Our last phone call was a disaster, and then my stupid cell died before I had the chance to say goodbye and to tell you that I love you. But I do. I love you so much. And I miss you like crazy."

She exhaled a sigh, one that felt weighted by more than just air. It was as if she'd been holding in a breath she'd been afraid to let go. In that moment it felt as if all had been restored between us.

"I love you too, Tyler. And I miss *you* like crazy."

"You do?" I whispered.

"*Ya.* I do."

We settled into the call and soon were chatting easily, this time with the focus on her end. Rachel caught me up on life in Lancaster County, and with every word, I found myself longing to be home more and more. Best of all, she and I were laughing and talking and getting along as if our last nightmarish phone call had never happened.

"I've been to two weddings this week. And both times I had to sit with the poor girls who weren't chosen by anyone."

I sat back in the deck chair, grinning like a fool.

"*Gut.* I'm happy to hear it. Though I'm surprised Wally Yoder didn't ask you to go to the table with him." Wally was a good friend of mine, but I knew he'd had his eye on the beautiful—and taken—Rachel Hoeck for years.

She was quiet for a moment. "Actually, Tyler, he did. So did Angus Fisher. But I told them no, that just because you were away didn't mean I was available for courting."

I swallowed hard, surprised at the impact her words had on me. I had never been the jealous type, but something about the thought of those two guys putting the moves on my girl the moment my back was turned made me a little crazy.

"So am I?" she asked, snapping my mind into focus.

"Are you what?"

"Available for courting?"

I took in a deep breath, wishing I could just will her to understand every single step of this complicated and confusing path I had been on.

"The answer to that is no. Definitely, positively no, you are *not* available for courting." After a beat, I added, "Unless, of course, you want to be."

I heard a soft intake of air on the other end of the line—I had caught her by surprise—and then she replied, "No, Tyler. I definitely, positively do not."

In that moment I wished I could simply fly through the phone, all the way to Pennsylvania, just so I could look into her sparkling blue eyes.

"So what's going on out there?" she asked. "You sound different. Has something happened?"

I wondered where to start. The last time we talked, I'd told her about the various elements of my quest—the mysterious conflict with Brady, the photography lessons, the word from God that I was to honor others before myself. So I started from there, summarizing all I had seen and done since and explaining how God had been moving in so many ways throughout every circumstance and conversation. I told her what Liz had shared with me the other day, how my mother had spent her years as an *Englischer* longing to return to the Amish world she'd left behind.

At that Rachel sighed. "Oh, Tyler, I'm so sorry for your *mamm*—but so glad you found that out. Don't you see? It would be the same for you too. I just know it would. If you left for good, you would spend the rest of your life regretting it."

"I know that now, but I didn't then. It took even more than that to finally open my eyes." With mounting excitement, I told her about my experiences yesterday, starting with my lesson being postponed and how I'd wanted to use the time to break into my father's storage unit and find my mother's photographs. I told her about the busyness of life out here and my search for a quiet place to pray and my time at the coffee shop. I told her about the puppies and that feeling of always being a visitor.

"Then I went for my final photography lesson, and it all just kind of came together for me there."

"Oh?"

"*Ya*. First, I realized I was never going to figure out the appeal that picture-taking had for my mother. It's just not that kind of a process."

"I could have told you that, even though I've never used a camera in my life."

"I know, I know. But I had to try."

"I understand."

"Next, Lark helped me see something important, that every person belongs where they love and are loved."

"You are loved here, Tyler."

"I know. But that's the beauty of it. Because I have love in both places, I can't lose by living in either one."

"Oh." Her tone was hesitant.

I continued quickly, "Not to worry, though, because what I finally came to understand is that the person I most am on the inside—the person God intends me to be—is the Amish Tyler, not the *Englisch* one. Something happened that gave me a real glimpse of myself in the outside world, of me being the man I would have become had my mother not died. And I realized that I didn't want to be that person. I want to be me. The Amish me. The me I really am."

Rachel was quiet for a long moment. "I'm so glad to hear that," she said finally. "You can't imagine how glad."

In her voice, I could hear the weeks of uncertainty begin to melt away. "So what happened to make you realize this at last?"

I blinked, speechless, amazed at how I had managed to bumble my way into this one. What could I say now? That the truth had come to me while making out with my photography tutor?

"Does it really matter? The point is, I get it now. Finally. I understand which world I belong in. I *am* Amish, Rachel, and I have been for years. I just need to make it official. I'm ready to join the church and be Amish for the rest of my life. I'm ready for all of it. For…us."

I wanted her to be happy, but instead she just wouldn't let it go.

"*Ya*, I understand, but I know you, Tyler. I know this voice. What is it you're not telling me?"

I exhaled, mentally kicking myself all the while.

"Look, it was just some spur-of-the-moment thing. Stupid, really. What matters is what I realized, not what I was doing when I realized it."

"Come on, Tyler. I want to understand."

I blew out a long, slow breath. "Fine. Lark and I kissed, if you have to know. But as soon as we did, it struck me that this guy kissing her was the other Tyler, the one I've always seen in the pond—and that *I don't want to be that guy.* I want to be the one who's looking *into* the pond, the Amish one. The one who loves you and wants to make a life with you. Do you understand what I'm saying?"

Not surprisingly, she remained quiet. I knew she needed to think over not just the promise of my words but the betrayal of my actions.

"I'm so sorry, Rachel," I whispered. "I shouldn't have let it happen. I had no business kissing anyone but you. It was just the situation and the timing and all of my confusion and everything. Nothing like that would ever—could ever—happen again. Ever. Please forgive me."

Still she said nothing. When she finally spoke, her voice sounded distant. Cold.

"I forgive you, Tyler. And I'm happy you have finally decided which world you want. But..."

I waited, taking in a breath and holding it as she continued.

"But now *I* have some thinking to do too."

"Thinking? About what? About us? About me?"

She sighed heavily. "Tyler, I've always thought it was you and me. Forever. Since we were children, you know? But I see now..."

"What? You see what?"

"That it's different for you. Unlike me, you've been holding on to the possibility that there might be someone else."

I groaned. "That's not true, Rachel. That's not it at all. This search hasn't been about choosing who I want to spend my life with. It's been about choosing a church, a home, a place to belong. A world."

"*Ya*, a world that could or could not include me as the person at your side."

I swallowed hard, unable to deny those words. "I couldn't join the church solely out of love for you," I whispered. "That would have been wrong."

"*Ya*, I know, and I've always understood that. I've been patient, but I've been waiting years now, Tyler, *years* for you to be ready to take that next step. I never quite understood why it dragged on for so long, but I see now what at least part of this delay has been about."

"I've had doubts about joining the *church*," I reiterated.

"*Ya*, but I have to believe you have also had doubts about taking me as your wife."

I closed my eyes, wondering how to make her understand. This had never been about her at all. If anything, it was my love for her that had kept me in Lancaster County for so long, that had kept me from asking these questions and going on this journey way before now.

"How can I convince you that my love for you is true? That I'm finally ready to take that next step?"

She didn't answer, but I could hear the telltale sounds of her crying.

"Look, I'll be home in less than two weeks," I pressed. "Once I can see you in person, once I can take you in my arms and ask you to be my wife, then you will know that my doubts have never been about you. Please, Rachel. I love you. I want it to be you and me, side by side, for the rest of our lives."

"Hold on," she whispered, and I heard the phone clunk down onto a hard surface, heard the soft whish of tissue being taken from a box as she pulled herself together. When she returned to the phone, she was hoarse with grief.

"Look, I gave you the freedom for you to do what you needed to do. I ask you to please do the same for me. I don't think we should talk again for a while."

"What do you mean?"

"I mean you can come back if you want, but I can't promise I'll still be here for you when you do."

"Rachel, you can't—"

"I'm hanging up now, Tyler. I have always loved you. And I wish you the best. But I have some decisions to make as well."

With that, she ended the connection between us, leaving me with a dead phone and two searing dilemmas.

I had hurt the person I most loved in the world.

And I didn't know how to make it right.

When I went inside, my expression must have shown everything. Liz did a discreet double take as I made a beeline for the stairs.

"Everything okay between you and Rachel?" she asked.

I paused, half of me wanting to be alone and half of me relieved to have someone to talk things over with. "No. Not really."

"I'm sorry, Tyler."

"I am too. I might…I might need to head back a little earlier than planned."

Brady looked up at me. "I can take care of my mom. You don't have to stay another day if you don't want to."

"Brady." Liz frowned at him.

"What? He doesn't. He can leave now if he wants."

"That's not what I want," I said. "I'm just saying I might head back before the end of the month since Dad's coming back early."

"And I'm just saying you don't have to wait for him. If you want to go back, go back. Now."

"Brady!" Liz exclaimed.

But my brother just stared at me, as though he had drawn a line in the dirt and dared me to step across.

The stress of the day overcame me. I could not stand another minute of the tension, especially as I had tried every angle I could think of to appease him.

"I'm really sorry I am such a dunce that I can't figure out what I did to make you mad at me, Brady. I've tried to understand your behavior toward me, I really have, but I just can't. You're going to have to tell me."

With a grunt, he turned his attention back to the TV. But I wasn't going to be put off that easily.

"I've only ever wanted to be a good brother to you."

"That is such a lie."

I could barely believe I heard him right. "I beg your pardon?"

"Brady, Tyler, I want you both to stop for a minute—" Liz pushed herself up on the couch, but Brady and I ignored her.

"You heard what I said. That's a lie." Brady turned toward me, his gaze steel on mine.

No one had ever called me a liar before. Ever. The accusation cut like a knife. Especially coming from my own brother.

"When have I ever lied to you? About anything?" I demanded.

He shook his head, a wounded half smile on his face, as if everything that came out of my mouth was a laughable but painful joke. "Go home, Tyler. Really. Just go home. It's obvious you want to. Just go." He stood and brushed past me to leave the room.

"Brady!"

He spun around, eyes blazing. "What?"

"Talk to me!"

"Fine." He stepped forward, his neck suddenly bulging and red with rage. "You want to know the truth? You want to know what I'm so mad about?"

"Yes. Please."

His eyes narrowed, and as I peered into them I realized that there was something else behind the anger. Pain. Hurt.

"All these years," he said in a voice low but strained, "my whole life, I thought Dad abandoned you in Pennsylvania, that he just went off and left you with your grandparents. For years I've blamed him that I never had a brother growing up because I thought it was his fault."

"I don't understand," I said, hoping the calm in my voice would calm him down as well. I bore my father no ill will for what had happened. I wanted him to sense that.

"Don't you get it, man? I've been blaming *Dad*. For years. Until I learned the truth."

"The truth?"

"That *you* were the one, not him. *You* decided to stay. He asked you to come with him and Mom, but you said no. It's *your* fault I grew up without a big brother around, *your* fault I'm practically an only child."

With that, he turned and left the room. I just stood there, the full force of his words falling onto me like a crushing weight.

I had done to my dad—and by default to my brother—what my dad had done to me. I had relinquished him. Walked away from him.

I wanted to call after Brady now, to say something, but no words would come.

Clarity pummeled me. It all made sense. All of it.

In all of these years, I'd never once considered how the choice I'd made at the age of eleven affected my family—my father and my brother and even my stepmother. But I realized now that the hurt had gone both ways.

They hadn't just abandoned me. I had rejected them.

TWENTY-EIGHT

O h, Tyler, I'm so sorry," Liz whispered from the couch.

I turned to her, still stunned and nearly speechless

My mind raced as I tried to decide what to do next. Go after my brother? Give him a chance to cool off first?

"Why don't you just sit down here for a minute," she said, as if reading my mind. I met her eyes and saw that they were shimmering with tears for her son and maybe for me too.

After a moment's hesitation, I did as she asked, taking a seat beside her on the couch.

"I'm sure Brady hasn't stopped to realize you were just a child back then."

I shook my head. "No, Liz, in a way he's right. I did make a choice. And that choice affected him. I just never realized it until now."

Fresh tears filled her eyes, and she dug a tissue from her pocket, dabbed at her cheeks, and blew her nose. We were both quiet for a moment.

"I think I know where all of this is coming from," she said finally, her expression growing distant. "A few weeks ago, the day after your dad called you and asked you to come, he and Brady had a big fight. Brady accused Duke of having abandoned you with your grandparents all those years and robbing him of having a brother to grow up with. And your dad, he lost his temper and…" Liz stopped as another tear slid down her cheek. She dabbed at her face. "He told Brady it was *you* who decided to stay. When you were eleven and we finally came for you, you didn't want to come with us."

I pictured the impact his words must have had. The moment Dad told him I'd chosen not to come, Brady's hurt and anger must have jumped from our father to me.

"Duke wasn't trying to throw you under the bus, Tyler, please don't think that," Liz said. "He didn't mean to deflect the blame or to drive a wedge between you and your brother. He was just trying to get Brady to understand that the situation back then hadn't been so cut and dried. It was more…complicated than that. For all of us."

I swallowed hard, feeling in the midst of my dismay a strong sense of relief as well. At least I knew now what was wrong, what had happened to make Brady's behavior toward me change so drastically.

Which meant I could set things to right at last.

"Should I go up there and apologize?" I asked. "That's what I'd like to do, but I'm not sure if this is the best time."

She shook her head. "Give him some space. Now that he's gotten that off his chest, I think he might need to settle down. Catch his breath. Maybe understand that what he's feeling isn't so much anger as it is hurt."

I nodded. "I can't believe I never thought about this before. Of course he's hurt. I would be too if I were him."

Then I realized that at the very least I could apologize to her. After all, I had unknowingly rejected her as my stepmother as well. I had not meant to communicate rejection—the Lord knows I was only eleven years old—but I had. I was too young to see it then and apparently had been blinded to it as I grew. I might have picked up on it later, except Dad never mentioned that day again. And neither had Liz. I grew up thinking I was the only one who had something to gain or lose that day.

"I'm sorry, Liz, if my decision hurt you too."

She held up a hand, palm out, as if to deflect my words. "Like I said, you were just a child. I would never hold you accountable for that choice. No way. I'll try talking to him first." Liz dug in her pocket for another tissue.

"Thanks," I said. Then I told her I'd be back later, that I needed to clear my head as well.

Still in a daze, I went to the garage, took the bike and helmet from the rack, and headed off into the hazy afternoon sunshine for a long ride, hoping it might help me to sort things out.

It didn't. By the time I returned, Brady was gone, off to spend the night at a friend's house. Liz told me she'd tried talking to him a bit, tried to explain more about the situation and why he shouldn't blame me for all that had happened back then.

"But to be honest," she added, "I don't think I got through to him. Maybe he'll think on it some more while he's gone. You never know."

I thanked her and headed upstairs. In my room, I took out pen and paper and wrote a long letter to Rachel, finally shedding a few tears of my own. It seemed that in a single day I had managed to alienate two of the most important people in my life. For now, all that was left to do was attempt to mend these fences and to pray.

And so pray I did, on my knees at the side of the bed, for more than an hour. During that time, I slowly came to understand something important, that the Lord was not nearly as concerned with where I lived my life, but how I lived it. I had chosen once before, as a child. And I was choosing again now, as an adult. I told God I wanted to spend my life in Lancaster County as a member of the Amish church, married to Rachel, and living in simplicity, surrender, and service to my community and Him. This was my decision to make, but I also felt strongly that it was God's will for my life.

When my prayer time was done, I grabbed pen and paper, climbed onto the bed, and wrote out three very important letters.

The first one was for the bishop, telling him I had heard my answer from God and that I was ready for the membership class and to take my vows.

The second was for *Daadi* and *Mammi*, telling them the same thing but in more detail, explaining the highlights of the spiritual journey I had been on. At the end, I also thanked them for raising me, and for being so wonderful and loving and wise.

The third was for Rachel, and it was by far the hardest one to write. After several false starts and crumpled pages, I finally ended up penning just a few quick sentences, telling her I would be getting home a little earlier than expected and would like the opportunity to see her and talk with her as soon as possible after that. I didn't know if she would even give me the time of day once I showed up at her door, but my hope was that if I asked her via letter, in advance, she might at least be willing to consider it.

After that, I felt much more at peace. In fact, despite the tension I was now experiencing in virtually all my human relationships, I had never been so connected to God. It was as if I'd been in a darkened room, trying to find my way, and with this decision finally made, a door had been thrown open, spilling light into every corner at last.

Brady didn't come back from his friend's house until late Sunday night, acting distant and aloof. Before he disappeared into his room for the night, I asked if we could talk.

"I have homework," he replied, and then he closed the door in my face.

The next few days were the most difficult I had ever known. I busied myself with little details on my dad's car, buffing out rust on the chrome, finishing the repairs to the upholstery inside, and cleaning out the trunk. But not since I was six, alone in an unfamiliar place and missing my mother so bad I could barely breathe, had I felt so disconnected from the people I loved. Rachel, Jake, and my grandparents seemed a million miles away; Dad was still in the Middle East; and Brady outdistanced them all. Liz, the one person who had always kept me at arm's length, was now my closest human connection. She offered me sympathetic nods and a kind word here and there, but she and I were both painfully aware that the long-buried emotions from the day they asked if I wanted to come live with them, and I'd said no, were out in the open.

She also felt bad for how Brady continued to treat me.

Liz had received an email with Dad's flight information, and he would be arriving at LAX early Wednesday afternoon, so I freely gave Brady the space he seemed to need all the way until Tuesday evening. I really didn't want Dad walking into this powder keg of a relationship, especially because it had been his words that had kicked things off in the first place. Liz had spoken to him at length on the phone after the fight, and I felt sure he was already beating himself up about it enough as it was.

I managed to corner Brady that night, just as he was turning off the TV to head upstairs to bed. Liz had turned in early, and I'd been in Dad's office for a while, reading through the rest of my mother's book on Germany. The moment I heard the TV go silent, I set the book aside and leapt up from my chair, heading straight for the living room. Fortunately for me, Brady had paused at the kitchen table to gather up the papers and books from where he'd been studying earlier. I seized the moment and went to the stairs, standing in place at the bottom. As soon as he zipped up his backpack, set it by the door, and headed my way, I spoke.

"Dad gets home tomorrow, and I think we need to settle this tonight. As men. As brothers." Startled, he hesitated. Then he crossed his arms over his chest, mouth shut tight, as he waited for me to say what I wanted to say.

Speaking softly so as not to wake Liz, I told my little brother how very sorry I was for not understanding the impact my decision from twelve years ago had had on him. I tried to describe that whole situation from my point of view, reminding him that I'd only been eleven years old at the time. But I didn't want to sound like I was making excuses, so I ended my plea by telling him, "Young or not, confused or not, the bottom line is that I rejected a life with my little brother. No wonder you've been feeling hurt and angry with me. I promise you, the greater loss was mine."

He nodded, his arms relaxing a bit but his expression still distant.

"Okay," he said finally, but from the tone of his voice I realized that it wasn't an apology he wanted. What he wanted, I felt sure, was to understand how I could have chosen the Amish life over a life with him and our father and his mother. He just really needed to get it—especially as I was about to make that same decision again, this time for good. But before I could help him, I realized with a start, I needed a few answers myself from our father.

I stepped aside and wished him a good night. He took the stairs two at a time.

This wasn't over.

On Wednesday morning I got up well before dawn to pray and ask God's favor on my remaining few days in Newport Beach. I didn't want to return to Lancaster County with unfinished business between my dad and my brother and me. It was clear to me now that this was the prime reason God had orchestrated that I come here. My decision to join the Amish church would affect my *Englisch* family, but it didn't have to affect them negatively. I had already come up with a few ideas on how to ensure that it didn't, but I had to deal with the unresolved issues of the past before charting a plan for the future.

All morning as I finished up the work on detailing my dad's car, I thought about the questions I wanted to ask him. Liz wasn't up to the long car ride, so I would be going alone to pick up my father. That meant he and I would have a chance to talk privately. He'd be tired from flying across multiple time zones, of course, but I thought it was important that he and I iron things out as soon as possible. I needed to make things right here, with everyone, so that I could go home and make things right there as well.

According to Liz, getting to LAX was going to be a much bigger ordeal than going to the John Wayne airport would have been. But this was my dad's only option, thanks to his point of origin, and so I steeled myself for the forty-mile drive. She'd tried to prepare me about the traffic congestion I would likely run into on the 405, and so I left extra early, hoping not to stress myself more than necessary.

She'd been right about the traffic. The sheer volume of cars and drivers was staggering. On the other hand, that made for a slower pace overall, which was worth it. In the end, I used the sluggish commute to continue to pray to God for wisdom and discernment.

With the GPS guiding me, I was able to find the turnoff for LAX and the right parking structure for Dad's arrival gate. He texted me when his plane landed, just a few minutes late, and again when he collected his bag and entered customs. The plan was to meet in the Ground Transportation area, so I headed there and found a bench along a wall. Forty-five minutes later, he finally emerged, bags in hand and a weary smile on his face.

I took the suitcase from him, and with his free hand he clapped me on the back. "Man, it's good to be home."

"I'm sorry you had to cut things short, but I'm really glad you're here too."

We headed for the parking structure.

"How is Liz?" he asked as we walked. "She keeps playing things down on the phone, but I know her well enough to know she's not giving me the whole truth."

"She really is okay, I think. She was in a lot of pain at first, but she seems to have finally figured out that the less she does, the less it hurts."

"Good. Glad to hear it."

As we neared the car, Dad said he was hungry and wanted to stop off and eat somewhere on the way home. I was relieved, especially because I had a feeling his true intention for the stop was to give the two of us time to talk. We both knew there were things that needed to be said.

"There's a coffee and pie place in Huntington Beach where we can eat," he added. "I'll drive if you want. Although you must have gotten here okay because you're still in one piece."

I reached into my pocket for the car keys and handed them over. "That would be fine with me."

Soon we were on the road, where Dad wove his way through the heavy traffic with ease, telling me all about his trip as we went. Forty minutes later, we were seated at a window table with a cup of coffee each and slices of triple berry pie.

Once the waitress had delivered our food, Dad finally launched into what was on both of our minds. "Liz told me all about the blowup with Brady on Saturday. I feel terrible about it. I never should have said to him what I did. You have no idea how much I regret it."

"I understand."

"I know you think you do, but I was so out of line, Tyler. He was accusing me of abandoning you and depriving him of having you for a brother. And I just...I couldn't let him think that about me. It was bad enough him knowing I had dumped you on your grandparents when you were six and then leaving you there. When he accused me of never going back for you, I lost it. I didn't stop to think that knowledge might change his relationship with you. Now that I know it did, I wish I could take it back."

"It's okay. It has to be okay. It's the truth."

"But he didn't have to hear it like that."

We were both quiet for a moment.

"*Daadi* and *Mammi* gave me a good life, Dad. I was happy there. I *am* happy there."

He winced slightly. "But you shouldn't have had to find your happiness outside of what I could provide for you. I'm your father."

"But you *did* provide it for me. You gave me *Daadi* and *Mammi* and all my uncles and aunts by letting them raise me."

He smiled tenderly. "Is that really how you see it?"

"Yes. It is. I'm not bitter about the decision you made to send me there. Or keep me there."

Dad took a drink of his coffee to let those words of affirmation settle in on him. "I'm glad, of course. But I wish...I wish I had come back for you when I said I would."

And there it was, the perfect opening to pose the question I'd been wanting to ask for days—for weeks. For years. "So why didn't you? Come back sooner, I mean."

Dad shook his head. "The truth?"

I nodded, my heart suddenly pounding in my chest.

"I was afraid of messing up what she had done in you."

I stared at him, not understanding, remaining silent until he continued.

"Your mom was so…she was such a good mother. She knew how to calm you when you were afraid and discipline you when you were ornery and talk to you and teach you things. You weren't like our friends' kids at all. They were always having tantrums and meltdowns and screaming at their playmates when they didn't get their way. But not you. Your mother had this way of dealing with you that was unlike any kind of parenting I had ever seen. Like super firm but super gentle, all at the same time. It's hard to explain, but I have to think it was how she was brought up. Even though she had left her Amish upbringing, her Amish upbringing never truly left her. I couldn't begin to measure up to her parenting skills. I still can't."

"You're not a bad father, Dad. You've always made it clear that you loved me, which is huge, especially to a kid."

He smiled. "Okay, so I'm not a complete failure. But I've never been very confident about it. Like I said, I was afraid of destroying what she had done. That's why I went on a second remote tour after that first one, because I knew your grandparents were doing a far better job raising you than I ever could. At least that's what I told myself. When I met Liz, I had another excuse for not coming for you. And then she got pregnant and I had another, and then we had a new baby and an upcoming move back to the States and I had another. I didn't come back for you until I had run out of excuses. By that point, I knew it was high time for me to take over from your grandparents, whether I was going to botch everything up for you as a father or not."

I took a sip of my coffee and swallowed it down. Once again, he'd given me the perfect opening for a question.

"So why didn't you just take me that day? You asked me if I wanted to come. Why didn't you just tell me to come?"

Dad fooled with the handle on his coffee mug as he considered his answer. "I wanted you to be where *you* wanted to be. You were turning into just the kind of boy you would have been had your mother lived. She would have been so happy to see you that way and in that environment. Before she died, I think she was torn between the life she had and the one she'd left. I don't know. I guess it felt like I was honoring her by giving you the choice—a choice she gave up the day she married me."

I sighed and looked out the window. "I thought it was because you had Brady and Liz and you didn't really need me to be a part of your new family. I wanted you to want me to come with you."

"And I wanted you to want to come."

I turned back to my father. "We didn't communicate very well, did we?"

"We were both making it up as we went along, I suppose. When I married your mother I thought it was for life. I didn't think I'd ever have to make the kinds of decisions I made in the years that followed. I made them on the fly."

"I'm sure you did the best you could."

He shrugged. "Yeah, that's what Liz tells me. I do know that my intentions were good. I really did want the kind of life for you that your mother could have given you. And Tyler, when I look at you now, I think you have it."

A cloak of peace seemed to fall across my shoulders when he said that, as warm as a down blanket. "I think I do too."

"You know, when you first told me on the phone that you would be able to stay with Brady while I was gone, I made a list of all the reasons why I was going to try to convince you to stay after I got back. Even to the day I left for the Middle East, I was hoping you would fall in love with the life you could have out here. But the longer I was gone and the more I agonized over it, the more I realized you are right where you belong. I'm not saying I don't want you close by because I do. But you've always seemed like an Amish man to me. And before that, an Amish boy. Even before your mother died, you were an Amish boy. You just didn't have the straw hat or the suspenders."

I smiled at this.

"I know you're going to have to decide to join or not join the Amish church, and I just want you to know I will stand behind you whatever decision you make. You will have always have a home with Liz and Brady and me, but I don't want you to ever think that to choose to be Amish means you're not one of us. You'll always be my son, Tyler. No matter where you live or how you worship God or whether or not you drive a car or use electricity or shave your beard. You'll always be my Amish son." He smiled, adding, "You always were, you know?"

Twenty-Nine

I felt good about our conversation, but I still had one last request for my father, which I made as soon as we got back in the car and continued on toward Newport Beach. I reminded him of the box of photos in the storage unit that he had promised to me before leaving on his trip and asked if we could stop by there and get them on our way home.

He looked so exhausted, I felt guilty for even bringing it up, but I was afraid if we didn't do this now, it might be days before he got around to it.

"We don't have the key," he said.

"Sure we do. It's on Liz's key ring," I replied.

He must have sensed how important this was to me because he agreed without further protest. Fifteen minutes later, we were finally pulling into the facility I'd been so drawn to since the moment I'd learned of the photos' existence.

Located just a few miles away from the house, the complex was protected by a thick iron fence. Dad pulled up to a little machine and punched in his security code, and then the gate slowly began to slide open. As he drove through and continued on inside, all I could see were rows and rows of separate buildings, each one alike, each one filled with what had to be at least a hundred separate units. The sign at the entrance had said there was no vacancy, but the further we went, the more astounding that fact grew. Every single unit was in use by people who, apparently, didn't have enough room at their homes to store all their belongings. Incredible. Add that to the list.

When my dad finally pulled into a parking slot, he said, "Be right back," and then he quickly climbed from the car.

"Need help looking for the box?" I asked, reaching for my door handle as well.

"Nope. You sit tight," he replied, no doubt preferring to do this alone. As he shut his door and walked off toward the building, I realized that it really would have been an infringement of his privacy to come here without his permission. As difficult as it had been to resist the urge, I was glad I'd waited. If he didn't even want me in there with him, I couldn't imagine how he would have felt if I'd gone there without him.

I thought again of my list and had a sudden realization. There was simply no way I could record all the differences between this world and mine. There were just too many to count.

My father was back a few minutes later, sliding into the driver's seat with the highly anticipated box in hand. I'd been expecting something along the lines of a shoebox, but this thing was made of solid metal, not cardboard, and was closer to the size of a boot box. It was also quite heavy for its size, which I commented on as he handed it over.

"It's a strongbox," he replied, sliding the keys into the ignition.

"A strongbox?"

He started the car and put it in gear. "You know, fireproof. Most people use them for documents, but they're good for pictures too."

We reached the gate and he again pulled to a stop and typed in the code, this time to let us out.

"She was always taking photos and getting them developed," he continued once we were on the road. "Used to make me nuts."

"It did? Why?"

"Oh, not the picture-taking. The part that happened afterward. She would always come back from the store with a packet of pictures, spread them out on the table, and study them for a while, and then end up throwing most of them away. Said she was saving just the good ones. Those she kept in there, where they would be safe."

He gestured toward the box in my lap, seeming perplexed at the thought of such waste. I totally understood, though, thanks to my time with Lark. Like her, my mother had approached photography as an art, I felt sure, bracketing each photo the way I'd been taught and then pulling the wheat from the chaff. For a moment I wondered how she might have known to do that. Had she hired a tutor too? Or perhaps researched photography at the library? Regardless, judging by what my father was saying now, she must have learned the technique and used it as well.

"When was the last time you looked through these?" I asked, holding the box firmly in my lap and gazing out at the houses we were moving past.

"Probably two years ago, when we moved here and set up the storage unit."

I nodded, aware that military families like my dad's typically took stock of everything in their possession every two to three years when they got orders to move somewhere new. No doubt their unit was neat and methodically organized, just like their garage and attic back at the house.

Still, with so many moves, unnecessary items were often jettisoned along the way. I asked my father why he'd kept these particular photos for so long.

He was quiet for a while before he responded.

"They're such great pictures. I don't know. I guess somehow holding on to them allowed me to hold on to the memory of your mom in a way that wasn't painful or complicated."

"Do you want to go through them with me, back at the house?" I asked, almost reluctantly.

He shook his head, much to my relief. "Nah, you enjoy them on your own," he replied. "Heaven knows you've waited long enough to see them."

When we arrived home, Brady had just been dropped off from football practice, and he and Liz and my dad all greeted each other warmly.

I felt obligated to stick around, one big happy family and all that, but when Dad finally settled down at the kitchen table with a beer and began sharing with them the same stories from his trip that he'd already told me in the car, I excused myself and headed upstairs, box in hand, hoping they wouldn't think me rude for slipping away.

In my room I closed the door and sat on my bed with the strongbox in front of me. I snapped open the metal clasp and lifted the lid, tilting it back on its hinges. Inside were dozens of envelopes, each one fat with photos and coffee-brown negative strips. I pulled out the first envelope, dated the year my parents were married, and began to go through it. It looked as if the pictures had all been taken in Germany and focused primarily on the rural countryside there. They weren't especially good—nothing like what Lark would have done—but they were okay.

Returning them to their envelope, I moved on to the next and then the next, pleased to see that my mother's talent as a photographer grew as time went on. I'd learned enough from Lark to notice the slow, subtle mastery of composition, exposure, technique.

From the packet dated the year I was born, I finally ran across a few shots of myself as an infant. But otherwise, my mother had continued to take mostly landscape shots, the only difference being the ongoing growth in her abilities as a photographer. Once we returned to Germany for a second tour, her pictures got even better, as they were especially sharp and clear and colorful.

I kept looking with great interest, occasionally running across another picture of myself as a child, usually outside, playing ball or patting a horse or jumping into a pile of autumn leaves. But primarily these were beautifully composed photos of rural Germany. There were farmhouses, fields of grain, half-timbered barns, horses, cows, laundry on the line, flowering hedges, hills of green, glistening brooks, and budding trees. No urban landscapes, no street scenes, no skylines. Every envelope that came after was that way as well, a few shots of me here and there, but mostly scenes as pastoral and peaceful as any Amish farm on any day of the year.

The envelopes came to an end once our second tour ended, the very last photo an aerial shot of the German countryside, probably snapped through the window of the plane that flew us home.

I sat back against the pillows and looked into the box, taking in the pictures in their entirety. Almost immediately, I realized what my mother had done here. Through the camera lens, she had managed to recreate an Amish-like world for herself from an ocean away. By focusing on scenes of the bucolic European countryside, she had found a way to tease out scenes reminiscent of Lancaster County.

This was what the photography had given her in the end, the ability to capture scenes that took her home, even if only in her imagination.

Feeling sad but settled somehow, those questions finally laid to rest, I said a prayer of thanks and then set the box on the dresser and headed back downstairs, expecting to find my family still gathered at the table, chatting happily and catching up with each other. Instead, Dad was gone, Liz had returned to the couch and was dozing there, and Brady was sitting on the floor wearing headphones and silently playing a video game on the TV. He didn't even glance my way when I came in the room, so I went in search of my father.

I was afraid he might have gone on to bed, but I found him in his study, going the through mail that Liz had sorted each day and had me put on his desk. He looked up as I came in, his eyes wide with curiosity.

"Well?"

I smiled, somewhat wistfully I'm sure, as I settled into the chair that faced the desk.

"I went through every single picture."

He grinned. "Didn't I tell you? Aren't they something?"

"They are. It was fun to see her grow as a photographer over the years, you know? She started out a little rough, but then she got better. Eventually, she was very good."

He nodded.

"Any idea what started her on that in the first place? I mean, photography isn't exactly a natural fit for someone who's been raised Amish."

Dad smiled. "You're right about that. Actually, it came from a dependents class at the army base."

"Dependents class?"

"Free courses offered to the dependents of military personnel stationed there. When we first went to Germany, she was struggling a little, trying to find her place both in the non-Amish world and as a new officer's wife. I talked her into taking a class or two, really just hoping that would give her something to do, maybe make a few friends. She chose photography—and almost right away she really got into it. As you saw when you looked through the pictures, she kept going with it, long after the course was over. Said it was sort of therapeutic, a way to help her merge her old life with her new one."

"You can say that again."

My father's eyes narrowed. "Huh?"

I shrugged. "All those scenes of the countryside…"

"Oh, I know. Your mother was always zipping out of town on her bicycle, heading off on the open road to take more pictures. Sometimes when I was gone, she would even bring the two of you on overnight car trips into the country. She'd find these little farmhouses in the Black Forest that took in renters. Half of the owners didn't speak a lick of English, but that didn't matter to her. She'd stay for four or five days just soaking up the rural scenery and letting you run around like a farmer's kid."

"Like an Amish kid, I think."

I realized that Dad hadn't put two and two together until that moment. His eyes widened, and then he sighed audibly.

"Of, course. They reminded her of home. I can't believe I didn't figure that out before now."

I nodded, and we both grew silent for a moment.

"I'm glad I gave them to you," he said at last.

I shook my head. "I'll keep the box with me, if you don't mind, but I'm not taking the pictures with me when I go, Dad. I am leaving them here with you."

He frowned. "Can't your grandfather make an exception just this once? They're your *mother's* photos, for crying out loud."

"This has nothing to do with that. I *want* you to have them. I want you to look at them whenever you need to picture what it's like to live a simpler life. I don't need the photos for that. But I think you and Liz and Brady might."

"What do you mean?"

I pondered how best to say it. "Your lives are very full here but also very complicated. Complex. Filled with distraction. I want you guys to consider coming to visit me more often. In fact, I think I am meant to show you the joys of a simpler life. I've been out here, doing it your way. Now it's your turn to come there and do it mine, at least for a little while."

Dad laughed lightly. "Trying to get us to become Amish, are you?"

I laughed too. "Merely trying to get you to unplug from time to time. Reconnect with each other. And with God. I think it would be great if the three of you came to Lancaster County for a quiet retreat from all of this."

He was thoughtful for a moment. "That sounds great, but I'm afraid Brady won't go for it. Not the way he's acting."

"I know. He and I still have a few things to figure out."

"Want me to talk to him?"

"Thanks, Dad, but this is between us. Brother to brother."

"I hear you."

He was just returning his attention to his mail when I added, "But you do need to talk to him about something else."

He looked up. "What's that?"

I told him what Brady had said about playing football and the pressure he was under from all sides—especially from his own father.

"He doesn't want to quit the team. He never did. What he wants is to be able to decide for himself how big a role football will play in his life. It needs to be his decision and only his. Not yours."

My father let out a long, slow sigh.

"I think the more you push," I added, "the more he's going to push back. If you keep going like you have been, I'm afraid you'll cause him to do the very thing you most *don't* want him to do, which is to quit the team."

"Okay. You're right. I know. Liz has been saying the same thing for a while now. I just didn't want to hear it."

"You need to hear it, though, before it's too late."

"Fine. I'll talk to him."

There was a sound behind me, and I turned to see if someone was there. I didn't see anything, but I realized we'd been speaking with the door not fully closed. Had Brady been standing just out of sight, listening to our conversation?

A part of me really hoped that he had.

I left my dad to his mail and returned to the living room to find Liz snoring gently from the couch and Brady nowhere in sight.

It was time to start thinking about what we should do for dinner, but before I went to the kitchen to rustle something up, I decided to search for my brother. I found him upstairs in his room, just sitting on the side of the bed and gazing out of the window.

Summoning my nerve, I gave a light rap on the doorway and stepped inside.

"Hey," he said.

"Hey."

From somewhere in the distance, I could hear the distinct whoosh of wood on metal. Skateboards. Stepping further into the room, I moved to Brady's bed and sat as well, watching through the window as Chris and some of his friends skated past on the street, whooping and hollering all the way.

"I heard what you said to Dad about football," Brady told me, his eyes still on the kids. "Thanks."

"No problem."

I glanced at him, at his innocent young face, so unmarked by time, and I could clearly see the sadness of too many lost yesterdays that we as brothers had never shared and never would.

"My mom was born Amish," I began softly. "I know you know that. And I'm sure you know she gave up everything about her Amish life when she married Dad. But she passed something on to me before she died. She passed on her love for that other life."

Brady shifted, his eyes still on the kids outside who were now just specks in the distance. "Why are you telling me this? You don't owe me any explanations about why you decided to stay."

"But you're wrong. I do. When Dad came back for me, I could barely remember that I had ever lived anywhere but right there in Lancaster County. My mother's parents treated me like their own son, and I felt safe and loved there. I was afraid to give up that security because I'd been forced to give it up once before, when my mom died and Dad sent me to live with people I had only just met. I didn't have the maturity to figure out what I was turning my back on, Brady. I didn't stop to think that my staying meant you would grow up with an older brother you hardly ever saw. The truth is, the three of you seemed complete without me. I didn't want to mess with that. And I confess I didn't want to be messed with, either."

He was quiet for a long moment. "I can't believe Dad let you go like that. He would never let me stay somewhere just because I wanted to. He should have made you come."

"I think he wrestles with that decision too. But I also know he was torn by wanting to do what would honor my mom. When she died, he didn't just lose a wife, you know? He lost the mother of his child. There were no easy fixes. I understand, and I have forgiven him. None of us is perfect."

Outside the window, the whirring sounds of the skateboard wheels had all but faded.

"You're going back, aren't you," he said, his voice flat. "For good this time."

"I am going to join the Amish church, yes. It's what I want. It's where I belong."

"Because we're not good enough for you."

I sought his gaze, but he still wouldn't look at me. "Because I am Amish to my very core. Because I can see now that this is God's will for my life."

He grunted.

"You told me, Brady, just after I got here, that you love football but that you would give it up before you would live your life as a slave to it. You have the right to decide what kind of life you're going to lead and if football is going to be a part of it. We all have the freedom to decide what kind of life we will lead. I am choosing to go back because it's the life I love. It's who I want to be. It's who God made me to be."

Finally, he turned to look at me, his eyes still filled with accusation. "If you'd made the right decision the first time, none of this would be happening now. Don't you get that?"

I let his question settle between us, his pain hanging there in the air. *Lord, show me how to make him understand.*

A burst of laughter wafted up from far down the street. Chris and his friends were racing back our way, and in that moment, I knew what to say.

"Look at Chris," I said, pointing out of the window.

Brady did as I said, turning back. "Yeah? So?"

"So what do you see when you look at him?"

He shrugged, defensive. "I don't know. He's a kid."

"Right. He's young. In fact, he's still just a child, right?"

Brady glared at me, as if to say, *Enough already.* "Fine. Yes. He's just a child. So what?"

I waited a beat and then replied, "So he's just about the same age I was when our father left the choice of where to live up to me. The same age I was when I made the choice that ended up having such a big impact on your life. On all our lives."

I wasn't trying to excuse what had happened. I wasn't trying to justify it. I was just trying to get my brother to see the truth, that a very adult decision had been thrust upon me when I was still just a little boy.

After a long moment, understanding began to dawn in his eyes. It was there for only a flicker and then he blinked it away, but I knew what I had seen.

My point was made. Maybe now Brady would finally find it within himself to forgive me.

THIRTY

Over the rest of that evening and the next, sure enough, my little brother slowly came around. As the chip on his shoulder melted away, he began to smile at me more, hang out with me more, take an interest in me more. By the end of Thursday night, we were lounging on the floor of the living room, fighting it out on the digital football field like any two brothers in any family in any house anywhere. It felt good, especially when Dad and Liz settled on the couch behind us, picked sides, and began hollering along with us as ad hoc cheerleaders.

My dad seemed to settle back into home life with ease, showing a tenderness with his still-injured wife that I hadn't known he possessed. As he took over my duties one by one, caring for her and serving up meals and managing things around the house, I found my own time freeing up more and more. By Friday morning, I knew I could start making plans to head home. Dad was expecting me to stay through Thanksgiving, but that meant waiting another whole week. I just didn't think I could risk taking that much time. I needed to get back to Rachel as soon as possible, to save what was left of our relationship. To convince her that all of our years together had not been in vain.

To convince her my commitment was real. And for a lifetime.

Once I explained the situation to Dad, he seemed to understand—especially when I told him that my intention was to marry Rachel in the following fall. He actually got tears in his eyes when I said that, and then he cleared his throat and clapped me on the back and said he wished us all the best.

After he and I talked, I decided to go online to try changing the date on the airline ticket myself. But as I logged in and started to pull up the website, I had an odd feeling, as if there was something important here I needed to understand. Confused, I sat back in the chair and thought about what else God might have for me to learn.

Closing my eyes, the image that came to mind was that of *Daadi* and of the bishop and elders who had so kindly and wisely given their blessing on this trip. That's when it struck me. By flying home, I was exercising the privilege they had granted me as the son of an *Englischer* and one not yet baptized into the church. That was all well and good, but if I truly wanted to come home in the right spirit—as a man ready to commit to the Amish life in full—then I should not fly, no matter how eager I was to get there. I should follow the standard Amish custom and go by ground instead. I hated risking more days away from Rachel, but I knew God would bless this sign of submission and patience and obedience. I would take the slow way—the Amish way—and trust Him to handle the rest.

After exploring my options, I ended up reserving a seat on the train. I'd be leaving Sunday evening at seven, which would get me home early Wednesday afternoon. That meant I would still get there before Thanksgiving—and I would have almost the entire weekend here to enjoy my California family before it was time to go.

Once the trip was booked, I called and left a message for *Daadi*, giving him the date and time of my arrival. I was going to tell my dad about the change in my travel plans as well, but Liz said he'd just run out to the store, so I went up to my room instead and spent the next half hour getting myself organized and partially packed.

I owed Lark a proper goodbye, not to mention her payment as my tutor, and it seemed as good a time as any to take care of both. I pulled my cell phone from my pocket and texted her to see if she was free for a few minutes.

She was.

Before I left, I brought the Leica downstairs to put back where it belonged. Dad had returned and was in the study, but before I could even tell him about the train trip, he looked up and spoke.

"I see you found your mother's camera."

I froze, staring first at him and then down at the device I was holding. "What?"

"The camera. It was your mother's. I gave it to her." He stood and came over to me for a closer look.

I blinked. "Are you serious? I figured it belonged to Liz."

"Nah, I bought it in Frankfurt for your mom at the beginning of our second tour to Germany." He took it from my hands. He held the thing to his eye and twisted the lens, and then he pulled back and shook his head as if to say he didn't understand the attraction. "She wasn't thrilled to be back, and I was trying to find a way to lift her spirits. I realized she hadn't fooled with photography for a while, so I sprang for the best German camera I could afford and surprised her with it."

I gaped at him, thinking of the photos in her box, of the gap in time and how much sharper and more beautiful the pictures had been when she'd started up again. Of course. She had taken them with the Leica.

My father handed it back to me and I took it from him carefully, as if it were a priceless vase or a newborn chick. "It's yours if you want it," he said. Then he added, "I mean, I know there are restrictions and all, but it was your mother's. Maybe you could just keep it as a souvenir and not actually use it."

Finally, I found my voice. "Are you sure? Lark said it's pretty valuable. You could probably sell it for a thousand dollars, maybe more."

He shrugged. "It's not mine to sell."

I thanked him, but a strange sadness filled me as I imagined taking it back to Lancaster County where it would cease to be useful to anyone. My mother had loved this camera. She had loved what it could do to a snippet of time and light.

When I got to Lark's, we headed to a neighborhood park a few blocks over, looking like two good friends out for a stroll in the generous California sun. But there was uneasiness between us.

"Did your dad get home okay?"

"He did. Thanks."

We took a few more steps in silence.

"You came to say goodbye, didn't you?"

"I came to say thank you."

She cracked a weak smile. "And then goodbye."

I felt bad for her, remembering how kind she had been since the night we met. As I glanced at her there beside me, I realized afresh how much she had helped me sort things out while I was here, and not just with Dad and Brady. With her kiss she had, unknowingly, shown me how much I loved Rachel and yearned for the life that awaited me back home. "Yes," I said. "I'm leaving Sunday night."

She shook her head and laughed lightly. "Just like that."

"No."

Lark looked at me. "What do you mean? If you're leaving, you're leaving."

"Lark—"

"Is it because I kissed you? Is it because I told you how I felt about you?" Her voice was tight with disappointment. "'Cause we can go back to being just friends for now, if you want."

I shook my head, wishing she could understand. "It's because that's my home. It's where I want to be, where I'm supposed to be."

"You're choosing Rachel over any kind of life here."

"I'm choosing to be Amish, Lark. That's who I am. That's the life I am suited for."

She was silent for a few moments. A runner jogged past us.

"You didn't even give living here a chance. And this thing with your brother? You're just going to take off with him so mad at you? Do you really think that's a good idea?"

"A lot has happened in the last couple of days. Brady and I finally talked. My dad and I finally talked. We understand each other now. And they understand why I need to go back. *I* finally understand why I need to go back."

She said nothing.

"Do you remember when I first met with you and I told you how I came to be raised by my grandparents? You said it was crazy how I ended up with them."

"I didn't say that." She frowned.

I smiled. "You did. I told you my dad made it my decision on whether or not to stay with my Amish grandparents and you said, 'Wow. That's crazy.'"

I glanced at her, seeing that her cheeks had turned a faint but rosy pink.

"No, it's okay," I assured her. "You said I belonged with my father, and you were right. Kids do belong with their parents. Most of the time, that's the best place for them to be. But when my mother died, my dad faced a decision no dad is prepared to make. Maybe what he did wasn't the wisest choice or even what my mother would have wanted him to do, but God brought good out of that decision, Lark. That's what He does. He can take even our most misinformed choices and make good out of them. And I can't help thinking that whatever desirable qualities you see in me were born out of the way I was raised. I was raised Amish."

"But you don't have to stay Amish."

We had reached the park. I motioned to a bench in a sunny alcove by a bed of still-blooming impatiens.

"You're right," I said as we both sat down. "That's the very thing I didn't realize until I came here. I thought I had to discover who I was. But who I am is not something I need to discover. Who I am is something, with God's guidance, I decide. Just like you will decide who you will be."

"But what about your family here? What about the life you could have here?"

I knew that there was more to her question than that. What she was really wondering was if I'd stopped to consider what part she might play in my life if I stayed.

"I am who I am because of how I grew up. I love my dad and my brother and I even love Liz as my stepmother, but their lives are so hectic and disconnected from each other. And none of them think much about how God fits into the picture. I probably would have grown up just like Brady is growing up now if I had been raised the way he's being raised. I wouldn't be who I am at all."

"But that's my point. If you leave now, you'll lose all influence over them. Do you think that's right, just to abandon them that way?"

I shook my head. "I'm not abandoning them. Trust me, Lark, I'll have a far greater influence on them as an Amish man than I would if I stayed. And even if that was the only reason to go back, that would be reason enough."

She breathed in deeply and looked down at her empty hands. "But that's not the only reason."

"No."

Lark raised her head to face me. "You're going to ask her to marry you."

I nodded.

We were quiet for a moment.

"I know maybe you don't want to hear this, but I have you to thank for helping me realize where I want to be. And who I want to be."

She shook her head and smiled thinly. "So I'm supposed to say, 'You're welcome'?"

I touched her arm, friend to friend. "I mean it. God has orchestrated every aspect of my time here to answer a prayer that's been on my heart for a long while. You were a part of that."

She sighed.

"You've been a good friend, Lark. You taught me a lot. Not just about photography but about so many, many things. I'm really glad God put you in my life for these few weeks."

She turned her gaze to a pair of children off in the distance, running at full speed toward a swing set. "Would you think me terribly selfish if I told you I still wish you had decided to stay?"

I squeezed her arm and let go. "I'm humbled and flattered. But that's not the path I'm on. I know that now."

We sat there for a few minutes watching the children across from us squeal in delight as they pumped their legs, sending their swings higher and higher into the sky. Watching them reminded me again of Rachel, of the day I fell in love with her on the swings so many years ago.

Lark and I were mostly silent as we walked back to her house. When we got there, she turned to give me one final goodbye hug, but I had something else I needed to do first. I led her over to my car, unlocked it, and reached inside, pulling out an envelope of cash with her name written on it.

"Your fee," I said, handing it over with a flourish. "Along with my thanks. You were an outstanding tutor."

I was smiling, but her expression quickly went blank. She was quiet for a moment, and then she told me she simply couldn't take it. "I know what we had started out as a financial arrangement, but it became much more. So much more. I wouldn't feel right taking your money."

I was not at all surprised. Before I left to come over, I'd realized she wasn't going to accept it. But then I'd had another idea, a good one. Without pressing things further, I slipped the envelope into my jacket pocket and gave her an understanding nod.

"I had a feeling you wouldn't," I said, and then I leaned back into the car, this time to retrieve the Leica. "This, on the other hand, might be a different story."

I held the camera out to her. She just stared at it for a long moment. "I don't understand," she whispered.

"I want you to have this. I honestly do."

"Holy cow. What? Why?"

"For two reasons."

Before I could even list those reasons, she was reaching out to touch it with the tip of one finger, gently, reverently, the way one might touch a child, or a lover.

"First, it needs to belong to someone who would really appreciate it—and really use it. I can't think of anyone who might enjoy it more than you. I want you to take it and make the most of it in my mother's memory."

In response, a sound bubbled from Lark's throat, a cross between a cry of joy and a sob. She put a hand to her mouth even as her eyes filled with tears.

"Second, I wanted to give you something special—"

"You can say that again," she whispered, blinking away the tears, her eyes still on the camera.

"Something that could symbolize how amazing you are and how very glad I am you came into my life. I owe you more than you could ever imagine."

After that, I grew silent, still holding out the camera, waiting for her to take it.

Slowly, she did. Cradling it her hands, she studied it as if she'd never even seen it before.

"I can't…I don't…"

I smiled. "Yes you can. Please. I want you to have it. It would make me happy."

She met my eyes, almost convinced. "What about your dad? Does he even know what this thing is worth?"

I nodded. "I told him. And then he said it belongs to me. And now I'm saying it belongs to you."

She looked down at her new treasure, a smile slowly spreading across her face even as tears filled her eyes. Lark wasn't the girl for me, but I knew she would make someone else very happy someday.

And there would be beautiful photographs all along the way.

Thirty-One

I spent the weekend with my family, enjoying every moment with them as I never had before. For the first time ever, I felt completely comfortable staying in my dad's house. Except for wanting to get back to Rachel, I wasn't overly anxious to head home, nor torn about leaving California. I knew where I was headed and that God was directing me there.

On Saturday Dad and Brady and I went to Disneyland, a place no one is ever too old—or too Amish—to enjoy. Then on Sunday, I convinced my family to attend Lark's church in hopes that a more contemporary style of worship would appeal to their highly contemporary lives. I was happy to see that all three of them appeared to enjoy the music and were intrigued by what the pastor had to say. We found Lark later among some of her friends, and I introduced my family to them so at least they now knew a few people there. My hope was that this would perhaps encourage them to go again. After lunch, we went for a long coastal drive in the muscle car—Dad was very grateful for the cosmetic work I had done on the upholstery—and I even got to drive it for a stretch, my final turn at a wheel before giving up my license for good.

On Sunday evening, before we left for the train station, I hung all of my *Englisch* pants and shirts Dad and Liz had given me in the closet and changed into the clothes I had worn on the flight out, my Amish clothes. Never had they fit so well. Never had they felt so right. Though I had laundered them before putting them away, I thought I could still smell the fragrance of Lancaster County in the threads of my shirt. Placing my hat on my head, I stood and looked at myself in the mirror, glad my hair had already begun to grow again. Standing there and regarding myself, I remembered a similar moment of mirror-gazing my first day there, when I was wearing my new *Englisch* clothes and was so eager to blend in. At the time, I wondered whether I was still Amish or not on the inside. Now that I knew the answer to that question, it was a relief to look Amish on the outside again as well.

I picked up my backpack to rearrange its contents and remembered the list I had been compiling. I opened the notebook, glanced at it, and couldn't help but laugh at what I had written there.

People drive with their windows rolled up, no matter what the weather.

Used clothes are undesirable.

Young people text to communicate.

The number of contacts in your cell phone is too numerous to keep in your memory.

Young women flirt with complete strangers.

Homes with just three people can have a dining table large enough to seat more than ten.

Fires are worked by remote control.

Houses can be kept by little work on your part.

One man can own three cars.

A house can have rooms that are never even used.

Individual cups of hot coffee can be made in a wide variety of flavors with the push of a button.

Dog mess must be picked up.

There are special plastic bags manufactured just for that purpose.

The Pacific Ocean shines like glass.

Some young women tint their hair with colors not found in nature.

Reading and researching simply for knowledge is uncommon, at least once one is no longer in school.

The first—and often only—step in any quest for knowledge is to search the Internet.

Young women ask for rides from near strangers.

People volunteer all sorts of personal information without provocation or invitation.

The generations are all so divided, even in church.

Opportunities for service and involvement abound.

Sometimes, technology really can bring people closer together instead of driving them apart.

People own so much stuff that they have to rent space in which to store it.

It seemed like a very long time ago that I had begun writing down what it meant to be a part of the *Englisch* world so that I might discover if I was meant to live in it. I didn't need the list to show me—I never had—and I didn't need it to prove to myself that I knew where I belonged. I crumpled the page into a ball and tossed it into the wastebasket.

Next, I turned to the strongbox of my mother's photos. Though I would leave them here with my father, I decided that I ought to bring a few home with me to show *Mammi* and *Daadi*. I thought perhaps they would find comfort in the knowledge that their prodigal daughter had spent her years in Germany trying to recreate, through photos, the world she had left behind in Lancaster County.

I opened the box and withdrew all of the envelopes of pictures, laying them across my bed so I could choose which ones I wanted. I flipped through the photos slowly, memorizing the images I wouldn't be taking with me, trying to pick the ones I would bring home to show my grandparents. Once I'd done that, I also decided to keep one as a memento for myself, the only picture in there that featured not just me but my mother as well. I looked to be about four, small and innocent and completely unaware of how my life would change. We were at a duck pond somewhere in Germany, and she had probably asked a passerby to take the photo of us, or maybe my dad had done it. In the image, she was crouched next to me so that our cheeks touched, her right arm tight around my shoulders. We were both smiling, but my gaze was on the creatures who were vying for the bread that I held in my hands. It was a mere second in time as my mother and I fed ducks on a sunny day in a little town I didn't even know the name of. I touched the edge of the photo, knowing Mom had also touched it many years ago, and then I reached into my backpack to slip it and the others into my Bible.

I gathered up the envelopes of photos and was about to lay them back in the strongbox when something round inside caught my eye. At first glance I thought it might be a coin, but when I looked closer I realized that it was a lock, a small metal circle with a keyhole at its center. Studying the box's interior even more closely, I realized that there was a seam running around its perimeter. This had to be a little door, one that opened to reveal a narrow, separate compartment underneath.

Heart pounding, I lifted the box and shook it, listening for the sound of moving objects inside. I heard only the faintest whiffle of paper on metal.

More photographs? Something else entirely?

If only I had a key! Intrigued to my core, I set the box down and started for the garage, intending to get a small screwdriver to try and work the lock free. Before I even reached the bedroom door, however, I froze in my tracks.

The key.

I did have a key.

I had the key from the day my mother died, the one she'd been clutching when she collapsed to the floor, never to awaken. It was a small key. Surely it fit a small lock. Perhaps this lock.

I came back and sat on the edge of the bed, my heart pounding even harder now. I knew it seemed like a long shot, but somehow I felt certain, deep in my soul, that the key I'd kept in my cigar box all these years was for this very lock.

Heart pounding, I stared at the keyhole for a long moment then finally went out to the top of the stairs and called down to my father.

"What's up?" he called back from somewhere not too far away.

"Can you come here for a minute? I need to show you something."

I don't know what I expected his reaction to be. Shock. Excitement. Enthusiasm. Instead, once he stepped into the room and I showed him the keyhole and the outlines of the hidden compartment, he just shrugged.

"Yeah?"

"What is this?" I demanded. Shaking the box, I added, "I can tell there's something in here. Something she locked beneath this little door."

His eyes narrowed as his expression grew distant. "I don't think it's any big deal, Tyler. I seem to recall…" His voice trailed off.

"What? Is it more photos?"

He shook his head. "Letters, I want to say. I think that's where she kept her letters from home."

"But why lock them away? Was there something secret about them?"

Again, he shrugged. "I guess there could've been. I never paid much attention. You're welcome to them. Take the whole box. Maybe once you get home, you can jimmy the lock."

I nodded, silent, not telling him that I was pretty sure I had the key.

"Thanks," I muttered, and then I shut the box and lowered it into my duffel bag.

"Or we can try it here. Maybe pry it open real quick before we go—"

"No. It's okay. I'll wait."

Without a doubt, we could have jimmied the lock with just a tool or two. But I knew I needed to resist that urge until I was finally home, no matter how excruciating the wait would be. Prying the little door off seemed disrespectful to my mother somehow, and far different from opening it with the key. Also, I was absolutely certain that this was what God expected of me. Patience was an important virtue—a vital one in Amish life—and I was already practicing patience by taking the train rather than flying. Now I would resist the urge to break open this lock. Shortcuts were not an option here, not if I wanted to be obedient to Him. I would wait until I was home to see what was inside.

At least I couldn't help feeling that this obedience was going to be rewarded. *With patience comes knowledge*, I could almost hear *Daadi* say in an oft-repeated Amish sentiment. And knowledge was something I still needed. Specifically, I needed knowledge about what my mother had been doing with that key when God called her Home.

Together, Dad and I headed downstairs, where Liz and Brady both did a bit of a double take at my transformation back into an Amish man. They didn't seem displeased, just surprised. I hugged Liz goodbye as Dad and Brady went into the garage to start the car.

"Thank you for coming," she said as we embraced. "And for my gardens. I can't tell you how much that means to me."

"You're welcome. And thanks for sharing with me about my mom. I can't tell you how much *that* means to me."

When we pulled apart her eyes were misted.

"She would be so very proud of you. I know I am."

Her words both cheered me and pierced me. "I'm sorry if I ever made it seem that I didn't need you as a mother."

Liz shook her head and dabbed at her eyes. "And I'm sorry if I ever made it seem that I didn't love you like a son."

We embraced again.

"Will you come to see me?" I asked when we parted a second time. "And I don't mean in Philly. I want you and Dad and Brady to come spend some downtime with me and *Daadi* and *Mammi* at the home place. And I want you to meet Rachel, even before she becomes my wife."

"I'd really like that."

"Goodbye, Liz. Take care of that ankle."

"Will do."

My next farewell was for the little pup yipping at my heels. Impulsively, I bent down and scooped him up for a quick hug, marveling at how light and tiny he was. Frisco was no Timber, but he was okay.

I handed him off to Liz, hiked my duffel to my shoulder, and stepped into the garage.

The drive to Union Station in Los Angeles was relatively quick. Though the tension between Brady and me was gone, I could tell he was struggling to accept my decision. As I embraced both him and my dad at the station, I again reiterated my invitation for them to come out and visit in the summer.

"We'll make a farmer of you yet," I teased my little brother, chucking him on the arm with my fist.

I was kidding, but his expression remained serious. "I just don't get how you could want to live that way for the rest of your life."

"I can only say God has given me a desire to live simply. You have a bit of that desire too. I saw it in you just the other day."

He rolled his eyes like the fourteen-year-old he was. "I'm pretty sure you didn't."

"I'm sure I did. When you told me you wanted to go backpacking in New Zealand, you said it would be nice to get away from school and homework and even other people."

"Okay, whatever."

"Not 'whatever,' Brady. This is important. When you said that, you were responding to that call on everyone's heart to live a simple, surrendered life. It might be a just barely perceptible itch for you, but it's there nonetheless."

He thought for a moment. "Okay. So?"

"So for me, it's not an itch. It's an irresistible, all-encompassing longing. And *that's* how I can live that way for the rest of my life."

Brady furrowed his brow as he considered the truth of my words.

"Come out next summer. Spend a month with me. Unplug."

Finally, he smiled. "I'll think about it, but I'm not making any promises. Especially if you try to make me milk a cow or slop a pig."

We shared a laugh.

With my time up, I gave Brady one last embrace. Then I turned to my dad. Though our hug was quick and our words simple, his final "I love you, son," stayed with me, keeping me warm my entire journey home.

I reached Lancaster County two and a half very long, uneventful days later. At least I'd had my thoughts and God's calming presence for company. From time to time I'd touch the strongbox inside my duffel and would sense there was one last thing I needed to do to complete my journey, and it had to do with what lay inside that locked compartment. I couldn't shake the notion that I had been given an opportunity to do something for my mother all these years after she had passed from this life to the next, something that only I could.

The trip had been exhausting, to say the least, but the last hour made every moment of it worthwhile. Watching the scenery outside my window grow ever more pastoral, ever more familiar, my heart began to race with a childlike anticipation. Drifted snow lay across the rolling hills like folds of white muslin. Pine trees seemed ready for Christmas. The subdued November palette was very different from California's perpetual vibrancy, and yet I found it comforting. As we rumbled on toward the Lancaster station, I could see Amish buggies here and there on the streets among the cars and trucks and motorcycles. I was almost home.

As soon as I reached the station and spotted *Daadi* and *Mammi* waiting for me there, I could tell they had gotten my letter. Gone were the worried looks and shared glances from prior to my trip. Now they were all smiles, so glad to see me, so eager to hear of every last adventure, so relieved and pleased to know I had made my decision for the church at last.

Back at the house, after an effusive greeting from Timber, I sat at the table while *Mammi* served me a late lunch of ham and cheesy potatoes and green beans and my favorite peach and raspberry crumble. She and *Daadi* both joined me there as I ate, asking all about my father and Liz and Brady and how they were, and then catching me up on all the news from home and from Jake, who was doing fine at farrier school out in Missouri.

As my grandparents and I sat in the warm Amish kitchen, I couldn't get over the quiet and peace that surrounded us, the lack of interruption. The absence of devices to divide us. Finally, I showed the two of them my mother's photos from Germany, explaining what I had managed to conclude from the entire collection, that she'd taken pictures as a way to capture scenes reminiscent of home. Gazing at the photos, they both seemed deeply touched at the thought—and somehow deeply healed as well.

I didn't want our time around the table to end, but before I saw Rachel, I wanted to take care of what lay locked inside the strongbox. Suddenly I didn't think I could wait another minute.

I excused myself to unpack and headed up to my room.

I retrieved the key first from the cigar box and then removed the strongbox from my duffel. I felt a strange sense of calm as I inserted the key into the lock. I knew it would fit. I knew it would open the lock.

The key turned as easily as if it were only a lever to open a door. Sure enough, inside was a small stack of envelopes—letters from home, just as Dad had said.

I gingerly pulled the stack from the box and laid each one out on the bed in front of me, counting seven in all. Studying the exteriors of the envelopes, I noted that five of them were all in the same handwriting, and though they bore no return addresses, they had all been mailed to my mother. The other two envelopes had nothing on them at all, no addresses or stamps or postmarks or anything. Taking a quick peek inside each, I saw that they were both in my mother's handwriting.

Perhaps those two were letters she'd been writing in return.

I sat back on the bed and considered how to proceed. After a moment, I reached out and arranged the five addressed envelopes by order of their dated postmark. I decided I would read through those first, in order, and save the other two—the ones she had written herself—for last.

With trembling hands, I picked up the oldest dated envelope and pulled out the letter from inside. Skimming its contents, I soon realized that it was a love letter, from someone named Jonah. He must have lived in Lancaster County, because throughout the whole thing he kept pleading with her to "come back home." Setting that one aside, I continued on with the next and then the next. Each one was more of the same, filled with urgings to come home and pledges of undying affection—apparently unrequited—all from this Jonah guy, whoever he was. It wasn't until I got to the fourth letter that the hairs on my arms began to stand on end.

As I read through various details in that note—about his family, about his personal life—I realized that this wasn't some random guy named Jonah my mom had won the affection of. This was a Jonah I knew—and knew well. It was *Uncle* Jonah. Jonah Bowman. Cousin Anna's father. Aunt Sarah's husband.

I gasped, looking up from the note as if the man might materialize right there in the room in front of me.

Jonah had been in love with my mother before he married her sister? I couldn't believe it. In all the years I had been here, I'd never heard one whisper of rumor or insinuation about a relationship between my mother and her future brother-in-law. In fact, I was having trouble believing it now, until I continued my reading and put more of the pieces together. From what I was seeing here and from what my aunt Sarah had already told me, Jonah had courted both my mom and my aunt when the three of them were on their *rumspringa*. Apparently, it had become something of a love triangle the day he secretly confessed to my mother that he loved her, even though they both knew that Sarah loved him.

Feeling as if I were moving through a dream, I read the fifth note.

Dearest Sadie: I know you told me you don't feel the same for me, but over time you could learn to love me. I know you could. I also know Sarah would understand eventually. She would forgive you. We are meant to be together, Sadie...

So many emotions were pounding inside my head as I tucked away his notes and moved on to the two unsent letters written in my mother's handwriting. I sensed only a momentary jolt of guilt as I opened the flaps and withdrew each one. Still, I knew I was meant to read all of this. I couldn't explain it, but I knew I was meant to. Even my dad thought so.

I smoothed out the stationery on the older of the two letters and began to read. It had been dated the year I was born.

Dear Jonah,

I am so pleased to hear the news that you and my sister will be wed at last. I know now you have come to understand that you and I were never meant to be together. Sarah is the soul mate I never could have been.

You should know that I don't blame you for what happened, but I do wonder, often, if you realize I had no choice but to leave so that Sarah could be spared the heartache of knowing the man she loved was in love with someone else—her own sister, no less—and so that you might forget about me and turn to her instead. Making this whole situation even more painful is the fact that she can never know the truth of my leaving, lest it break her heart twice over.

Hearing now that the two of you are to be wed, I am finally at peace about my decision to go. If it spared my beloved sister such heartache, and it led you to love her at last and to make a life with her as your wife, then it has been worth all of the sacrifice in the end.

That is why I am writing now, to say that I forgive you and that I am so happy to hear the news. May your life together be blessed!

I am not even sure if I will be able to send you this letter. I do not have an address for you where it would be assured to escape the notice of others. I shall end it here and try to figure out how to get it to you. If you are reading these words, it means that I succeeded.

Please know that I wish the two of you all the best and I hope you find love as deep and true and everlasting as I have with Duke.

All the best,
Sadie

I sat back, realizing that I held in my hand the final answer I sought. My mother left Lancaster County out of love for her sister. But because of the circumstances, she could never tell that to another living soul.

I reached for the final envelope, expecting it to be dated around the same time as the other. Instead, what I saw in the date line made me gasp aloud. It hadn't been written then. It had been written eight years later.

On the day before she died.

It, too, was a letter, but to Sarah this time. Far less formal than the one she'd written years before to Jonah, this seemed to be an olive branch of sorts, a reaching out from sister to sister. I held it up and began to read.

My dear sister Sarah,

I don't know how many times I have tried to write this letter to you. And here I am trying again. I only have a few minutes before Tyler gets home from kindergarten, so I'll make it quick.

This time of year, my heart always grows so heavy as I think of you celebrating your birthday without me there at your side. It has been eight and a half years since I left, and every year I have thought of you on this day and missed you more than words can say.

We are back in the States now, as Mamm may have told you, and I am eager to finally, finally come home for a visit. I spoke to Mamm on the shop phone just a few days ago about coming to visit. Her heart was still as hardened to me as ever, but I plan to persist. If I do make it home, perhaps you will bring yourself to speak to me this time? That is my most fervent prayer!

You should know that I believe God gifted me Duke in a way I don't think I could explain to anyone, least of all Mamm and Daed. I am aware of how very much I have grieved them, but I will honor my commitment to my marriage vows. And though I miss Lancaster County with every breath in my body, I know I cannot return, at least not for more than a visit. I will be forever torn, but it helps to know that you are happy, as Mamm said. On the phone, she spoke of your sweet little ones, your beautiful girls. And I am so grateful to God that Jonah has found his soul mate in you.

I know you have forgiven me for leaving because that is your way, as it is mine. All I can say is that I had my reasons, and I am at peace with them. Regardless, you still are and will always be my best friend. Even as time and distance separate us, I hope

The letter ended there, midsentence. I could almost picture it, the sight of my mother scribbling away until I came home from school, then being interrupted before she was done. She must have tucked the letter away and planned to finish writing it the next day.

But the next day she died. She died with the key in her hand.

I folded the letter and placed it back inside the envelope, knowing without question I would give it to my aunt Sarah. It wasn't quite complete, but it said enough. It said what my mother had longed to say for years. That she loved her sister. That she had held on to hope. That she thought of Sarah as her best friend to the end.

Her other letter, the one to Jonah, I would not deliver. I knew it would serve no purpose. Nor was there any reason to keep any of the notes he had written to her either. After setting the one for Sarah aside, I took all of the others and stuffed them into my pocket. Downstairs, I grabbed some twine from the mudroom, pulled on my jacket and boots, and headed outside to the pond, thankful that it was not yet frozen solid.

I looked about for the right-sized rock, and then I withdrew the pages from my pocket. With the twine I secured to the rock the pages that revealed the truth of why my mother left, making sure the knots were taut. Then I flung the rock with its cargo to the center of the pond my mother loved and missed so very much, where it sank out of view.

The paper would become fragments, the fragments would become nothing. Even the twine would eventually disintegrate. In time, there would be only a rock at the bottom of a lovely pond.

I waited until the water's surface was calm again and then I turned back toward the house. I would save the delivery of Sarah's letter for another day, as God would lead.

Right now, there was someone vitally important I needed to see.

I made it to Rachel's a little after five, though it felt later. Thanks to the early-setting sun, it was already dark. The moment she opened the door, the blue of her eyes was the only spot of color I saw in the whole room.

"Rachel," I said, removing my hat.

"You're back," she said softly.

"*Ya*. I'm home."

I wanted her to drop the pan and towel she was holding in her hands and run into my arms. Instead, she simply turned and led the way back to the kitchen.

"Can you come out for a walk?" I asked, now gripping the hat brim nervously in my hands.

She shared a look with her mother, who was busy dropping dumplings into a large vat of bubbling broth.

"*Ya*," Rachel said finally, and then she went to pull on her winter coverings.

Outside, we ambled down the driveway in the crisp evening air toward a small grove of walnut trees that flanked the nearest pasture. We were silent as we moved from the shoveled pavement of the drive to the crunchy snow of the lawn and then continued on, side by side, our boots breaking twin paths in the snow as we went. I wanted so much to hold her hand, but I knew I didn't dare try. Not yet, anyway.

For the first time that I could ever remember, I felt nervous around her. If only I could know what was going through her mind. She seemed deep in thought. Far, far away. Before I began what I had come there to say, I asked if she'd had a chance to think things over herself since we talked.

"That's all I've been doing since we last spoke. Thinking. And praying."

She didn't offer up more than that, so I began to share my heart with her.

"I have so much to tell you, Rachel. It's amazing, really, everything that God showed me while I was in California."

Praying for the right words as we continued to stroll, I launched into a summary of all that I had questioned and explored and come to understand during my time away. I knew she'd heard much of it before, in our phone calls and my letters. But this time I needed to make sure she understood fully the path I'd been on and how it had led me directly back home, back to the Amish life and back to her—for good.

Once we were standing in the midst of the grove, I took her elbow and slowed to stop, giving her arm a gentle tug so that she would turn to face me. Even there in the darkness, her eyes were sapphire against the white.

"I'm sorry it has taken me so long to reach this point," I told her, releasing my hold on her arm. "You deserved better."

She looked down, so I reached out and put a finger to her chin, tilting her face up toward mine.

"You did, Rach, but the point is, I'm here now. I'm finally where you've been wanting me to be all along."

She nodded and then glanced away.

"Now that I am here, there's just one question left to ask," I whispered.

To my dismay, she took a step back, away from me.

"I think I know what that question is," she said. Again, I sensed fear from her.

"Rachel, I—"

"And it's not that I don't want to marry you, Tyler, because I do. I always have. I just...I..." Her voice trailed away.

"You're afraid."

She turned to me. "*Ya!*" she exclaimed, obviously relieved she didn't have to say those words herself. "I am afraid! I hear what you are saying, but how am I to believe you? How am I to know you will still feel this way ten, twenty, fifty years from now?"

I stepped forward, taking both of her hands in mine, wishing she could see straight into my heart. "I know you're afraid I might regret joining the church, that I'll find out some day down the road that I don't want to be Amish anymore, and that my other life is calling to me. And I'll be stuck."

"*Ya,*" she whispered.

"But I'm not my mother, Rachel. That is not going to happen."

Tears welled up in the corners of her eyes. "How do you know that? You can't know that."

I didn't tell her what I had learned from the hidden part of my mother's box, the true reason she had run away all those years ago. Perhaps someday I might share that knowledge with Rachel, but for now, she would just have to trust me. Love had been the thing that sent my mother away from Lancaster County, but love—not just for Rachel but for God and for the entirety of my Amish life—had been the thing that brought me home.

"I don't want any other life. This is who I am. This is who I choose to be."

"But what if someday you wish you had chosen differently?" The tears that rimmed her eyelids spilled down her cheeks.

I squeezed her hands and pulled her close to me. "I have faith. I am being sure of what I cannot see. I can't know the future, Rachel. And neither can you. But this spring when I am baptized I will promise to serve God, to be a member of this district with all of its rights and responsibilities and blessings. I will promise those things on faith, trusting that God will empower me to keep those promises. And I know He will. God was with me when I came here at six, and He's led me back here again at twenty-three because this is His will for my life. This is where I belong. And now I am asking you to have faith in me. I love you, Rachel. I am asking you to trust the man I have become, the man I will be for the rest of my life. Will you? Will you trust me?"

She paused for a long moment, searching my eyes for some truth she might find there. Then finally, slowly, she brought my hands to her lips and kissed them, brushing my folded fingers across her moist cheek.

"*Ya*," she whispered. "I will."

I bent to touch my forehead to hers, the brim of my hat covering the top of her winter bonnet as joy swept over me.

Our hands were still clasped together, our foreheads still touching, as I began to whisper, "Thank you, thank you," over and over, in gratitude to God and to Rachel. She was crying softly, but her tears were sweetly happy.

"Will you marry me, Rachel?" I murmured.

She laughed through her tears. "I would love to marry you, Tyler."

I bent down to steal a kiss from her, but she let me have it willingly.

An eager breeze, bitter cold in the darkness, spun around us, lifting the strings of Rachel's bonnet and tickling my nose.

With a grunt, I broke off our kiss, brushed the strings away. Then I pulled her closer and kissed her again, already counting the days until I could call her my wife.

The morning of my baptism, I walked out to my mother's pond, knowing it was still partially frozen and I wouldn't be able to see my reflection in the murky mid-March water. But I didn't care. It almost seemed appropriate that the man who had stared back at me all those years was hidden from my view now. There on the bank, I sank to my knees on the wet ground, Timber nosing me worriedly. I coaxed his face away and patted his head. Then I whispered a prayer of gratitude to God for protecting me from the moment I arrived in Lancaster County as a six-year-old—alone and afraid—and for surrounding me with people who loved me. I thanked Him for my family, for Rachel, and for the new life we would forge together, starting this fall. Since returning from my father's in November and making things right with her, I had seen our relationship grow by leaps and bounds as she slowly came to see for herself that she really did have nothing to fear.

I thanked Him for faith, for grace and mercy.

For loving me when I was *Englisch* and loving me no more and no less now that I would be Amish.

I thanked Him for giving me the freedom to choose the life I wanted to live and for showing me His will for that life.

I thanked Him for the capacity to love other people.
I rose from the frosted ground. Timber barked joyfully.
Let's run, the dog seemed to say.
And so we did.

I'd witnessed plenty of baptisms in my seventeen years in Lancaster County, including Rachel's, but I had never listened as fully to the words of commitment as I did later that morning at the worship service.

I knelt with the five other young adults who were to be baptized alongside me. I renounced the devil and the world. I committed myself to Christ and Christ alone, and I promised to uphold the *Ordnung* of my district and to serve in ministry should the lot ever fall to me. One of the deacons then poured water through the bishop's hands over my head. The water was cool and cleansing, and tiny rivers slid down my collar to trail down my back. I stood and the bishop leaned forward to kiss me on my cheek, a holy kiss of welcome.

I had never felt more connected. I had never felt more a part of anything in my life.

In July, that feeling strengthened when my California family remained true to their promise and came out for a stay at the farm. I think we were all a little nervous at first, but they seemed game to unplug and experience the "simple life" for the ten days of their visit. In turn, I did my best to keep them occupied and show them a good time.

That first day, I introduced Brady to several Amish cousins close to his age, and they hit it off right away, much to my relief. My dad wanted to explore the workshop, where he began peppering me with questions, marveling at the ingenious ways our tools had been adapted for nonelectrical use. While we were busy out there, Liz spent time in the kitchen with *Mammi*, learning to make biscuits from scratch.

The first few days of their visit went well, though at times they seemed to grow antsy and uncomfortable—and I heard a few under-the-breath remarks about the lack of air-conditioning, the early-to-bed-early-to-rise hours we kept, and the smell of manure wafting over from the farm next door. But by about the fourth day, I noticed that all three seemed to have relaxed significantly. Here there were no cell phones, no email, no iPads or voice mail or any other digital connections to their world back home and, thus unplugged, they began to flourish.

Brady's new friends taught him how to handle a horse and buggy and play Dutch Blitz, and he impressed them in turn with his prowess at our nightly volleyball games in the yard. As the week went on, my dad happily pitched in with buggy repairs, and one night at dinner Liz declared as her goal to take on all of *Mammi's* chores the next day so that the woman could put her feet up and rest. We all chuckled—both at the thought of Liz doing everything and of *Mammi* doing nothing—but in the end she came close to achieving her goal. Liz also endeared herself to me when she made a special effort to get to know Rachel, spending a day at her house canning with her and her mom, and then later taking both of them for a "girls day out" of lunch and shopping in Strasburg. Throughout everything, I was glad that Dad, Liz, and Brady seemed to find a comfortable familiarity with my way of life, which had always felt so foreign and unapproachable to them before.

In the beginning, I knew that my California family was just humoring me, but by the end of their stay, they seemed genuinely glad they had come. And we all knew that I had been right. The simpler life was good for them. Even Brady had managed to break the habit of reaching for his cell phone every few minutes and instead focused on the people around him.

Best of all was the look on my father's face during our nightly Bible time. To my surprise, for the duration of their visit, *Daadi* tucked away the King James Bible and read from a more modern, easy-to-understand translation instead—an act which touched me deeply. As his gentle voice shared the Word of the Lord by candlelight, I could sense a willing eagerness in my father's eyes, a hunger, one I had never seen before. Each night, I silently prayed that he would come to know God on a personal level—and ultimately lead his wife and younger son there as well.

Despite the wonderful week we shared, it wasn't too difficult to say goodbye once it was over, because we knew they would be returning in just a few months for the wedding.

Rachel and I were finally joined together as husband and wife in October, in the very first ceremony of the fall marriage season because neither of us could wait a moment longer. With Jake serving as my *newehocker* and Brady sitting nearby as unofficial groomsman, Rachel and I took our vows and fulfilled at last the promise first begun on a school playground so many years before.

At the reception afterward, I was thrilled to see how easily Brady and my dad and Liz fit in with everyone else—Amish or not—and simply laughed and talked and helped us celebrate this special day. Their trip here over the summer had definitely made changes in all of them and had helped cement our relationships in a whole new way.

I also continued to feel a deeper connection with the other members of my district. The boy who had never belonged finally felt a part of something—fully—at last.

And then there was the woman sitting next to me. The whole day, I couldn't stop smiling, especially each time I caught the beautiful blue eyes of my bride. Gazing at her, I realized I wasn't just a full-blown member of my father's family out there or my mother's family back here or of this loving Amish community. Now I was also a part of something even more special—of Rachel and me and our own little family of two. God willing, that number would grow with the passing years. But I couldn't imagine my joy ever being more complete than it was now.

More than once that day, I thought of my mother and how much I wished she could have been at the wedding with us. But I had a peace about it, thanks to the legacy she had given me, the legacy of an Amish life.

For months I had saved the letter she'd written to Sarah, never quite feeling led to give it to her prior to now. But something told me this would be the day, especially given the sad moment she and I had shared together at Anna's wedding the year before. Perhaps now Sarah could finally find some peace.

This time, I was the one who found her at the fence, focused on the horses.

"Missing your best friend?" I said, coming to a stop behind my aunt.

Sarah startled, and then she smiled when she turned and realized it was me. Her smile faded away just as quickly.

"Best friends don't leave," she said, shaking her head. "They don't just run off without a word."

Stepping closer, I pulled the letter from my pocket and handed it to her. "I wouldn't be so sure about that," I said. Then I explained how I had found the item she was holding and that it was an unfinished letter to her, one that my mother had started writing the day before she died.

Sarah's face grew so pale that I took her arm and led her to a nearby stump, where she sat. As she unfolded the pages with trembling hands and began to read, I gave her shoulder a pat and then went in search of her husband.

I found Jonah in the barn and pulled him aside, telling him that his wife needed him out back.

"Is something wrong?" he asked, and for a moment, as I looked into his eyes, I felt a surge of bitterness. If not for the persistence of his affections, she would never have had to leave here in the first place.

Then again, I realized, had she never left, she never would have met my father—and I never would have been born.

"Just go to her," I said, forgiveness surging in my chest as I realized God's hand had been in all of it, every step of the way.

When I once again reached Rachel's side, she gripped my hand under the table and held on tight.

"Where were you?" she whispered, a flash of fear in her deep blue eyes. "Not having second thoughts, are you?"

"Of course not."

"No whispering to you from the outside, pulling you away?"

Looking back at her, all I could do was smile. "Oh, Rachel," I said, holding her hand even tighter. "If you only knew. Trust me, I am *exactly* where I want to be. From now on, the only whisper I'll be hearing in my ear is yours."

She smiled back at me, the twinkle returning to her eye. "For the rest of your life?"

"For the rest of my life." And then, in a very non-Amish display of affection, I kissed my new wife.

Afterward, I looked around the room at all who had gathered there, my mind returning to the words my mother had said that first time she'd told me about the pond on her parents' farm.

There's always another place besides the one where you are.

For such a long time I thought I had no place, neither here nor there. Now I knew that nothing could be further from the truth.

I had a place, all right. It was here in Lancaster County, right here amid my community, my family, my loved ones. Right by Rachel's side.

Right where I had been all along.

DISCUSSION QUESTIONS

1. The pond at his grandparents' farm holds a special place in Tyler Anderson's heart. What are some of the reasons he is drawn to it?

2. What do you think the pond symbolizes? Is there a place or object at your childhood home that affects you in a similar way?

3. Was Duke's decision to leave his son in the care of his grandparents the right thing to do? How might Tyler's personality and character have been different had his mother not died? How about if Duke had kept him instead of sending him away?

4. Tyler's little brother felt cheated of a relationship with his big brother. How valid are Brady's feelings? Would you have felt the same way? What has been the influence of sibling relationships in your life?

5. When Tyler arrives in California, he is intent on fitting in

and masking his Amish upbringing. Why do you think he felt the need to do that?

6. Tyler made a list of distinctions that were true of the *Englisch* world as he saw it. If you were to make a similar list about the non-Amish world, what would you include?

7. Had you been in Sadie's shoes, would you have told Sarah the full truth about why you left Lancaster County? Why or why not?

8. What was Rachel afraid of when Tyler returned to Lancaster County? To what degree do love and trust work together?

9. Do you think Tyler's *Englisch* family will continue to visit him in Lancaster County? Do you think Tyler will still have an influence on them even after he takes his membership vows?

10. Where do you see Rachel and Tyler in ten years? Do you think Tyler will still be drawn to visit the pond, or has he found peace at last?

About the Authors

The Amish Groom is Mindy Starns Clark's twenty-second book with Harvest House Publishers. Previous novels include the bestselling, Christy Award-winning *The Amish Midwife* (cowritten with Leslie Gould), *Whispers of the Bayou*, *Shadows of Lancaster County*, *Under the Cajun Moon*, and *Secrets of Harmony Grove*, as well as the popular Million Dollar Mysteries. Mindy lives with her husband, John, and two adult daughters near Valley Forge, Pennsylvania. You can connect with Mindy at her websites: www.mindystarnsclark.com and www.amishfaqs.com.

Susan Meissner is a multi-published author, speaker, and writing workshop leader with a background in community journalism. Her novels include *The Shape of Mercy*, named by *Publishers Weekly* as one of the 100 Best Novels of 2008 and a Carol Award winner. She is a pastor's wife and the mother of four young adults. When she's not writing, Susan writes small-group curriculum for her San Diego church. Visit Susan at her website: www.susanmeissner.com, on Twitter at @SusanMeissner, or at www.facebook.com/susan.meissner.